Guillaume Musso is the number one bestselling author writing in French today. To date he has had nine novels published. He lives in the south of France.

Emily Boyce's most recent translation is *How's the Pain?* by Pascal Garnier.

Anna Aitken translated Guillaume Musso's previous title, *Where Would I Be Without You?* in conjunction with Anna Brown.

The Girl on Paper
Guillaume Musso

Translated by Emily Boyce
and Anna Aitken

Gallic Books
London

The Girl on Paper

A Gallic Book

First published in France as *La Fille de papier*
By XO Éditions
Copyright © XO Éditions, 2010

English translation copyright © Gallic Books, 2011
This edition 2012
First published in Great Britain in 2011 by Gallic Books
59 Ebury Street, London, SW1W 0NZ

A CIP record for this books is available from
the British Library
ISBN 978-1-906040-88-8

Typeset by Gallic Books in Helvetica
Printed and bound by CPI Group (UK) Ltd, Croydon, CR0 4YY

For my mother

*What is the point of books, if not to bring us
closer to real life, if not to make us all
the more eager to live it?*
Henry Miller

Prologue

*Wanting to meet an author because you like his work is
like wanting to meet a duck because you like pâté*
Margaret Atwood

(USA Today, 6 February 2008)

ANGEL TRILOGY CAPTIVATES AMERICA

The tale of a doomed love affair between a young woman and her guardian angel has proved to be the literary sensation of the year. Here, the true story behind the phenomenon.

No one at Doubleday really believed in it. Yet the first novel of 33-year-old unknown Tom Boyd (original print run just 10,000 copies) has become one of the biggest bestsellers of the year in just a few months. *In the Company of Angels*, the first volume of what is to be a trilogy of novels, has topped the bestseller lists for twenty-eight weeks. With sales of over 3 million copies in the United States, the novel is about to be translated and distributed in more than forty countries.

Set in a Los Angeles where romance meets fantasy, the novel tells the story of the forbidden love between Delilah, a young medical student, and Raphael, the guardian angel who has been watching over her since she was a child. But the supernatural framework is really just an excuse for the author to explore more emotive subjects such as rape, incest, organ donation and mental illness. Just like Harry Potter and the Twilight series, *In the Company of Angels* has found a receptive audience for its rich mythology. Boyd's most committed readers have formed a community with its own moral codes and its own theories. Hundreds of websites dedicated to Tom Boyd's fictional characters have already been set up. Known to be quiet and unassuming, the author is a teacher from the MacArthur Park neighborhood. Before he unexpectedly found fame, Boyd taught English to troubled teenagers at the local high school, where just fifteen years ago he himself was a pupil.

Following the success of his first novel, Boyd has quit teaching after signing a $2 million contract with Doubleday for the two remaining books in the trilogy.

*

(Gramophone, 1 June 2008)
FRENCH PIANIST AURORE VALANCOURT RECEIVES PRESTIGIOUS AVERY FISHER PRIZE
On Saturday, the renowned 30-year-old pianist Aurore Valancourt was awarded the prestigious Avery Fisher Prize. This highly sought-after honor comes with a monetary award of $75,000 and is given to a musician for his or her outstanding achievement in music.

Born in Paris on July 7, 1977, Aurore Valancourt is

considered to be one of the most talented musicians of her generation.

A piano virtuoso

Valancourt received her classical training at the Curtis Institute in Philadelphia, and was discovered in 1997 by the conductor André Grévin, who invited her to go on tour with him. This marked the beginning of her international career. She started performing regularly with some of the world's leading orchestras, but quickly became disillusioned with the elitism of the system. Without warning, Valancourt abruptly withdrew from the public eye in January 2003. She then embarked on a two-year round-the-world motorcycle tour which ended in Sawai Madhopur, India. Valancourt spent several months there, surrounded by the lakes and cliffs of the nearby national park.

In 2005, Valancourt relocated to Manhattan where she returned to the stage and the recording studio, but also became a passionate environmental activist. This brought her even more media attention and her fame spread beyond the music world.

Taking advantage of her natural good looks, Valancourt began to appear on the pages of fashion magazines (a glamorous spread in *Vanity Fair*, a slightly more revealing one in *Sports Illustrated*...) and became the face of a well-known brand of lingerie. This publicity turned Valancourt into the world's highest-paid classical musician.

An eccentric and controversial star

Despite her youth, Valancourt is a highly accomplished pianist, but she is often criticized for being somewhat cold, especially when it comes to her Romantic repertoire.

Valancourt has always been quick to assert her independence and she is never afraid to do as she pleases. A 'nightmare' for concert organizers, she has become known for last-minute cancellations and diva behavior.

Valancourt's off-stage personality is no different. A perpetual bachelorette, she claims not to be interested in any serious romantic attachment, preferring to live for the moment, which has resulted in no small number of conquests. Her high-profile flings with countless celebrities mean that she is the only classical musician regularly to appear in the pages of celebrity gossip magazines, which has raised a few eyebrows in more traditional music circles.

*

(Los Angeles Times, 26 June 2008)

AUTHOR OF ANGEL TRILOGY DONATES $500,000 TO LA HIGH SCHOOL

As his second novel, *The Memory of Angels*, rapidly climbs the bestseller lists, author Tom Boyd has donated half a million dollars to Harvest High School in Los Angeles, its principal announced today. As a teenager, Boyd attended the school, located in the underprivileged MacArthur Park neighborhood. After becoming a teacher himself, Boyd returned there to teach English, until the success of his book allowed him to resign his position.

When contacted by this newspaper, the author declined to confirm the donation. The fiercely private novelist, who rarely talks to the press, is said to be working on the third and final volume of his saga.

*

(Stars News, 24 August 2008)
GORGEOUS AURORE SINGLE AGAIN!
One man's loss is another man's gain. At 31, the pianist and model just announced she has split from her boyfriend, Spanish tennis pro Javier Santos, who she had been dating for several months.

So now it looks as if, after his impressive performance at Roland-Garros and Wimbledon, the sports star will spend his well-deserved holiday in Ibiza with only his friends from Barcelona as company. As for his ex-Queen of Hearts, you can be sure she won't stay single for long.

*

(Variety, 4 September 2008)
ANGEL TRILOGY TO BE MADE INTO A MOVIE

Columbia Pictures has just purchased film rights to the *Angel Trilogy*, Tom Boyd's fantasy-romance saga.

Millions of readers have enjoyed the nail-biting suspense of the first two books of the trilogy, *In the Company of Angels* and *The Memory of Angels*. Shooting of the film version of the first book is due to start in the near future.

*

From: patricia.moore@speedaccess.com
Subject: Healing
Sent: September 12, 2008
To: thomas.boyd2@gmail.com

Hello, Mr Boyd. I have been wanting to write to you for a long time now. My name is Patricia, I am 31 and bringing up my two children alone, following the death of my beloved husband who suffered from a brain tumour which gradually sapped his strength. His dying left me more devastated than I care to admit. We had so little time together ... It was in the months following my husband's death that I discovered your books.

I escaped into your stories, and when I had finished I finally felt I had regained some harmony in my life. In your novels, people often get the chance to turn their lives around and right their wrongs. All I hope for is the chance to love again, and find someone to love me back.

Thank you for giving me the courage to rebuild my life.

*

(Paris Matin, 12 October 2008)

AURORE VALANCOURT: GENUINE TALENT OR CELEBRITY FAKER?

The crowd was buzzing yesterday evening at the Théâtre des Champs-Élysées.

The notoriety of the brilliant young musician continues to excite the curiosity of the media and the public. The programme began with Beethoven's *Emperor* concerto, followed by Schubert's *Impromptus*, an enticing selection which nevertheless failed to deliver.

Although performed with flawless technique the concerto was soulless, lacking any lyrical quality. To be brutally frank, Aurore Valancourt is more a marketing product than the extraordinarily gifted pianist that the media makes her out to be. If it were not for her attractive physique and angelic features, she would be nothing more than a run-of-the-mill musician, because the 'Valancourt Phenomenon' in fact relies on a well-oiled media machine that has managed to turn an ordinary performer into an international idol.

Sadly her musical immaturity wasn't enough to stop the audience, obviously taken in by her image, from giving her a standing ovation.

*

From: myra14.washington@hotmail.com
Subject: Extraordinary books
Sent: October 22, 2008
To: thomas.boyd2@gmail.com

Hello, Mr Boyd. My name is Myra and I'm 14 years old. I live in the projects in LA, the ones you read about in the papers. I go to school in MacArthur Park and I went to your lecture that time you came to my school. I never thought I would get into reading. But your books were so exciting. I saved up to buy your second book, but I didn't have enough money, so I went to Barnes & Noble every day until I finished it.

I guess I just want to say thanks.

*

(TMZ.com, 13 December 2008)

AURORE AND TOM TOGETHER AT KINGS OF LEON CONCERT?

The Kings of Leon played to a full house on Saturday night at the Los Angeles Forum. The pianist Aurore Valancourt and the writer Tom Boyd were spotted in the crowd… and it looks like their relationship is heating up. Boyd and Valancourt shared flirtatious glances, whispered in each other's ears and put their arms around each other. These two are obviously more than friends. The photos speak for themselves. We'll let you be the judge!

*

(TMZ.com, 3 January 2009)

AURORE VALANCOURT AND TOM BOYD'S JOGGING DATE

Fitness kick or romantic outing? Whatever the reason, Aurore Valancourt and Tom Boyd enjoyed a long run yesterday along the snow-covered paths of Central Park.

*

(TMZ.com, 18 March 2009)

AURORE VALANCOURT AND TOM BOYD APARTMENT HUNTING IN MANHATTAN

*

(USA Today, 10 April 2009)

TOM BOYD'S NEW BOOK DUE OUT LATER THIS YEAR

Doubleday announced yesterday that the last chapter in Tom Boyd's saga is to be published this fall. Great news for the novelist's enthusiastic fans.

Entitled *Mix-up in Heaven*, the last volume of the *Angel Trilogy* looks set to be one of the biggest books of the year.

*

(Entertainment Today, 6 May 2009)

TOM SEEKS PERFECT RING FOR AURORE

The writer recently spent three hours in Tiffany's

in New York trying to find the perfect ring for his girlfriend of several months.

According to the sales assistant, 'He seemed so in love, and was very anxious to find a ring that would really make her happy.'

*

From: svetlana.shaparova@hotmail.com
Subject: Remembering a love affair
Sent: May 9, 2009
To: thomas.boyd2@gmail.com

Dear Mr Boyd,

First of all, please forgive any spelling mistakes. I am Russian and my English is not so good. Your book was given to me as a gift by a man that I was in love with, who I met in Paris. When he gave me the book, all he said to me was: 'Read it and you'll understand.' This man (his name was Martin) and I are no longer together, but your story reminded me of the bond we once had that made me so happy. When I read your books I can escape. Thank you if you are reading this message, and I wish you a happy life.

Svetlana

*

(Onl!ne, 30 May 2009)

AURORE VALANCOURT AND TOM BOYD SEEN FIGHTING IN RESTAURANT

(Onl!ne, 16 June 2009)
AURORE VALANCOURT: CHEATING ON TOM BOYD?

(TMZ.com, 2 July 2009)
AURORE VALANCOURT AND TOM BOYD: IT'S OVER!

The celebrity pianist, who has been romantically involved with the author Tom Boyd for several months, was spotted last week with James Bugliari, the drummer of rock band The Sphinx.

＊

You will certainly have seen this video already; it's received record numbers of hits on YouTube and Dailymotion and attracted scores of comments – some mocking, others more sympathetic.

The venue is the Royal Albert Hall in London during the Proms.

At the beginning of the clip, Aurore Valancourt walks onstage to a standing ovation. Dressed in a plain black dress with a discreet pearl necklace, she greets the orchestra and sits down at the piano. The opening chords of Schumann's *Piano Concerto* fill the auditorium.

During the first five minutes, the audience is silent,

21

captivated by the music. After the allegro opening, Aurore begins to play around a little with the phrasing and the music is beautifully soft, until suddenly a man climbs onto the stage, having eluded the security guards, and makes for the pianist.

'Aurore!'

The young woman jumps and lets out a small cry.

At this point the orchestra stops playing, two bodyguards appear on the stage, catch the unwelcome intruder and wrestle him to the ground.

'Aurore!' he repeats.

The pianist, who has recovered from her initial panic, stands up and indicates to the bodyguards that they should let go of the troublemaker. The audience is stupefied and an eerie silence has fallen.

The man stands up, tucking his shirt back into his trousers, as if to salvage some of his lost dignity. His eyes are glistening and bloodshot from alcohol and lack of sleep.

He is no terrorist, nor is he a madman.

Just a man in love, a man in despair.

Tom approaches Aurore and makes a clumsy, slurring declaration of love, clinging to the vague hope that this will be enough to change the mind of the woman he still loves. But she cannot hide her discomfort and turns away from his intense gaze, cutting him off.

'It's over, Tom.'

He looks at her with pathetic confusion.

'It's over,' she says again, gently, not meeting his gaze.

(Los Angeles Daily News, 10 September 2009)

AUTHOR OF ANGEL TRILOGY ARRESTED FOR DRUNK DRIVING

On Friday evening, the bestselling author was arrested for driving under the influence. Police reportedly clocked Boyd going 90 mph in a 40 mph zone.

Tom Boyd didn't submit quietly, and is reported to have insulted several police officers at the scene, threatening to have them fired. Handcuffed and placed in a cell, Boyd is said to have had a blood alcohol concentration of 0.16, double the legal limit in California.

When the author was released a few hours later, he issued an apology through his agent, Milo Lombardo: 'I behaved like a total idiot and apologize for having acted so irresponsibly, putting not only my own life but the lives of others in danger.'

*

(Publishers Weekly, 20 October 2009)

FINAL VOLUME OF ANGEL TRILOGY DELAYED

Doubleday has just announced that Tom Boyd's new novel will not be published until next summer. This means readers will have to wait another eight months to find out what happens at the end of the bestselling saga.

The delay may be due to the author's recent unsavory behavior following a painful break-up, which has reportedly plunged Boyd into a deep depression.

These reports are, however, strongly denied by Boyd's agent, Milo Lombardo: 'Tom is not suffering from any kind of writer's block. He is working hard every day to ensure that his new novel will not disappoint his readers. I'm sure that everyone can appreciate that this takes time.'

However, this doesn't seem to have convinced some of his fans. Doubleday has already been inundated with angry letters from outraged readers. An online petition has even been set up, demanding that Tom Boyd honor his professional commitments.

*

From: yunjinbuym@yahoo.com
Subject: Greetings from South Korea
Sent: December 21, 2009
To: thomas.boyd2@gmail.com

Dear Mr Boyd,

I'm not going to tell you my life story. I just want to let you know that I was recently admitted to a psychiatric clinic to be treated for severe depression. Several times I even tried to end it all. While I was there, a nurse persuaded me to open one of your books. I had heard of you already – it's hard to miss your book covers on the subway, on buses or at tables outside cafés.

I thought your stories weren't for me. I was wrong. I know that life isn't like a book, but I found in your plots and your characters a little spark of something that gave me hope.

With deepest thanks,
Yunjin Buym

*

(Onl!ne, 23 December 2009)
WRITER TOM BOYD ARRESTED IN PARIS
The bestselling author was arrested at Charles-de-Gaulle airport last Monday after a scuffle with a waiter who refused to serve Boyd, claiming that he was drunk. Boyd was taken into police custody. Following an investigation, the public prosecutor set a date for a hearing at Bobigny criminal court in late January. Boyd faces charges of disorderly conduct and assault and battery.

*

From: mirka.bregovic@gmail.com
Subject: Your most avid reader in Serbia!
Sent: December 25, 2009
To: thomas.boyd2@gmail.com

Dear Mr Boyd,

This is the first time I've ever written to anyone that I only know through their books! I teach literature in a small village in the south of Serbia, where we have no bookstore and no library. On this day, I would like to wish you a Merry Christmas, as night falls on the snowy landscape around me. I hope one day you will come and visit our beautiful country, and while you're at it, why not my little village, Rakovica!

Thank you for allowing me to escape a little.

Yours,
Mirka

PS I would also like to tell you that I don't believe a word of what they are saying in the papers and on the news about your private life.

*

(*New York Post*, 2 March 2010)

THE RISE AND FALL OF TOM BOYD

At 11 p.m. the night before last, for reasons as yet undisclosed, the bestselling author came to blows with another patron at the Beverly Hills hotspot Freeze. What started as an argument between the two men quickly escalated into a fistfight. Police quickly arrived on the scene and arrested the young author after finding ten grams of crystal meth on his person.

Boyd has been charged with drug possession and was released on bail, but is expected to appear before the Los Angeles Superior Court shortly.

It's a safe bet that this time Boyd will need an excellent attorney if he expects to avoid jail.

From: eddy93@free.fr
Subject: One of the good guys
Sent: March 3, 2010
To: thomas.boyd2@gmail.com

Let me introduce myself: my name is Eddy, I'm 19 and I'm training to be a baker in Stains, on the outskirts of Paris. I completely screwed up high school because I never turned up, and because I liked weed a little too much.

But last year I met a great girl. I didn't want to lose her so I decided to get my act together for her. I went back to school, and now I'm not just learning new things, I understand them too. Out of all the books she told me to read, yours are my favourite: they bring out the best in me.

I can't wait for your next book, but I don't like some of the stuff I've read about you in the papers. My favourite characters in your novels are the ones that stay true to what they believe in, no matter what. So if you really believe in what you write, you should take better care of yourself, Mr Boyd. Don't let alcohol or dope take over your life.

Don't be a loser like I was.

With all my respect,
Eddy

1

The house by the sea

*Sometimes, women meet men who have nothing and decide
to try to give them everything. Sometimes, they succeed.
Sometimes, women meet men who have everything, and
decide to leave them with nothing.
They always succeed*
Cesare Pavese

'Tom, open the door!'

The shout was drowned out by the wind and there
was no reply.

'Tom! It's me, Milo. I know you're in there. Come out
of your hole for crying out loud!'

Malibu
Los Angeles County
A beach house
For the last five minutes, Milo Lombardo had been
hammering incessantly on the wooden shutters
overlooking the terrace of his best friend's house.

'Tom! Open up or I'll kick the door down. You know
I'm strong enough!'

Wearing a tailored shirt, a well-cut suit, and
sunglasses, Milo nevertheless looked as if he had
seen better days. At first, he had thought that with

time Tom's wounds would heal, but, far from moving on, Tom seemed to have plunged into an even blacker depression. The writer had barely left the house in six months, preferring to barricade himself in his luxurious prison, refusing all phone calls and visitors.

'Last chance, Tom: let me in!'

Every evening Milo came to bang on the door of the luxury house, but every evening all that greeted him was the angry complaints of annoyed neighbours and the inevitable intervention of the security guards who were employed to protect the houses of the mega-rich residents of Malibu Colony.

But he had had enough of waiting around for Tom to open up. It was time for more extreme measures.

'OK, you asked for it,' he said, taking off his jacket and grabbing the metal crowbar lent to him by Carole, their childhood friend who was now a detective with the LAPD.

Milo glanced back at the view behind him. The sandy beach was basking in the warm early-autumn sun. Lined up like sardines, the luxury villas extended along the seafront, as if creating a kind of barrier against unwelcome intruders. The area was home to countless Hollywood stars and business tycoons. Tom Hanks, Sean Penn, Leonardo DiCaprio and Jennifer Aniston were all said to own properties here.

Milo blinked, dazzled by the sunlight. Fifty yards away, a tanned Adonis was standing in front of a small hut on stilts. He was clearly a lifeguard and was looking through his binoculars, apparently mesmerised by the surfer girls enjoying the powerful Pacific waves. As no one was watching, Milo got to work with the crowbar.

He wedged the curved end of the metal lever into one of the small slits in the shutter and pushed down with all his might until the wooden slats broke away from the frame.

Do you have the right to save your friends from themselves? he wondered as he broke into the house.

But the moment of moral doubt didn't last long; apart from Carole, Milo had only ever had one friend and he was prepared to do anything to help him forget his heartache and start living again.

*

'Tom?'

In the half-light it felt as if the house was in an eerie state of suspended animation, and it smelt stale and musty. The kitchen sink was overflowing with dirty plates and the living room looked as though it had been vandalised: the furniture had all been turned over, while the floor was littered with dirty laundry and broken plates and glasses. Milo had to pick his way through pizza boxes, empty Chinese takeaway cartons and beer bottles to get to the windows, which he opened to bring some light and air back into the room.

The two-storey house was built in an L-shape with an underground swimming pool. In spite of the mess, the house seemed calm, with its maple furniture, pale wooden floors and abundant natural light. The interior design was a blend of modern and vintage, mixing more up-to-date pieces with furniture that harked back to the days when Malibu was just a surfing beach, before it became the luxury haunt of millionaires.

He found Tom on the sofa, curled up in the foetal position. He was a shocking sight; pale, with a Robinson Crusoe-style beard, he looked nothing like the stylish photos on the back of his novels.

'Anyone in there?' shouted Milo.

He moved closer to the sofa. The coffee table was littered with crumpled prescriptions from Dr Sophia Schnabel, the 'psychiatrist to the stars', whose Beverly Hills clinic kept a significant proportion of the area's jet-set population in legal drugs.

'Tom, get up!' Milo barked as he knelt down beside his friend.

Warily, he inspected the pillboxes that were scattered around the floor and table: Vicodin, Valium, Xanax, Zoloft, Stilnox. A lethal modern cocktail of painkillers, tranquillisers, antidepressants and sleeping pills.

'My God!'

Suddenly fearing an overdose, he was seized by panic and took his friend by the shoulders to try and rouse him from his drug-induced slumber. Violently shaken back to consciousness, the writer finally opened his eyes.

'What the hell are you doing here?' he slurred.

2
Two friends

*I kept repeating over and over all the things you're
meant to say to help a broken heart, but words are no help at
all... There are no words that have the power to heal the guy
who feels he has nothing left, because
he has lost the one he loves*
Richard Brautigan

'What the hell are you doing here?' I slurred.

'I'm worried about you, Tom. You've been locked
away here for months, stuffing yourself with sedatives.'

'Well, that's my problem!' I shouted back, trying to
get up.

'No, Tom, your problems are my problems. I thought
that's what friends were for.'

I sat on the sofa with my head in my hands and
shrugged my shoulders, half ashamed, half in despair.

'Anyway,' Milo continued, 'if you think I'm just going
to sit here and watch a woman put you through all
this—'

'You're not my father, OK?' I answered, slowly and
laboriously trying to stand upright.

As I got to my feet, I suddenly felt dizzy and had to
lean on the back of the sofa for support.

'That's true, but if Carole and I don't take care of
you, who will?'

I turned away from him, ignoring his question.

Although I was only in my boxers, I made my way to the kitchen to pour myself a glass of water. Milo followed me, dug out a trash bag and began to sort through the contents of my fridge.

'Unless you're planning on death by out-of-date yoghurt, I'd get rid of all of this dairy stuff if I were you,' he said, sniffing a rather dubious-looking pot of fromage frais.

'It's not as if you have to eat it.'

'And these grapes – was Obama even in office when you bought them?'

He then turned his attention to the living room, clearing the floor of all the takeaway boxes and empty bottles.

'Why are you still hanging on to this thing?' he asked disapprovingly, pointing at a digital photo frame which was playing a slideshow of photos of Aurore.

'Because this is MY HOUSE and in MY HOUSE I can do what I want.'

'Maybe, but that girl broke your heart into a thousand pieces. Don't you think it's time you took her down from her pedestal?'

'Listen, Milo, I know you never liked Aurore—'

'I'll admit I wasn't her biggest fan. And, if I'm honest, I always knew she wouldn't stick by you.'

'Oh, really? May I ask why?'

Things he had obviously been wanting to say for a long time came pouring out.

'Because Aurore isn't like us! Because she looks down on people like us. Because she was born with a silver spoon in her mouth. Because for her life is a game, whereas for us it's always been a struggle—'

'As if it were really that black and white. You don't know anything about her.'

'Stop defending her! Look what she's done to you.'

'Of course, you'd never be in this situation, would you? You've never been in love; all you have is your bimbos!'

The argument had unintentionally escalated and now we were trading retorts like blows.

'But what you're going through has nothing to do with love,' Milo raged. 'It's something else entirely, a mixture of suffering and dangerous obsession.'

'At least I'm not afraid to take risks. You, on the other hand—'

'What, you think I'm afraid of taking risks? I parachuted from the top of the Empire State Building. The video was all over the internet.'

'Yeah, and what did you get out of that, apart from a huge fine?'

Milo carried on as if he hadn't heard me.

'I've skied down the Cordillero Blanco in Peru. I've paraglided off the top of Everest. I'm one of the handful of people in the world who have climbed K2—'

'I'm not saying you're not a daredevil. But I'm talking about daring to fall in love. And that's a risk you've never taken, not even with—'

'SHUT UP!' he exploded, grabbing the collar of my T-shirt to stop me finishing my sentence.

He stayed like that for a few seconds, fists clenched, glaring at me, until he remembered where he was; he had come to help me, and there he was about to punch me in the face.

'Sorry,' he said, releasing his grip.

I just shrugged and walked out onto the wide terrace that looked out over the ocean. Out of sight of prying eyes, the house was connected to the beach by a private flight of steps, which were currently lined with terracotta pots of dying plants I had not bothered to water for months.

To protect my eyes from the sun I put on an old pair of Ray-Ban Wayfarers that were lying around on the teak table, then flopped down into my rocking chair.

Milo appeared from the kitchen a few minutes later carrying two cups of coffee and offered me one.

'Right, let's stop acting like kids and talk about this,' he said, leaning on the table.

I said nothing, lost in the view of the rolling waves. At that moment I only wanted one thing: for him to tell me whatever it was he had come to say and then leave so I could go and throw up in the toilet, then swallow a handful of pills that would take me far away from reality.

'How long have we known each other, Tom? Twenty-five years?'

'Something like that,' I said, taking a sip of coffee.

'You've always been the sensible one,' Milo said. 'You've stopped me from making more than one mistake in the past. If it weren't for you, I would have ended up in prison, or worse, ages ago. If it weren't for you, Carole would never have become a cop. And, if it weren't for you, I would never have been able to buy my mother a house. Look, what I'm trying to say is, I owe everything to you.'

I felt embarrassed and tried to brush his words aside with a dismissive gesture. 'If you've just come round to go all soft on me—'

'I'm not going all soft on you. Think of everything we've had to face together, our lousy childhood, the drugs, the gang violence...'

This new line of attack got to me and I felt a shiver down my spine. Despite how far we had come from those days, a part of me was still that fifteen year-old from MacArthur Park, with its dealers, its dropouts and its stairwells filled with shouting and screaming. And the fear that followed you everywhere.

I turned away and looked out at the ocean. The water was calm and shimmered a thousand shades of blue from turquoise to ultramarine. Just a few gentle, regular waves rippled the surface of the Pacific. The tranquillity was a million miles away from our turbulent adolescence.

'We're clean now,' Milo carried on. 'We earn an honest living. We don't carry guns under our jackets any more. There are no bloodstains on our T-shirts, no traces of cocaine on our banknotes—'

'I don't see how this has anything to do with—'

'We have everything we could possibly ask for, Tom. Health, youth, jobs that we love – you can't just throw all of that away for some girl. It's stupid. She's not worth it. Keep your mourning for when real pain comes around.'

'Aurore was the love of my life! Why can't you understand that? Why can't you just let me be?'

Milo sighed. 'Do you really want me to say it? If she truly was the love of your life, she would be the one here with you now, trying to keep you from self-destruction.'

He gulped down his espresso, then observed, 'You've done everything possible to get her back.

You've begged her, you've tried to make her jealous, you made a fool of yourself in front of the whole world. It's over: she's not coming back. She's moved on and you should too.'

'But what if I can't?' The question I hadn't wanted to ask.

He seemed to consider this for a moment. His expression was anxious and unreadable.

'I think you don't really have much choice any more.'

'Why do you say that?'

'Take a shower and get dressed.'

'Where are we going?'

'To have a steak at Spago's.'

'I'm not hungry.'

'I'm not taking you there for the food.'

'So why are we going?'

'Because you're going to need a stiff drink after you hear what I have to tell you.'

3

A man possessed

Jef, you're not alone
But stop your crying
Like that, everyone can see,
Just cos some girl
Just cos some fake blonde
Let you go...
I know your heart's heavy
But you've got to move on, Jef
Jacques Brel

'Why is there a tank parked outside my house?' I asked, pointing at the ostentatious sports car whose giant tyres dwarfed the kerb on Colony Road.

'It's not a tank,' Milo replied irritably, 'it's a Bugatti Veyron, the Black Blood model. It's one of the most powerful racing cars in the world.'

Malibu
A sunny afternoon
Wind rustling the trees
'You've bought *another* car? Are you collecting them or something?'

'But this is so much more than a car, my friend. This is a work of art!'

'Looks more like a babe magnet to me. Do girls really go for the whole car thing?'

'Like I need a car to get girls!'

I wasn't so sure. I'd never understood my peers' obsession with coupés, roadsters and convertibles.

'Let's go take a look at her.' Milo suggested, his eyes shining with excitement.

Not wanting to spoil his fun, I let him give me the full tour. With its sleek, elliptical shape and smooth lines, the Bugatti looked like a cocoon with a few growths on its exterior that glinted in the sunlight and contrasted sharply with the pitch-black bodywork: a chrome grille, metallic wing mirrors and glinting wheel-trims, where you could just make out the flaming blue of the disc brakes.

'Do you want to check out the engine?'

'But of course.'

'You know they only ever made fifteen of these engines?'

'No, but I'm so glad you told me.'

'You can go from nought to sixty in under two seconds. At top speed, you can hit 250 mph.'

'That's great news, especially considering how expensive gas is now and how there are speed cameras every hundred yards around here, and I bet it's really good for the environment!'

Milo couldn't hide his disappointment.

'Do you have to be such a killjoy, Tom? You don't know how to appreciate the good things in life. You need to learn to relax.'

'Well, one of us has to be like that. And since you chose your role first I took the one that was left.'

'Come on, get in.'

'Can I drive?'

'No.'

'Why?'

'You know perfectly well your licence has been suspended.'

*

The racing car left the shaded streets of Malibu Colony and joined the Pacific Coast Highway, which followed the coastline. The car hugged the road beautifully. The interior was lined with smooth leather that glinted a warm orange in the light. There was something extremely comfortable about it; I felt protected in the cosy surroundings and closed my eyes, letting the sound of Otis Redding on the radio wash over me.

I knew full well that this sense of calm, fragile as it was, was only due to the tranquillisers I had taken after my shower, but the moments of relief were so rare I had learned to appreciate them whenever they came around.

Ever since the day Aurore had left me it had felt as though a cancer were eating away at my heart, lodged there permanently like a rat in a pantry. Hungry for fresh meat, my ravenous grief had left me drained of all emotion and all willpower. During the first few weeks after the break-up, the constant threat of depression had kept me alert – I was determined to fight tooth and nail against despair and bitterness. But now I had lost my fear too and with it all dignity and even the desire to keep up appearances. The parasite that was growing inside me had gnawed away at me mercilessly, turning everything monochrome, sapping all my energy, extinguishing the last embers of hope. At the first sign of any intention on my part to regain control of my life, this canker turned into a hideous serpent, poisoning me with its venom, which seeped into my brain in the form of painful memories: Aurore's quivering body, her scent, the fluttering of her eyelashes, the way her eyes would suddenly flash gold as they reflected the light.

Soon even these memories became less vivid. I had so numbed myself with pills that everything had become blurry around the edges. I had started to let myself drift away, spending whole days sprawled on my couch in the darkness, protected by my chemically induced shield, knocked out cold by Xanax, which on bad days brought nightmares full of pointy-snouted rats with rough tails, nightmares from which I would awake covered in sweat, shivering and stiff with fear, wanting only one thing: to escape from reality once more by taking an even stronger dose of antidepressants than before.

In this comatose haze, days had turned into months without my noticing, so loose was my grip on reality. But reality was still there: I was still being eaten alive by my grief and I hadn't written anything in over a year. My mind felt blocked, paralysed into inactivity. Words no longer came to me, any will to write had deserted me, my imagination had dried up.

*

When we reached Santa Monica beach, Milo turned onto Interstate 10, following signs to Sacramento.

'Did you see the game?' he asked excitedly, handing me his iPhone, which was displaying a sports website. 'The Angels beat the Yankees!'

I glanced briefly at the screen, my mind on other things.

'Milo?'

'Yes?'

'You should be concentrating on the road, not me.'

I knew that my friend found what I was going through difficult to relate to; it brought him face to face with things he didn't really understand. As far as he was concerned, the breakdown, the emergence of that unbalanced side that we all have inside us, was something that he had wrongly believed would never happen to me.

We turned right toward Westwood, going into Los Angeles's Golden Triangle. As people like to point out, there is no cemetery and no hospital in this part of town. Just pristine streets and expensive boutiques, which operate on an appointment-only basis, like a doctor's surgery. From a demographic point of view, no one is ever born or buried in Beverly Hills.

'I hope you're hungry,' said Milo, turning onto Canon Drive.

He screeched to a halt outside a stylish restaurant.

After handing the keys to the valet, Milo led me confidently into this regular haunt of his.

The former street kid from MacArthur Park saw the fact that he could walk into Spago's without reservation, whilst mere mortals had to wait weeks for a table, as a kind of social payback.

The maître d' showed us to a chic patio area where business tycoons and Hollywood celebrities enjoyed the best tables. Milo made a discreet gesture: just a few feet away from us, Jack Nicholson and Michael Douglas were finishing their drinks, whilst over at another table, a sitcom actress who had fed our teenage fantasies picked at a lettuce leaf.

I sat down, immune to the 'important people' around me. Over the last two years I had had the opportunity to meet people I had once idolised. At private parties, at various nightclubs, or in palatial houses, I had been able to talk to actors, singers and authors who had been my childhood heroes. But any illusions I had were utterly destroyed by these conversations. You don't want to know what happens on the inside of the Dream Factory. In 'real life' these people I had once looked up to often turned out to be nothing more than a bunch of losers, predators methodically seeking out young girls that they would lure in, only to drop them as soon as they had served their purpose, before once more going out prowling for fresh meat. Just as sad were the actresses who were so charming and witty onscreen, but off camera staggered between lines of coke, anorexia, Botox and liposuction.

But who was I to judge these people? Had I not myself become one of the crowd that I despised so much? Was I not also a victim of the loneliness that comes with fame, the dependence on medication, and the same selfishness which, in my more lucid hours, inevitably filled me with self-loathing?

'Enjoy!' announced Milo enthusiastically, pointing to

the canapés that had come with our apéritifs.

I took a small bite of a slice of bread topped with a sliver of tender meat.

'It's Kobe beef,' he explained. 'You know, in Japan they massage them with saké so that the fat is absorbed by their muscles?'

I frowned slightly.

He continued, 'To tame them, their food is mixed with beer, and to relax them they are played classical music. Could be that the meat on your plate has listened to Aurore's concertos. Maybe he fell in love with her music. See, now you have something in common!'

I knew he was trying his hardest to try to lighten the mood, but even my sense of humour had abandoned me.

'Come on, Milo, I'm getting tired. What is it that you wanted to tell me?'

He wolfed down a last canapé without even tasting the meat, then took out a tiny laptop that he opened on the table.

'OK, for now you have to keep in mind that I'm talking to you as your agent, and not your friend.'

He always said this at the start of our so-called business meetings. Milo was the backbone of our little business. Cell phone surgically attached to his ear, he never seemed to stop, permanently on the phone to editors, foreign agents and journalists, always searching for a new way to promote the work of his only client: me. I don't know how he managed to convince Doubleday to publish my books. In the competitive world of publishing he had learned his trade on the job, with no experience and no qualifications to help him, and had become one of the best, just through believing in me more than I believed in myself.

He always said that he owed everything to me, but I knew that it was really the other way round: *he* was the one who had made me into a star by getting my first book onto all the bestseller lists. After this early success, I was offered contracts by some of the best agents in the business, but I had turned them all down.

Because, above and beyond being a good friend, Milo possessed a rare quality that I prized above all others: loyalty.

At least, that's what I had always thought, until I heard what he had to say to me that day.

4

The inside world

*The outside world is so empty of hope that the inside
world has become twice as precious to me*
Emily Brontë

'Well, let's start with the good news: your first two
books are selling as well as ever.'

Milo turned the computer screen so I could see the
red and green lines shooting up to the top of the graph.

'The international market has followed America's
lead, and your book is well on the way to becoming
a global phenomenon. It's only been six months and
you've already received more than fifty thousand
emails from readers! It's incredible, isn't it?'

I turned to look at him. What he had just told me
meant nothing to me. Heavy clouds hung in the smog-
filled LA air. I missed Aurore. What was the point of
being successful if I had no one to share it with?

'Some more good news: shooting starts on the movie
next month. Keira Knightley and Adrien Brody have
both said yes and the big shots at Columbia are pretty
excited. They've just managed to get the set designer
from *Harry Potter*, and they think they're looking at a
July release across three thousand screens. I've been
to a few casting sessions: they were amazing – you
should have come.'

As the waitress served the dishes we had ordered – crab tagliatelle for him and a chanterelle mushroom omelette for me – Milo's phone started to vibrate.

He glanced at the number on the screen, frowned a little, hesitating for just a second before deciding to take the call. He got up from the table and withdrew to the glass-covered walkway that led from the restaurant to the patio.

The phone call was soon over. I had only caught snatches of the conversation because of the chatter from surrounding tables. I could tell that it was heated, with recriminations and references to problems that I knew nothing about.

'That was Doubleday,' explained Milo as he sat back down. 'They were calling about one of the things I want to discuss with you. It's nothing to worry about: just a problem with the printing of the special edition of your last book.'

That edition was very important to me, and I had wanted every last detail to be perfect. It was to be bound in imitation leather, with watercolour illustrations showing the main characters, and a previously unpublished preface and postscript.

'What sort of problem?'

'To satisfy the huge public demand, they tried to rush the printing. They put the printer under enormous pressure and someone somewhere screwed up, which means they now have 100,000 faulty copies on their hands. They're going to pulp them, but the annoying thing is that some of the copies have already been delivered to bookstores. They're going to email all the stores and get them back.'

He pulled a copy out of his bag and handed it to me. Even in my distracted state I spotted the problem straight away when I flicked through the copy. Only half of the 500 pages that made up the book had been printed. The story stopped abruptly on page 266, midway through a sentence:

Billie wiped her eyes, which were blackened where her mascara had run.

'Please, Jack, don't leave like this.'

But the man had already put on his coat. He opened the door, without so much as a backward glance at his mistress.

'I'm begging you!' she cried, falling

And that was all there was. Not even a full stop. The book finished at 'falling', which was followed by 200 blank pages.

Because I knew all my novels by heart, I had no trouble remembering what was supposed to come next: '"I'm begging you!" she cried, falling to her knees.'

'Well, no point worrying about that too much,' Milo cut in, picking up his fork. 'It's up to them to sort out the mess. The most important thing, Tom, is—'

I knew what he was going to say before he even finished his sentence.

'The most important thing now, Tom, is your next book.'

My next book.

He swallowed a large mouthful of pasta then started tapping keys on the computer.

'The hype is unbelievable. Just take a look at this!' Milo had gone to Amazon's homepage. From advance orders alone, my 'next book' was already number one, just above the fourth *Millennium* book, which was in second place.

'What do you think of that then?'

I sidestepped the question. 'I thought Stieg Larsson was dead, and that they were never going to publish the fourth book.'

'I'm talking about your book, Tom.'

I turned my attention back to the screen, amazed by the fact that they were selling something that didn't even exist yet, that would probably never exist. My next novel was due to be published on 10 December, just three months away. So far I had yet to write a single line and had only the vaguest idea of a plot in my head.

'Look, Milo—'

But my friend didn't seem to want to let me speak.

'This time, I promise I'll get you a launch that will make Dan Brown jealous. You'd have to be living on another planet to miss this book coming out.'

Milo was getting so carried away that it was difficult to stop him:

'I've already started to hype the book, and there's plenty of buzz on Facebook and Twitter, and a lot of discussion on book blogs between your supporters and your detractors—'

'Milo—'

'For the US and UK alone, Doubleday has ordered an initial print run of 4 million copies. The big names are expecting a great first week. We'll have bookstores opening at midnight, like they did for *Harry Potter*!'

'Milo— '

'And you will have to put yourself in the spotlight a little more. I can get you an exclusive interview with NBC— '

'Milo!'

'Everyone's really going crazy for you, Tom. No one wants to bring out their new book in the same week as yours, even Stephen King, who's pushed the release date of his paperback to January so you don't steal all his readers.'

To shut him up, I slammed my fist down on the table. 'STOP THIS!'

Glasses shook and people around us jumped, shooting disapproving looks in our direction.

'There isn't going to be a next book, Milo. Not for a few years, anyway. I can't do it any more; you know that as well as I do. I'm all washed up. I can't even put a few words down on paper and, most importantly, I don't have any desire to.'

'Well, at least try. Work is the best medicine. And, anyway, writing is your life. It's your best hope for getting out of your depression.'

'Don't think I haven't tried. I've sat in front of my screen for hours on end, but just looking at my computer makes me feel sick.'

'Maybe you could get another computer, or start writing by hand in exercise books, like you used to.'

'I could try writing on parchment or wax tablets – it still wouldn't change anything.'

Milo seemed to be losing patience.

'You used to be able to work anywhere! I've seen you writing at a table in Starbucks, in plane seats, sitting on a basketball court, surrounded by guys yelling at each other. I've even seen you type out whole chapters on your cell phone, waiting for the bus in the rain.'

'Well, I can't any more. That's finished.'

'Millions of people are waiting to find out what happens next in the story. You owe it to your readers!'

'It's just a book, Milo, not the cure for AIDS.'

He opened his mouth to reply, but suddenly froze, as though he were finally realising that there was no way of making me change my mind.

Unless telling me the truth could.

'Tom, there's *another* problem.'

'What do you mean?'

'With the contracts.'

'Which contracts?'

'The ones we signed with Doubleday and with your foreign publishers. They paid us huge advances on condition that you would keep to the deadline.'

'I never agreed to that.'

'I agreed to it for you, and maybe you didn't read the contracts all the way through, but you signed them.'

I poured myself a glass of water. I didn't like the way this conversation was going at all. For years we had each played our parts perfectly: I had let him take care of the business side of things, and I let my imagination take care of the creative side. Until now, this arrangement had suited me perfectly.

'We've already pushed back the publication date several times. If you haven't finished the book by

December, we'll run into serious financial problems.'

'Surely all we have to do is give them back the advance they paid us.'

'It's not quite as simple as that.'

'Why not?'

'Because we've already spent it, Tom.'

'What, all of it? How?'

He shook his head in exasperation. 'Do you need me to remind you how much your house cost? Or the price tag on that diamond ring you gave to Aurore and that she never even returned to you?'

How dare he?

'What are you talking about? I know perfectly well how much I earn, and how much I can afford to spend!'

Milo avoided my gaze. Beads of sweat were starting to appear on his forehead. He pursed his lips, and his expression, so animated a few minutes earlier, had become serious.

'I've … I've spent everything, Tom.'

'What do you mean? What have you spent?'

'Your money and mine.'

'What are you talking about?'

'I put almost everything in a fund that went up in smoke with the Madoff affair.'

'I sincerely hope you're joking.'

But, no, he was not joking.

'Everyone was fooled by it,' he said sadly. 'Banks, lawyers, politicians, artists, Spielberg, Malkovich, even Elie Wiesel.'

'So how much do I have left, apart from my house?'

'Your house was mortgaged three months ago,

Tom. And, to be honest with you, you don't even have enough to pay your property tax.'

'But what about your car? That must have cost at least a million.'

'Try two million. But I've had to park it outside my neighbour's house for the last month so it's not repossessed.'

Shell-shocked, I fell silent for a moment before something clicked.

'I don't believe you! You just made all that up so I'd do some more writing, didn't you?'

'If only.'

Now it was my turn to pick up my phone, to call the accountants who took care of my taxes and therefore had access to all of my various accounts. My adviser confirmed that, yes, all of my accounts were completely empty, something that he had apparently been trying to bring to my attention for weeks, sending a constant stream of recorded delivery letters and voicemail messages.

But when was the last time I had emptied my mailbox or listened to my answering machine?

Once I had regained my composure, I felt neither panicked nor seized by a desire to throw myself across the table at Milo and hit him in the face. I just felt incredibly weary.

'Look, Tom, we've got ourselves out of far worse situations than this.'

'Do you realise what you've done?'

'But you can fix it,' he reassured me. 'If you manage to finish your novel in time, we can easily get back to where we were before.'

'And just how do you think I'm going to be able to write 500 pages in less than three months?'

'You already have a few chapters tucked away somewhere – I know that.'

I put my head in my hands. It was obvious he didn't understand the first thing about how powerless I was feeling.

'I've just spent the last hour telling you that I'm washed up, that my mind is behind bars, that it's as dry as a rock. The fact that I apparently now have no money doesn't change any of that. It's over!'

But he wouldn't drop it.

'You've always said that writing was what kept you balanced, what kept you sane even.'

'Well, clearly I was wrong: it wasn't not writing that pushed me over the edge, it was love.'

'All the same, do you see that you are self-destructing for the sake of something that doesn't exist?'

'Are you saying that love doesn't exist?'

'Of course love exists. But you're so damn obsessed by the idea of soul mates. As if there were some invisible link between two people destined to be together.'

'So you think it's ridiculous to believe that there's someone out there who can make you happy, someone you would want to grow old with?'

'Of course not, but that's not what you believe in: you believe that there is only one person on earth for everyone. Like some kind of missing part seeking to reunite with its original other half to re-form a whole.'

'Well, that's what Aristophanes seems to think in Plato's *Symposium*!'

'Maybe, but your whole Aristo-thingy with its plate or whatever doesn't say that Aurore is your missing part. Believe me: you have to give up this idea. Mythology is fine for your books, but in the real world it doesn't work so well.'

'No, you're right – in the real world it isn't enough for my best friend to ruin me; he also thinks it's OK to lecture me about my life!' I exploded, getting up to leave.

Milo also got up, with a despairing look on his face. At that moment, I could tell he would have done anything in the world just to inject a little inspiration into me.

'So you have no plans to start writing again any time soon?'

'No. And there's nothing you can do to change that. Writing a book isn't like building a car or making washing powder,' I shouted at him in the doorway.

As I left the restaurant, the valet handed me the keys to the Bugatti. I got into the driver's seat, turned on the engine and put it into gear. The leather seats had a lingering smell of mandarin, and the lacquered-wood dashboard, embellished with aluminum, made me feel as though I were in a spaceship.

The force of the sudden acceleration threw me back in my seat. As the screeching tyres left skid marks on the asphalt, I caught sight of Milo in the rear-view mirror, running after me, hurling insults at me as he went.

5

Shards of paradise

Hell exists, and now I know that its horror comes from the very fact that it is made from broken shards of paradise
Alec Covin

'Here's the tool you lent me – you can return it to its owner,' Milo announced, handing Carole a steel crowbar.

'Its owner is the State of California,' answered the young policewoman, putting the metal lever in the trunk of her car.

Santa Monica
7 p.m.
'Thanks for coming to pick me up.'

'Where's your car got to?'

'Tom's borrowed it.'

'But Tom's had his licence taken away.'

'Let's just say he was annoyed with me,' Milo said, not meeting her gaze.

'Did you tell him the truth?' she asked anxiously.

'Yes, but that doesn't seem to have encouraged him to start writing again.'

'I told you it wouldn't.'

She locked her car and together they walked over the suspension bridge that led to the sea.

'But seriously,' said Milo irritably, 'don't you find the whole thing a bit over the top, letting yourself go like that just because of a love affair?'

She looked at him sadly.

'It may be a little melodramatic, but it happens all the time. I think it's awfully sad.'

He shrugged and let her walk slightly ahead of him.

With her tall frame, olive skin, raven hair, and sky-blue eyes, Carole Alvarez had something of the Mayan princess about her.

Originally from El Salvador, she had arrived in the United States when she was nine. Milo and Tom had known her since they were kids. Their families – what families they still had – lived in the same dilapidated apartment block in MacArthur Park, the Spanish Harlem of Los Angeles, a hangout for heroin addicts and people who had violent scores to settle.

The three of them had grown up together against a backdrop of poverty, broken-down buildings, pavements lined with trash and shopfronts with metal shutters that had been smashed in and covered in graffiti.

'Shall we sit down for a bit?' she asked, unfolding a towel.

Milo joined her on the white sand. The little waves lapped the shore gently, leaving a silvery foam that tickled the bare feet of passers-by.

The beach, which was always extremely crowded in the summer, was much quieter on this early-autumn evening. The familiar outline of the Santa Monica pier loomed, welcoming Angelenos who wanted a release from their stressful jobs and busy city life, as it had been doing for over a century.

Carole rolled up her shirtsleeves, took off her shoes and leant back to take in the light breeze and Indian-summer sun. Milo watched her tenderly.

Life had not been any kinder to Carole than it had to him. She had only just turned fifteen when her stepfather was killed by a bullet to the head after his grocery store was raided in the violent protests that had shaken the impoverished parts of town in 1992. After the incident, she had played hide-and-seek with social services to avoid being put in a foster home, preferring instead to take up residence with Black Mama, a former prostitute and dead ringer for Tina Turner. At least half the men in MacArthur Park had lost their virginity to her. Somehow Carole had managed to keep up with her studies whilst holding down a job on the side. She had been a waitress at Pizza Hut, a sales clerk in a cheap jewellery shop and a receptionist for the local council. Most importantly, she had passed her exams to get into the police academy the first time round, joining the LAPD on her twenty-second birthday. She was climbing the ladder incredibly quickly. She had risen through all three ranks of officer, before being made a sergeant just a few days ago.

'Have you spoken to Tom recently?'

'I send him two messages a day,' Carole replied, turning to face him. 'But at best I get sarcasm.'

She looked searchingly at Milo. 'What can we do for him at this point?'

'Well, for starters we can stop him throwing his life away,' he answered, pulling from his pocket the bottles of sleeping pills and tranquillisers that he had managed to swipe without Tom noticing.

'I hope you realise that you're at least in part responsible for what's happening to him.'

'What, so it's my fault Aurore left him?' Milo countered.

'You know perfectly well what I'm talking about.'

'Are you saying that it's my fault there was a worldwide financial crash? That it's because of me that Bernie Madoff decided to embezzle $50 billion? And, be honest, what did you really think of that girl?'

Carole shrugged her shoulders helplessly.

'I didn't really know her, but I always knew she wasn't for him.'

In the distance the atmosphere on the pier was buzzing. Children's shrieks of excitement mingled with the smell of candyfloss and toffee apples. The theme park's Ferris wheel and rollercoasters were built directly over the water, facing the small island of Santa Catalina, which was just visible through the evening mist.

Milo sighed.

'I'm starting to worry that no one will ever find out how the *Angel Trilogy* ends.'

'I know how it ends,' Carole said calmly.

'You know the end of the story?'

'Tom told me.'

'Really? When?'

Her face darkened.

'Oh, it was a long time ago,' she replied vaguely.

Milo frowned. His surprise was tinged with disappointment. He had believed he knew everything about Carole's life: they saw each other almost every day, she was his best friend, his only real family, and –

although he would never admit it – the only woman he had ever had true feelings for.

He looked out at the sea, his mind elsewhere. Just like on TV, a few plucky souls were braving the waves on surfboards, whilst impossibly good-looking lifeguards surveyed the beach from their little wooden huts. Milo watched the surfers without really seeing them; all he could think about was Carole.

Their bond was a particularly strong one that had formed when they were children and was based on mutual respect. Even if he had never said it out loud, Carole meant more to him than anyone else in the world, and the nature of her job meant he worried about her constantly. Unbeknownst to her, in the evening he would sometimes park outside her apartment block, because it comforted him to know that he was close to her. The truth was, his single greatest fear was that one day he might lose her, even though he himself was not really sure what exactly he was so afraid of. That she would get hit by a train? That she would take a bullet whilst arresting a junkie? Or the more likely option, that he would have to watch her fall in love with another man.

*

Carole put on her sunglasses and undid the top button of her shirt. In spite of the heat, Milo resisted the temptation to roll up his sleeves. His upper arms were covered in tattoos of cabalistic symbols, indelible reminders of his days in MS- 13, also known as Mara Salvatrucha, an extremely violent gang that ruled the streets of MacArthur Park, which he had joined at the age of twelve for lack of anything else to do. Born to an Irish mother and a Mexican father, Milo had been considered a Chicano by the other clan members, all Salvadoran immigrants, who had subjected him to the *cortón* initiation ceremony. This was a hazing that for girls was a gang rape and for boys a group beating that lasted around fifteen minutes. It was an absurd rite of passage that was somehow supposed to prove your courage, toughness and loyalty, but often ended tragically.

Although barely a teenager, Milo had nevertheless survived the ordeal and for two years he stole cars, dealt crack, worked the black market and sold arms, all for the Mara. By the time he turned fifteen he had become a savage who knew nothing beyond fear and violence. Trapped in a downward spiral, and seeing only prison or death in his future, he owed his eventual salvation entirely to Tom's intelligence and Carole's love. They had managed to get him out of his personal hell, and he was living proof of the fact that it was possible to leave the Mara alive.

The last rays of the setting sun glittered on the sand. Milo blinked, both to protect his eyes from the glare and to chase away the past.

'Can I take you out for some seafood?' he asked, jumping to his feet.

'I think, considering the state of your bank balance, it's me that should be taking you out for dinner,' Carole pointed out.

'Come on, it's to celebrate your promotion,' he said, holding out his hand to help her up.

They left the beach in pensive silence and walked along the cycle path that linked Santa Monica to Venice Beach. They then turned onto Third Street Promenade, a wide palm-lined street that contained several art galleries and fashionable restaurants.

They sat down at a table outside Anisette, whose menu was written in French and filled with exotic-sounding dishes such as *frisée aux lardons*, *entrecôte aux échalotes* and *pommes dauphinoises*.

Milo insisted that they have an aperitif of pastis served 'California style' in a tall glass filled with ice cubes.

Despite the jugglers, buskers and fire-eaters that enlivened the street with light and music, the dinner was a serious, gloomy affair. Carole seemed sad and Milo was crippled with guilt. The conversation soon turned back to Tom and Aurore.

'Do you know why he writes?' Milo asked abruptly, as he realised he had no idea how this part of his friend's mind worked.

'What do you mean?'

'I know Tom's always liked reading, but writing is a different matter. And you knew him better than I did when we were teenagers. What drove him back then to write his first story?'

'I don't know,' Carole was quick to reply.

But she was lying.

*

Malibu
8 p.m.

After I had driven around town for a while, I parked the Bugatti outside the house that I now knew no longer belonged to me. A few hours earlier, I had been at rock bottom but with tens of millions of dollars. Now, I was just at rock bottom.

I felt exhausted and out of breath, as though I had been running, and flopped down on the couch, staring absently at the tangle of beams holding up the sloping ceiling.

I had a splitting headache, my back was killing me, my hands were clammy and my stomach was tied up in knots. I had violent palpitations that shook my chest. Inside I was empty, consumed by a terrible pain that had finally managed to defeat me.

For years I had spent my evenings writing. That was where all my emotion, all my energy had always gone. Then I started giving lectures and countless book readings all over the world. I had set up a charity that gave kids from my neighbourhood the chance to study art. I had even played a few gigs on drums with my idols: the Rock Bottom Remainders.

But now I couldn't be bothered with anything: people, books, music and even the rays of the sun as it set over the ocean, it was all meaningless.

I got up gingerly and went outside onto the terrace. Further down the beach, an old Chrysler with faded yellow paintwork, a hangover from the Beach Boy era, proudly displayed the town's motto on its back window: Malibu, where the mountain meets the sea.

I stared at the flaming border of light just above the horizon until it dazzled my eyes, and then it was swallowed up by the waves. This phenomenon, which had once fascinated me, now left me with no sense of wonder. I felt totally numb, as though all my emotional reserves had been used up.

There was only one thing that could save me: being with Aurore again – her supple body, her smooth ivory skin, her eyes that sparkled with golden lights and the way she smelt of sand. But I knew that wasn't going to happen. I knew I had lost the fight and that now there was nothing left for me to do but dull my senses with hits of crystal meth, or whatever I could get my hands on.

I needed to sleep. I searched anxiously for my medication in the living room, suspecting that Milo had got rid of most of it. I ran into the kitchen and searched through the bin. Nothing. Seized by panic, I ran upstairs and raided the wardrobes and cupboards until I finally found my travel bag. Hidden away in a side pocket was a little box of sleeping pills and some tranquillisers left over from my last promotional trip to Dubai, where I had given a reading in a bookstore in the Mall of the Emirates.

Almost in spite of myself I poured the entire contents of the box into my hand and for a moment I just stared down at the small blue and white capsules that seemed to be taunting me.

Go on, do it!

I had never come so close to the edge. My mind played out a slideshow of terrifying images – my neck in the noose of a rope, my lungs filling with gas from the stove, the barrel of a gun pressed against my temple. Sooner or later I was going to end up like that. Had some part of me not known it all along?

Go on, do it!

I swallowed the handful of pills to make it all stop. When they wouldn't go down, I drank water to help them on their way.

I dragged myself to the bedroom and collapsed on the bed. The room was cold and empty, with a vast wall of luminous turquoise glass, just transparent enough to let the sunlight in.

I curled up in a ball on my mattress, haunted by my thoughts of death.

Hanging on the wall opposite me was Marc Chagall's painting of the two lovers, who seemed to look down on me with compassion, as if they wished they could do something to relieve my suffering. Before I had even bought my house (which was no longer mine) or Aurore's ring (she was no longer mine), the Russian painter's work had been my first extravagance. Simply entitled *Lovers in Blue*, Chagall's canvas had been finished in 1914. I had fallen in love with the painting the second I saw it. It showed a man and a woman entwined, united in their mysterious, yet peaceful love. For me, it symbolised the healing of two wounded beings, who had become one to share the burden of each other's pain.

As I gently slipped into a deep sleep, I felt as though I were cutting myself off from the problems of this world. My body was disappearing, my mind was drifting away from me, life was leaving me.

6

The day I met you

There has to be chaos inside you to give birth to a dancing star
Friedrich Nietzsche

EXPLOSION!
A WOMAN SCREAMS!
A CRY FOR HELP!

The sound of breaking glass wrenched me out of my nightmare. I opened my eyes with a start. The room was plunged in darkness and rain lashed against the windows.

I sat up, slowly and painfully, my throat dry. I felt feverish and I was soaked with sweat. I was having difficulty breathing, but I was still alive.

I looked over at the alarm clock:

                    03:16

I heard noises coming from the ground floor, and I could make out the sound of the shutters slamming against the wall.

I tried to turn on the bedside lamp, but, as was often the case, the storm had cut the power in Malibu Colony.

I forced myself to get out of bed. I felt nauseous and my head was heavy. My heart was thumping in my chest as if I had just run a marathon.

Feeling dizzy, I had to lean against the wall for

support. The sleeping pills might not have killed me, but they had thrown me into a kind of limbo that I was struggling to climb out of. My eyes were what worried me the most: it was as though someone had peeled them, and they felt so raw that I was having difficulty just keeping them open.

Tortured by my headache, I dragged myself down the stairs, clutching the banister for support. With each step I took, I felt my stomach churning, as though I might throw up at any moment.

Outside, the storm raged. With every lightning flash, the house resembled a lighthouse in the middle of a tempest. When I finally reached the bottom of the stairs, I took stock of the damage. The wind had rushed in through the bay window, which had been left wide open, knocking over a crystal vase which had smashed on the floor. The torrential rain had started a small flood in my living room.

Damn it!

I hurried over to shut the window and then went to the kitchen to dig out a box of matches. It was only when I went back into the living room that I suddenly became aware that someone else was in the room with me.

I turned round.

*

The slim, graceful outline of a woman stood out against the bluish light from outside.

I jumped with fright, then peered closer into the

darkness. As far as I could tell, the young woman was naked, covering her modesty with her hands.

Well, this is all I need!

'Who are you?' I asked, moving closer to see her more clearly.

'Oh! Don't worry about that,' she replied, grabbing hold of a tartan rug to wrap around herself.

'What do you mean, "Don't worry about that"? What on earth's going on? Can I just point out that you're in my house?'

'Maybe so, but that's no reason to—'

'Who are you?' I asked for the second time.

'I would have thought you'd recognise me.'

I was having difficulty making her out in the darkness, but in any case I didn't recognise the voice, and I was in no mood for guessing games. I struck a match to light an old Chinese hurricane lamp that I had found in a flea market in Pasadena.

The soft light illuminated the face of my intruder. A young woman of around twenty-five stared back at me with an expression that was half alarmed and half defiant. Water streamed from her honey-coloured hair.

'I don't see how I'm supposed to recognise you; we've never met.'

She let out a mocking laugh, but I refused to play her game.

'Right, that's enough, miss! Tell me what you're doing here!'

'It's me, Billie!' she said, as if this were perfectly obvious, pulling the rug around her shoulders.

I saw that she was shivering and that her teeth were

chattering. It was hardly surprising: she was soaked to the bone and the room was freezing cold.

'I don't know anyone called Billie,' I replied, turning to the large walnut cupboard which held all kinds of junk.

I slid open the door and rummaged around in a sports bag until I found a beach towel patterned with Hawaiian palm trees.

'Take this,' I said, throwing the towel across the room to her.

She caught it and dried her face and hair, still fixing me with that defiant stare.

'Billie Donelly,' she said, watching me carefully for my reaction.

I stood motionless for a few moments, not really understanding what she was saying to me. Billie Donelly was one of the secondary characters in my novels. She was appealing but something of a lost soul. She worked as a nurse in a hospital in Boston. I knew that a lot of my female readers identified with her 'girl next door' personality, and her string of failed relationships.

Taken aback, I stepped toward her and shone the light at her. Like Billie she was slim, energetic but sensual-looking, with a perfect heart-shaped face and slightly angular features, scattered with a few discreet freckles.

But who was this girl? An obsessive fan? A reader who identified a little too much with my character? An attention- seeking admirer?

'So you don't believe me then?' she asked, sitting

herself down on a stool at the breakfast bar in the kitchen and picking up an apple from the fruit bowl, which she began to devour greedily.

I put my lamp down on the wooden counter. Even though my head was still throbbing, I was trying to remain calm. Intruders breaking and entering into celebrity homes had become commonplace in Los Angeles. I had heard that one morning Stephen King had found a man armed with a knife in his bathroom; that an aspiring screenwriter had broken into Spielberg's house just to get the director to read his script; and that one of Madonna's more unbalanced fans had threatened to cut her throat if she refused to marry him.

For a long time I had been spared this unfortunate phenomenon. I shied away from television studios, turned down most interviews and, much to Milo's despair, rarely appeared in public to promote my books. It was a source of personal pride that my readers enjoyed my books and my characters for what they were, rather than for me as a celebrity. Recently, however, the media attention that my relationship with Aurore had attracted had turned me, against my will, from a respected author into a less respected 'star'.

'Hello? Anybody there?' Billie interrupted my train of thought, waving her arms around in front of my face. 'God, I thought you'd died for a second there, with your eyes like a cat's butt.'

That sounds exactly like something Billie would say.

'OK, that's enough now. You're going to put some clothes on and go back to where you came from.'

'I think it would be a little difficult for me to go back there.'

'Why?'

'Because I come from the pages of your books. For someone who's meant to be a literary genius, you're a little slow on the uptake.'

I sighed, trying not to give in to my growing exasperation. I attempted to reason with her. 'Look, as you well know, Billie Donelly is a fictional character.'

'Yeah, she certainly is.'

That's something at least.

'But this is the real world.'

'I would have thought that was obvious.'

Now we're getting somewhere.

'So, if you really were a character out of my novels, you couldn't be standing here now.'

'Oh yes, I could.'

This girl was really something.

'Explain to me how that's possible, and explain fast, so I can go back to bed.'

'I fell.'

'Where from?'

'From a book. From your book, to be precise!'

I looked at her disbelievingly. I did not have the first clue what she meant.

'I fell from a line, in the middle of an unfinished sentence,' she added, pointing to the book Milo had given me at lunch, as if this proved her point.

She got up and brought me the copy, which she opened at page 266. For the second time that day, I read the passage where the story came to an abrupt end:

Billie wiped her eyes, which were blackened where her mascara had run.

'Please, Jack, don't leave like this.'

But the man had already put on his coat. He opened the door, without so much as a backward glance at his mistress.

'I'm begging you!' she cried, falling

'You see, it's written right there: "she cried, falling". So I fell into your world.'

The more she spoke, the more shell-shocked I felt. Why did these things always fall (literally this time) on me? What had I done to deserve this? True, I was probably a little out of it, but not enough to have made all of this up. I'd only taken a few sleeping pills, not LSD! Whatever it was that I was seeing, this girl was nothing more than a figment of my imagination. She was probably just an unpleasant physical manifestation of the overdose I had taken a few hours earlier.

I tried to hang on to this idea, eager to convince myself that all this was just a hallucination that had lodged in my mind, but I couldn't stop myself from replying, 'You're crazy, and that's putting it mildly. I'm guessing this isn't the first time someone's told you this?'

'Well, you should probably just go back to bed, because you clearly have your head stuck up your ass, and that's not putting it mildly.'

'I will go back to bed, because I don't want to waste any more of my time with a lunatic like you!'

'That's fine – I've had enough of your insults!'

'Well, I've had enough of dealing with a madwoman who's dropped out of bloody nowhere into my house at three in the morning!'

I wiped the beads of sweat off my forehead. I was finding it difficult to breathe again, and spasms brought on by anxiety were making the muscles in my neck tense up.

My cell phone was still in my pocket. I took it out to punch in the number of the security guards who protected the Colony.

'Oh, that's great, chuck me out!' she shouted angrily. 'Much easier than actually helping me!'

I was not going to get involved in her games. Still, there was something touching about her: her comic-book features, her cheerful freshness, that slight tomboyishness, which was softened by her deep blue eyes and endless legs. But what she was suggesting was so incomprehensible that I didn't think I could help her.

I typed in the number and waited.

The first ring.

My face was flushed and my head felt heavier than ever. Then my vision blurred and I started seeing double of everything.

Second ring.

I needed to splash my face with water, I needed to —

But everything around me grew hazy and the room started to swim. I heard the phone ring a third time as though the sound were coming from very far away. Then I lost consciousness completely and collapsed on the floor.

7

Billie in the moonlight

The muses are ghosts, and sometimes
they come uninvited
Stephen King

The rain was still beating down incessantly, lashing the window panes, which shook in the howling wind. The power had finally come back on, although the lamps were still flickering precariously.

Malibu Colony
4 a.m.
Bundled up in a quilt, Tom had fallen into a deep sleep on the sofa.

'Billie' had turned the heating on and put on a dressing gown that was far too big for her. With her hair wrapped in a towel, she looked around the house, holding a cup of tea. She opened all the wardrobes and drawers, setting out on a meticulous inspection of the contents of every cupboard, right down to the food in the fridge.

In spite of the mess in the kitchen and living room, she liked the edgy, bohemian decor: the surfboard that hung from the ceiling, the coral lamp, the antique brass telescope, the vintage jukebox.

She spent half an hour examining the shelves of the

bookcase, plucking books here and there whenever one caught her attention. She found Tom's laptop on a desk and turned it on without any hesitation, but discovered she needed a password to log on. She tried a few words from his books, but none of these granted her access to his files.

In one of the drawers, she found a bundle of letters addressed to Tom, with postmarks from all over the world. Some envelopes contained drawings, pressed flowers and lucky charms. For an hour she pored over each of the letters and noticed with some surprise that a large number of them mentioned her.

On the desk itself, more mail lay in heaps, mail that Tom had not even got around to opening yet: receipts, bank statements, invitations to premieres, press clippings that had been sent to him by the publicity department at Doubleday. Without pausing to think about what she was doing, she opened most of the envelopes, leafing through the writer's bank statements and immersing herself in the story of his break-up with Aurore, which had been carefully chronicled by several newspapers.

Occasionally, she glanced over at the sofa as she read, to make sure that Tom was still asleep. Twice, she got up from her seat to cover him properly with the quilt, as if he were a sick child.

She also studied with great interest the slideshow of photos of Aurore that were displayed in the digital photo frame on the mantelpiece. There was something extraordinarily calm and graceful about the pianist. Something intense, yet pure. Looking at the photos,

Billie couldn't help wondering why some women were so blessed at birth – with beauty, talent, education and wealth – while others had to start life with so little.

She sat herself down on a windowsill and watched the rain as it drummed on the glass. She looked at her reflection in the window and felt dissatisfied with what she saw. She had always been ambivalent about her looks: she thought her features were too pointy, and her forehead too high. Her lanky, long- limbed frame made her look like a grasshopper. She certainly didn't find herself attractive, with her modest bust, narrow hips, awkward posture and freckles, which she particularly disliked. Of course, her legs, which went on for ever, weren't too bad. They were her 'deadly weapon', to use an expression from Tom's novels. They were legs that drove men wild, but they weren't always the nicest men. She banished these thoughts, abandoning the 'enemy in the mirror' to continue her investigation of the house.

In the dressing room of the guest suite, she discovered an impeccably ordered walk-in closet. These were probably clothes that had been left behind by Aurore and were an indication of how quickly the relationship had ended. She walked around this Aladdin's cave in amazement, eyes wide like a child in a sweet shop. It held some of fashion's most prized treasures: a Balmain jacket, a beige Burberry trench coat, a Birkin bag – a real one! – a pair of Notify jeans …

In the shoe section, which slid out, she found the Holy Grail: a handmade pair of Christian Louboutin stilettos. Miraculously, they fitted her perfectly. She couldn't resist trying them on in front of the mirror, allowing herself to play Cinderella for fifteen minutes, with a pair of pale denim jeans and a satin blouse.

She ended her tour of the house in Tom's bedroom. She was surprised to find the room bathed in a bluish light, even though there were no lights on. She turned to face the canvas on the wall and stood fascinated in front of the lovers' embrace.

In the half-light, the Chagall had an otherworldly quality and seemed almost phosphorescent in the shadows.

8

She stole my life

Life isn't going to do you any favours, believe me.
If you want a life, steal it
Lou Andreas-Salomé

A sensation of warmth enveloped my body and brushed over my face. I felt better in the warm; I felt protected. I kept my eyes closed for a few moments longer to prolong the sensation of being asleep in the comforting padded cocoon. I thought I could hear a song playing somewhere in the distance. The notes of the chorus of a reggae song were accompanied by a smell that took me back to my childhood – banana pancakes and caramelised apple.

The room was flooded with light. My headache had disappeared completely. I turned my head towards the terrace, shielding my eyes with my hand to protect them from the dazzling sun. The music was coming from my little radio, which stood on a polished teak sideboard.

Something was moving next to the table: the billowing folds of a dress slit to the thigh floated in the light. I sat up to lean against the back of the sofa. I knew that dress, the pale-pink dress with the shoulder straps! I knew that body that was just seductively visible under the translucent fabric!

'Aurore,' I murmured.

But the gauzy, shimmering outline moved toward me until it was almost completely blocking out the sunlight, and…

No, it wasn't Aurore, it was in fact that crazy from last night who thought she was a character out of my novels!

I leaped up from the sofa, before immediately sitting down again when I realised I was as naked as the day I was born.

The madwoman undressed me in the night!

I scanned the floor for my clothes, or even just a pair of boxers, but I couldn't see anything within arm's reach.

This has to stop now!

I grabbed hold of the quilt to wrap it round my waist before hurrying out onto the terrace.

The wind had chased away the last of the clouds. The sky had cleared up completely and was a bright cornflower blue. In her summer dress, Billie's doppelgänger was buzzing around like a bee chasing rays of sunlight.

'Why the hell are you still here?' I demanded furiously.

'That's a funny way to thank me for making you breakfast!'

As well as serving little pancakes, she had poured two glasses of grapefruit juice and made a pot of coffee.

'And what made you think you had the right to undress me then?'

'What goes around comes around. You got a pretty good look at me last night.'

'But you're in my house!'

'Oh, come on! You're not going to get all upset just because I saw your little friend, are you?'

'My what?'

'You know, your pecker, your little winkle.'

Little? I thought indignantly as I pulled the quilt tighter round my waist.

'I'm only saying that out of affection, mind you, because, to be honest, there's nothing little about—'

'OK, you've had your joke!' I interrupted. 'And if you think you can win me over with flattery…'

She offered me a cup of coffee.

'Are you capable of speaking to someone without yelling at them?'

'And who gave you permission to wear that dress?'

'Don't you think it suits me? It belongs to your ex, doesn't it? I don't really see you as the cross-dressing type.'

I collapsed into a chair and rubbed my eyes, trying to get myself together. Last night, I had naively hoped that the girl might be nothing more than a hallucination, but unfortunately this was clearly not the case: she was a real-life woman, the spitting image of the first-class nuisance I had created in books.

'Drink that coffee before it gets cold.'

'I don't want it, thanks.'

'Are you sure? You look like death warmed up.'

'It's *your* coffee that I don't want.'

'Why?'

'Because I don't know what kind of crap you might have spiked it with.'

'Surely you don't think I want to drug you?'

'I know what crazies like you are capable of.'

'Crazies like me?'

'Yeah. Nymphos who are totally convinced that the actor or writer they are obsessed with is also in love with them.'

'Me, a nymphomaniac? Now you really are confusing your sick fantasies with reality, pal. And if you think I'm obsessed with you, you're even more stupid than I thought.'

I kneaded my temples as I looked up at the sun dominating the horizon. My back hurt and all of a sudden my headache had returned, only this time it had decided to attack the back of my head.

'We're going to stop this once and for all now. You're going to go home before I have to call the police, OK?'

'Look, I can see that you don't want to face up to the truth, but—'

'But?'

'I really am Billie Donelly. I really am a character from your books and, believe me, that is as terrifying for me as it is for you.'

Speechless, I took a gulp of coffee, then after a brief hesitation I finished the cup. The brew may well have been poisoned, but, if it was, the effects were not immediate.

I still wasn't going to let my guard down. I thought of a television programme I had seen as a child about John Lennon's assassin, who had apparently been motivated by the idea that by killing the musician he would win some of his victim's celebrity for himself.

Granted I was no Beatle, and this woman was a little prettier than Mark David Chapman, but even so I knew that many stalkers suffered from psychotic illnesses, and that at any moment they could become violent. For this reason, I was at my calmest and most reassuring as I tried reasoning with her again.

'Look, I think that maybe you're a little…disturbed. It happens. We all have our bad days, right? Maybe you lost your job recently, or someone you love? Maybe you just broke up with your boyfriend? Or you're feeling rejected and resentful? If that's the case, I know a very good psychologist who could—'

She interrupted my pep talk by waving a prescription written by Dr Sophia Schnabel in my face.

'As far as I can tell, you're the one who needs a shrink.'

'You went through my things!'

'Affirmative,' she replied, refilling my coffee cup.

I was completely baffled by her behaviour. What was I meant to do now? Did I call the cops or the men in white coats? From what she'd said, I was willing to bet she had a criminal record or a history of psychological problems. The simplest way to get rid of her would have been to throw her out with my own two hands, but I was afraid that if I laid even a finger on her she would claim that I had abused her, and that was not a risk I was willing to take.

'You didn't go home last night,' I pointed out, in a final attempt to make her leave. 'Your family or friends must be getting really worried about you. If you want to let anyone know where you are, feel free to use the phone.'

'Oh, I don't think so. For starters, no one ever worries about me, which I'll admit is quite sad. As for your phone, I think you've just been cut off,' she answered without missing a beat as she wandered back into the living room.

I watched her move toward the large table that I used as a desk. She waved a stack of bills at me with a grin.

'Hardly surprising, really,' she remarked. 'You haven't paid your phone bill in months!'

That was the final straw. Without thinking, I threw myself at her and knocked her to the ground. So what if I was accused of assault? At that moment I would have preferred that to having to hear one more word from her. I held her down, one hand behind her knees and the other round her waist. She struggled as much as she could, but I was not going to let go. I dragged her out onto the terrace where I deposited her unceremoniously on the ground, as far away as possible, before marching back into the living room and shutting the glass door behind me.

Much better! Nothing like doing things the old-fashioned way, works every time.

Why had I put up with the intruder for so long? In the end, it hadn't proved difficult to get rid of her! Whatever I said to the contrary in my novels, sometimes physical force speaks much louder than words.

I watched the young woman I had locked out with a satisfied smile. She responded to my sudden good mood by giving me the finger.

Finally I was alone again!

I needed to relax. The house being empty of

all medication, I turned to my iPod and, with the precision of an alchemist preparing a soothing potion, I concocted an eclectic playlist centred around Miles Davis, John Coltrane and Philip Glass.

I plugged the iPod into my speakers and the room was suddenly filled with the opening notes of *Kind of Blue*, the loveliest jazz album ever composed, even to people who didn't like jazz.

In the kitchen I made some more coffee, then went back into the living room, hoping that my strange visitor would have disappeared.

I was wrong.

Clearly annoyed – again, that was putting it mildly – she had started to destroy the breakfast that she herself had served. The cafetière, the plates, the mugs, the glass tray; in short everything that could be smashed was being thrown onto the terracotta paving stones. Then, shaking with rage, she slammed her fists repeatedly against the sliding doors, before hurling a garden chair at them with all her might. The chair just clattered to the floor, repelled by the bulletproof glass on the doors.

'I AM BILLIE!' she yelled over and over again, but her words were muffled by the triple glazing, and I guessed rather than heard what she was saying. All this racket was going to wake the neighbours soon, and then hopefully filter down to the security team at the gates, who would come and relieve me of this pain in the butt.

By this point, she had collapsed by the door. Holding her head in her hands, she finally seemed to have given up. I felt moved by her obvious distress, and watched her intently, realising that what she had said to me had aroused if not quite fascination, then at least curiosity.

She lifted her head and through the strands of honey-gold hair I saw her forget-me-not eyes take on a troubled expression.

I moved closer and sat down on my side of the glass wall, looking at her intently, trying to find the truth of the situation, if not an explanation. It was then that I saw her blink as though she were trying to hold back tears. I moved back and saw that the pale-pink dress was stained dark red with blood. Then I spotted the bread knife in her hands and realised that she had cut herself. I got up to try to help her, but this time she was the one who locked the door, jamming the outside handle with the table.

Why? I looked at her questioningly.

I saw that there was still a defiant flicker in her eyes and her only response was to slam the bloody palm of her left hand against the window. Through the glass, I made out the three numbers she had slashed into her hand:

144

9

The shoulder tattoo

The bloody numbers danced in front of my eyes:

144

Normally, my immediate reaction would have been to call 911 for an ambulance, but something held me back. There was blood pouring from the wound, but it didn't look deep. What was she trying to tell me with this dramatic gesture? What had possessed her to do such a thing?

She's crazy.

True, but what else was behind it?

I didn't believe what she told me, that's why she did it.

What did the number 144 have to do with what she had told me?

Once again she slammed her palm violently against the window pane. This time I saw that her right index finger was pointing at the book on the table next to me.

My novel, the story, the characters, fiction – what?

Then suddenly it was obvious.

Page 144.

I grabbed the copy and leafed through it hurriedly until I came to the crucial page. It was the opening lines of a chapter, which started like this:

The day after the first time she made love with Jack, Billie visited a tattoo parlour.

The needle moved across her shoulder, pushing the ink under her skin, gradually carving out a slanting inscription. It was a symbol that a Native American tribe used to define what it was to be truly in love: a part of you has entered me for good, and its poison has bewitched me. A permanent epigraph that she would now carry with her always, protection against life's inevitable suffering.

I looked up at my 'visitor'. She was hugging her knees to her chest on the terrace. She looked sadly back at me, her chin resting on her knees. Was I the one in the wrong? Was there in fact something more to the situation I found myself in? No longer sure what to think, I moved closer to the window. Suddenly the eyes that were watching me through the glass lit up. She lifted her hand to pull down the strap of her dress, to reveal her shoulder.

Just next to her shoulder blade I saw the tribal symbol that I knew so well. There was the Native American symbol used by the Yanomamis to distil the essence of love: *a part of you has entered me for good, and its poison has bewitched me.*

10

The paper girl

Novelists, minds are inhabited, indeed possessed,
by their characters, just as the mind of a peasant is possessed
by Jesus, Mary and Joseph, or that of
a madman by the devil
Nancy Huston

The house was calm after the storm. Having agreed to come back inside, the young woman had disappeared into the bathroom while I made some tea and laid out what was left of my medicine cabinet on the breakfast bar.

Malibu Colony
9 a.m.
She joined me at the kitchen table. She had showered, put on my bathrobe and stopped the bleeding by bandaging her wounds with a hand towel.

'I have a first-aid kit,' I said, 'but it's not very well stocked.'

Nevertheless, she was able to find some antiseptic wipes in it and used them to carefully clean her wounds.

'Why did you do it?'

'Because you wouldn't believe me, for crying out loud!'

I watched her open the cuts gently to see how deep the knife had gone in.

'I'll drive you to the hospital. It looks like you need stitches.'

'I'll do them myself. I am a nurse, don't forget. All I need is ome surgical thread and a sterile needle.'

'Damn! That's just what I forgot to put on my grocery list!'

'Don't you even have any sticking plasters?'

'What do you think? This is a beach house, not a health centre.'

'Or just some ordinary silk thread or horsehair? That would do fine. But wait! You have something better, I think. I'm sure I saw the miracle cure somewhere around here, in the—'

She got up off her stool in mid-sentence and started rummaging through the drawers in my desk as if she were in her own home.

'Found it!' she announced triumphantly, sitting back down at the table with a tube of Super Glue in her hand.

She unscrewed the lid of the small tube whose label read 'for use on ceramics and porcelain' and squeezed a thin line of glue onto her cuts.

'Wait a second – are you sure you know what you're doing? We're not in a movie, you know.'

'No, but I am a literary heroine,' she replied sardonically. 'Don't worry, this is why you make up people like me.'

She pushed the edges of the cut together and held them there for a few seconds until the glue took effect.

'There we go!' she exclaimed proudly, holding up her skilfully sutured palm.

She took a large bite of the slice of toast that I had

just buttered for her, then gulped down some tea. Behind her mug I could see those large eyes trying to read my mind.

'You're being much nicer to me, but you still don't believe me, do you?' she said, wiping her mouth with her sleeve.

'A tattoo isn't *exactly* concrete evidence,' I said carefully.

'But the mutilation is, right?'

'It's concrete evidence that you have violent and impulsive tendencies, sure!'

'So interrogate me!'

I refused, shaking my head. 'I'm an author, not a journalist or a cop.'

'But it wouldn't be that difficult, would it?'

I threw the contents of my mug into the sink. Why was I forcing myself to drink tea when I had always hated the stuff?

'Look, I'll make you a deal.' I left my proposition unfinished as I considered the best way to put it to her.

'Yes?'

'I'm quite happy to put you to the test by asking you a series of questions about Billie, but if you hesitate, or give a wrong answer, even once, you leave here no questions asked.'

'Deal.'

'So we're agreed: at the first mistake you're gone, otherwise I'll call the police. And this time – you can cut yourself up all you like, I'll leave you leaking blood on the terrace.'

'Have you always been such a charmer, or do you have to work at it?'

'Do we have a deal?'

'Yes. Fire away.'

'Name, date of birth, place of birth?'

'Billie Donelly, born August 11, 1984, in Milwaukee, near Lake Michigan.'

'Mother's name?'

'Valeria Stanwick.'

'What did your father do for a living?'

'He worked for Miller, the second largest brewery in the state.'

She never missed a beat, seeming to answer my questions instinctively.

'What's the name of your best friend?'

'One of my greatest regrets is that I don't really have one. Just a few girlfriends.'

'First sexual encounter?'

She took a moment to think about this question, looking at me solemnly. I understood that her unease came solely from the personal nature of the question.

'I was sixteen. It happened in France; I was on a language course on the Côte d'Azur. His name was Théo.'

I was becoming more and more unsettled by the accuracy of her answers, and, judging by her smile, I could tell that she knew she had finally caught my attention. Whatever was behind this, one thing was certain: she knew my novels inside out.

'What's your favourite drink?'

'Coca-Cola. The proper one, not Diet or Zero.'

'Favourite film?'

'*Eternal Sunshine of the Spotless Mind*. It captures

so exactly the pain of being in love. It's so poetic, so melancholy. Have you seen it?'

She unfolded her long limbs and wandered over to lie down on the sofa. I was once again struck by her resemblance to Billie; she had the same luminous fair complexion, the same unspoilt natural beauty, the same street-smart humour, the same tone of voice that I remember describing in my books as 'provocative and mocking, at once confident and childlike'.

'Most prized quality in a man?'

'Did you get your questions out of Proust?'

'Something like that.'

'I like *men to be men*. I don't have much time for those guys who are so obsessed with their "feminine side". You know what I mean?'

I looked doubtfully at her. I was about to fire another question at her, when she suddenly spoke up again.

'What about you? What quality do you value most in a woman?'

'Imagination, I think. Humour is the foundation of intelligence, isn't it?'

She pointed at the digital picture frame which was playing the slideshow of photos of Aurore.

'You say that, but your pianist doesn't look like she has much of a sense of humour.'

'How about we stick to the point?' I suggested, joining her on the sofa.

'You're starting to like this interrogation thing, aren't you? Are you enjoying the power trip?' she joked.

But I was not to be distracted, and I continued with my questioning.

'If you had to change one thing about the way you looked, what would it be?'

'I'd like to be a bit curvier, more feminine.'

I didn't know what to say. She knew everything. Either this woman really was mad and had identified with Billie to the point where she had started to become her, or she *really was* Billie, and it was me that was going mad.

'Come on then,' she taunted.

'All this shows is that you know my books really well,' I said, doing all I could to hide my surprise.

'OK, ask me some more questions then.'

That was exactly what I intended to do. Just to provoke her, I chucked the copy of my book into the chrome-metal trash can, then opened my compact laptop and typed in my password to access my desktop. I actually knew much more about my characters than what went into my novels. To really get inside the heads of my 'heroes' I had got into the habit of writing a detailed biography of about twenty pages or so for each one. I put as much information as possible into these biographies, from their date of birth to their favourite song, including things like the first name of their nursery-school teacher. At least three-quarters of this information did not end up in the published version of the book, but it was all part of the invisible framework necessary for the mysterious alchemy of writing. I had convinced myself that this exercise gave my characters a certain level of credibility, or at least a little humanity, which perhaps explained why many of my readers identified with them.

'Do you really want to keep going?' I asked, bringing Billie's file up on screen.

The young woman pulled a small silver lighter and an opened pack of Dunhills out of a drawer in the coffee table, a pack that I hadn't even known was there; it had no doubt belonged to one of the women I had dated before Aurore.

She lit a cigarette with a peculiar elegance.

'That's exactly what I want to do.'

I looked at the screen and picked something at random.

'Favourite rock band?'

'Um ... Nirvana,' she said before changing her mind. 'No, the Red Hot Chili Peppers!'

'Not a particularly original choice.'

'But it's the right answer, isn't it?'

She had a point. Probably a lucky guess. Who didn't love the Red Hot Chili Peppers?

'Favourite meal?'

'If it's a friend from work asking, I'd say Caesar salad, so I don't look like a total pig, but really it's a nice greasy portion of fish and chips!'

This time, she couldn't have just been guessing. I felt beads of sweat forming on my forehead. No one, not even Milo, had read these 'secret' biographies of my characters. The only place I kept them was on my computer, where they were well protected by a password. Still refusing to take this as evidence that she was telling the truth, I hit her with another question.

'Your favourite position?'

'Fuck off.'

She got up from the sofa and stubbed out her cigarette.

The lack of reply renewed my confidence.

'How many people have you slept with? And, this time, answer me! You don't get lives, you know, and you've already taken one! '

For this, I received an icy glare.

'You're just like all the others, aren't you? You're only interested in one thing.'

'I never claimed to be any different. So, how many?'

'You know that already. Ten, maybe.'

'I want an exact number.'

'I'm not going to start listing them in front of you!'

'Because it would take too long?'

'What are you implying? Are you saying I'm a slut?'

'I never said that.'

'No, but you were obviously thinking it.'

Ignoring her modesty, I persisted with what was quickly turning into torture for her.

'So, how many?'

'Sixteen, I think.'

'And out of this "sixteen, I think" how many were you in love with?'

She sighed.

'Two. The first and the last: Théo and Jack.'

'A virgin and a womaniser. You have extreme tastes.'

She looked at me contemptuously.

'Classy! You're clearly a gentleman.'

Despite my provocative questions, I had to admit she was getting it right every time.

Drrring!

Someone was ringing the doorbell, but I had no intention of answering it.

'Are you done with your stupid questions?' she asked defiantly.

I tried a trick question.

'What's your favourite book?'

She shrugged, looking embarrassed.

'I don't know. I don't read much – I don't have the time.'

'The classic excuse!'

'If you think I'm dumb, you only have yourself to blame!

May I remind you that I'm a product of your imagination. You invented me!'

Drrring! Drrring!

At the door, my new visitor was getting impatient, and was taking it out on the doorbell, but they would just have to wait.

Baffled by the entire situation, and increasingly thrown off balance with each correct response, I got carried away, not realising that my interrogation was turning into harassment.

'Your greatest regret?'

'I don't have any children yet.'

'At what point in your life were you happiest?'

'The last time I woke up in Jack's arms.'

'The last time you cried?'

'I can't remember.'

'Try.'

'I don't know. Lots of things make me cry.'

'The last time it meant something.'

'Six months ago, when I had to have my dog put down. He was called Argos. Is that not written down in your little file?'

Drrring! Drrring! Drrring!

I ought to have left it at that. I had more proof than I needed, but I was still overwhelmed by what was happening. My little game had hurled us violently into another dimension, another reality that my mind didn't want to adjust to. In my panic, I directed my anger toward Billie.

'Your greatest fear?'

'The future.'

'Can you remember the worst day of your life?'

'Please don't ask me that.'

'It's my last question.'

'Please, don't.'

I grabbed her by the arm. 'Answer me!'

'Let me go! You're hurting me!' she yelled, struggling to break free.

'TOM!'

cried a voice from behind the door.

Billie had managed to free herself from my grasp. Her face was flushed with rage and her eyes flashed with pain.

'TOM! OPEN THE DOOR NOW!! DON'T MAKE ME COME IN THERE WITH A BULLDOZER!'

Milo, of course.

Billie had taken refuge on the terrace. More than

anything I wanted to go and apologise for the pain I had caused her, because I knew full well that her anger and sadness were genuine, but what had just happened had disturbed me so deeply that I welcomed the prospect of a new perspective on the situation.

11

The little girl from
MacArthur Park

*Friends are the angels that lift us when our wings
have forgotten how to fly*
Anonymous

'You narrowly avoided the bulldozer!' joked Milo as he marched into the living room. 'Wow. I see things aren't getting any better. You look like someone who's just been snorting sodium bicarbonate.'

'What do you want?'

'I've come to pick up my car, if that's all right with you! I just want to take her for one last spin before she's repossessed.'

Malibu Colony
10 a.m.
'Morning, Tom,' said Carole, as she too stepped into the house.

She was still in uniform. I glanced at the street below and saw a police car parked outside my house.

'Have you come to arrest me?' I laughed, pulling her into my arms for a hug.

'My God, you're bleeding!' she exclaimed.

I frowned, but soon noticed the bloodstains that

had bloomed on my shirt: a reminder of Billie's slashed hand.

'Don't worry, it's not my blood.'

'Oh, well, that's all right then! And it looks fresh,' she pointed out, a note of suspicion creeping into her voice.

'Listen to this. You'll never guess what's happened to me. Yesterday evening—'

'Whose dress is this?' Milo interrupted, holding up the bloodstained silk tunic.

'It belongs to Aurore, but—'

'To Aurore? Don't tell me that you've—'

'No! It wasn't her that was wearing it. It was another woman.'

'Oh, so you're seeing someone else now? That can only be a good thing, right? Is it someone we know?'

'Well, sort of.'

Carole and Milo exchanged astonished looks before demanding in unison, 'Who is it then?'

'Take a look on the terrace. You're in for a big surprise.'

They hurried across the room and stuck their heads out of the glass doors. They were silent for about ten seconds, until finally Milo observed, 'There's no one there, buddy.'

Taken aback, I went out onto the terrace with them, where a cool breeze was blowing.

The table and chairs had all been overturned, and the tiles were covered in broken glass. The ground was smeared with mashed banana, coffee and maple syrup. But there was no sign of Billie.

'Has the military been conducting nuclear tests on your terrace?' Carole enquired.

'She has a point – it's like a war zone out here,' Milo chimed in.

To avoid the glare, I shielded my eyes and scanned the horizon. Last night's storm had transformed the beach into a wild jungle. The swirls of foam that were still breaking on the shore had left in their wake tree trunks, seaweed, a surfboard and even the skeleton of a bike. But I had to accept the fact that Billie had vanished.

Ever the policewoman, Carole had crouched down by the door and was examining the traces of blood that were beginning to dry on the glass. She looked worried.

'What happened here, Tom? Did you get into a fight with someone?'

'No! It's just—'

'I really think we have a right to know the truth this time!' my best friend interrupted again.

'If you want explanations, shut up and let me finish my sentences!'

'Well, start finishing them! Who did this to your terrace? And whose blood is on this dress? The Pope's? Gandhi's? Marilyn Monroe's?'

'It's actually Billie Donelly's.'

'Billie Donelly? The character from your novels?'

'The very same.'

'I suppose it amuses you to make a fool of me?' Milo exploded. 'I would do anything, anything in the world for you. If you asked me to, I would bury a body in the middle of the night for you. But you obviously couldn't care less, you take me for an idiot—'

Carole got up suddenly from where she had been

crouching and came and stood between us like the referee in a boxing match. Then, in the exasperated tone of a mother scolding her children, she said, 'Time out, boys. Stop arguing. Why don't you both sit down and Tom can explain everything calmly, OK?'

*

And that is what happened.

For fifteen minutes straight I recounted in minute detail the incredible story, from my bizarre first encounter with Billie in the dead of night to this morning's interrogation, which had finally convinced me that she was real.

'So if I've understood you properly,' Milo clarified, 'one of your heroines "fell out" of a badly printed sentence straight into your house. Because she was naked, she put on a dress belonging to your ex-girlfriend, then made you banana pancakes for brekkie. To say thank you, you locked her out on the terrace and while you listened to Miles Davis she slashed up her palm, getting blood all over the place, then stuck herself back together with special ceramic and porcelain Super Glue. Then you made peace by playing twenty questions, after which she decided that you were a pervert and you implied she was a slut, before she said abracadabra and disappeared just as we both arrived. Did I get that right?'

'Just forget it,' I said. 'I knew you'd find some way to turn it against me.'

'Just one last question: what exactly have you been smoking?'

'That's enough out of you!' interrupted Carole.

Milo looked concerned. 'You need to see your psychiatrist again.'

'That's ridiculous, I feel fine.'

'Look, I know that I'm responsible for your financial situation. I know I shouldn't have put pressure on you to finish your book within the deadline, but you're really scaring me now, Tom. You're losing it.'

'You're just a little burned out.' Carole tried to soften Milo's words. 'You've been under a lot of strain recently. For three years you barely stopped: writing through the night, meeting fans, lectures, tours all over the world to promote your books. Anyone would collapse under that kind of pressure. Your break-up with Aurore was just the final straw. You need to rest, that's all.'

'Stop treating me like a kid.'

'You have to start seeing your shrink again,' Milo repeated.

'She mentioned a course of sleep therapy to us—'

'What do you mean, "to us"? Have you been talking to Dr Schnabel behind my back?'

'We're on your side, Tom,' said Milo, trying to calm me down.

'Then why can't you just leave me alone? Why don't you sort out your own life instead of always interfering with mine?'

Hurt by this retort, Milo shook his head and opened his mouth as if to reply, but his expression darkened and he remained silent. Instead, he took a Dunhill from the open pack on the table and went out to the beach to smoke alone.

I was alone with Carole. She also lit a cigarette, inhaling deeply before passing it to me, just like when we were ten years old and we used to share a cigarette, hidden behind the scrawny palm trees in MacArthur Park. No longer on duty, she shook her hair out of its knot, letting the ebony waves cascade over her dark-blue uniform. With her hair loose, and her familiar clear gaze, she could have passed for the teenage girl she had once been. The bond between us was more than just mutual understanding and affection. Nor was it just an ordinary friendship. It was one of those unbreakable connections that can only be formed in childhood, but which last a lifetime, for better or worse. More often for worse.

As always when we found ourselves alone together, the memories of our chaotic adolescence flooded back. The empty lots that were the only view we had, the suffocating air of the asphalt quagmire imprisoning us, the painful memory of the conversations we used to have after school out on the basketball courts.

This time more than ever it felt like we were twelve years old again. As though all the books I had sold, all the criminals she had caught were just part of an act we were both putting on for the rest of the world, when really we were still back there.

After all, it was no coincidence that none of the three of us had ever had any children. We still had too many of our own demons to fight to have enough energy to create new life. I did not know much about Carole's life any more. Recently we had seen less and less of each other, and when we did meet up we both avoided talking about what really mattered.

Maybe we were both living in the naive hope that if we ignored our past long enough it would just disappear. But it wasn't that simple. To forget his childhood, Milo played the fool the whole time, acting as if everything were a joke. As for me, I poured everything I had onto the page, swallowed dangerous cocktails of pills and inhaled crystal meth.

'I don't like big emotional scenes, Tom,' she began nervously, toying with a little spoon.

Now that Milo was no longer in the room, she looked sad and anxious; she no longer had to pretend.

'You know that we will always be there for each other, no matter what,' she continued. 'I'd donate a kidney for you; I'd give both, if you asked me to.'

'I'm not asking you to.'

'For as long as I can remember, it was always you who fixed everything. Now it's my turn to fix you, and I can't seem to help.'

'Don't start with all that crap. I'm fine.'

'No, you're not fine. But there's one thing you have to know: neither Milo nor I would be where we are today if it weren't for you.'

I shrugged. I wasn't even sure that we had come very far at all from where we started. Sure, we lived in better areas, and our lives were no longer dominated by fear, but as the crow flies we were still just a few miles from MacArthur Park.

'However we got here, when I wake up in the morning you're the first thing I think of. And if you sink, Tom, we go down with you. If you let go, my life won't make sense any more.'

I opened my mouth to tell her to stop talking crap, but other words came out instead.

'Are you happy, Carole?'

She looked at me as though she hadn't understood the question. As though in her struggle just to get by she had forgotten all about being happy, as though that idea had fallen by the wayside long ago.

'This thing about the character from your books,' she carried on, 'it's totally implausible, isn't it?'

'It is a little far-fetched,' I admitted.

'Look, I don't know what I can do that would help, other than remind you that I'm your friend, that I love you and that I'm always here. And this sleep therapy thing, it might be worth a try, don't you think?'

I looked at her affectionately. Touched as I was by her desire to help, I was absolutely determined to avoid any kind of therapy.

'Well, even if I wanted to, I couldn't pay for it!'

She brushed my objection aside. 'Do you remember the day you got your first royalty payout? The amount was so large that you insisted on sharing it with me. I refused, of course, but you still found a way of getting my bank details and putting the money in my account yourself. Do you remember my face when I got my bank statement and my balance was suddenly over $300,000!'

As she told the story, Carole began to look a little happier, and her eyes regained some of their sparkle.

I couldn't help but smile, as I remembered that happy time when I had believed that money would solve all our problems. For a few moments, life seemed a little brighter, but it didn't last long, and there were tears of distress in her eyes as she begged, 'Accept the offer. Please. I want to pay for it.'

She was once again the abused little girl that I had met all those years ago, and it was to make her happy that I agreed to the treatment.

12

Rehab

Death will come for me,
and she will have your eyes
Title of a poem found on Cesare Pavese's
bedside table after his suicide

At the wheel of the Bugatti, Milo drove slowly, which was not like him at all. We sat in tense silence.

'It's going to be fine. Don't look like that. It's not as if I'm checking you into Betty Ford!'

'Yeah, whatever.'

Back at my house, we had clashed again whilst looking for the keys to the car. We had searched for an hour without finding them. For the first time in our lives we had almost come to blows. Finally, after throwing a few home truths at each other, we had sent a runner over to Milo's office to pick up the spare keys.

He turned on the radio to lighten the mood, but the snippet of Amy Winehouse's refrain only increased the tension.

I said NO, NO, NO

I lowered my window and watched the palm trees that lined the seafront whip past us, feeling even worse than before. Maybe Milo was right. Maybe I was losing my mind. Maybe I was seeing things. After all, I was aware that whenever I wrote I was on a knife edge. Writing plunged me into a strange limbo where reality began to fade and my characters became more and more real to me, so much so that they would follow me wherever I went. I shared their suffering, their doubts and their joy, and they would continue to haunt me well after the novel had been completed. My characters dominated my dreams and sat with me at breakfast. They were with me when I bought my groceries and when I went out for dinner. They were even there when I made love. It was at once exhilarating and pathetic, intoxicating and disturbing. However, up until now, I had always been able to stop this temporary delirium from tipping over into madness. If previously my imagination had occasionally gone too far, it had never threatened to make a madman of me. Why should it start now, when I had not written so much as a line in months?

'Oh, I almost forgot. I brought this for you,' said Milo, throwing a small plastic bottle into my lap.

I picked it up.

My tranquillisers.

I unscrewed the lid and studied the little white pills that seemed to be taunting me from the bottom of the bottle.

Why give them to me now, when you've tried so hard to get me off them?

'It wasn't a good idea to make you go completely cold turkey,' he explained.

My heart started racing and I felt suddenly anxious and alone. I hurt all over, like a drug addict waiting for the next hit. How was it possible to be in this much pain without having sustained any actual injuries?

I found it odd that, in this instance, my best friend was my dealer.

'This sleep therapy thing is going to make you feel like a new man,' Milo reassured me. 'They make you sleep like a baby for ten days straight!'

He was trying to cheer me up, but I could tell he didn't really believe what he was saying.

I gripped the orange bottle tightly, so tightly that the plastic felt as though it were about to crack. I knew that all I had to do was let just one of the small white tablets dissolve under my tongue to feel instantly relieved. I could even take three or four and just go to sleep. They had a lovely effect on me – 'You're lucky,' Dr Schnabel had told me. 'Some people suffer very nasty side effects.'

Determined to show I wasn't dependent, I put the bottle in my pocket without opening it.

'If the treatment doesn't work, we'll try other things,' Milo promised. 'I've heard about this guy in New York – Connor McCoy. Apparently he works wonders with hypnosis.'

Hypnosis, artificially induced sleep, bottles of pills. I was beginning to tire of fleeing reality, even if at the moment my reality was a difficult one. I did not want to spend ten days in a coma induced by neuroleptic drugs. I didn't like the lack of responsibility on my part that this treatment involved. Now I was keen to deal with my demons head-on even if it killed me.

I had long been fascinated by the links between mental

illness and creativity. Camille Claudel, Maupassant, Nerval and Artaud had all gradually succumbed to madness. Virginia Woolf had drowned herself in a river; Cesare Pavese had ended his life with an overdose of barbiturates in a hotel room; Nicholas Staël had thrown himself out of a window; John Kennedy Toole had run a hose from the exhaust pipe of his car to the inside of the vehicle; not to mention the great Hemingway, who had blown his face off with a rifle. Same again for Kurt Cobain: a bullet in the skull on a pale Seattle morning, leaving nothing but a note addressed to his imaginary childhood friend: 'It's better to burn out than fade away.'

As good a way to go as any, I suppose.

Each one of these artists had tried to make their way in the world, but it always ended the same way. If art exists because real life isn't enough, perhaps there comes a point where even art is no longer enough and the only logical conclusion is madness and death. And even if I was not as gifted as these particular individuals I was unlucky enough to share their neuroses.

*

Milo pulled into the parking lot of a modern building surrounded by carefully planted trees. The building was a striking combination of pink marble and glass: Dr Sophia Schnabel's private clinic.

'We're your allies, not your enemies,' Carole reminded me, as she met us on the steps leading to the entrance.

The three of us went in together. At reception, I was surprised to find an appointment had already been made for me, and that my stay in the clinic had been planned the previous evening.

Resigned to my fate, I followed my friends into the lift without putting up a fight. The glass capsule took us up to the top floor, where a secretary led us into a huge office, assuring us that the doctor would soon be with us.

The room was light and spacious, with a large desk and white leather sofa.

'Cool chair,' whistled Milo in admiration as he sat down on a seat shaped like a hand.

There were several Buddhist sculptures dotted around the room, which created a serene atmosphere, no doubt useful for relaxing more difficult patients. A bronze bust of Siddhartha, a Wheel of Law made of sandstone, a pair of marble gazelles complete with fountain in the middle – all the usual suspects were there.

I watched Milo trying to come up with one of his customary jokes. Between the statues and the interior design, there was enough material for an entire stand-up show, but he remained silent. That's when I realised that he was hiding something serious from me.

I looked at Carole for reassurance, but she avoided my gaze by pretending to study the various diplomas that Dr Schnabel had hung on the walls.

Ever since the murder of Ethan Whitaker, Schnabel had been the hottest psychiatrist to the stars. She counted some of the biggest names in Hollywood as patients: actors, singers, producers, politicians, sons of this one, sons of sons of that one.

She even had her own television series, where viewers caught a glimpse of the inner life of 'real people', who got the chance to have a live session with the 'Celebrity Shrink' (that was the programme's title) and describe in detail their unhappy childhood, their addictions, their sexual exploits and how they'd always wanted to try a threesome.

Half the entertainment industry adored Sophia Schnabel. The other half feared her. After practising for twenty years, it was rumoured that she possessed files that rivalled those of Edgar Hoover. She had thousands of hours of recorded therapy sessions that must have contained some of the darkest, most unspeakable secrets in Hollywood history. These files were of course completely confidential and kept under lock and key, but they nevertheless had the power to destroy the entire entertainment industry, not to mention the havoc they could wreak in the world of politics.

A recent event had further consolidated Sophia's hold on the entertainment world. A few months earlier, Stephanie Harrison, the widow of the billionaire Richard Harrison, founder of the Green Cross chain of supermarkets, had died of an overdose at the age of thirty-two. At the autopsy, traces of sedatives, antidepressants and slimming pills were found in her blood. There was nothing unusual in that. Except that the doses were worryingly high. The deceased's brother had accused Schnabel on live television of being entirely responsible for his sister's death. He had engaged an army of lawyers and detectives who searched Stephanie's apartment and found more than fifty prescriptions. They were made out to five different pseudonyms, but all signed by Sophia Schnabel. The discovery had proved extremely damaging to the psychiatrist. With the shock of Michael Jackson's death still fresh in the public's mind, the media suddenly turned on the vast network of doctors that was more than happy to write out endless prescriptions on demand for its wealthier clients. Anxious to limit this dangerous practice, the State of California lodged a complaint against the psychiatrist for writing fraudulent prescriptions, a complaint that was then suddenly and inexplicably withdrawn. This was highly unusual as the prosecutor had all the evidence he needed to charge her. The change of heart, which many put down to a lack of courage on the part of the magistrate, effectively rendered Sophia Schnabel untouchable.

To enter into the privileged inner circle of patients, you had to be recommended by one of her former clients. She was one of the 'hot tips' that celebrities liked to pass around amongst themselves, like the answers to *Where do you find the best coke? Which trader will get you the best investments? How do you get courtside seats at the Lakers' game? Who do you ring to get a call-girl-who-doesn't-look-like-a-call-girl?* (the men) *or Who do you call to get breasts-that-don't-make-it-look-like-you've-had-your-breasts-done?* (the women).

I had been given Sophia's number by a Canadian soap actress that Milo had tried to chat up, without much success. Schnabel had treated her for a severe form of agoraphobia. At first I had thought this girl bland and uninteresting but she was in fact cultured and discerning, and through her I discovered the charms of John Cassavetes' films and the paintings of Robert Ryman.

Sophia Schnabel and I had never really seen eye to eye. Our sessions now mostly consisted of me simply picking up my medication, which made us both happy: she got paid for a full consultation for only five minutes' work, and I had access to all the chemicals I wanted to pump into my body.

*

'Good morning,' Dr Schnabel greeted us as she walked into her office. She always used her trademark welcoming smile from her television programme, but today she also sported the familiar tight leather jacket left open to reveal a low-cut blouse underneath. Some people thought she was stylish.

As always, it took me a few moments to get used to her shock of hair, which she tried to tame with a strange perm that made her look as if she were wearing the still-warm corpse of a small poodle.

I could tell by her greeting that she had already spoken with Milo and Carole. I was excluded from the conversation as if they were my parents and they had already taken a decision on my behalf that I had no say in at all.

What I found most disturbing was seeing Carole

so distant and cold after the emotional conversation we'd had just an hour ago. She was uncomfortable and hesitant, visibly upset at being part of a scheme she didn't approve of. On the surface, Milo looked more sure of himself, but I sensed that this was an act for my benefit.

As I listened to Sophia Schnabel's ambiguous words, it became obvious that a course of sleep therapy had never been the plan. The battery of tests she wanted me to undergo were just an excuse to lock me up in here. Milo was trying to have me put away so he didn't have to deal with the financial mess he had made! I was familiar enough with California law to know that a doctor could enforce involuntary committal of a patient for up to seventy-two hours if they judged the patient to be so unstable as to present a danger to society, and in my present state I fitted into that category pretty well.

I had clashed with the authorities more than once over the past year, and it would be a long time before I was off their radar. I was currently on bail awaiting trial for possession of drugs. My encounter with Billie – which Milo was currently recounting to the doctor in vivid detail – would be enough to class me as psychotic and prone to hallucinations.

Just when I thought there could be no more surprises, I heard Carole describing the bloodstains on my shirt and the terrace windows.

'Was it your blood, Mr Boyd?' asked the psychiatrist.

I chose not to explain; she wouldn't have believed me anyway. Her mind was already made up, and I could almost hear the report that she would later dictate to her secretary:

> The patient has self-harmed, or has tried to inflict serious wounds on another party. The patient's judgement, clearly impaired, renders him incapable of understanding his need for treatment. This justifies involuntary committal.

'If you don't mind, we're going to start the tests.'

Yes, I did mind. I didn't want any testing, I didn't want to be put to sleep, I didn't want any more pills! I got up to end the conversation.

I walked over to the polished glass screen that stood in front of the sculpture representing the Wheel of Law, decorated with little flames and floral motifs. The Buddhist emblem was about three feet tall and had eight spokes, which were supposed to indicate the path that led away from suffering. Dharma's wheel worked thus: follow the path toward 'what must be', and explore the path until you find 'the right decision'.

I had a sudden epiphany and lifted the wheel, hurling it with all my strength at the bay window, which shattered into a million tiny glass diamonds.

*

I can still hear Carole's scream.

I still see the satin curtains fluttering in the wind.

I still feel the gust of wind that rushed in through the gaping hole, scattering papers and overturning a vase.

I still hear the cry that seemed to come from the heavens.

I still feel how I just let myself fall into the void.

I still feel my body tumbling.

I still remember the tears of the little girl from MacArthur Park.

13
The escapees

*People ask me when I'm going to make a film with
real people. What's real?*
Tim Burton

'You took your time!' I heard a voice complain.

It was not an angel, much less St Peter.

It was Billie Donelly.

Clinic parking lot
Midday

I had fallen two storeys and now found myself tangled in
a curtain on the roof of a beaten-up old Dodge, parked
exactly under the window of Sophia Schnabel's office.

I had a cracked rib, and my knees, neck and ankle
were killing me. But I was alive.

'I don't want to hurry you,' said Billie, 'but I'm worried
that if we don't get out of here pretty damn quickly
they'll stick you in a straitjacket.'

I saw that she had once again helped herself to
Aurore's clothes and was wearing a white camisole
with a pair of faded jeans and a belted jacket with
silvery edging.

'Come on, unless you want to spend all night on this
roof!' she said, jangling a bunch of keys on a Bugatti
key-ring.

'So you're the one who nicked Milo's keys!' I exclaimed, climbing down from the Dodge.

'You're welcome!'

Incredibly, I seemed only to have sustained a few minor injuries, but when I put weight on my foot I couldn't stop myself crying out in pain. I had a badly sprained ankle and found I couldn't walk properly.

'THERE HE IS!' shouted Milo, who had suddenly appeared in the parking lot and was now sending three male nurses built like rugby players after me.

Billie got into the driver's seat of the Bugatti and I threw myself in beside her.

She slammed down the accelerator and headed for the parking lot exit just as the barrier was coming down. Without a second's hesitation she screeched to a halt on the gravel.

'TOM! COME BACK!' Carole begged as we hurtled past her.

The three giants tried to block our path, but Billie just accelerated, clearly enjoying herself.

'You must admit you're glad I'm here!' she announced triumphantly as the car smashed through the barrier and we sped toward freedom.

14

Who's that girl?

Rage, rage against the dying of the light
Dylan Thomas

'Where are you taking me?' I asked, clutching my seat belt.

Turning onto Pico Boulevard, the Bugatti was now heading toward the Pacific Coast Highway at full speed.

At the wheel, Billie, clearly under the impression she was the new Ayrton Senna, had adopted an aggressive driving technique, favouring sudden braking, rapid acceleration and abrupt turns at top speed.

'This thing goes like a rocket!' she said happily, instead of answering my question.

Thrown back against the headrest, I felt as though I were on an aircraft about to take off. I watched her change gears with surprising dexterity. She was obviously having a field day.

'The engine's a little noisy, don't you think?'

'*Noisy*? Are you kidding? It's like Mozart!'

She had obviously forgotten my question, so I repeated it, feeling annoyed.

'Where are you taking me?'

'Mexico.'

'Huh?'

'I packed a suitcase and a washbag for you.'

'What? I never agreed to this! I'm not going anywhere.'

I demanded instead to be dropped off at a hospital so I could get my ankle looked at. I was not at all happy with the way things were going. But she ignored my request.

'Stop the car!' I commanded, grabbing her arm.

'You're hurting me!'

'Stop the damn car!'

She slammed on the brakes and swerved to the side of the highway. The tyres of the Bugatti screeched over the asphalt before coming to a halt in a cloud of dust.

*

'Why on earth do you want to go to Mexico?'

We had both got out of the car and were arguing on the strip of grass that bordered the road.

'I'm taking you where you're not brave enough to go on your own!'

'Oh, of course! And where might that be then?'

I had to shout over the roar of the passing traffic, exacerbating the pain in my chest.

'We're going to find Aurore!' she yelled, just as a truck narrowly missed colliding with the Bugatti and sped past with its horn blaring.

I stared at her in a daze.

'I don't see what Aurore has to do with any of this.'

The air was thick with fumes. Beyond the wire fencing I could make out the runways and control towers of Los Angeles airport.

Billie opened the trunk of the car and took out a copy of *People Magazine*. There were several headlines splashed across the cover: Brangelina's potential break-up, yet another Pete Doherty scandal, the holiday snaps of the latest Formula 1 champion and Rafael Barros with his new fiancée – Aurore Valancourt.

Just to torture myself, I opened the gossip magazine at the relevant page to find glamorous photos taken in some utopian beach resort. Surrounded by steep rock faces, white sand and turquoise water, Aurore radiated beauty and serenity in the arms of her Hispanic hero.

My vision blurred. Paralysed by shock, I tried to concentrate on the words in the article but I couldn't. Only the highlighted quotes managed to leave their painful imprint on my mind.

Aurore: *We only met recently, but I know that Rafael is the one for me.*
Rafael: *Our joy will be complete when we have a child.*

Disgusted, I sent the rag flying to the side of the highway, then, despite my current lack of a licence, climbed into the driver's seat, slammed the door shut and turned the car round to head back into town.

'Hey! You can't just leave me by the side of the road!' Billie shouted after me, waving her arms and positioning herself in front of the hood.

I let her get in, realising that I was not going to have a moment's peace.

'I understand what you're going through,' she said.

'There's no need to feel sorry for me; you have no idea what you're talking about.'

As I drove, I tried to get my head straight. I needed time to think about the events of the morning, I needed to...

'So where are you taking us?'

'Back to my place.'

'But there's no such thing as "your place" any more! And there's definitely no such thing as "my place".'

'I'll get myself a lawyer,' I muttered. 'I'll find a way to get my house back, and all the money that Milo lost.'

'It won't work,' she interrupted, shaking her head sadly.

'I didn't ask for your opinion – mind your own business!'

'But this *is* my business! May I remind you that I'm stuck here because of your mistake, because of that stupid badly printed book!'

At the traffic lights, I scrabbled around in my pockets until I found my tranquillisers. I had a cracked rib, a swollen ankle and a broken heart. So I felt justified in swallowing three tablets in one go.

'That's right, take the easy way out,' said Billie reproachfully, her voice heavy with disappointment.

At that precise moment, I could happily have murdered her. Instead I took a deep breath and tried to stay calm.

'You won't get your girlfriend back by just sitting on your butt stuffing yourself with pills, you know.'

'You don't know anything about my relationship with Aurore. And, for your information, I've tried everything to get her back.'

'But maybe you didn't try the right way, or at the right time. Maybe you think you know what women want, but really you don't know anything about them. I think I could help you—'

'If you really wanted to help me, you'd shut up for a minute! Just for one minute!'

'You want to get rid of me? Well, get back to work then! The sooner you finish your novel, the sooner I can return to the world of fiction.'

Clearly pleased with her retort, she sat back and crossed her arms, waiting for a reaction that never came.

'Listen,' she said excitedly, 'I'll make you a deal: we go to Mexico, I help you get Aurore back, and in exchange you write the third part of your trilogy, because that's the only way to get me back where I belong.'

I rubbed my eyes, unsure of how to respond to this extraordinary proposition.

'I brought your laptop with us,' she added, as if this fact would somehow sway my decision.

'It doesn't work like that,' I explained. 'You can't write a novel to order. There's a kind of alchemy to it. I would need at least six months of dedicated hard work to finish the book. It demands an ascetic commitment that I have neither the strength nor the desire to give to it.'

She looked at me mockingly, imitating my voice: '"You can't write a novel to order. There's a kind of alchemy to it …"'

She paused for a few seconds before bursting into hysterical laughter.

'My God, you need to stop wallowing in your own misery. If you don't snap out of it soon, it'll get the better of you for good. It's so much easier to self-destruct gradually than to try and pull yourself together, isn't it?'

Touché.

I didn't reply, although I took her point. She wasn't totally wrong. Earlier in the psychiatrist's office, when I had hurled the statue through the window, something inside me had been released: an inner protest, a need to regain control of my life. But I had to admit that that desire had disappeared as quickly as it had surfaced.

Now, however, I had the impression that Billie was not going to drop this, and was not afraid to confront me with difficult truths.

'You know what will happen if you don't really start to fight your natural inclinations?'

'No, but I'm sure you're about to tell me.'

'You'll keep taking the pills and you'll keep snorting drugs. Each time you'll sink a little lower into self-hatred and self-disgust. And when you're stone broke, you'll end up on the street where one day they'll find your corpse with a syringe still sticking out of your forearm.'

'Charming.'

'You should also be aware that if you don't act now, you'll never find the energy or the strength to write another line.'

With both hands on the steering wheel, I gazed absent-mindedly at the road ahead. She was right, of course she was, but it was probably too late to do anything about it now. I was probably destined to go under for good, when my destructive side finally won out.

She looked intently at me. 'And all those lofty morals you preach in your books – resilience in the face of adversity, second chances, inner resources you have to find in yourself to recover from life's blows – they're much easier to write about than to put into practice, aren't they?' All of a sudden her voice faltered unexpectedly, as if overcome with emotion, tiredness and fear. 'And what about me? You don't give a damn about me! I've lost everything in your story: my family, my job, my home and I'm stuck in a reality where the only person who can help me would prefer to wallow in self-pity!'

I was taken aback by her reaction and turned my head to look at her, not knowing what to say. Her face was haloed by the sun, and her eyes glittered with distress.

I glanced in my rear-view mirror and slammed down the gas pedal, overtaking a long line of cars, before doing another U-turn and heading for the south again.

'Where are we going?' she asked, wiping away a stray tear.

'To Mexico,' I said, 'to get my life back, and to change yours.'

15
The pact

*No magic tricks, no special effects. It was created by
words thrown down on the page, and words on the page
are the only thing that will rid us of it*
Stephen King

We stopped at a service station just past Torrance
Beach. I don't know if the Bugatti had a rocket engine,
but it certainly consumed as much fuel.

Pacific Coast Highway
South Bay, LA
2 p.m.
The gas station was crowded. To avoid waiting too
long, I decided to fill the tank at one of the self-service
stands. I almost cried out in pain when I stepped out
of the car; my ankle was hurting more than ever and it
had started to swell up. I inserted my card, put in the
PIN code, but

```
TRANSACTION NOT PERMITTED
```

The message was splashed across the screen
in angry digital lettering. I pulled my card from the
machine and wiped it with my sleeve then tried again,
still without success.

Damn it.

I rummaged around in my wallet, but found only a lone $20 bill. I stuck my head angrily through the passenger window.

'My card doesn't work!'

'Of course it doesn't! You don't have a penny to your name, remember? It's not a magic card!'

'You don't have any money by any chance, do you?'

'And where would I have stashed that then?' she answered calmly. 'I was as naked as the day I was born when I landed on your terrace!'

'Well, thanks for the help!' I fumed, limping over to the till.

The shop was crammed with customers. In the background Stan Getz and João Gilberto's magical version of 'The Girl from Ipanema' could be heard, a masterpiece sadly ruined by being played to death in countless elevators, supermarkets and places like this.

'Cool car!' someone called admiringly from the line.

Several customers and cashiers looked curiously through the window at the Bugatti, and a crowd quickly gathered around me. I explained my credit card problem to the guy on the till who listened to me patiently. I had a trustworthy face and a car worth $2 million, even if I didn't have enough money to put two gallons of gas in its tank. People in the crowd started to fire questions at me that I didn't have the first clue how to answer: was it true that you had to put down a deposit of $300,000 when you ordered the car? Was there a secret key that allowed you to go up to 250 mph? Was the gearbox really worth $15,000 all on its own?

A customer who had just paid his bill, an elegant man in his fifties, with salt and pepper hair and a white shirt with a mandarin collar, jokingly offered to buy my watch so I could pay for my fuel. He offered me $50 for it. Then more serious bids started to roll in: an employee called $100, then $150 before the manager trumped him with an offer of $200.

It had been a gift from Milo and I loved it for the simplicity of its discreet metal casing, off-white face and black crocodile strap. However, I knew as little about watch-making as I did about cars. The watch told me what time it was and that was all I ever asked of it.

Everyone in the queue had joined in with the auction, and the bidding stood at $350. It was at this point that the man in the mandarin collar decided to take a thick wad of notes out of his wallet. He counted out ten $100 bills and laid them on the counter.

'I'll give you $1,000 for the watch if we do this quickly, no questions asked,' he said solemnly.

I hesitated. I had paid more attention to my watch in the last three minutes than I had in two years of owning it. Its rather unpronounceable name meant nothing to me but I was no expert on the subject. I could have recited entire pages of Dorothy Parker but I would have been hard pressed to name more than two brands of watch.

'You have yourself a deal,' I finally replied, undoing the strap.

I pocketed the dollar bills and gave $80 to the guy behind the counter to pay for my gas in advance. I was just about to leave when I remembered something, and asked him if he had any bandages for my ankle.

Fairly satisfied with my purchases, I went back to the Bugatti and inserted the nozzle in the fuel tank. As he pulled away, I saw my buyer give me a brief wave before speeding off in his Mercedes.

'How did you get on then?' asked Billie, lowering the window.

'Fine, no thanks to you.'

'Go on, how did you do it?'

'I used my natural wiles,' I said proudly as I watched the numbers flash past on the machine.

I had aroused her curiosity.

'And?'

'I sold my watch.'

'Your Portuguese?'

'My Portuguese what?'

'Your watch. It's the IWC Portuguese model.'

'Well, that's useful information.'

'How much did you sell it for?'

'One thousand dollars. That should keep us in gas all the way to Mexico. And I'll even buy you lunch before we set off.'

She ignored that and said, 'How much did you really sell it for?'

'I really sold it for $1,000,' I repeated, replacing the hose on the pump.

Billie put her head in her hands.

'That watch is worth at least twenty grand!'

My immediate reaction was that she was joking. Surely people didn't pay that much for watches? But, judging from her obvious disgust, I was forced to admit that I'd been had.

*

Half an hour later
A roadside fast-food restaurant near Huntington Beach

In the men's room, I washed my face and strapped up my ankle, then went back to join Billie at our table.

Perched on a stool, she was working her way through a giant banana split that she had ordered as dessert after two cheeseburgers and a large portion of fries. How did she manage to stay so skinny with an appetite like that?

'Mmm, delicious. Youwannatastesome?' she asked, her mouth full.

I shook my head, choosing instead to wipe some whipped cream off the tip of her nose with my napkin.

She smiled at me then spread a map out on the table between us to show me the route we were taking.

'Right, it shouldn't be too hard. According to the magazine, Aurore and her boyfriend are on vacation until the end of the week in a luxury hotel in Cabo San Lucas.'

She leaned over the map and with a marker pen made a small cross on the southern tip of Mexico's Baja California peninsula.

I had heard of the place before; it was a popular destination for surfers because of its extremely powerful waves.

'It's not exactly down the road, is it? Don't you think it would be better to fly there?'

She looked at me darkly.

'Taking airplanes costs money, and selling your most valuable possessions at discount prices isn't a great way of holding on to it!'

'We could always sell the car.'

'Enough stupid suggestions! Concentrate! Any-way, you know perfectly well I don't have a passport.'

She traced an imaginary route across the map with her finger.

'At the moment I think we're about 125 miles from San Diego. I suggest we avoid the freeways and toll roads so we don't waste any more money, but if you let me drive we could be at the Mexican border in under four hours.'

'And why would I let you do that?'

'I'm a bit more in my element, aren't I? Cars don't seem to be your cup of tea. You seem more interested in book stuff than in mechanics. And, anyway, with that ankle—'

'I'm not so sure—'

'You look offended! I hope it's not that you have a problem with being driven by a woman. I would have thought you were past that macho bullshit by now!'

'All right! No need to go off at the deep end – you can drive us to San Diego but after that we'll take it in turns because it's a long journey.'

She seemed satisfied with this arrangement and continued with the explanation of her master plan.

'If all goes well, we'll be in Tijuana by this evening

134

and we'll be able to look around for a nice little motel to stay the night in.'

'A nice little motel.' *As if we were on vacation!*

'And then tomorrow we'll wake up early and get going straight away. Cabo San Lucas is 750 miles from Tijuana. We could do that in a day, and get to your one true love's hotel by sundown.'

When she put it like that, it sounded easy enough.

My phone vibrated in my pocket – I could still receive calls, even if I could no longer make them. Milo's number flashed on the screen. He had been leaving me voicemails every ten minutes for the last hour, but I was systematically erasing them, without even listening.

'So we're agreed: I'm going to help you patch things up with your sweetheart and in exchange you're going to write this damned third volume!' she summarised.

'What makes you think I've still got any chance with Aurore? She's madly in love with her Formula 1 man.'

'That's my problem, not yours. You just con-centrate on writing. But no messing around, got it? I want a full-blown proper novel. And don't forget my terms and conditions.'

'I'm sorry? Terms and conditions?'

She nibbled the end of her pen, like a small child about to start her homework.

'Firstly,' she began, marking a large 1) on the paper tablecloth in front of her, 'I want you to stop making me the fall guy in your plotlines. Does it amuse you to lump me with every scumbag on the planet? Do you enjoy setting me up with married men whose wives no longer excite them and who see me as nothing more than a sure thing to satisfy their frustrated sex drives? Maybe my unhappiness makes your female readers feel better about themselves but it's killing me bit by bit.'

This unexpected tirade left me speechless. It was certainly true that I hadn't cut Billie much slack in her life, but as far as I was concerned, that wasn't a problem: she was a fictitious character, a purely abstract creation who existed solely in my imagination and in the imaginations of my readers. She was a heroine whose material form consisted of nothing but words on a page, but now the creature was attacking the creator!

'Secondly,' continued Billie, tracing a 2) on the tablecloth, 'I've had enough of being broke. I love my job, but I work on the cancer ward and I can't deal with watching people suffer and die every day. I've become a human sponge: I absorb my patients' emotions. And I'm also up to my ears in student debt! I don't know if you know what nurses get paid, but it's not exactly Wall Street!'

'So what can I do to make you happy?'

'I want to be transferred to the paediatric ward. I want to deal with life, rather than death. I've been asking to move for two years now, but that shrew Cornelia Skinner says no every time. She claims we're understaffed. And—'

'And what?'

'I'd love to come into a little money sometime soon, just to oil the wheels.'

'Now hang on—'

'What difference does it make to you? It's so easily

done! It would only take a line! Look, I'll even write it for you: "Billie suddenly inherited half a million dollars from an uncle whose sole living relative she was."'

'Yeah, I guess I could do that. You clearly have no scruples about me killing off an uncle of yours!'

'No, no, not my real uncle obviously, just some great-uncle once removed that I never knew, you know, like in the movies.'

She wrote down her sentence, obviously pleased with herself.

'Is that the end of your letter to Santa? Shall we get going?'

'One more thing,' she said, calmly. 'The most important thing of all.'

She wrote a 3) at the edge of the tablecloth, and then a name:

Jack

'That's it,' she said. 'I want Jack to leave his wife for good to come and live with me.'

Jack was Billie's lover. He was a married man, a selfish jerk with devastating good looks, and the father of two small boys. She had been having a passionate and painful affair with him for the past two years. He was a jealous and possessive narcissist who kept her firmly under his thumb, flipping between declarations of love and humiliating put-downs, always keeping her in the role of a mistress whom he could screw and then discard as he pleased.

I shook my head in disgust.

'Jack thinks with his dick.'

I didn't even see her hand coming. She slapped me as hard as she could, almost knocking me off my stool.

The few customers left in the restaurant had all turned to stare at us, waiting for my reaction.

How can she defend that jerk? wondered the angry voice in my head. *Because she's in love with him, for God's sake!* answered the more rational voice.

'You have no right to pass judgement on my personal life, any more than I have the right to judge yours,' she said defiantly. 'I'm helping you get Aurore back, and you're going to invent a life for me where I wake up every day in Jack's arms – deal?'

She signed the contract that she had drawn up on the tablecloth, then carefully tore it free and offered me her pen.

'Deal,' I said, rubbing my face.

I signed on the proverbial dotted line and threw a few dollar bills on the table so we could leave.

'You'll pay for that slap,' I promised her, giving her a withering look.

'Yeah, we'll see about that,' she said, walking back to the car.

16
Speed limits

That's thirty minutes away. I'll be there in ten.
From *Pulp Fiction*, directed by Quentin Tarantino

'You're driving way too fast!'

We had been travelling for about three hours.

For the first sixty miles or so we had followed the seafront, passing Newport Beach, Laguna Beach and San Clemente, but the coast road was so busy that we'd turned onto California Route 78 after Oceanside, cutting through Escondido.

'You're going way too fast!' I repeated, having got no reaction the first time.

'Are you joking?' replied Billie. 'We're barely doing seventy- five!'

'But the limit here is fifty!'

'So? This thing works fine, doesn't it?' she said, pointing to the radar detector that Milo had installed.

I opened my mouth to protest, but suddenly a red warning light started to flash on the dashboard. An alarming rattling noise came from the engine, which then gave out completely. The vehicle ground to a halt a few yards down the road, giving me the opportunity to vent the anger that had been building up inside me since we had started driving.

'I knew it was a ridiculous idea to go chasing after

Aurore! We'll never get to Mexico – we have no plan, no money and now no car!'

'It's OK, there's no need to get wound up; we might be able to fix this ourselves,' she said, getting out of the car.

'What do you mean, fix it? It's a Bugatti, not a bicycle!'

Unruffled, Billie opened the hood and started to rummage around in the engine. I followed her, continuing my tirade.

'These things are all electronic now; you need twelve engineers just to work out what the problem is in the first place. I've had enough: I'll hitch a ride back to Malibu.'

'Well, if you thought the car breaking down was going to let you off the hook, you can think again,' she retorted, closing the hood.

'What makes you say that?'

'I fixed it.'

'What? Seriously?'

She turned the key in the ignition and the car started up immediately.

'There wasn't really anything wrong with it; one of the radiators in the cooling system got disconnected, which automatically cut off the fourth turbo compressor and turned on the warning light for the central hydraulic system.'

'Right,' I replied, nonplussed. 'Nothing wrong with it at all, really.'

When we were back on the highway, I had to ask: 'Where did you learn to do stuff like that?'

'You of all people should know that!'

I had to think back over the details of my various characters to come up with the answer.

'Your two brothers!'

'Of course!' she replied, accelerating. 'You gave me mechanics for brothers and they passed on their passion to me.'

*

'You're driving way too fast!'

'Oh, you're not going to start that again, are you?'

Twenty minutes later

'Indicate! Normally people indicate before they suddenly pull into another lane!'

She stuck out her tongue impishly.

We had just passed Rancho Santa Fe and we were trying to get back onto State Route 15. The air was warm and the afternoon sun cast a soft light on the trees and brought out the red ochre tones of the hills. We were not far from the Mexican border.

'And while you're at it,' I said, looking pointedly at the car radio, 'would you turn off the crappy tunes you've been inflicting on me for hours?'

'You have such a refined turn of phrase – it really shows how well read you are.'

'Seriously, how can you listen to this stuff? Remixes of remixes, bad rap lyrics, plastic R & B singers that all look and sound exactly the same—'

'It's just like being in the car with my father.'

'So what's this trash playing now?'

She rolled her eyes dramatically. 'Trash? It's the Black Eyed Peas!'

'Do you ever listen to real music?'

'What do you class as "real music"?'

'Bach, the Rolling Stones, Miles Davis, Bob Dylan—'

'All right, well, why don't you get your gramophone out for me sometime, Grandpa?' she replied playfully, turning off the radio.

For three minutes she was completely silent – a feat worthy of *The Guinness Book of World Records* as far as she was concerned – before piping up again.

'How old are you?'

'Thirty-six,' I answered, frowning.

'Ten years older than me,' she pointed out.

'Yes, and?'

'And nothing,' she said, whistling to herself.

'Look, if you're going to start going on about generation gaps, you can stop right there, honey.'

'That's what my grandfather used to call me.'

I turned the radio back on and started hunting for a station that played jazz.

'Still, don't you think it's quite strange that you only listen to music that was recorded before you were born?'

'Tell me, lover-boy Jack, how old is he again?'

'Forty-two,' she conceded, 'but he's a bit more on it than you are.'

'What are you talking about? Every morning he does his Frank Sinatra in the bathroom, belting out "My Way" in front of the mirror! He uses his hair dryer as a microphone!'

She looked at me with big, round eyes.

'That's right,' I said. 'Author's privilege. I know all your secrets, even the ones you don't like to admit to yourself. Joking aside though, what do you see in the guy?'

She just shrugged. 'He got under my skin. I can't explain it.'

'Try.'

She looked at me earnestly.

'From the first time we met, there was something between us, something instinctive, like animal attraction. We recognised each other. As if we had been together before we even met.'

What a load of crap. A string of banalities that I was unfortunately responsible for.

'But this guy couldn't care less about you. When you first met, he hid his wedding ring. He waited six months before he told you he was married!'

She blanched, clearly stung by the painful memory.

'And, between you and me, Jack was never planning on leaving his wife.'

'That's exactly what I'm relying on you to change!'

'Time and time again he humiliates you, and instead of telling him where to stick it you hero-worship him!'

This time, she didn't even try to excuse him and concentrated on driving, which made us speed up again.

'Do you remember last winter? He promised you, swore to you, that you would spend New Year's Eve together. I know it meant a lot to you, symbolically, to start the year with him. So you took care of everything.

You booked a beautiful little bungalow in Hawaii and paid for the whole thing yourself. And what happened? The night before, he told you he wouldn't be able to leave his family. Always the same story – his wife and kids first. And do you remember what happened next?'

As I waited for an answer that I knew wasn't coming, I studied the dashboard, which showed we were going at over 100 mph.

'You really are driving too fast.'

She took one hand off the steering wheel to give me the finger, at the precise moment a speed camera flashed, photographing us going faster than we had gone all day.

She slammed on the brakes, but the damage was done.

The classic trap: a speed camera just at the edge of some godforsaken hole in the middle of nowhere, at least half a mile from the nearest house.

We heard the screech of a siren, accompanied by flashing lights.

Tucked out of sight behind a thicket, the local sheriff's Ford Crown had just come out of its hiding place. I turned round to see the blue and red lights of the vehicle that was now giving chase.

'I told you about ten times you were going too fast!'

'Well, if you weren't so annoying—'

'Oh, it's so easy to blame other people, isn't it?'

'Shall I try to lose them?'

'Stop messing around and pull over.'

Billie flicked on her indicator and reluctantly did as I asked, while I kept on at her.

'Now we really are in trouble: you don't have a licence,

you're driving a stolen car and you've definitely set a record for the worst case of speeding in the history of San Diego County!'

'OK, OK, are you done yet? I've had enough of your self-righteous preaching! No wonder your girl ran off!'

I glared at her, furious. 'There really are no words to describe you! You're the ten plagues of Egypt all by yourself!'

I didn't even wait for a response; all I could think about was what being pulled over might mean. The sheriff's officer would seize the Bugatti, call for reinforcements, take us to the station and inform Milo that his vehicle had been found. Things would only get worse when they discovered that Billie didn't have a driver's licence. Not to mention the fact that I was still a celebrity on bail, which wasn't going to help matters.

The patrol car had pulled over several yards behind us. Billie had switched off the ignition and was fidgeting nervously in her seat like a child.

'Don't try to be smart. Just stay still and keep your hands on the steering wheel.'

She innocently undid a button of her shirt to better expose her chest, which was the final straw.

'As if that's going to make any difference! You don't realise what you're doing, do you? You just broke the speed limit by 50 mph! You'll most likely have to make a court appearance and spend the next month in prison!'

She paled visibly and turned round, watching the police officer anxiously.

Even though his lights were still flashing, and it was broad daylight, the officer shone a harsh flashlight on us.

'What's he playing at?' she asked, sounding worried.

'He just put the licence plate number into his database and he's waiting for the results.'

'We're probably not going to get to Mexico now, are we?'

'You could say that.'

I waited a few seconds before deciding to twist the knife further.

'And you're probably never going to get Jack back now either.'

There was a deathly silence as we waited for the officer to deign to get out of his sedan.

In the rear-view mirror I saw him come toward us like a calm predator, stalking a prey that he already knew was his, and a feeling of despair crashed over me.

So this is how it all ends.

My insides felt hollow. I was overwhelmed by a sudden feeling of emptiness. It was probably to be expected that I felt strange: I had after all just lived through the most inexplicably bizarre day of my life so far. In less than twenty-four hours I had lost all my money, the most maddening of all my heroines had landed naked in my living room, I had thrown myself through a window to avoid being committed, fallen two storeys onto the roof of a Dodge, confidently sold for $1,000 a watch that was worth $20,000 and signed a hare-brained contract written out on a tablecloth, just after being sent flying by a slap around the face.

But I was feeling much better now, fresher and more optimistic than I had felt in a while.

I looked at Billie as if we were about to part for good,

as if this were the last time we would ever be alone together. As if the spell were about to be broken. For the first time, her eyes looked sad and full of despair.

'I'm sorry I hit you,' she apologised. 'I got a bit carried away.'

'Oh, that's OK.'

'And you couldn't possibly have known about the watch.'

'Apology accepted.'

'And I should never have said that thing about Aurore—'

'OK, OK! No need to overdo it.'

The police officer was circling the car as if he were a potential buyer trying to decide whether he wanted it or not, then he double-checked the licence plate, taking his time, clearly enjoying himself.

'We're not going to give up that easily though,' I said, thinking aloud.

I was beginning to suspect that characters from novels were not really meant to function in the real world. I knew Billie; I knew all her flaws, the things in her life that made her unhappy, her candour, her vulnerability. In a way I felt responsible for what happened to her, and I didn't want her to experience the trauma of prison. She looked up at me and I saw a flicker of hope in her eyes. It was us two against the world.

The officer rapped on the window, indicating that we should open it.

Billie obeyed meekly.

He was the cowboy type, a macho man in the Jeff Bridges mould, with a suntanned face, aviator sunglasses and a gold chain that hung down over his hairy chest.

Clearly delighted to find himself with a pretty young girl in his clutches, he seemed not even to have noticed I was in the car.

'Afternoon, ma'am.'

'Afternoon, Officer.'

'Know how fast you were going?'

'Kind of. Pretty near a hundred, right?'

'Any particular reason for going so fast?'

'I'm in a hurry.'

'A real beauty you've got here.'

'Yeah, not like your shitheap,' she said, looking back at his car. 'That thing probably can't do much more than seventy.'

The cop's face darkened and he realised it was probably better just to go through the whole procedure by the book.

'Licence and vehicle documents.'

'Good luck…' she said, calmly turning on the ignition.

His hand went straight to his holster.

'Please switch off the engine immediately—'

'… because you're going to find it pretty hard to catch us in that old thing.'

17

Billie and Clyde

One of these days they'll get us,
But I don't care, Bonnie's the one I need
I don't care what they do to us,
I am Bonnie and it's Clyde Barrow for me
Serge Gainsbourg

'We need to get rid of the car!'

The Bugatti was tearing along a narrow road lined by eucalyptus trees. The sheriff had made no attempt to follow us, but we were sure he would have called for back-up. Even if he couldn't get anyone to help him, the marine base camp a few miles away meant this area was under constant surveillance. Basically, we were trapped.

Suddenly, a dull whine that seemed to be coming from the sky above us added to our troubles.

'Is it us they're after?'

I rolled down the window and, craning my neck, looked up to see a police helicopter hovering above the forest.

'I have a horrible feeling it is.'

Record-breaking speed on a public highway, insulting a law enforcement officer, fleeing arrest; if the sheriff had decided to pull out all the stops, we were risking everything.

Billie swerved sharply down the first forest path we came to, and drove the Bugatti as far into the undergrowth as she could to camouflage us.

'We're only twenty-five miles from the border,' I said. 'We could try and get hold of another car in San Diego.'

She opened the trunk, which was crammed with luggage.

'That's for you to take; I put some of your things in there,' she said, chucking an old hard-sided Samsonite at me, almost knocking me to the ground.

She, on the other hand, hesitated in front of the mountain of suitcases full of clothes and shoes that she had swiped from Aurore's wardrobe.

'We probably won't be going to any balls in Mexico,' I said, to hurry her up.

She grabbed a large monogrammed canvas bag and a silver vanity case. As I turned to leave, she held me back.

'Wait, there's a present for you on the back seat.'

I raised an eyebrow, expecting another cheap trick, but nevertheless looked in the back of the car to find the Chagall canvas, covered by a beach towel.

'I figured it probably means a lot to you.'

I looked gratefully back at her. I could have kissed her.

Lying across the back seat, the Lovers in Blue looked as though they were passionately embracing, like two schoolkids on a first date at the drive-in.

As always, just looking at the picture did me good, lifting my spirits and filling me with calm. The lovers were there, as they always had been, anchored to one another, and the strength of their connection was like a soothing balm on my wounds.

'That's the first time I've seen you smile,' Billie observed.

I put the painting under my arm and we started to make our way through the trees.

*

In our efforts to escape the helicopter we scrambled over endless banks, weighed down like mules, sweating and out of breath – well, especially me. We had obviously not yet been picked up by their radar, but every now and again we could hear the ominous drone of the helicoper overhead.

'I have to stop,' I said, panting like a dog. 'What did you put in this suitcase? I feel like I'm dragging a safe behind me!'

'So sports aren't really your thing either?' she asked,turning to face me.

'I might have let myself go a bit these past few months,' I admitted, 'but maybe if like me you'd fallen out of a second- floor window you'd be a little more sympathetic.'

Barefoot, Billie weaved gracefully in and out of the trees, with her shoes slung over her shoulder.

We walked down a small slope and came to a road. It wasn't a freeway, but was wide enough to allow cars to go in both directions.

'Which way do you think?' she asked.

I gratefully put my suitcase down and placed both

hands on my knees, trying to get my breath back.

'No idea. I'm not Google Maps.'

'We could try hitching a ride,' she suggested, choosing to ignore my remark.

'Not with all this stuff – no one will want to take us.'

She crouched down and started to rummage around in her bag, pulling out a new outfit. Unselfconsciously she undid her jeans, replacing them with a pair of white hot pants, and swapped her jacket for a pale-blue fitted Balmain number with dramatic pointy shoulders.

'We'll be in a car within the next ten minutes,' she promised, readjusting her sunglasses and adopting a more seductive pose.

I found myself once again taken aback by the apparent duality of her nature. She could go from a playful and candid young girl to an arrogant and alluring femme fatale in the blink of an eye.

'Looks like Pretty Woman has cleaned out the boutiques on Rodeo Drive,' I called after her as I followed her down the road.

'Pretty Woman has had just about enough of you.'

*

We had been waiting for a few minutes. Only about twenty cars had driven past. None of them had stopped. We'd passed a sign that told us we were in the vicinity of San Dieguito Park, and then a second sign at the junction for Interstate 5. We were on the right road, but going in the wrong direction.

'We should cross the road and try to get a lift from the other side,' she said.

'I don't want to hurt your feelings, but your seduction routine isn't getting us very far, is it?'

'In five minutes you'll be sitting comfortably on a leather seat. Want to bet on it?'

'Sure, why not?'

'How much money do you have left?'

'Just over $700.'

'OK, five minutes. Are you timing us? Oh, wait, I forgot, you don't have a watch any more.'

'What about me? What do I get if I win?'

She didn't reply, her expression suddenly turning serious.

'Tom, we're going to have to sell the painting.'

'No. Out of the question.'

'How else do you expect to be able to get hold of a car and pay for somewhere to sleep?'

'We're in the middle of nowhere! A painting like this should be sold in an auction room, not in the first gas station we come across!'

She frowned and seemed to be thinking hard.

'Fine, maybe we don't have to sell it, but we should at least pawn it.'

'*Pawn it?* This is a masterpiece, not my grandmother's wedding ring!'

She shrugged, just as a rusty old pick-up truck slowed down near us.

'Get ready to pay up,' she said, grinning.

In the truck were two Mexicans, who worked as gardeners in the park during the day and drove back to Playas de Rosarito every evening. They offered to take us as far as San Diego. One looked like an older, fatter version of Benicio del Toro while the younger one, Esteban…

'He looks just like that gardener from *Desperate Housewives*!' whispered Billie excitedly. He was obviously her type.

'*Señora, usted puede usar el asiento, pero el señor viajará en la cajuela.*'

'What did he say?' I asked, sensing bad news.

'He said that I can sit in the front if I want, but you'll have to go in the back,' she translated, taking pleasure in delivering the news to me.

'But you promised me a leather seat!' I protested, climbing into the back to sit amongst the tools and bags of dry grass.

*

I've got a Black Magic Woman

The rich, full sound of Carlos Santana's guitar streamed out of the open window of the pick-up. It was a real boneshaker an old 1950s Chevrolet that looked as though it had been repainted dozens of times, and clearly had a few miles on the clock.

Perched on a bale of straw, I brushed off the dust that had accumulated on the painting and addressed the *Lovers in Blue* directly.

'I'm sorry about this, but it looks like we're going to have to go our separate ways for a while.'

I had been thinking about what Billie had said and an idea had come to me. The year before, *Vanity Fair* had asked me to write a short story for their Christmas issue. The idea was to 'rework' a well-known classic – some called this heresy – and I had decided to rewrite a truncated version of my favourite Balzac novel. In the first lines the reader followed the fortunes of a young heiress, who, having frittered away her inheritance, is lured in by a pawnbroker, who gives her a talisman with the power to fulfil its owner's every desire. I was prepared to admit that even though it had gone down well with readers, it was not the best thing I had ever written, but in the course of my research I had come across the colourful figure of Yochida Mitsuko, the most influential pawnbroker in California.

Much like Sophia Schnabel's clinic, Mitsuko's little shop was one of the must-have addresses that circulated amongst the beautiful people in the Golden Triangle in Los Angeles. Just like everywhere else, the need for ready cash pushed even the wealthiest stars to offload some of their more extravagant purchases and, out of the twenty or so pawnbrokers in Beverly Hills, Yochida Mitsuko was the favourite among those in the know. With the help of *Vanity Fair* I had been granted a private interview with him at his workshop near Rodeo Drive. He proudly described himself as 'pawnbroker to the stars' and had plastered his walls with photos of himself standing next to various celebrities, who all looked rather embarrassed to have been captured on camera at a time when their financial fortunes had so obviously taken a turn for the worse.

His warehouse was a real Aladdin's cave, overflowing with an assortment of treasures. I remember seeing the baby grand piano that belonged to a famous jazz singer, the captain of the Dodgers' lucky bat, a magnum of '96 Dom Pérignon, a Magritte painting, a customised Rolls-Royce belonging to a rapper, the Harley of a well-known crooner, several cases of '46 Mouton Rothschild and, despite the Academy's strict rules, the gold statuette of a legendary actor who shall remain nameless.

I looked at my phone. I was still barred from making calls, but I could access my address book and I quickly located Mitsuko's number.

I leaned forward to whisper in Billie's ear, 'Could you ask your boyfriend if I could possibly use his phone?'

She seemed to negotiate with the gardener for a few minutes, and then, 'Esteban says that's OK, but it will cost you $50.'

I didn't want to waste time haggling, so I handed him a bill in exchange for an old nineties Nokia. A wave of nostalgia washed over me as I held it in my hand: it was ugly, heavy and dull, no camera and no Wi-Fi. But it worked.

Mitsuko picked up after the first ring.

'It's Tom Boyd here.'

'What can I do for you, my friend?'

I wasn't sure why, but he had always seemed to like me, even though in my story I had not painted him in a particularly flattering light. Far from being offended, this 'artistic' portrayal had given him a certain cachet, for which he was extremely grateful, and he had thanked me by sending me a signed first edition of *In Cold Blood*.

I asked politely how he was getting on, and he confessed that since the recession and the credit crunch his business had flourished like never before: he had already opened a second store in San Francisco and had plans for a third in Santa Barbara.

'Every day, doctors, dentists and lawyers come into my shop to pawn their Lexus, their golf clubs or their wives' mink stoles because it's the only way they can afford to pay their bills. But you must have a reason for calling. Do you have something interesting for me to look at?'

I started to describe my Chagall, but it was immediately obvious he was only listening to me out of politeness.

'The art market hasn't recovered from the financial crisis yet, but come and see me tomorrow and I'll see what I can do for you.'

I explained that I couldn't wait until tomorrow, that I was in San Diego and I needed cash in the next two hours.

'I suppose your phone has been cut off as well,' he guessed. 'I didn't recognise the number you called me on, and you know how it is: with the number of gossip whores in this town, word gets around fast.'

'What are they saying?'

'That you're done for, and that these days you prefer swallowing pills to writing novels.'

My silence was all the response he needed. Still, at the other end of the line I could hear he was typing something into his laptop, and I guessed he was looking up the current value of Chagall paintings and what kind of bids they were attracting at auction.

'I can get your phone working again in the next hour,' he said. 'You're with TTA, aren't you? It'll cost you $2,000.'

Before I had even given my consent, I could hear him sending a message on his computer. If Sophia used people's secrets against them, Mitsuko used their wallets.

'As for the painting, I'll give you $30,000 for it.'

'I hope you're joking. It's worth about twenty times that amount!'

'About forty times, in my opinion. Give it two or three years, at somewhere like Sotheby's in New York, when the new-money Russians feel like spending again. But if you need cash by tonight, and you factor in the huge commission I'm going to have to give to my colleague in San Diego, $28,000 is all I can offer you.'

'You just said thirty grand!'

'Minus the 2,000 to get your network coverage back. And all this providing you carefully follow the instructions I'm about to give you.'

Did I have any choice at this point? I reassured myself that I had four months to pay him back – plus 5 per cent interest – and be reunited with my most prized possession. I wasn't sure I could do it, but it was a risk I had to take.

'I'll text you my instructions,' concluded Mitsuko. 'Oh, and by the way, tell your friend Milo that he's only got a few days left to pick up his sax.'

I hung up and gave Esteban back his phone, just as we cruised into the city centre. The sun was setting.

San Diego was beautiful, bathed in a pink and orange glow that put me in mind of nearby Mexico. At a red light, Billie clambered into the back with me.

'Man, it's freezing in here!' she said, hugging her knees to her chest.

'Well, dressed like that—'

She waved a piece of paper in my face.

'They gave me the address of one of their friends who's a mechanic. He might be able to get us a car. How are you getting on?'

I looked at the screen on my phone. As if by magic, I was suddenly able to send texts and make calls again. Mitsuko's text told me to use the camera on my phone to take a picture of the painting and send it to him.

With Billie's help I brought the painting into focus on the screen, and took shots from all angles, taking special care to take a few of the certificate of authenticity on the back of the painting. Then, using an app downloaded from the internet in a few seconds, every photo was dated, encrypted and saved, before being sent via a secure server. According to Mitsuko, these photos would count as valid evidence in a court of law.

The whole operation took about ten minutes, and by the time the pick-up truck dropped us off at the main station we had received a text from the pawnbroker giving us the address of his colleague in San Diego where we were to drop off the painting in exchange for the $28,000.

I helped Billie down onto the sidewalk with our luggage and we thanked the gardeners for their help.

'*Si vuelves por aqui, me llamas, de acuerdo*?' said Esteban, holding on to Billie's hand for a moment too long.

'Sí, sí!' she replied, running her hand through her hair flirtatiously.

'What did he say to you?'

'Nothing! He just wished us luck.'

'Oh sure, that's exactly what he said to you,' I said, getting in line for a taxi.

She gave me a complicit smile, which prompted me to promise her, 'Well, anyway, if everything goes according to plan, you'll be eating chilli con carne and quesadillas with me tonight!'

The mention of food was enough to get her talking again, but now instead of being exasperated by her incessant chirping, I heard it as cheering music.

'And enchiladas, you've had enchiladas before, right?' she exclaimed. 'God, I love them, especially the chicken ones, when they're all crispy. But you know you can also get them with prawns, and pork as well, right? Oh and nachos, urgh, I don't like them at all. And escamoles? You've never tried them? Oh, we'll have to find you some then. You know what they are? Ant larvae! It's a really, like, posh thing to eat; some people even say it's like insect caviar. Weird, huh? I've only ever tried them once. I was on vacation with some friends...'

18

Motel Casa del Sol

Hell is contained entirely in this word: solitude
Victor Hugo

'Obviously, anything was going to be a let-down after the Bugatti,' Billie pointed out, a hint of disappointment creeping into her voice.

Southern outskirts of San Diego, 7 p.m.
A dingy, run-down garage

She sat down in the front seat of the car, a 1960s Fiat 500 missing its hubcaps and chromework, which Santos, the mechanic who had been recommended to us, was trying to pass off as a solid station wagon.

'Sure, it's not the most comfortable ride, but believe me it's reliable!'

'Whose idea was it to paint it pink?'

'It was my daughter's car,' explained the Mexican.

'Ow!' cried Billie, banging her head against the roof as she got out. 'You sure you don't mean your daughter's Barbie's car?'

It was my turn to look inside.

'The back seat has been ripped out,' I said.

'More space for your luggage!'

I inspected the headlights, indicators and hazard lights, pretending I knew what I was doing.

'Are you sure it's all OK?'

'According to Mexican standards, yes.'

I checked the time on my phone. We had picked up the $28,000 as planned, but we had wasted a lot of time getting from the pawnbroker's warehouse to the garage. This car was almost certainly on its last legs, but without a driver's licence between us, we could neither buy nor rent one the legal way.

This car also had the advantage of a Mexican licence plate, which would make it easier for us over the border.

Santos finally agreed to sell it to us for $1,200, but we had to struggle for fifteen minutes just to get my suitcase and Madam's effects into such a cramped space.

'Isn't this the car they called "the yoghurt pot"?' I asked, pushing down on the door of the trunk with all my strength.

'*El bote de yogur?*' he translated, pretending not to understand the connection I was making between the dairy product and the pile of junk that he was only too happy to offload on us.

This time it was me at the wheel, and it was with slight apprehension that we hit the road again. It was already dark. We weren't in one of the nicer areas of San Diego, and I found it difficult to orient myself amongst the endless parking lots and shopping malls, but we finally got ourselves back onto the 805, which led to the border.

The tyres squealed on the asphalt and the powerful roar of the Bugatti had been replaced by the nasal whine of the Fiat's little engine.

'Come on, let's go up to second gear,' suggested Billie.

'I'm already in fourth!'

She glanced at the speedometer, which had barely reached 40 mph.

'That's as fast as it goes then,' she said, crestfallen.

'Well, at least now we won't be breaking any speed limits.'

The battered old thing just about got us to the Tijuana border crossing. It was a typical day there, lively and traffic-clogged. As we joined the 'Mexico only' line, I went over the procedure with my passenger.

'We shouldn't have a problem going in this direction, but if we do we're going straight to jail. So no messing around this time, OK?'

'I'm all ears,' she said, blinking her Betty Boop eyes.

'It's not complicated: you keep your mouth shut and you don't move a muscle. We're just two innocent Mexican workers coming home after a day's work. Got it?'

'*Vale, señor.*'

'And if you could quit fooling around for one second I would be eternally grateful.'

'*Muy bien, señor.*'

For once, we got lucky. We were through in less than five minutes, no searches, no questions asked.

We stayed close to the coast, as we had done for most of the journey. Luckily the mechanic had installed a radio-cassette player. Unluckily, the only cassette we could find was an Enrique Iglesias album, which sent Billie into raptures, but made my ears bleed all the way to Ensenada.

When we got there, a storm broke out of nowhere, and torrential rain beat down on us. The windshield was tiny and the flimsy wipers were so ineffectual that I often had to stick my arm out of the window to keep them working.

'Let's stop at the first place we find.'

We passed a motel, but it had a 'no vacancy' sign outside it. We couldn't see three yards ahead of us. Forced to keep my speed at 15 mph, I was getting a lot of grief from drivers stuck behind me, and the angry blare of horns accompanied us as we crawled along.

We finally found shelter in San Telmo, in the Casa del Sol Motel, a rather inappropriate name given the circumstances, whose neon 'vacancy' sign flickered comfortingly in the rain. Judging by the state of the cars in the parking lot, I guessed that this place was not going to be a nice little B&B, but we weren't exactly on our honeymoon anyway.

'We'll just get one bedroom, right?' she teased, walking into reception.

'One bedroom with two beds.'

'Don't worry, I'm not going to be throwing myself at you any time soon.'

'Oh, I'm not worried. I'm not a Mexican gardener – I'm not your type.'

The receptionist grunted at us. Billie asked if we could see the room first, but I grabbed the key and paid up before she could say anything else.

'Well, we don't have anywhere else to go, it's pouring out there and I'm exhausted.'

The one-storey building formed a U-shape round

a courtyard planted with scrawny, dead-looking trees that were bending in the wind.

Unsurprisingly the room was extremely basic and badly lit, and a strange smell hung in the air. The furniture must have been in vogue when Eisenhower was in office. There was an enormous television set on a stand with four wheels and a large speaker behind the screen. The kind of 'antique' you might pick up at a yard sale.

'Think about it,' joked Billie. 'People probably watched the moon landing and Kennedy's assassination on this screen!'

I switched it on, curious to see what would happen. It made a vague crackling noise, but no image appeared on the screen.

'Well, I guess we won't be watching the Superbowl in here.'

The shower was roomy, but the taps were covered in rust.

'I'll let you in on a secret,' said Billie, grinning. 'You can tell by looking behind the bedside table if they've done the dusting properly.'

Putting her words into action, she moved the table aside, then let out a scream. 'Gross!' she said, throwing her shoe at a cockroach. She turned to look at me, hoping to be comforted.

'Shall we go and have our authentic Mexican dinner?'

I was less than enthusiastic. 'Look, there's no restaurant around here, it's pissing down out there, I'm totally wiped out and not particularly inclined to get back behind the wheel.'

'Yeah, you're just like all the others, all talk and no action.'

'I'm going to bed, OK?'

'Come on, let's at least have a drink somewhere! We passed a little bar on the way here, just down the road.'

I started to take off my shoes, then lay down on one of the beds.

'Go without me. It's already late and we have a long way to go tomorrow. And anyway I don't like bars, especially not ones by the side of the road.'

'Fine, I'll go without you.'

She went into the bathroom with a few of her things, to emerge moments later in a pair of jeans and a fitted leather jacket. She was ready to go, but looked as though she had something she wanted to get off her chest first.

'Earlier, when you said you weren't my type...'

'Yes?'

'What do you see as my type?'

'Well, take that asshole Jack, for example. Or even Esteban, who didn't stop leering at you the whole time we were in that truck, probably led on by your come-hither stares and provocative outfit.'

'Is that really how you see me, or are you trying to be cruel?'

'Honestly, that's how I see you, and I know I'm right, because I created you.'

Her face darkened and she left without saying another word.

'Wait,' I said, getting up to follow her. 'At least take some money with you.'

She held my gaze defiantly.

'If you really knew me at all, you'd know that I've never had to buy my own drinks.'

*

Suddenly alone, I had a lukewarm shower, strapped up my ankle again and opened my suitcase to find something to sleep in. As Billie had promised, I found my laptop staring up at me like a physical manifestation of my guilt. I paced up and down the room for a while then opened the cupboard, hoping to find a pillow. In the drawer of one of the bedside tables, next to a cheap copy of the New Testament, I found two other books, no doubt left behind by previous occupants. The first was Carlos Ruiz Zafón's bestseller *The Shadow of the Wind*, a book I had once given to Carole as a present, and the second was called *La Compañía de los Ángeles*. It took me a few seconds to work out that this was the Spanish translation of my first novel. I leafed through it curiously. The last person to read it had taken the time to underline certain sentences and had even made a few notes here and there. I couldn't tell whether the person had loved or hated the book, but they had obviously felt strongly about it and that was what mattered to me the most.

Feeling encouraged by this discovery, I sat down at the tiny Formica desk and switched on my computer.

What if I got it back? I could start writing again; I could want to start writing again!

The screen demanded my password. I felt the

familiar anxiety resurfacing, but I tried to tell myself it was just nervous excitement. When the image of a beach appeared on the desktop I launched Word and a gleaming blank page appeared on the screen. At the top of the page, the cursor blinked expectantly, waiting for my fingers to start moving across the keyboard. My pulse sped up as if someone had put my heart in a vice. I suddenly felt dizzy and so nauseous that I had to switch off the computer again.

Damn it.

Writer's block, blank-page syndrome, whatever you called it, I had never thought it would affect me. As far as I was concerned, a lack of inspiration was something that only afflicted pretentious intellectuals who wrote self-consciously, striking poses as they went along, not scribblers like me, who had been making up stories in their heads since the age of ten.

Some artists had to invent their misery in order to create something of value, because there was not enough real misery in their lives. Others used their personal sorrow as a kind of trigger. Frank Sinatra had written 'I'm a Fool to Want You' after his break-up with Ava Gardner. Apollinaire had written 'Sous le pont Mirabeau' after his separation from Marie Laurencin. And Stephen King had always been very open about the fact that he had written *The Shining* under the influence of alcohol and drugs. Although I could not put myself in the same league as these greats, I had never needed chemical stimulation to write. For years I had spent every moment of every day – Christmas and Thanksgiving included – channelling my imagination onto the page. When I was on a roll, nothing else mattered: I was in a different place, in a trance, in a kind of hypnotic dream. During these fertile periods, writing itself became a drug, more euphoric than the purest coke, more delightful than the most intoxicating drunkenness.

But all of that felt very far away now. I had given up writing and writing seemed to have given up on me.

*

One tranquilliser. It was important not to imagine I was stronger than I was. To humbly accept my addiction.

I went to bed and turned out the light. I tossed and turned; sleep would not come. I felt utterly powerless. Why was I no longer capable of doing my job? When had I stopped caring about what became of the characters I had created?

I saw from the ancient radio-alarm clock that it was 11p.m. I was starting to worry about Billie; she still hadn't come back. Why had I been so harsh on her? I suppose because I still hadn't quite come to terms with her sudden appearance and intrusion in my real life, and also because I didn't feel capable of sending her back to hers.

I got up, dressed quickly and went out into the rain. I had been walking for a good ten minutes before I saw the greenish neon sign that told me I was close to the Linterna Verde.

The bar was busy, and the clientele almost entirely male. There was a lively atmosphere. The tequila was flowing freely and the old stereo blasted out classic rock. Her tray loaded with bottles, a waitress weaved between the tables, refuelling those who had finished their drinks. A wizened old parrot in a cage kept the drinkers sitting at the bar amused, while another barmaid – whom the regulars seemed to call Paloma – attracted catcalls as she took orders. I asked for a beer and she served me a Corona with a wedge of lime. I scanned the room. It was decorated with wooden screens, which looked vaguely Mayan. On the walls, old scenes from westerns jostled for space with photos of local football teams.

Billie was sitting at the back of the room with two macho-looking guys. They were laughing raucously. I approached the group, beer in hand. She saw me, but acted as if she hadn't. Judging by her dilated pupils I guessed she had already downed quite a few drinks. I knew all of her weaknesses, and I knew that alcohol often didn't agree with her. I could also tell what these guys were like, and what they were after. They might not have been the sharpest tools in the box, but they obviously had a radar for vulnerable women, who were their prey.

'Come on, I'm taking you back to the motel.'

'Leave me alone. You're not my dad and you're not my husband. I asked if you wanted to come with me and you chewed me out.'

She shrugged her shoulders and dipped a tortilla in her guacamole.

'Don't be so childish. You can't hold your drink and you know it.'

'I can take my drink perfectly well, thank you,' she said provocatively, grabbing the bottle of mescal that was standing in the middle of the table and pouring herself another glass. She then passed it to her companions, who both swigged straight from the bottle. The more muscly of the two, who was wearing a T-shirt that bore the name 'Jesus', offered me the bottle, like some kind of initiation.

I looked suspiciously at the little scorpion at the bottom of the bottle, a sign of the local belief that the animal represented power and virility.

'I'm fine,' I said.

'If you don't want to drink, you can leave, buddy! You can see the little lady is having a good time with us.'

Instead of doing as he said, I took another step toward the table and looked Jesus straight in the eye. For all that I was an avid reader of Jane Austen and Dorothy Parker, I had also been raised on the streets. I had thrown as many punches as I had taken, from guys with knives, from guys much more intimidating than the one I was looking at now.

'You can shut the hell up.'

Then I turned to Billie again.

'The last time you got drunk, it didn't end well, remember?'

She looked back at me disdainfully.

'You really know how to wound people with your words, don't you? They always hit right where it hurts. You've got a real talent for that, you know?'

Just after Jack had cancelled their vacation to Hawaii at the last minute, she had made straight for the Red Piano, a bar near the Old State House. She was devastated, pretty much at rock bottom. To dull the pain, she had let a certain Paul Walker, who ran several local convenience stores, buy her a succession of vodka tonics. She didn't say no, which he took to mean yes. In the taxi he had started to feel her up. She resisted, but perhaps not enough, because the guy clearly thought he was owed some kind of reward for all the drinks he had paid for. Her head was spinning so much that she didn't even know what she wanted any more. Paul had followed her into her apartment block and invited himself up for another drink. Tired of the struggle, she had let him come up in the elevator with her, afraid he would wake the neighbours if she said no. After that point she had no recollection of what had happened. She had woken up the next morning on the sofa, her skirt up around her waist. She had spent the next three months in a permanent state of panic, taking endless pregnancy and HIV tests, but hadn't been able to bring herself to press charges, feeling partly responsible for what had happened to her.

I had brought this awful memory back to her and now she looked up at me with tears in her eyes.

'Why do you make me go through these things in your books?'

The question hit home. I gave her the honest answer.

'Probably because I gave you a lot of my personal demons to wrestle with. My darkest side, all the things I hate myself for, manifest themselves in you. The side that makes me lose all self-respect and self-esteem.'

Stunned into silence, she still didn't seem to want to come with me.

'I'll take you back to the motel,' I insisted, offering her my hand.

'*Como chingas!*' Jesus whistled between his teeth.

I ignored the provocation and kept my eyes on Billie.

'The only way to get out of this is together. You're my lifeline and I'm yours.'

She was about to answer when I heard Jesus call me *joto*, faggot, an insult I was familiar with because it was the favourite swearword of Tereza Rodriguez, the old lady from Honduras who worked as my cleaner and who had been my mother's next-door neighbour in MacArthur Park.

The punch came out of nowhere. A proper right hook, straight from my teenage glory days, which knocked Jesus onto the next table, sending beer bottles and nachos flying. A great first blow, but sadly there were no more to come.

In less than a second the atmosphere in the room was electric. Delighted to see things hotting up, the punters joined in with cries of 'Fight! Fight!' From behind, two guys lifted me up off the ground, before a third made me regret ever having set foot in the bar. Blows came from all angles at terrifying speed, striking me in the face, stomach and groin, but, in some perverse way, the vicious beating was doing me good. Not because I took any masochistic pleasure in it, but perhaps because this martyrdom was one small step on my road to redemption. Lying on the ground, my mouth was filled with the metallic taste of blood. Flashing images danced in front of my eyes, a mixture of things that were happening in the room and memories of other times, other places: Aurore looking lovingly at another man in the pages of a gossip magazine, Milo's betrayal, Carole's far-away look, the tattooed hip of Paloma, the Latina babe who had just turned up the music, and whom I could make out shaking her booty to the rhythm of the blows that were raining down on me. And Billie, I could see Billie moving toward me with the mescal bottle in her hand, ready to crack it over the head of one of my attackers.

*

All of a sudden everything calmed down. I understood, with intense relief, that the show was over. I felt myself being lifted up and carried through the crowd, before landing with a thud outside in the pouring rain, face down in a muddy puddle.

19

Road movie

Happiness is a bubble on a bar of soap
that changes colour as an iris does,
and that bursts when you touch it
Balzac

'Milo, open the door!'

Dressed in uniform, Carole hammered at the door with the force and authority conferred on her by the law.

Pacific Palisades
A small two-storey house, swathed in morning mist
'I'm warning you, I'm here as a cop, not as your friend. As a member of the LAPD, I demand that you let me in.'

'The LAPD can go screw itself,' groaned Milo, half opening his door.

'Well, that's exactly the kind of attitude we need!' said Carole reproachfully, following him into the house.

He was in his boxer shorts and a Space Invaders T-shirt. He was pale, with dark circles under his eyes and hair that looked as though he'd stuck his fingers into an electric socket. The satanic symbols of the Mara Salvatrucha inked permanently onto his arms stood out harshly.

'Can I just point out that it's seven in the morning, I

was asleep and I've got someone here?'

On the glass coffee table, Carole could see an empty bottle of cheap vodka as well as a half-empty bag of weed.

'I thought you'd given all that up,' she said sadly.

'No actually. In case you hadn't noticed, my life is going down the drain, I ruined my best friend and I can't even help him when he needs me, so yeah, I had a few drinks and smoked a couple of joints.'

'And you found some company.'

'Yeah, and that's my business, OK?'

'Who was it this time? Sabrina? Vicky?'

'No. Two $50 whores I picked up on Creek Avenue. That good enough for you?'

Taken aback, she couldn't work out whether he was telling the truth, or just trying to wind her up.

Milo switched on the Nespresso machine and inserted a capsule, yawning.

'OK, so you must have a reason for coming to wake me up at the crack of dawn.'

Carole looked troubled for a moment, but soon pulled herself together.

'Yesterday I left a description of the Bugatti at the police station, and I asked them to let me know if there was any news of it, and guess what? They've just found your car in a forest near San Diego.'

For the first time that morning, Milo looked pleased.

'And Tom?'

'No news yet. The Bugatti was pulled over for speeding, but the girl at the wheel just drove off again.'

'The girl?'

'According to the local sheriff, it wasn't Tom driving the car, but a young woman. But the report does say there was a male passenger in the vehicle at the time.'

She listened to the sounds coming from the bathroom. A hair dryer blasted away while the shower was running. So two people really had stayed over.

'Near San Diego, you said?'

Carole looked at the report.

'Yep, some place near Rancho Santa Fe.'

Milo scratched his head, making his hair stick out even more.

'I think I'll go straight there in my rental car. If I hang around long enough, I might find a clue that will put me on Tom's tracks.'

'I'm coming with you,' she decided.

'Don't bother.'

'I'm not asking your opinion. I'm coming with you whether you like it or not.'

'What about your job?'

'I can't remember the last time I took a day off. Plus we'll find him more quickly with two of us on the case.'

'I'm so worried he's going to do something stupid,' Milo suddenly confessed, staring into the distance.

'Him? What about you? What about last night?' she answered harshly.

The bathroom door opened, revealing two Latina girls chattering loudly as they left the room. One was half naked, with a towel around her head, the other was wrapped up in a bathrobe.

As she stared at them, Carole realised something that made her stomach flip: these two girls looked exactly like her! Maybe a little more common, a little more worn down, but one of them had light eyes just like hers, while the other was exactly her height and shared her distinctive dimples. They embodied what she might have become, had she not dragged herself out of MacArthur Park through sheer force of will.

She tried to disguise how uncomfortable she felt, but Milo had already noticed.

He tried to hide his shame, but she knew it was there.

'I'm going to go back to the station and let them know I'm taking a few days off,' she said, finally, to break the awkward silence. 'You have a shower, drive your girlfriends home and meet me back at my place in an hour, OK?'

*

Baja peninsula, Mexico
8 a.m.

I opened one eye cautiously. The morning sunlight bounced off the wet road and rain-spattered windshield.

Huddled up in a blanket, with stiff, aching muscles and a blocked nose, I slowly came to and found that I was curled up on the passenger seat of the Fiat 500.

'Nice nap, was it?' Billie asked me.

I sat up, wincing at the crick in my neck.

'Where are we?'

'On a road between nowhere and somewhere else.'

'Have you been driving all night?'

She nodded cheerfully, as I caught sight of my reflection in the rear-view mirror, and the ugly reminders of the blows I had taken last night.

'It suits you,' she said, quite seriously. 'I didn't like the look you were working before, all preppy and conservative. You looked like maybe you needed a slap.'

'You've got a real talent for giving compliments, you know that?' I looked out the window. The landscape had become wilder. The narrow, uneven road led through rocky desert terrain, where tufts of vegetation had sprouted here and there. I saw cacti, agaves with full, plump leaves, and thorny bushes. The traffic was flowing freely, but the road was so tight that meeting a bus or truck was a life-threatening experience.

'I'll take over so you can get some sleep.'

'We'll stop at the next gas station.'

But service stations were thin on the ground and not many of them were open. Before we found one, we went through several abandoned villages that looked like ghost towns. It was while passing through one of these that we came across an orange Corvette that had stopped by the side of the road, its hazard lights flashing. A young hitchhiker – who wouldn't have looked out of place in a Calvin Klein underwear advert – was leaning against the hood holding a small sign that said 'out of gas'.

'Shall we help him out?' Billie suggested.

'No, he's obviously just pretending to have broken down so he can take advantage of some stupid tourist.'

'Are you implying that all Mexicans are thieves?'

'No. I'm implying that your desire to get involved with every good-looking guy we come across is going to get us into even more trouble.'

'You weren't complaining when it got us a ride!'

'Look, it's so frickin' obvious this guy's out to steal our money and our car. If that's what you want, then please feel free to stop, but don't ask for my blessing!'

Luckily she decided not to risk it, and we continued on our way.

When we had filled up on gas, we stopped off at a family-run grocer's. There was a basic selection of fruit, vegetables, pastries and dairy products on display in the old-fashioned store window. We bought enough to make a small picnic for two and sat down at the foot of a nearby Joshua tree.

As I sipped my piping hot coffee, I watched Billie with a kind of fascination. Sitting on a rug, she devoured cinnamon polvorones and churros covered in icing sugar with great relish.

'So good! Don't you want any?'

'There's something I don't understand,' I said thoughtfully.

'In my books you eat like a bird, but, since I've known you, you've wolfed down everything you can get your hands on.'

She seemed to think about this for a few moments, as if she too had just realised something, then she said, 'It's because of *real life*.'

'Real life?'

'I'm a character in a novel, Tom. I belong in the world of fiction and not in real life. I don't belong here.'

'What has that got to do with how much you eat?'

'In real life, everything has more taste, more substance to it. And not just food. The air has more oxygen, the landscapes are filled with colours that take your breath away. Everything in fiction is so bland.'

'Fiction, bland? I spend my life hearing the opposite. Most people read novels precisely to escape reality.'

She said seriously, 'You might be very good at telling stories, creating emotions, pain, heartache, but you don't know how to describe the spice of life, its flavours.'

'Well, how nice of you to point that out to me,' I said, realising that my skills as a writer were being put under the microscope. 'What kind of flavours are you talking about, exactly?'

She looked around her, trying to find an example.

'Take the taste of this fruit,' she said, cutting off a piece of the mango we had just bought.

'What about it?'

She looked up at the sky and closed her eyes, as though offering her pretty face to the early-morning breeze.

'Or the feeling of the wind on your face.'

'Yeah …'

I looked sceptical, but I knew she had a point. I was incapable of capturing the magic of an instant in words. It was impossible. I didn't know how to pin it down. I didn't know how to enjoy such moments either, and so was unable to properly share them with my readers.

'Or,' she said, opening her eyes and pointing into the distance, 'that pink cloud that's melting away behind that hill.'

She got up, and carried on, her enthusiasm growing.

'In your books, you might write "Billie ate a mango",

but you would never take the time to describe the flavour of the mango.'

She carefully placed a piece of the fruit in my mouth.'So, what's it like?'

Stung by her criticism, I threw myself wholeheartedly into the game and tried to describe the fruit as accurately as I could.

'It's fresh and perfectly ripe.'

'You can do better than that.'

'It has a sweet pulp that melts in the mouth, bursting with flavour, with a scent of—'

I saw her grinning. I carried on.

'It's golden, like a mouthful of sunlight.'

'Don't overdo it; you're not making an advert!'

'I can't do anything right!'

She folded up the rug and started walking back to the car.

'Now you know what I mean!' she called back to me. 'So try to remember this when you're writing your next book. Put me in a world filled with colours and flavours, where fruit tastes like fruit and not cardboard!'

*

San Diego Freeway

'I'm freezing my balls off here. Can you shut the window?'

Carole and Milo had been driving for an hour. They were listening to a news station and were both pretending to be absorbed in a debate about local politics in order to avoid having to talk about what was really bothering them.

'Well, since you asked so nicely,' she retorted, winding up her window.

'What, you've got a problem with the way I talk now?'

'Yeah, actually. Why do you have to be so crude the whole time?'

'Sorry, I'm not some sensitive writer type. I've never written a novel.'

She looked at him, stunned.

'What do you mean by that?'

Milo scowled and turned up the radio as if he were just going to ignore the question, then, apparently changing his mind, blurted out, 'Has there ever been anything between you and Tom?'

'*What?*'

'You've always been in love with him, haven't you?'

Carole looked astonished. 'Is that really what you think?'

'I think that for years you've been waiting for one thing: for Tom to see you as a woman, instead of as a best friend.'

'You've really got to stop drinking and smoking weed, Milo. When you come out with crap like that, it makes me want to—'

'Makes you want to what?'

But she just shook her head. 'I don't know, to... to cut you up into little pieces, so you die a slow and painful death, then clone 10,000 copies of you so I can kill each and every one with my own hands, slowly—'

'All right, all right, I think I get the picture.'

*

Mexico

Despite the fact that our car refused to go at more than a snail's pace, we were gradually racking up the miles. We had just passed San Ignacio and, against all odds, our little yoghurt pot was holding up just fine.

For the first time in a long while, I felt good. I liked the landscape, the smell of the road with its intoxicating scent of freedom, the shops without signs and the carcasses of abandoned cars, which gave me the sensation of cruising down Route 66.

The icing on the cake was that in one of the rare service stations we came to I had unearthed two cassette tapes knocked down to ninety-nine cents apiece. The first was a compilation of classic rock gems, from Elvis Presley to the Stones. The second was a pirate recording of three Mozart concertos by Martha Argerich. It was the perfect way to start Billie's musical re-education.

Our progress was halted, however, in the early afternoon as we drove through some rather wild countryside with no fences or gates. A huge flock of sheep had decided they had nothing better to do than congregate in the middle of the road, with no intention of budging. We were in the vicinity of several farms and ranches, but no one seemed in a hurry to move the animals out of the road.

They weren't going anywhere: long blasts of the horn and Billie's agitated gestures could do nothing to shift them. Resigning herself to the wait, Billie lit a cigarette whilst I counted out the money we had left. A photo of Aurore fell out of my wallet and Billie grabbed it before I could do anything to stop her.

'Give me that!'

'Wait, let me have a look. Did you take this?'

It was a simple black and white shot, which had a certain innocence about it. In tiny little shorts and a man's shirt, Aurore smiled at me from a Malibu beach, with a sparkle in her eyes that I had once mistaken for love.

'Honestly, what is it that's so special about your pianist?'

'What's so special?'

'OK, so she's pretty. Well, if you're into the "perfect woman with the body of a supermodel" thing. But, apart from that, what do you see in her?'

'Please… You're in love with a total scumbag. You're not in a position to give me any lectures.'

'Is it because she's so sophisticated?'

'Yes, Aurore is sophisticated, and cultured. And I don't give a damn if you think that's pretentious. I was brought up in a really bad area. It never stopped: everywhere you went, screams, insults, threats, gunshots. The closest thing to a book was *TV Guide* and I had never heard of Chopin or Beethoven. So, yeah, I liked that I was with a Parisienne who talked to me about Schopenhauer and Mozart rather than pussy, dope, rap, tattoos or false nails!'

Billie rolled her eyes. 'That's very nice, but you also liked Aurore for her looks. If she'd been 100 pounds heavier, I'm not so sure you would have been quite so obsessed with her, even with all that Mozart and Chopin stuff.'

'You've made your point, OK? Just drive!'

'And where should I go exactly? This pile of junk isn't going to survive a head-on collision with a sheep.'

She took a drag of her Dunhill before continuing to have a go at me.

'So your deep and meaningful conversations about Schopenhauer, was that before or after you screwed?'

I looked at her, stung by this last comment. 'If I were saying these things to you, you'd have slapped my face by now.'

'Come on, I was only joking. I like how you blush when you're embarrassed.'

And to think I created you myself.

*

Malibu

As she did every week, Tereza Rodriguez arrived at Tom's house to do the cleaning. For the last few weeks the author had not wished to be disturbed and so had taped a note to his front door telling her to go home again, but he always attached an envelope with her pay. Today there was no note on the door.

Finally.

The old lady hated being paid to do nothing, but, more than that, she was worried about the boy she had watched grow up in MacArthur Park.

Back then, Tereza's apartment had been on the same floor as Tom's mother's place, and directly next door to Carole Alvarez's family. Because she had been living alone since the death of her husband, the young boy and his friend would come and do their homework at her place after school. It had to be said that the atmosphere there was a lot less volatile than in their respective homes: on one side of the landing a flighty and neurotic mother who ricocheted from lover to lover, breaking up homes as she went, and on the other a tyrannical stepfather who delighted in taking out his rage on his tribe.

Tereza opened the door with her set of keys, and stared in horror at the bombsite that greeted her. Then she pulled herself together and started to attack the mess. She put on the dishwasher, mopped then vacuumed the floor, did a load of laundry and cleaned up the remains of the tsunami that had devastated the terrace.

She left the house three hours later, after sorting and putting out the trash.

*

It was just after 5 p.m. when the truck came to empty the garbage cans in Malibu Colony.

As he loaded the contents of one of the dumpsters into the truck, John Brady – one of the workers on duty that evening – caught sight of a new-looking copy of the second volume of the *Angel Trilogy*. He rescued it, and at the end of his shift took a closer look at it.

Whoa! And it looks like some kind of special edition! Nice watercolour illustrations and Gothic lettering and all that.

His wife had read the first book and was impatiently waiting for the sequel to appear in paperback. This would make her so happy.

When he got home, Janet was indeed overjoyed with the present. She started to read it in the kitchen, whipping through the pages with feverish excitement, so absorbed in it that she forgot to take her macaroni and cheese out of the oven. She was still devouring chapter after chapter when she got into bed and John realised that he was not going to get any action and would be sleeping at the Cold Shoulder Hotel that night. Grudgingly he resigned himself to sleep, furious at having shot himself in the foot by bringing that damned book home, ruining both his dinner and his plans for the rest of the evening. He nodded off, comforted by a dream in which the Dodgers, his team, won the World Series by thrashing the Yankees. So Brady was in a very happy place when suddenly he was woken up by a shriek.

'John!'

He opened his eyes, filled with panic. Sitting up in bed next to him, his wife seemed deeply upset.

'You can't do this to me!'

'Do what?'

'The book stops right in the middle of page 266!' she said reproachfully. 'The rest is nothing but blank pages!'

'How is that my fault?'

'I know you did this on purpose.'

'Of course I didn't! What makes you say that?'

'I want to know what happens next!'

Brady put on his glasses and looked at the alarm clock.

'But, baby, it's two in the morning! Where do you

expect me to find the rest of the story?'

'The 24 Market is open all night. Please, John, go and buy me a new copy. The second one is even better than the first.'

John Brady sighed. He had married Janet thirty years ago, for better or for worse. This evening it was definitely for worse, but he put up with it. He wasn't so easy to live with himself, after all.

He dragged his old bones out of bed, still half asleep, and pulled on a pair of jeans and a jumper, before going down to get his car out of the garage. When he reached the 24 Market on Purple Street, he threw the faulty copy into a nearby trash can.

Stupid damned book!

*

Mexico

We were almost there. If the road signs were to be believed, we were less than 100 miles from Cabo San Lucas.

'We're down to our last tank,' remarked Billie, pulling up at a service station.

She hadn't even switched off the engine when Pablo – according to the name badge on his T-shirt – rushed over to fill our tank and clean our windshield.

It was getting dark. Billie squinted, trying to read a wooden sign in the shape of a cactus that listed the specialties of the station restaurant.

'I'm starving. Do you want to grab something to eat? I'm sure they have some amazing junk food in there.'

'You're going to give yourself indigestion with all this eating, you know.'

'It's fine – I've got you to take care of me. I'm sure you'd make a very sexy doctor.'

'You're sick in the head, that's what you are!'

'And whose fault is that? Seriously, Tom, you have to learn to let go. Worry a bit less. Let life be good to you, instead of always being afraid it might hurt you.'

Look who thinks they're Paulo Coelho all of a sudden.

She got out of the car and I watched her walk up the wooden steps that led into the restaurant. With her spray-on jeans, fitted leather jacket and silver vanity case, she was working a cowgirl look that blended in well with the general decor of the place. I paid Pablo for the gas and followed Billie up the steps.

'Give me the keys so I can lock it.'

'It's fine, Tom! Relax. Stop looking for danger everywhere. Forget the car for a second; right now you're buying me tortillas and stuffed peppers and then you're going to describe them for me!'

I gave in and walked into the saloon-style restaurant, where I guessed we would be spending some time. But that was without taking into account the bad luck which had plagued us along every step of this surreal journey.

'The… the car…' stammered Billie, just as we sat down at a table outside, about to tuck into our corn tortillas.

'What about it?'

'It's not there any more,' she said, a note of panic creeping into her voice, and pointed at the parking spaces opposite us.

I stormed out of the greasy spoon, leaving my food untouched on the plate.

'Stop looking for danger everywhere, huh? Relax? Great advice you give! I knew that something like this was going to happen. We even filled up the tank for the bastards!'

She looked ashamed for about half a second before her usual sarcasm came to her rescue.

'Well, if you were so sure we were going to get robbed, why didn't you lock the door? Everyone has to take responsibility for their actions, you know.'

Yet again, I had to keep myself from trying to strangle her. This time, we had no car and no luggage. It was now pitch dark and it was getting cold.

*

Rancho Santa Fe
Sheriff's office

'Wait, Sergeant Alvarez is with you?'

'Yeah, and?' said Milo, handing the officer his driver's licence and the insurance papers for the Bugatti.

Looking a little shifty, the sheriff rephrased his question, gesturing towards Carole, who was filling out some paperwork with the secretary on the other side of a glass partition.

'Your friend, Carole, is she your girlfriend, or just a friend who's a girl?'

'Why, you planning on asking her to dinner?'

'If she's available, I wouldn't mind, I'll admit it. She's so…'

He stopped for a moment, searching for the right word, careful not to say anything stupid, but then thought better of it and left the description unfinished.

'Go for it, buddy,' said Milo. 'Try it, then see whether I punch your lights out or not.'

Looking as though he had just received an electric shock, the sheriff's officer checked the vehicle documents before handing the keys over to Milo.

'You can pick it up now. Everything should be in order, but try not to go lending your car to just anybody from now on.'

'I didn't lend it to just anybody – I lent it to my best friend.'

'Well, then maybe you should pick your friends more carefully.'

Milo was about to respond in kind when Carole came back into the office.

'When you stopped them, Sheriff, are you absolutely sure it was a woman who was driving? Absolutely one hundred per cent sure?'

'Trust me, Sergeant, I know a woman when I see one.'

'And the guy in the passenger seat was definitely him?' she asked, holding up a book with Tom's picture on the back.

'To be honest, I didn't really get that good a look at him. I mainly spoke to the blonde chick. A real pain in the ass, she was.'

Milo saw they were wasting their time and asked for his documents.

The sheriff handed them over, before asking a question he'd been dying to ask ever since he'd laid eyes on Milo.

'The tattoos on your arms, they're from the Mara Salvatrucha, aren't they? I've read about them on the internet. I didn't think it was possible to get out of gangs like that.'

'You shouldn't believe everything you read on the internet,' said Milo, turning to leave.

In the parking lot, he inspected every inch of the Bugatti. The car seemed fine. There was gas in the tank, and some luggage in the trunk, a sign of the previous occupants' hasty departure. He opened the bags to find they were stuffed with women's clothes and toiletries. In the glove compartment he discovered a road map and a gossip magazine.

'What is it?' asked Carole. 'Have you found something?'

'Maybe,' he answered, showing her the route that had been marked out on the map. 'So did that jerk ask you out to dinner then?'

'He asked for my number, and if I wanted to go out sometime soon. Why, does that bother you?'

'Not at all. He's no Einstein though, is he?'

She was on the point of telling him where to stick it when something suddenly occurred to her.

'Have you seen this?' she exclaimed, showing him the photos of Aurore and Rafael Barros in their little corner of paradise.

Milo pointed at a small cross on the map and looked at his childhood friend.

'What would you say to a weekend in a luxury hotel on the Mexican coast?'

Mexico
El Zacatal service station

Billie seductively caressed the silky fabric of a short nightdress, edged with Chantilly lace.

'If you give her this, your girlfriend will do things to you she's never done before. Things you haven't even heard about, they're so dirty.'

Pablo's eyes widened. For the last ten minutes Billie had been trying to swap her vanity case for the gas-pump attendant's scooter.

'And this really is the latest thing,' she carried on, producing a crystal bottle with a stopper that sparkled like a diamond.

She opened it and looked at him mysteriously, like a magician about to perform her most impressive trick.

'Smell that,' she said, waving the bottle under his nose. 'It's an enchanting scent, isn't it? It's so seductive, so alluring. Just let the violet, pomegranate, pink peppercorns and jasmine take over your senses.'

'Stop trying to seduce the poor boy!' I said. 'You're going to get us into even more trouble!'

But Pablo seemed only too happy to be hypnotised by Billie, smiling as she opened her mouth to continue her spiel.

'Experience the intoxicating top notes of musk, freesia and ylang-ylang.'

I looked at the scooter doubtfully. It was ancient, a knock-off Italian Vespa that a local manufacturer must have introduced to Mexico in the 1970s. It looked as though it had seen more than a few paint jobs, and was covered in vintage-looking stickers that had started to blend in with the paintwork. One of them read: World Cup, Mexico 1986.

Behind me Billie's monologue continued.

'Trust me, Pablito, when a woman wears this perfume, she enters a magical secret garden, overflowing with sensual scents which turn her into a wild tiger, desperate to—'

'All right, show's over!' I cut in. 'Anyway, the two of us will never fit on that scooter together.'

'It'll be fine, I'm not exactly obese, you know!' she shot back, completely forgetting Pablo and the essence of feminine charm, apparently contained in Aurore's vanity case.

'And it's too dangerous. It's dark and the roads around here are in such bad condition, full of pot holes and humps.'

'*Trato hecho*?' asked Pablo.

Billie grinned at him. 'It's a great deal! Trust me, your girlfriend's gonna think you're a god,' she promised, grabbing his keys.

I shook my head.

'This is ridiculous! This thing is going to give out after ten miles. The belt is probably totally worn down and—'

'Tom.'

'What?'

'This kind of scooter doesn't have a belt. Stop playing macho man; you don't know the first thing about mechanics.'

'I bet no one's even been on it for twenty years,' I said, turning the key in the ignition.

The engine spluttered a few times before settling into a low hum. Billie climbed on behind me, put her arms round my waist and laid her head against my shoulder. The scooter sputtered off into the night.

20

The city of angels

It's not how hard you hit. It's how hard you get hit...
and keep moving forward
Randy Pausch

Cabo San Lucas
La Puerta del Paraíso Hotel
Suite 12

Pale morning light filtered in through the curtains. Billie opened one eye, stifling a yawn, and stretched out languorously on the bed. The digital clock showed it was after nine. She rolled over. A few feet away on a separate bed, Tom was curled up in the foetal position, still fast asleep. They had arrived at the hotel in the dead of night, exhausted and aching all over. Pablo's ancient scooter had given up the ghost a few miles before they'd reached their destination, and they'd had to finish their journey on foot, calling each other every name under the sun as they slogged towards the resort.

Wearing underwear and a camisole top, Billie hopped out of bed and crept towards the couch. Along with the two queen-size beds, the suite had a central fireplace and a spacious living room furnished with a mixture of traditional Mexican furniture and hi-tech gadgets, like a flat-screen TV, wireless internet and an impressive set of decks. Shivering, Billie slipped on Tom's jacket, wrapping it around her like a cape, then walked out onto the balcony.

The sight that greeted her as she stepped outside was enough to take her breath away. When they'd collapsed into bed the night before, it had been pitch dark, and they had been far too worn-out to appreciate the view. But this morning was a different story.

Billie stood on the sun-drenched balcony that looked out over the tip of the Baja peninsula, that magical place where the Pacific Ocean met the Sea of Cortés. Had she ever seen such an incredible landscape? Not that she could remember, anyway. She leant on the balustrade, smiling to herself. A row of little houses lined a white sandy beach lapped by a sapphire sea, the mountains towering behind. The name of the hotel – La Puerta del Paraíso – promised a door to paradise, and she had to admit it lived up to its billing.

She looked into the telescope mounted on the balustrade. It was meant for budding stargazers, but instead of looking up at the sky or at the mountains, she pointed the lens at the hotel swimming pool. Three infinity pools, each on its own level, led down to the beach and seemed almost to merge with the sea itself.

Exclusive little islands were dotted about on the water, where the beautiful people sunned themselves under straw parasols.

Looking into the distance, Billie did a double take.

I swear that guy in the stetson is Bono! And the tall blonde with her kids, she looks exactly like Claudia Schiffer…

This was enough to keep her entertained for a few minutes, until a cool gust of wind made her curl up in a wicker armchair. As she rubbed her arms to warm herself up, she felt something in the inside pocket of the jacket. It was Tom's wallet. It was old and tattered, made of rough leather, with corners that curled. She had no scruples about opening it, curious to explore the contents. It was stuffed full of bills, the result of pawning the picture. But she wasn't interested in the cash. She pulled out the photo of Aurore that she had noticed the night before and turned it over to find a handwritten message:

I love you because you are the knife that
I use to search within myself.
A.

Hmm, a quotation that the pianist must have copied from somewhere. It was self-obsessed, tormented and full of pain, aiming for a Gothic-Romantic effect.

Billie replaced the photo and examined the rest of the contents. There wasn't much, just some credit cards, Tom's passport and some Advil tablets. And that was it. But what was this bulge at the bottom? On closer inspection, she discovered a cut in the lining that had been sewn up with thick thread.

She took out her hairclip and used it to unpick the stitches. Then she shook the wallet upside down until a metal object fell into her hand.

It was a spent cartridge from a shotgun.

Her heart was racing. Realising that she had just violated someone's secret, she quickly shoved the cartridge back into the lining. Then she felt there was something else in there too.

It was a yellowing, slightly faded Polaroid. It showed a young man and woman hugging in front of a metal gate and a row of concrete high rises. She recognised Tom immediately; he couldn't have been more than twenty at the time, and the girl a little younger, more like seventeen or eighteen. She was beautiful, with South American looks. Tall and slim, she had strikingly light eyes, which glittered in the photo despite its poor quality and age. Judging from her pose, she had been the one taking the photo by holding the camera up above them.

'Enjoying yourself?'

Billie jumped, dropping the Polaroid. She turned round.

*

La Puerta del Paraíso Hotel
Suite 24

'Enjoying yourself?' shouted a voice.

His eye glued to the telescope, Milo was scrutinising the attractive physiques of two half-naked nymphs who were soaking up the sun at the edge of one of the swimming pools, when Carole burst onto the balcony. He started and turned round to find his friend looking at him disapprovingly.

'You know that thing's meant for studying Cassiopeia and Orion, not for ogling girls!'

'They might be called Cassiopeia and Orion, you

never know,' he said, pointing out the two pin-ups.

'You think you're so witty.'

'Look, Carole, you're not my wife and you're definitely not my mother. Anyway, how did you get into my room?'

'I'm a cop, remember? A hotel-room door is no obstacle to me,' she said, throwing a canvas bag down on one of the wicker chairs.

'I call that breaking and entering!'

'Call the police then.'

'You think you're pretty funny too, don't you?' He was obviously irritated and changed the subject. 'Anyway, I asked at reception. Tom and his "girlfriend" have already checked in.'

'I know, I asked too. Room 12, twin beds.'

'Does that make you feel better? Twin beds?'

She sighed. 'You can be a real jerk when you put your mind to it.'

'And Aurore? Did you ask about her as well?'

'Of course!' she said, walking over to the telescope to have a look for herself, turning it towards the shoreline. She studied the long stretch of fine white sand for a few seconds, watching the waves lap the shore. 'And if I've got my facts straight, Aurore should be right... there.'

She focused the lens for Milo to have a look.

Near the water's edge, in a sexy one-piece, the very lovely Aurore was climbing onto a jet-ski with Rafael Barros.

'He's not bad at all, is he?' remarked Carole, looking into the telescope.

'Really? Him?'

'You'd have to be pretty picky not to find him attractive!

Look at those broad shoulders, and those abs. The guy has the face of a Hollywood star and the body of a Greek god!'

'Are you done?' growled Milo, nudging Carole out of the way so he could look into the lens again. 'I thought you said this was for Orion and Cassiopeia.'

She smiled to herself, while he looked for a new object to spy on.

'The brunette over there, the one who looks totally wasted, with the breast implants and all that hair, is that—'

'Yes, that's her!' Carole cut him off. 'When you're done having fun with that thing, you can work out how we're going to pay for this room.'

'I've no idea,' admitted Milo dejectedly.

He looked up from his new toy and lifted the sports bag so he could sit down opposite Carole.

'This thing weighs a ton – what's in it?'

'Something I brought for Tom.'

He frowned, waiting for an explanation.

'I went to his place yesterday morning before I came to see you. I wanted to check the house for other clues. I went into the bedroom and guess what? The Chagall's gone!'

'What?'

'Did you know there was a safe behind it?'

'No.'

Milo suddenly saw a glimmer of hope. Maybe Tom

had some hidden savings that would help them pay off some of their debts.

'I was curious, and I tried out a few combinations.'

'And you managed to guess it,' he finished for her.

'Yes, by entering 07071994.'

'Did that just come to you? Divine inspiration, was it?'

She chose to ignore the sarcasm.

'It's just the date of his twentieth birthday: July 7, 1994.'

At the mention of this date, Milo's face darkened and he muttered, 'I wasn't with you guys then, was I?'

'No, you were in prison.'

Milo felt arrows of remorse pierce his heart. His demons still lurked in the background, ready to resurface the moment he let his guard down. His head was filled with clashing images: the luxury hotel around him and the walls of a prison cell, the wealthy paradise and hellish poverty.

Sixteen years ago, he had spent nine months in a penitentiary in Chino. It had been a dark time in his life, but the painful purging process had nevertheless marked the end of the bad years. Ever since, he had felt as though he were teetering on the edge of a precipice, that despite all he had done to put his life back together, he might at any moment go over the edge. His past was a ticking time bomb that was constantly threatening to explode and shatter everything he had worked so hard to rebuild.

He blinked several times to banish the memories that were trying to pull him under again.

'So what was in the safe then?' he asked, trying to keep his tone neutral.

'The present I gave him for his twentieth birthday.'

'Can I see?'

She nodded.

Milo picked up the bag and put it on the table to open it up.

*

Suite 12

'Are you going through my stuff?' I said angrily, snatching my wallet out of Billie's hands.

'No need to stress out.'

Still half asleep, I was finding it difficult to emerge from my comatose state. My mouth was dry and my body ached all over. My ankle was still agony, and I felt as though I had spent the night in a tumble dryer.

'I hate people that snoop around! You really do have all the character flaws under the sun, don't you?'

'Oh, and whose fault is that?'

'People have a right to privacy, you know! I know you've never opened a book in your life, but, if you ever do, have a look at Solzhenitsyn. He once said, "Our liberty is based on what others do not know about us." Have a think about that.'

'Well, I was just trying to even things up a bit,' she said in her defence.

'What do you mean?'

'You know everything about my life, so surely it's normal for me to want to know a bit more about yours?'

'No, it's not normal! Nothing about this is normal! You should have stayed in the pages of my book, and I should never have agreed to come here with you.'

'Well, someone woke up on the wrong side of the bed this morning!'

You've got to be kidding me – now she's the one getting annoyed with me!

'Look, you might normally be able to charm your way out of arguments, but it won't work with me.'

'Who's the girl?' she asked, pointing at the Polaroid.

'The Pope's sister – are you happy now?'

'Come on, surely you can come up with something better than that. Even in your books you'd make more of an effort.'

She's got some nerve...

'That's Carole. We've been friends since we were kids.'

'And why do you keep a photo of her in your wallet like a relic or something?'

I gave her a black, scornful look.

'Fine! Fine!' she shouted, storming back inside. 'I don't give a shit about your precious Carole anyway!'

I looked down at the yellowing photo in my hand. I had sewn it into my wallet years ago, and hadn't looked at it since.

Memories started to drift up to the surface. My thoughts became confused, taking me back sixteen years, to Carole tugging impatiently at my arm.

'Stop! Stop moving, stay still, Tom! Cheeeeese!'

Click. I could hear the whirr of the instant camera as it spat out the photograph.

I saw myself grabbing the photo as it came out, while Carole protested.

'Be careful! You'll get fingerprints all over it; it's still drying!'

I remembered her chasing after me as I shook the Polaroid to get it to dry faster.

'Let me see! Let me see!'

Then the magic of the next three minutes as she leaned against my shoulder, waiting for the image to slowly emerge, laughing hysterically at the final result.

*

Billie set the breakfast tray down on the teak table.

'OK,' she admitted, 'I shouldn't have gone nosing around in your stuff. I agree with your Solzy-thingybob. Everyone has the right to keep a few secrets.'

We had both calmed down a little. She poured me a cup of coffee while I buttered her a slice of bread.

'What happened that day?' she persisted, after a moment's silence.

But there was no longer any desire to pry or unhealthy fascination in her voice. Perhaps she could sense that, despite appearances, I wanted to confide in her about that part of my life.

'It was my birthday,' I began. 'My twentieth birthday.'

*

Los Angeles
MacArthur Park
7 July 1994

That summer, the heat was unbearable. It was

overwhelming, turning the streets into furnaces. On the basketball court, the sun had warped the surface, but that hadn't stopped a group of bare-chested guys who thought they were Magic Johnson from slamming the ball through the hoop time after time.

'Hey, freak! Wanna show us what you've got?'

I didn't even look up. I didn't even really hear them. I'd turned my Walkman up to full volume. Loud enough that the pulse of the bass and the pounding beat drowned out the taunts. I walked along the wire-mesh fence until I reached the parking lot where a lone tree with a few sad leaves offered a patch of shade. It was not exactly an air-conditioned library, but it was fine for reading. I sat down on the dry grass, leaning back against the trunk of the tree.

Protected by my wall of sound, I was in my own world. I looked at my watch: one o'clock. I had another half-hour before I had to catch the bus to Venice Beach where I sold ice creams on the boardwalk. Enough time to get through a few pages of one of the eclectic selection of books recommended to me by Miss Miller, a young and rather brilliant teacher at my college who had a soft spot for me. In my bag, *King Lear*, *The Plague* by Albert Camus, and Malcolm Lowry's *Under the Volcano* nestled beside the thousand or so pages of James Ellroy's four-volume *LA Quartet*.

My Walkman blasted out the dark lyrics of the latest REM album. Lots of rap as well. These were the glory days of West Coast hip hop: Dr Dre, Snoop Dogg, the powerful anger of Tupac. I had a love-hate relationship with that kind of music. It's true most of the lyrics weren't exactly poetry: hymns to cannabis, insulting the police, explicit sex, celebrations of gun violence and fast cars. But they did give a voice to our experiences and the things we lived with every day: the streets, the ghetto, the despair, gang rivalry, police brutality and the girls who found themselves pregnant at fifteen, giving birth in the school johns. And, above all else, the thing that dominated both the songs and our everyday reality: drugs. Drugs were everywhere, the cause and the effect, the explanation at the root of everything: money, power, violence and death. Listening to the rappers, it felt like they knew what we were going through. They too had hung out around towering apartment blocks, exchanged gunshots with the cops, ended up in jail or in hospital. Some of them even died here, on the streets.

I caught sight of Carole walking toward me. She wore a light-coloured dress, which gave her a kind of ethereal, fairy-like air – not her usual look. Like most of the girls around here, she tended to hide her femininity under hooded sweatshirts, XXL T-shirts and basketball shorts three sizes too big. Carrying a large sports bag, she walked past the guys on the court, ignoring their passing jibes and catcalls as she came over to join me on my little patch of grass.

'Hey, Tom.'

'Hey,' I said, pulling out my headphones.

'What you listening to?'

We'd known each other for ten years. Apart from Milo, she was my only friend. The only person (apart from Miss Miller) that I could have real conversations with. The bond we shared was unique, probably stronger than if Carole were actually my sister. We were closer than girlfriend and boyfriend. It was something else, something you couldn't put a name to.

So we had known each other a long time, but four years before that summer everything had changed. It changed the day I discovered that hell on earth existed in the apartment next to mine, only feet away from my own bedroom. That something inside the girl I met every morning on the stairs was already dead. That she was treated like an object, a thing, suffering unspeakable horrors night after night. That, bit by bit, someone was sapping the life, the vitality, the youth, out of her.

I didn't know how to help her. I was alone. I was sixteen, I had no money, no gang, no gun, no muscles. Just a brain and the desire to help, but that wasn't much use against the reality she faced.

She asked me not to tell anyone, and I respected her wishes. I did the one thing I could, which was to write her a story. A never-ending story that followed the main character, Delilah – a teenager with more than a passing resemblance to Carole – and her guardian angel, Raphael, who had been watching over her since she was a child.

For two years I saw Carole almost every day, and every new day brought with it another instalment of my story. She used to say that the story was her shield against the blows life dealt her. That my characters and their adventures pulled her into a fantasy world, far away from her troubles.

I spent more and more time thinking up new

adventures for Delilah, all the while wishing there was more I could do. Most of my free time was dedicated to creating a mysterious and romantic vision of Los Angeles in widescreen. I did extensive research, poring over ancient mythologies and histories of magic. I spent my nights bringing my characters to life, as they battled their own personal demons.

As the months passed, my story took shape, becoming more than just a supernatural fairy tale. It slowly grew from a coming-of-age story into an epic adventure, an odyssey. I put my heart and soul into it, never for a moment suspecting that it would one day bring me fame beyond anyone's wildest dreams, and be read by millions of people all over the world.

And that's the reason why I so rarely give interviews, why I am so reticent with journalists. The inspiration behind the *Angel Trilogy* is a secret I would never share, not at any price.

'So, what are you listening to?'

Carole was then seventeen, and beautiful, especially when she smiled. She was full of energy, full of life and plans for the future. And I know she thinks that all this is thanks to me.

'A Prince cover by Sinead O'Connor – you probably don't know it.'

'You're kidding. Everyone knows "Nothing Compares 2 U"!'

She stood looking down at me, framed against the summer sky.

'Want to go and see *Forrest Gump* at the Cinerama

Dome? It came out yesterday. Everyone says it's really good.'

'Oh, I dunno,' I said, without much enthusiasm.

'Or we could rent *Groundhog Day* from the store, or watch some more *X-Files*?'

'I can't, Carole, I'm working this afternoon.'

'OK, well, in that case—'

She interrupted herself to look mysteriously in her bag and pulled out a can of Coke, which she shook with a flourish as though it were a bottle of champagne.

'We'll just have to celebrate your birthday right now.'

Before I could protest, she opened the can and sprayed the contents all over me.

'Stop it! What's wrong with you?'

'Oh, come on, it's only Diet. It won't leave a stain.'

'Oh, really!'

I dried myself off, trying to look angry, but her smile and infectious happiness were irresistible.

'Well, it's not every day that you turn twenty. I wanted to do something special,' she said, suddenly sounding serious.

She turned to her bag again and handed me a huge package. Just from looking at it I could tell it had been wrapped carefully and came from a 'fancy' store. As I took it from her, I could feel how heavy it was, and I was embarrassed. I knew Carole was as broke as I was. She worked several jobs, but most of her savings went straight into paying for her classes.

'Open it, you idiot! Don't just sit there looking at it!'

Inside the box, there was something I could never

have hoped for. A kind of Holy Grail for scribblers like me. Better than Charles Dickens's pen, better even than Hemingway's Royal typewriter: it was a PowerBook 540c, the king of all laptops. For the past two months, every time I'd passed the window of Computer Club, I'd had to stop and look at it. I knew all of its functions by heart: the 33 Mhz processor, the 500 Mb hard drive, the LCD colour screen, the internal modem, the three-and-a-half-hour battery life. It was the first computer to have its own trackpad. Seven pounds of unrivalled technology, which cost a grand total of $5,000.

'I can't accept this from you,' I said.

'Well, you're going to have to.'

I was lost for words, and so was she. Her eyes shone, probably mine did too.

'It's not just a present, Tom. It's a responsibility as well.'

'I don't understand.'

'I want you to turn Delilah's story and *In the Company of Angels* into a proper book. I want this story to help other people like it helped me.'

'But I can write with a pen and paper!'

'Maybe, but by accepting this gift you're committing yourself. You're committing yourself to me.'

I didn't know what to say.

'Where did you find the money to pay for it, Carole?'

'Don't worry about that, I found a way.'

Neither of us spoke for a few minutes. More than anything I wanted to take her in my arms and maybe kiss her, maybe tell her I loved her. But we were not ready for that. All I could do then was promise her that one day I would write the story.

To break the heavy silence, she pulled one last thing from her bag, an ancient Polaroid camera, which belonged to Black Mama. She put her arm round my waist, lifted the camera above our heads and posed.

'Stop! Stop moving! Stay still, Tom! Cheeeeese!'

*

La Puerta del Paraíso Hotel
Suite 12

'Wow, she's some girl, your Carole,' murmured Billie when I had finished telling my story.

Her eyes were full of compassion as though she were seeing me for the first time.

'What does she do now?'

'She's a cop,' I said, swallowing a mouthful of lukewarm coffee.

'And the laptop?'

'It's at my house, in a safe. I used it to type up the first drafts of the *Angel Trilogy*. So I kept my promise.'

But she wasn't going to let me off that easily.

'You'll have fulfilled your promise when you finish the third book. Some things are easy to start, but it's only once you've completed them that they take on their true meaning.'

I was just about to ask her to stop the lecture, when there was a knock on the door.

I opened it without thinking, assuming it would be

room service, or a chambermaid, but I was wrong.

We've all had a similar experience, when it seems as if some higher power has engineered invisible links so that we get exactly what we need, at the precise moment that we need it most.

'Hello,' said Carole.

'Hi, buddy,' Milo shot at me. 'Good to see you again.'

21

Love, tequila and a mariachi band

She was as beautiful as another man's wife
Paul Morand

The hotel gift shop
Two hours later

'Come on! Stop acting like a child!' Billie ordered, tugging at my sleeve.

'Why do you want me to go in there anyway?'

'Because you need some new clothes!'

She gave me a shove and I found myself swallowed up by the revolving doors, before being spat out into the plush hotel store.

'What's wrong with you?' I exclaimed, stumbling. 'What about my ankle? Sometimes you act like a total airhead!'

She crossed her arms like an angry schoolteacher.

'Listen, you look like you've been dragged through a hedge backwards, you haven't seen the sun in six months and, judging by your haircut, your hairdresser died last year.'

'So?'

'Well, you're going to have to look a bit sharper if you want to get your woman back! So follow me.'

I limped grudgingly after her; a long shopping trip was the last thing in the world I felt like. The room was vast and airy, covered by a glass dome, and was more reminiscent of the chic Art Nouveau stores I had visited in London, New York and Paris than anything I had come across in Mexico. Immense crystal chandeliers hung from the ceiling and large black and white, vaguely artistic, photos adorned the walls, all of celebrities, such as Brad Pitt, Robbie Williams and Cristiano Ronaldo. The place was all about vanity and ostentation.

'OK, we'll start with skincare,' Billie said firmly.

Skincare… I groaned inwardly.

All of the impeccably turned-out make-up girls looked as though they had been cloned from the same model. They offered their help, but Billie, who seemed to know exactly what she was doing, declined.

'The seven-day beard, caveman thing really doesn't work for you,' she announced.

I decided not to argue. It was certainly true that over the last few months I had let myself go a little.

She grabbed a basket and dropped the three tubes she had just picked up into it.

'Cleanse, tone and moisturise,' she chanted.

She moved on to the next shelf, continuing her running commentary.

'I really like your friends. Your buddy, he's a funny guy, isn't he? He seemed so pleased to see you. It was really something.'

We had just spent the last two hours with Carole and Milo. Seeing them had done me good, and I felt I was getting back on my feet.

'Do you think they believed our story?'

'I don't know,' she admitted. 'It's a bit difficult to believe the unbelievable, isn't it?'

*

Hotel pool
Jimmy's Bar

The bar, with its straw roof, looked out onto the swimming pool and boasted a spectacular view of the sea and the golf course, whose eighteen holes ran along the edge of the beach.

'So what do you think of this Billie girl?' asked Carole.

'Great legs,' answered Milo, taking a sip of his cocktail,served in a coconut shell.

She looked up in irritation.

'One day you'll have to explain to me why you insist on making everything about sex.'

He shrugged dismissively, like a child who had just been told off. The barman shook his shaker vigorously, making a show of mixing the 'Perfect After Eight' that Carole had ordered.

Milo tried to carry on the conversation.

'So what do you think of her? Don't tell me you bought all that stuff about her being a character who's fallen out of one of his novels?'

'I know it seems crazy, but something about the story appeals to me,' she said thoughtfully.

'The resemblance between her and the character is uncanny, I'll give you that. But I don't believe in magic, or fairy stories.'

Carole thanked the waiter with a nod of her head. The pair left the bar to go and sit on two deckchairs overlooking the water.

'Like it or not, there is something magical about the *Angel Trilogy*,' she said, gazing at the ocean.

Feeling enthused, she shared her theory with Milo.

'The trilogy isn't like other bestsellers. Readers relate to the flaws of the characters, but it also helps people discover an inner strength they never knew they had. The story changed my life all those years ago, and it changed the course of all of our lives for good. It got us out of MacArthur Park.'

'Carole?'

'What?'

'This girl who's claiming to be Billie, she's just a gold-digger. Some chick trying to take advantage of Tom so she can bleed him dry.'

'Bleed him dry?' she cut in. 'What's left to take? Thanks to you, he's stone broke!'

'I wish you wouldn't keep bringing that up! Don't you think I feel bad enough about it already? I'll never forgive myself for screwing up like that. I think about it constantly; for weeks I've been trying to come up with a way to make it right.'

She got up from her chair and looked down at him coldly.

'For a guy consumed by guilt, I've got to say you're looking pretty comfortable lying there with your feet up and your coconut cocktail!'

She turned her back on him and marched off in the direction of the beach.

'That's not fair!'

He jumped up from his deckchair and ran after her, trying to stop her getting away.

'Wait for me!'

As he ran, he slipped on a wet tile and went flying. *Damn it.*

*

Hotel gift shop

'This is what you need: a moisturising soap with goat's milk extracts. And then this gel to exfoliate with.'

Billie continued dropping items into her basket, firing recommendations and beauty tips at me as she moved from aisle to aisle.

'You should also start using anti-wrinkle cream. You're at a crucial stage in your life in terms of skincare. Up until now, the surface of your skin has held up, but not for much longer. Your wrinkles are going to deepen. And don't tell me that women find wrinkles attractive, because they don't!'

Once she got going, there was no need to respond. She kept up both sides of the conversation and talked enough for the two of us.

'And your eyelids are drooping. With those bags and dark circles, you look like you've been out on the town three nights running. You know you need at least eight hours' sleep every night to flush out all your toxins?'

'Well, for the last two nights, you haven't let me get much sleep, have you?'

'Oh, so it's my fault, is it? Oh! And some collagen

serum. And some self-tan lotion, just to give you a bit of colour. If I were you, I'd spend some time at the spa. They've got these really hi-tech machines that blast fat cells. No? Sure? How about a manicure? Your nails look pretty horrible.'

'My nails? You're finding fault with my nails now?'

Suddenly, as we turned into the perfume aisle, I found myself face to face with a life-size cut-out of Rafael Barros. Sporting a whiter-than-white smile, toned pecs, broad shoulders, smouldering eyes and James Blunt-style designer stubble, the Hispanic Apollo was the face of a luxury brand's new fragrance, Unstoppable.

Billie gave me a moment to recover from the shock, then attempted to comfort me.

'I'm sure that photo has been airbrushed to death,' she reassured me gently.

But I wasn't in the mood for her sympathy.

'I don't want to talk about it.'

Refusing to let me wallow in self-pity, she dragged me along in her wake, determinedly pursuing her treasure hunt.

'Look!' she exclaimed, stopping in front of a display unit. 'Our secret weapon to give your skin a bit of a lift – an avocado face mask!'

'I am not slapping that all over my face, like some pansy!'

'Well, don't blame me for your dry, dull skin!'

And, just as I was starting to get really annoyed, she added fuel to the fire.

'And as for your hair I give up completely – good luck

dealing with that mop! We could always just buy some keratin shampoo, but I think it would be better to make you an appointment with Giorgio, the hotel hairdresser.'

Carried along by her enthusiasm, she moved toward the men's fashion section.

'Right, now for the serious stuff.'

Like a master chef carefully selecting ingredients for an elaborate dish, she plucked items from various shelves.

'OK, we'll try this… and this… and… that.'

As she pulled it off the shelf, I snatched a fuchsia shirt out of her hands before it could reach the basket, along with a mauve jacket and some satin trousers.

'Um… are you sure these are for men?'

'Oh please, you're not going to have some kind of male identity crisis, are you? These days, real men care about what they wear. See this fitted shirt? I gave this to Jack as a present—'

She stopped herself mid-sentence, realising too late that this was the wrong thing to say.

She was right. I threw the shirt back at her and stormed out of the shop without saying another word.

Women… I sighed to myself as I stepped into the revolving doors.

*

Women… Milo sighed to himself.

He walked out of the hotel's in-house clinic with a bloody wad of cotton in his nose and his head tilted backwards to slow the bleeding. Thanks to Carole, he had completely humiliated himself by the pool, falling flat on his face in front of 'Orion and Cassiopeia', smacking into the thighs of one girl and oafishly spilling his coconut cocktail all over the other.

I can't do anything right lately.

As he reached the forecourt of the shopping area, he slowed his pace; the floor was slippery and there were people everywhere.

Now would definitely be a bad time to go flying again, he thought to himself, just as a man came shooting out of the revolving doors at top speed, crashing straight into him.

*

'Hey! Look where you're going!' he grumbled, wiping dirt from his face.

'Milo!' I exclaimed, steadying him.

'Tom!'

'Are you hurt?'

'No, it's fine. I'll explain what happened.'

'Where's Carole?'

'She had a hissy fit; you know what she's like.'

'Wanna get a beer and a bite to eat?'

'Do you even need to ask?'

The Window on the Sea was the hotel's more informal restaurant. Spread over three levels, it provided a buffet with specialities from twelve different countries. The terracotta walls were decorated with paintings by local artists – still-lifes and vividly coloured portraits reminiscent of María Izquierdo and Rufino Tamayo.

Diners could choose to sit inside the air- conditioned dining room, or outside on the terrace. We sat outside at a table that gave us a stunning view of the sun-drenched swimming pool and the sea beyond it.

Milo was obviously in a good mood.

'I'm so happy to see you again. You're feeling a bit better, right? Well, anyway, you look better than you have done in ages. Is it to do with that girl?'

'It was her that got me out of my depression,' I admitted.

A host of waiters was hurrying from table to table, carrying trays of champagne, California rolls made with foie gras, and langoustines.

'You shouldn't just have taken off like that,' he said reproachfully, stopping a waiter to grab two glasses of champagne and a plate of canapés.

'But it's this trip that saved me! Anyway, if I'd hung around, you would have had me committed!'

'Maybe the sleep-therapy idea was a mistake,' he conceded, looking ashamed. 'But I was so desperate to do something, anything, to help you that I panicked and went straight to Sophia Schnabel.'

'Let's just forget it.'

We clinked glasses in a toast to our future, but I could see something was still bothering Milo.

'Just to make sure…' he said finally. 'This woman, you don't actually believe she's the real Billie, right?'

'As unbelievable as I know it sounds, I'm afraid I do.'

'Maybe having you committed wouldn't have been such a bad idea after all,' he quipped, swallowing a mouthful of langoustine.

I was going to tell him where to go, when my phone vibrated with a text message.

Hi Tom!

The name of the sender sent shivers down my spine. I couldn't ignore it.

Hi Aurore!

What are you doing here?

Don't worry, I'm not here for you, if that's what you think.

Milo got up from his seat and, true to form, stood behind me so he could shamelessly read the messages over my shoulder.

Well, why are you here then?

I'm taking a vacation. I don't know if you've noticed, but I've had a difficult year.

I hope you're not trying to make me jealous with that bimbo I saw you with in the shop.

'She's got some nerve, that chick!' Milo interjected angrily. 'Tell her she can go screw herself.'

But before I could start typing a reply she sent another missile my way.

And tell your friend not to be so rude about me.

'What a bitch!' snarled the friend in question.

And not to read other people's text messages over their shoulder.

Milo looked as though he'd been slapped in the face, and scanned the tables surrounding us.

'She's down there!' he said, pointing to a table tucked away in a little alcove near the open-air buffet. I looked over the balustrade. Aurore, in a pair of ballet pumps and a silk sarong, was having lunch with Rafael Barros, her eyes glued to her BlackBerry.

I wasn't in the mood for her games. I switched off my phone and told Milo to calm down.

It took another two glasses of champagne for him to do so.

*

'So, now that you're feeling a bit better, what's next for you?' he asked, looking worried.

'I think I'm going to start teaching again,' I said. 'But not in the States. There are too many bad memories in Los Angeles.'

'Where will you go?'

'Maybe France. There's an international lycée on the Côte d'Azur that seems interested in taking me on. I might try my luck there.'

'So you're leaving us,' he concluded bitterly.

'We have to grow up sometime, Milo.'

'And what about writing?'

'I'm done with writing.'

He opened his mouth to protest, but before he could say anything all hell broke loose behind me.

'What do you mean, done with writing? What about me?' yelled Billie.

Everyone on the terrace turned to look at us reproachfully. What with Milo's cursing and Billie's sudden explosion, we weren't fitting in very well with the clientele of billionaires and celebrities. We belonged back in the projects, barbecuing sausages, drinking beer and shooting hoops on an abandoned basketball court.

'You promised to help me!' said Billie angrily, still standing at our table.

Milo decided to put in his two cents' worth.

'It's true that if you promised to—'

'That's enough out of you!' I interrupted, holding my hand up to silence him.

I grabbed Billie by the arm and led her over to one side.

'We're both in denial,' I said. 'I can't write. I won't write. That's just the way it is. I'm not asking you to understand, I'm just asking you to accept it.'

'But I need to go back to my life!'

'Well, maybe your life is here now. In this damned "real world" that you claimed you were so in love with.'

'But I want to see my friends.'

'I thought you didn't have any friends!' I shot back.

'At least let me see Jack one more time.'

'If you want someone to screw, you'll find them by the dozen here.'

'You've got problems, you really do! And what about my mom? Am I going to find dozens of them here too?'

'Look, I'm not responsible for what happens to you.'

'Maybe, but we had a contract!' she said, pulling from her pocket the crumpled piece of tablecloth that had sealed our deal. 'You may have a lot of faults, but I at least thought you were a man of your word.'

Still holding her by the arm, I made her walk with me down to the buffet by the pool.

'Don't talk to me about contracts – you haven't honoured your side of the deal either!' I said, gesturing toward the table where Aurore and her boyfriend were sitting watching our little show.

I'd had enough of deluding myself.

'Our pact is null and void. Aurore has moved on – you'll never get her back for me.'

She looked at me defiantly.

'Wanna bet?'

I shrugged in confusion.

'Go ahead, I guess.'

Slowly, she moved a little closer to me, gently placed her hand behind my neck and kissed me lightly on the lips. Her mouth tasted fresh and sweet. I shivered, caught off guard, and stepped back slightly. I felt my heart start to pound in my chest, as feelings I had buried for so long came bubbling to the surface. If Billie had stolen the first kiss, I was eager to give the second away.

22
Aurore

We were both lost in the forest of a cruel
period of transition. Lost in our loneliness...
lost in our love of the absolute... mystical pagans
with no graves and no God.
Victoria Ocampo, in a letter to
Pierre Drieu La Rochelle

Bourbon Street Bar
Two hours later

Flashes of lightning lit the sky. Thunder rumbled in the distance and rain beat relentlessly down on the hotel, shaking the palm trees, battering the thatched parasols and studding the open water with thousands of little drops. I had been sheltering for the last hour on the covered terrace of a wine bar in a colonial-style planter's house, which reminded me of parts of New Orleans. Holding my cup of coffee, I watched the holidaymakers fleeing the storm for the comfort of their hotel rooms.

I needed to be alone, to gather my thoughts. I was angry with myself, annoyed that I had been so thrown by Billie's kiss, and that I had joined in her childish and degrading attempt to make Aurore jealous. We were not fifteen any more and this kind of petty game no longer worked.

I rubbed my eyes and tried to get back to work. I

watched the cursor in the top left-hand corner of my screen blink at me reproachfully. I had switched on the old Mac that Carole had brought for me in the vague hope that this ancient machine, which had once been everything to me, would somehow kick-start the creative process. In my glory days I had typed out hundreds of pages on this keyboard, but the computer wasn't a magic wand.

Unable to concentrate even for a few seconds, incapable of stringing two words together, I had lost my belief in myself, along with the thread of my story.

The storm made the air heavy and oppressive. I felt the old nausea rising as I sat frozen in front of the screen. Everything started to swim before my eyes. My mind was wandering, distracted by other cares, and at that moment, writing even the beginnings of a chapter seemed as daunting as climbing Everest.

I took one last sip of coffee and got up to order another. Inside, the room had the look of a British pub, with wood panelling and leather sofas adding to the warm and cosy feel. I went up to the counter, studying the impressive collection of bottles lined up behind the mahogany bar. I felt as though I ought to be sipping whisky or cognac, instead of coffee, and puffing on a Havana to the crackling sound of a Dean Martin record.

And, sure enough, someone went over to the piano and picked out the opening notes of 'As Time Goes By'. I turned around to have a look, half expecting to see Sam himself, the piano player in *Casablanca*.

Aurore was sitting on a leather stool, dressed in a long cashmere jumper and lacy tights. Her seemingly endless legs were tucked under her and made even longer by a pair of ruby-red heels. She looked up at me as she played. Her nails were painted purple and on her left index finger she wore a cameo ring. I noticed the stone cross she often wore to perform hanging round her neck.

Unlike mine, her fingers danced nimbly across the keys. She moved effortlessly from *Casablanca* to 'La Complainte de la Butte' before teasing out a little improvised variation on 'My Funny Valentine'.

The bar was almost empty but the few remaining drinkers watched her with total fascination, bewitched by the aura that surrounded her, a heady mix of Marlene Dietrich mystery, Anna Netrebko sex appeal and Melody Gardot sensuality.

I was no different; neither cured nor immune to her charms, I fell under her spell. Seeing her again was painful. When she left me, she had taken all the vitality out of me: my hopes, my self-confidence, my faith in the future. She had bled me dry, banished laughter and colour from my life. But, most of all, she had numbed my heart, stifling any possibility of loving again. My insides were like scorched earth: nothing grew there; there were no trees and no birds; I was trapped in a never-ending winter. I lost any appetite or desire, save that of dulling all my senses by stuffing myself full of drugs to smother memories that were too raw to confront.

*

Falling in love with Aurore was like catching a fatal and virulent illness. I met her in the airport in Los Angeles, in the boarding line for a flight to Seoul. I was going to South Korea on a promotional tour; she was going to perform Prokofiev. I loved her from the moment I saw her, for the most insignificant reasons, or perhaps the most significant: a sad smile, eyes that sparkled as they caught the light, the way she pushed her hair off her face, turning her head almost in slow motion. Then I fell in love with the inflections in her voice, her intelligence, her wit, her practical attitude to her own beauty. Later, I loved her for her secret flaws, for her melancholy nature, the chinks in her armour. We spent a few precious months wrapped up in each other, consumed by a happiness that carried us far above everyday reality – moments that seemed to last for ever, spinning in a giddy, intoxicating whirl.

Of course, I always knew there would be a price to pay. After all, I did teach literature, and I always bore in mind the warnings of my favourite authors: Stendhal and his 'crystallisation' theory; Tolstoy's Anna Karenina throwing herself under a train, having sacrificed everything for the man she loves; the sad decline of Ariane and Solal, the two lovers in *Belle du Seigneur*, numbed by an ether overdose, in the sordid solitude of a hotel room. But passion is like a drug: knowing its devastating effects has never stopped anyone destroying themselves once they're hooked.

Under the mistaken impression that she completed me, I told myself our love would last, that we'd succeed where others had failed. But the truth was that Aurore didn't bring out the best in me. She revived the worst aspects of my character, habits I'd long fought to suppress: a tendency for possessiveness; for being fooled by a pretty face, falling for the illusion that beauty might be more than skin deep; and a feeling of smug self-satisfaction at having got one up on all the other males of my species by bagging such a gorgeous girl.

Although Aurore had learned to take fame with a pinch of salt and claimed to have her feet firmly on the ground, celebrity rarely has a positive effect on those admitted to its club. Far from healing wounds to your self-esteem, it tends to cut them even deeper.

I knew all that. I knew Aurore's greatest fear was losing her looks or her artistic talent: the two magic powers bestowed on her from on high, marking her out from all others. I knew how her steady voice could falter, that behind the facade of a self- assured icon hid a woman lacking in confidence, strugglingto find inner balance. A woman who dealt with her complexes by cramming her diary full, rushing between world capitals, booking concert dates three years ahead and having a string of affairs followed by meaningless break-ups.

Yet right up to the end I still imagined I could be her anchor, and she mine. For it to work, we'd have had to put our trust in one another. As it was, she was so used to playing games and making people jealous to get what she wanted that the waters between us weren't exactly calm. Ultimately, our ship had sailed, and sunk. We could probably have been happy stranded together on a desert island, but life is not a desert island. Her friends – wannabe intellectuals in Paris, New York and Berlin – sneered at my 'trashy' novels, while on my side, Milo and Carole found her snobbish, superior and self-obsessed.

*

The storm raged, veiling the windows with a thick curtain of rain. In the hushed, classy surroundings of the Bourbon Street Bar, Aurore was striking the last few chords of 'A Case of You', which she had just finished singing in a smooth, bluesy voice.

While the crowd applauded, she took a sip from the glass of Bordeaux perched on the piano and thanked her audience with a nod. Then she closed up the instrument to make it clear that the show was over.

'Pretty impressive,' I said, walking toward her. 'Norah Jones had better watch out if you go down that road.'

She held out her glass, challenging me.

'Let's see if you've still got it.'

I placed my lips where hers had been and sampled the mysterious potion. She had encouraged me to share her passion for studying wines, but left me before I had a chance to learn the basics.

'Um... Château-Latour 1982,' I plucked at random.

My uncertainty brought a faint smile to her lips, before she corrected me, 'Château-Margaux 1990.'

'I think I'll stick to Diet Coke. Fewer vintages to remember.'

She laughed the way she used to laugh before, back when we loved one another. She moved her head very slowly, as she did when she wanted to be admired, and a golden lock fell from the clip holding back her hair.

'How are you?'

'Fine,' she replied. 'You, on the other hand, look like you've just walked in from the Stone Age,' she quipped, alluding to my beard. 'Oh, and how's your mouth doing? Did they manage to stitch you up?'

I frowned, confused. 'Stitch what up?'

'The piece that blonde took out of your lip at the restaurant. New girlfriend, is she?'

I dodged the question by turning to the counter to order 'the same as the lady'.

But she wouldn't be put off.

'She's a pretty girl. Not exactly classy, but pretty all the same. Anyway, looks like things are pretty explosive between you.'

I fought back. 'So how's it all going with Mr Sporty? OK, so he's not the sharpest knife in the drawer, but he's easy on the eye, I guess. You were made for each other. He's the love of your life, or so I've read.'

'So that's the kind of paper you read these days? They wrote such a load of crap about me and you that I'd have thought you'd know better. And as for "the love of my life"? C'mon, Tom, you know perfectly well I've never gone in for all that.'

'Even with me?'

She took another sip of wine, got up from the stool and leaned on the window ledge.

'Before you, I never had passionate love affairs. My relationships have always been fun, but I've never let myself get too carried away.'

It was one of the things that had come between us.

For me, love was like oxygen. It was what made life sparkle, gave it drama and intensity. For her, however magical it might be, at the end of the day it was all just illusion and deception.

Staring into space, she explained.

'You make ties and then they come undone – that's life. Eventually you go your separate ways, without necessarily knowing why. I can't give everything to another person, with a Sword of Damocles hanging above my head. I don't want to build my life on feelings, because feelings change. They're fragile and uncertain. You think they're deep and solid and then they're swept away by a passing bit of skirt or a smooth smile. I make music because there will always be music in my life. I like reading because there will always be books. Plus I can't say I know any couples who've stayed together for life.'

'That's because you surround yourself with artists and celebrities who are constantly jumping in and out of bed with each other!'

She was quiet for a moment, walking slowly out onto the terrace and placing her glass down on top of the rail.

'Our problem was, we didn't know where to go after the excitement of the early days had gone,' she concluded. 'We didn't work hard enough—'

'You didn't work hard enough,' I corrected her, feeling increasingly sure of myself. 'You're the one who gave up on us.'

One last bolt of lightning ripped through the sky and the storm was over, vanishing as suddenly as it had arrived.

I went on. 'All I wanted was to share my life with you. I think that's all love means, in the end: wanting to experience things together, learning from your differences.'

The grey sky began to clear and a patch of blue appeared amongst the clouds.

'All I wanted,' I tried to drum home, 'was to build a future with you. I was ready to take anything on, to go through anything with you by my side. I'm not saying it would have been easy – nothing ever is – but it's all that mattered to me. We would have overcome everything life threw at us if we'd just stuck together.'

In the main room, someone was playing the piano again. A few notes from a sultry variation on 'India Song' drifted through to us.

I turned and in the distance saw Rafael Barros approaching, carrying a surfboard under his arm. I started toward the wooden staircase to avoid having to meet him, but Aurore held me back, clutching my wrist.

'I know all that, Tom. I know you can't take anything for granted; nothing's ever guaranteed.'

There was a fragile note in her voice. It was unsettling; the femme fatale's varnish was cracking.

'I know you only really deserve love if you give your whole body and soul to it, throwing yourself in and risking everything… but I just wasn't ready to do that, and I'm still not now.'

I broke free of her grip and walked down the steps. Behind me, she added, 'I'm sorry if I made you believe otherwise.'

23

Solitude

Solitude is the profoundest fact of the human condition. Man is the only being who knows he is alone, and the only one who seeks out another
Octavio Paz

La Paz area
Early afternoon

With her rucksack on her back, Carole leapt between the rocks along the jagged coastline. She stopped to look up at the sky. The downpour had lasted less than ten minutes, just long enough to soak her from head to toe. Her clothes drenched, her face streaming with rain, she felt the warm water seeping under her T-shirt.

I'm such a klutz! she thought to herself, wringing her hair out with her hands. She'd remembered to bring a first-aid kit and a snack, but no towel or change of clothes!

A pleasant autumn sun had chased away the clouds, but it wasn't warm enough to dry her off. She started running again at a swift, steady pace, drinking in the beauty of each little cove against a backdrop of cactus-covered mountains. At a bend in the steep track leading down to the shore, a man burst out from behind a bush. She tried to run round him, but caught her foot on a root. She let out a cry as she fell spectacularly into the arms of the stalker.

'It's me, Carole!' Milo reassured her as he gently caught her.

'What the hell are you doing here?' she shouted, freeing herself from his grasp. 'Did you follow me? What the hell is wrong with you!'

'Jeez, will you calm down a minute?'

'And you can stop gawping at me!' she screamed, suddenly aware of her wet clothes clinging to the contours of her body.

'I've got a towel,' he offered, rummaging in his bag. 'And some dry clothes.'

She grabbed the bag out of his hands and went behind a tall umbrella-shaped pine tree to change.

'Don't even think about trying to get an eyeful, you creep. I'm not one of your Playmates, you know!'

'I'd have my work cut out trying to see you behind that thing,' he replied, catching the damp T-shirt and shorts she had just thrown off.

'Why did you follow me?'

'I wanted to spend some time with you. And I also wanted to ask you something.'

'Go on then, do your worst.'

'Why did you say that the story of the *Angel Trilogy* saved your life?'

She fell silent for a moment, before responding bitterly.

'One day, when you're a bit less of a jackass, maybe I'll tell you about it.'

He had rarely known her to be so vindictive, and was

239

taken aback. Still, he tried to carry on the conversation.

'Why didn't you ask me to come with you?'

'Because I wanted to be on my own, Milo. Is that so hard to understand?' she asked, pulling on a cable-knit jumper.

'But what good does it do to be lonely? Being alone is the worst thing in the world.'

Carole came out from her shelter, dressed in men's clothes that hung off her.

'No, Milo. The worst thing in the world is being stuck with guys like you.'

He felt as if he'd been punched.

'What exactly are you so mad at me for?'

'Drop it. We'll be here all night if I have to list everything,' she said, starting back down towards the beach.

'No, no, go right ahead! I want to know,' he admitted, falling into step with her.

'You're thirty-six years old, but you act like you're eighteen,' she began. 'You're irresponsible and immature. You'd like to think you're a player, but you're pathetic. All you live by is the ABC…'

'Huh?'

She spelled it out. 'Ass, beer and cars.'

'You done?'

'No.' She turned to him as they reached the sand. 'You're not the kind of guy a woman can rely on.'

'And what does that mean?'

She stood in front of him with her hands on her hips, looking him straight in the eye.

'You're one of the "good-time guys", one of those

cowboys women can have a bit of fun with when they're feeling lonely.

They might spend a night with you, but they'll never think of you as the father of their kids.'

'That's not what they all think!' he protested.

'Yes, it is, Milo. Any woman with an ounce of sense would say exactly the same. How many nice girls have you ever introduced us to? None, that's how many. There've been heaps of them and they're always the same: strippers, half-hookers and poor little lost girls you pounce on in crappy clubs, picking off the weak ones.'

'OK, and how many guys have you brought home? Oh no, that's right, we've never seen you with a man! Kind of weird, don't you think, honey? Past thirty and no love life to speak of?'

'Maybe it's just that I don't send you a fax to let you know every time I'm seeing someone.'

'Whatever! You saw yourself as the writer's wife, didn't you? Getting a mention on the back cover. Wait, here it is: "Tom Boyd lives in Boston, Massachusetts, with his wife Carole, their two children and their Labrador." That's what you wanted, isn't it?'

'You need your head looked at. Maybe cut out the wacky baccy.'

'And you won't tell the truth. You're like a goddamn Wonderbra.'

'Does everything have to come back to sex? You sure got a problem there.'

'It's you who has a problem with it!' he retorted. 'Why don't you ever wear dresses or skirts? How come you never put on a bathing suit? Why d'you come up in a rash if someone brushes against your arm? You like girls or what?'

Before Milo could finish his sentence, she slapped his face, hard, with the force of a punch. He grabbed Carole's wrist just in time to stop another one.

'Get off me!'

'Not until you calm down!'

She was thrashing around like a madwoman, tugging with all her might until she threw her opponent off balance. Eventually she tumbled backwards onto the sand, bringing Milo with her, his weight landing squarely on top of her. He was about to lift himself off when he found the barrel of a pistol pressed to his head.

'Get off!' she ordered, cocking her gun. She had managed to get it out of her bag. She might sometimes forget to pack a change of clothes, but Carole never forgot her weapon.

'Right away,' Milo said quietly.

Bewildered, he slowly got up and watched with sadness as his friend ran away from him, both her hands gripping the butt of the pistol.

He stood, dazed, in the little lagoon surrounded by white sand and turquoise sea, long after she had disappeared.

That afternoon, the shadow of the MacArthur Park projects stretched all the way to the very tip of Mexico.

24

La cucaracha

Love is like quicksilver in the hand. Leave the fingers
open and it stays. Clutch it, and it darts away
                                              Dorothy Parker

La Hija de la Luna restaurant
9 p.m.
Perched on the cliff top, the high-class restaurant
overlooked both the swimming pool and the Sea of
Cortés. The landscape was as impressive by night as it
was in daylight, gaining in romance and mystery what
it lost in clarity. Brass lanterns hung from the trailing
vines, and candles in coloured holders bathed each
table in a warm glow. Wearing a silver sequined dress,
Billie walked ahead of me toward the entrance area.
We were greeted cheerfully and shown to the table
where Milo was waiting for us. It was clear he'd been
drinking, and he couldn't explain why Carole wasn't
there. A few tables away, sitting in the middle of the
terrace like jewels in a crown, Aurore and Rafael Barros
were displaying their new-found love.

The atmosphere at dinner was gloomy. Even the
usually bubbly Billie seemed to have gone flat. She
looked tired and pale, and was feeling sorry for herself.
Earlier that evening I had found her huddled up in bed
in our room, having slept all afternoon. 'The journey

must have caught up with me,' she guessed. Whatever the reason, I had a hard time convincing her to come out from under the covers.

'What's happened to Carole?' she asked Milo.

Judging by his bloodshot eyes and deflated expression, it looked as though my friend might be about to fall under the table. Just as he began to mutter a few words of explanation, the peace of the restaurant was shattered by the strains of a tenor voice.

La cucaracha, la cucaracha,
Ya no puede caminar

A group of mariachis had rushed up to our table to serenade us. With two violins, two trumpets, a guitar, a guitarròn and a vihuela, the band made an impressive amount of noise.

Porque no tiene, porque le falta
Marijuana que fumar

Their outfits were a sight to behold: black trousers with embroidered seams, short jackets with silver buttons, smartly knotted ties, belts with eagle-shaped buckles, shiny boots, and, of course, sombreros the size of flying saucers.

After the mournful wail of the soloist came the rest of the band singing with a rather forced jollity, as though it were a duty rather than a pleasure.

'Pretty tacky, huh?'

'You have to be kidding!' exclaimed Billie. 'These guys are pure class.'

I looked at her doubtfully. Clearly we meant very different things by the word 'class'.

'Gentlemen, look and learn!' she said, turning to Milo and me. 'What you're seeing here is the ultimate expression of masculinity.'

The lead singer smoothed his moustache and treated his adoring audience to another number, with accompanying dance moves.

Para bailar la bamba,
Se necesita una poca de gracia.
Una poca de gracia pa mi pa ti.
Arriba y arriba

The concert continued along the same lines for a good part of the evening. Moving from table to table, the mariachis churned out their repertoire of folk songs on the themes of love, courage, beautiful ladies and arid landscapes. To me it was an old-fashioned, irritating spectacle; to Billie, the embodiment of the proud spirit of a people.

As the show neared its end, a far-off hum could be heard. All the diners turned to look at the sea in unison. A light appeared on the horizon. The whirring noise became more and more deafening and an old seaplane could be seen silhouetted against the sky. Flying low, the metal bird swooped over the restaurant to drop flowers onto the terrace. Within seconds, hundreds of roses of every colour came raining down, carpeting the shiny wooden floor. This unexpected floral shower was met with rapturous applause. Then the seaplane reappeared above our heads before launching into a chaotic choreographed display. Luminous plumes of smoke came together to form an unconvincing heart shape which quickly blew off into the Mexican night.

The crowd roared once again when all the lights were turned out and the maître d' walked toward the table where Aurore and Rafael Barros were sitting. He was carrying a diamond ring on a silver tray. Then Rafael got down on one knee, while a waiter stood to one side, ready to uncork the champagne when Aurore said yes. Everything was perfect, planned down to the tiniest detail – just as long as you liked your romance piled on thick and appreciated off-the-shelf, mail-order moments.

But wasn't this exactly the kind of thing Aurore couldn't stand?

*

I was sitting too far away to hear her response, but close enough to read her lips.

'I'm sorry,' she whispered, though whether these words were meant for herself, the audience or Rafael Barros, I wasn't sure.

How come guys didn't put a bit more thought into it before popping the question like this?

There followed an unbearably heavy silence in which it seemed that the entire restaurant was sharing the embarrassment of this fallen demigod, who was now nothing but a sad case kneeling on the floor, a pillar of salt frozen in shame and shock. I'd been there too, some time before him, and at that moment I felt more sorry for him than gleeful at getting even.

Well, that was before he got up, strode across the room oozing wounded pride, and out of nowhere threw me a right hook worthy of Mike Tyson.

*

'And so the bastard came up and smacked you right on the nose,' summed up Dr Mortimer Philipson.

Hotel clinic
Three-quarters of an hour later

'That's pretty much it in a nutshell,' I agreed, while the doctor cleaned up the wound.

'You're lucky. It's bled a lot, but your nose isn't broken.'

'Well, that's something.'

'Having said that, your face looks like it's taken a bit of a battering. Been in any scraps lately?'

'I had a disagreement with a guy named Jesus and his followers in a bar,' I replied vaguely.

'You also have a cracked rib, as well as a nasty sprained ankle. It's badly swollen. I'll put some ointment on it, but you'd better come back tomorrow morning so I can put a compress on it. How did you wind up with that?'

'I fell onto the roof of a car,' I replied, as though it was the most normal thing in the world.

'Hmm … you live dangerously.'

'For the last few days, you could say that.'

The hotel's health centre was no small-time clinic, but a modern complex with state-of-the-art equipment.

247

'We treat the biggest stars on the planet in here,' the doctor responded when I pointed this out.

Mortimer Philipson was approaching retirement. His languid air didn't seem to match his tanned, strong-featured face and his bright laughing eyes. He had the look of Peter O'Toole playing a somewhat older incarnation of Lawrence of Arabia.

He finished rubbing my ankle and asked a nurse to bring me a pair of crutches.

'I'd advise you not to put any weight on that foot for a few days,' he warned as he handed me his card, with my appointment for the next day written on it.

I thanked him for his help and, using my sticks, dragged myself slowly back to my suite.

*

The bedroom was filled with a gentle light. Pale flames flickered in the fireplace in the middle of the room, casting a glow over the walls and ceiling. I looked for Billie, but she wasn't in the living room or the bathroom. I could hear the chorus of a Nina Simone song coming faintly from somewhere.

I pulled back the shutters that looked onto the balcony and found her lying, eyes closed, in the overflowing Jacuzzi. The curved sides of the pool were covered in blue mosaic tiles, and it was fed by a cascade of water pouring from a large swan's beak, illuminated in all the colours of the rainbow by an advanced lighting system.

'Coming in?' she challenged me, keeping her eyes closed.

I moved closer to the hot tub. It was surrounded by

twenty or so little candles, forming a wall of tiny flames. The surface of the water shimmered like champagne, with golden bubbles floating up from the bottom.

I put down my crutches, unbuttoned my shirt and pulled off my jeans, and slipped into the water. It was very hot, almost unbearably so. Thirty-odd jets distributed around the inside of the tub massaged you in a way more invigorating than relaxing, while seductive music played out from waterproof speakers in each corner. Billie opened her eyes and reached over to stroke the plaster that Philipson had just stuck on my nose. Lit up from below, her face appeared translucent, while her hair seemed to have turned white.

'Does the returning soldier need a little light relief?' she teased, snuggling up to me.

I tried to brush off her advances. 'I don't think it's a good idea to repeat the kissing episode.'

'Look me in the eye and tell me you didn't enjoy it.'

'That's not the point.'

'It worked though, didn't it? Just a few hours later, your beloved Aurore was back on the market in spectacular style.'

'Maybe. Aurore's not in the Jacuzzi with us now though, is she?'

'How do you know she's not watching us?' she asked, slipping into my arms. 'All the rooms have telescopes on the balconies and everyone spends all day checking each other out. Haven't you noticed?'

Her face was now only a few inches away from mine. Her eyes were pale blue, the pores of her skin had opened up in the steam and beads of sweat were forming on her forehead.

'Maybe she's looking at us right now,' she carried on. 'Don't pretend that doesn't turn you on just a little bit.'

I couldn't stand this game; it was so unlike me. And yet, spurred on by the thought of our previous kiss, I couldn't stop myself placing one hand on her hip and the other behind her neck.

She gently pressed her lips against mine and then my tongue reached for hers. It was just as magical as before, but it lasted only a few seconds before something overwhelmingly bitter forced me to stop.

There was a strong, sharp taste in my mouth that caught the back of my throat and made me pull away suddenly. Billie looked stunned. It was then that I noticed her lips had gone black, her tongue tinged purple. Her eyes had lit up but her skin was becoming paler and paler. She was shivering, her teeth were chattering and she bit her lips. I scrambled out of the Jacuzzi, helped her out and rubbed her down with a towel. I could feel her legs wobbling, on the verge of folding beneath her. Racked by a violent coughing fit, she pushed me away so she could bend over, suddenly overcome by the urge to vomit. With visible discomfort, she brought up a thick, sticky paste before falling to the floor.

But what I was looking at wasn't vomit. It looked like ink.

25

The danger of losing you

With a gun barrel between your teeth,
you speak only in vowels
From the film *Fight Club*, by Chuck Palahniuk

Hotel clinic
1 a.m.
'You her husband?' asked Dr Philipson, closing the door of the room where Billie was now sleeping.

'Um, no, it's not like that,' I replied.

'We're her cousins,' claimed Milo. 'We're the only family she's got.'

'Often take baths with your "cousin", do you?' the doctor asked, looking at me with irony.

An hour and a half earlier, just as he was preparing to make a difficult putt, he'd had to throw a white coat on over his golf clothes and rush to Billie's bedside. He immediately saw that the situation was serious and put all his effort into reviving her, getting her admitted to the clinic and carrying out first aid.

Since his question didn't require a response, we followed him silently into his office. It was a corridor-like room which looked out over a sunny lawn, as smooth as a putting green, with a little flag flying in the middle. As you got closer to the window, you could make out a golf ball eight or nine yards from the hole.

'I'm not going to lie to you,' he began, gesturing to

us to sit down. 'I have absolutely no idea what's wrong with your friend, nor what brought on the attack.'

He took off his coat and hung it up, before settling down in front of us to list her symptoms.

'She has a very high temperature, her body is abnormally stiff and she's brought up the entire contents of her stomach. She's also suffering from headaches, she's having trouble breathing and she can't stand upright.'

'Which means what?' I pressed him, anxious to hear some kind of diagnosis.

Philipson opened the top drawer of his desk and took out a cigar, still in its metal tube.

'She's showing clear signs of anaemia,' he added, 'but what I'm really concerned about is this black substance she's regurgitated in some quantity.'

'It looks like ink, doesn't it?'

'Could be...'

He took the Cohiba cigar out of its tube and stroked it, as if hoping that contact with the tobacco would offer some revelation.

'I've requested a blood test, as well as an analysis of the black paste and one of her hairs which, you say, suddenly turned white.'

'It happens, doesn't it? They say that when you've suffered some kind of trauma your hair can go white overnight. It happened to Marie Antoinette the night before her execution.'

'Bullshit,' the doctor scoffed. 'The only way to take all the pigment out of the hair that fast is by pouring bleach on it.'

'Do you really have the facilities to investigate all this?' Milo asked.

The doctor cut the tip off his Havana cigar. 'As you'll have seen, our equipment is cutting edge. Five years ago, the eldest son of an oil baron sheikh was staying at the hotel when he had a jet-ski accident. He crashed into a speedboat and was in a coma for several days. His father promised to make a substantial donation to the hospital if we managed to get him out of danger. More by chance than anything, he pulled through without any lasting damage. The sheikh kept his word, and that's why we're so well set up.'

As Mortimer Philipson stood up to usher us out, I asked if I could spend the night by Billie's bedside.

'No point,' he said abruptly. 'We've got a nurse on call and two medical students who'll be working all night. Your "cousin" is our only patient. She'll be monitored 24-7.'

'Really, Doctor, I insist.'

Philipson shrugged and returned to his office, muttering, 'If you want to break your back sleeping in a chair, that's your funeral, but don't come running to me tomorrow morning when that sprained ankle and cracked rib of yours are giving you hell.'

Milo left me outside Billie's room. I could tell he was on edge.

'I'm worried about Carole. I've left dozens of messages on her voicemail, but I still haven't heard anything. I've got to find her.'

'OK, good luck, bro.'

'G'night, Tom.'

I watched him walk off down the corridor, but after a few yards he stopped in his tracks and turned back toward me.

'You know, I wanted to say... to say I'm sorry,' he admitted, looking me right in the eye.

His eyes were red and shining, his face haggard, but he had an air of determination about him.

'I really screwed up, taking risks with my investments,' he went on. 'I thought I was smarter than the rest. I let you down and now you've lost everything. I don't know if you'll ever be able to forgive—'

His voice cracked. He screwed up his eyes and a tear ran down his cheek. Seeing him cry for the first time in my life made me uncomfortable. I didn't know how to react.

'It's just so dumb,' he added, rubbing his eyes. 'You know, I thought we'd done the hard part, but I was wrong. The hardest thing isn't getting what you want; it's keeping hold of it once you have it.'

'Milo, I don't give a shit about the money. It never filled a void; it never solved anything. You know that.'

'We'll get out of this mess, the same way we've always done, you'll see,' he promised, trying to pump himself up again. 'Our luck won't run out now.'

Before leaving to look for Carole, he slapped me on the back and assured me, 'I'll sort this out, I swear. Maybe it'll take some time, but I'll do it.'

*

I turned the handle quietly and peered round the door.

Billie's room was enveloped in bluish shadow. I walked over to her bed, making as little noise as I could.

Her sleep was fitful and feverish. A thick sheet covered her body, with only her pale face peeking out above it. The sparky vivacious blonde, who just this morning had been playing havoc with my life, had aged ten years in the space of a few hours. I sat beside her for some time, choked up, before laying my hand gingerly on her forehead.

'You're one hell of a girl, Billie Donelly,' I whispered, leaning toward her.

She wriggled and, without opening her eyes, murmured, 'I thought you were going to say "one hell of a pain in the ass".'

'That too,' I said, trying to hide my emotion.

I stroked her face and told her, 'You've pulled me out of a black depression. Because of you, all the feelings that have nagged away at me are fading. You've filled the silence with your laughter and wisecracks.'

She tried to say something, but her breath was so short that she couldn't get it out.

'I won't give up on you, Billie. I swear to you,' I promised, taking hold of her hand.

*

Mortimer Philipson struck a match and lit his cigar, then walked out onto the green holding his putter. The golf ball was a little over eight yards away, on a slight slope. Mortimer took a long drag on his cigar, then crouched down to get a better feel for the shot. It

255

would be a tricky putt, but he'd got hundreds in from this distance. He got into position and focused. 'Luck is what happens when preparation meets opportunity,' Seneca had said. Mortimer played the shot as if his life depended on it. The ball rolled over the green and seemed to hesitate before skirting round the hole, without actually falling into it.

Opportunity was thin on the ground tonight.

*

Milo rushed out to the hotel forecourt and asked the valet to fetch the Bugatti from the underground car park. He headed towards La Paz, using the satnav to find the spot where he'd left Carole. That afternoon on the beach, he'd seen just how raw her wounds were, wounds he hadn't known even existed before.

How often we fail to notice the suffering of those we love most, he thought to himself sadly.

The broad-brushed portrait she'd painted of him had got to him too. She'd always thought of him as a low-down, good-for-nothing, tacky, trailer-trash male chauvinist pig, just like everyone else did. He had to admit he hadn't done much to set her straight. It suited him to hide behind this image, which protected a sensitive side he was scared to acknowledge. He would have done anything to get Carole to love him, yet he didn't feel able to reveal his true self to her.

He drove for half an hour through the bright night. The shadow of the mountains loomed out of the clear sky, so unlike the sky above our polluted cities. He turned down a wooded track to park the car, shoved a blanket and a bottle of water into his bag and took the stony path down towards the beach.

'Carole! Carole!' he shouted as loud as he could. But his cries were carried off by the capricious warm wind, which blew over the sea, moaning sadly.

He found the cove where they had argued that afternoon. The air was mild and the pale full moon was admiring its own reflection on the surface of the water. Milo had never seen so many stars in the sky, but there was no sign of Carole. With a torch to light his way, he carried on, clambering over the craggy rocks that lined the shore. About 500 yards further on, he slipped down a narrow path which opened out into a small bay.

'Carole!' he shouted again as he stepped onto the beach.

His voice carried better this time. The cove was sheltered from the wind by granite cliffs which softened the sound of waves breaking on the shore.

'Carole!'

With all his senses primed, Milo walked the length of the cove until he caught sight of something moving at the far end. As he approached the cliff face, he saw that the rock was split almost from the top by a long fault line, which opened out into a cave. There he found Carole curled up on the sand with her legs tucked under her and her head hanging down, shivering. She looked utterly crushed. She was still clutching her pistol tightly.

Milo knelt down beside her. He was nervous approaching her, but his anxiety quickly gave way to real concern for his friend. He wrapped her up in the blanket he had brought with him and lifted her up to carry her back to the car.

'I'm sorry about what I said earlier,' she mumbled. 'I didn't mean it.'

'It's all forgotten,' he reassured her. 'Everything's going to be fine.'

The wind blew colder and stronger. Carole ran her hand through Milo's hair and looked up at him, her eyes brimming with tears.

'I'll never do anything to hurt you,' she whispered in his ear.

'I know,' he said, holding her tightly to him.

*

Keep going, Anna. Don't give up. Keep going!

On the same day, some hours earlier, in a blue-collar district of Los Angeles, a young woman by the name of Anna Borowski was hurrying up the road. If you'd seen her running along in her fleece-lined hoodie, you'd probably have thought she was out for a morning jog. But Anna wasn't going jogging. She was going through trash.

Just a year before, life had been good for Anna. She ate out several times a week and didn't bat an eyelid at spending a thousand dollars on shopping trips with her girlfriends. But when the economic crisis came everything changed. One day she had a job, the next her firm was laying off half its staff and her management role no longer existed.

For a few months, she had told herself she was just

going through a bad patch, and stayed upbeat. She was prepared to take any job she was qualified for, spending her days on job sites, sending out thousands of CVs, going to careers fairs and even spending a sizeable sum on careers coaching. But all her attempts came to nothing. In six months, she hadn't even managed to land a proper interview. To get by, she'd had to take a cleaning job at a retirement home in Montebello, but the few measly dollars she earned weren't nearly enough to cover her rent.

Anna slowed down as she reached Purple Street. It wasn't yet 7 a.m. The road was beginning to come to life, but it was still quiet. Nevertheless, she waited for the school bus to go by before delving into the garbage can. The more she did it, the better she became at putting aside her dignity and pride. Anyway, she didn't really have a choice. Thanks to her former spend-now-think-later mentality and a few debts that had seemed insignificant in the days when she was earning $35,000 a year, she was now in danger of losing the roof over her head.

At the beginning, she had merely rummaged in the dumpsters out the back of the supermarket below her apartment, looking for food that had gone past its sell-by date. But she was far from the only one to have had that idea. Each evening, an ever-growing crowd of homeless people, casual workers, students and hard-up pensioners swarmed around the metal containers, until the management put an end to it by spraying all the food with detergent. So Anna had been forced to look further afield. To begin with, she had been traumatised by the experience, but the human being was an animal, able to adapt to all kinds of humiliation.

The first garbage can she came across was full to the brim, and her explorations bore fruit: a half-eaten box of chicken nuggets, a Starbucks cup with a fair amount of black coffee left in it, and another containing a cappuccino. In the second, she found a torn Abercrombie shirt which could easily be washed and mended and, in the third, a nearly new book with an attractive imitation-leather cover. She put the meagre hoard in her rucksack and carried on.

Half an hour later, Anna Borowski returned home to her little apartment in a modern, well-kept block, which now contained only the bare minimum of furniture. She washed her hands and poured the two coffees into a mug which she put in the microwave along with the nuggets. While she waited for her breakfast to be ready, she spread out the day's haul on the kitchen table. The elegant Gothic-lettered book cover leapt out at her. A sticker in the left-hand corner told the reader, 'by the author of *In the Company of Angels*'.

Tom Boyd? She remembered the girls at the office talking about him. They couldn't get enough of his books, but she'd never read anything by him. As she wiped a blob of milkshake off the cover, it occurred to her she might be able to get a good price for this. She logged on to the internet by hacking into her neighbour's Wi-Fi once again. The book cost $17 to buy new on Amazon. She went into her eBay account and put it on sale for $14 to buy now. Worth a shot.

Then she washed the shirt, took a shower to scrub

herself clean and got dressed, pausing in front of the mirror to look at herself.

She had just turned thirty-seven. For years she had looked younger than her age, and then all of a sudden it was as if a vampire had sucked out all her freshness. Since losing her job, she had resorted to eating rubbish, which meant she had put on at least twenty pounds. It had all gone on her ass and face, giving her the appearance of a giant hamster. She tried to smile, but hated what she saw.

She was all at sea, the signs of shipwreck writ large across her ugly face.

Get moving, you're gonna be late!

She put on a pair of pale-blue jeans, trainers and a hoodie.

That'll do, it's not like you're going to a club. No point getting all dressed up to go and wipe up old guys' shit!

No sooner had she thought this than she was ashamed of being so cynical. She felt so utterly lost. What did she have to cling on to in her darkest moments? There was no one who could help her, no one at all to turn to. No real friends, no man in her life – the last had left the scene several months ago. As for family, she hadn't told either of her parents about her problems, for fear of losing face. And you had to admit they weren't exactly hanging around the phone waiting for her news. Some days, she almost wished she had stayed in Detroit like her sister, who still lived five minutes away from the family home. Lucy had never had an ounce of ambition. She'd married a big fat hillbilly who worked in insurance and had a little brat of a child with him, but at least she didn't have to worry about whether she'd have enough to eat from one day to the next.

Anna went to open the door, but couldn't bring herself to walk through it. Like everyone else, she was on medication: painkillers for her back and extra strong ibuprofen tablets that she gobbled up like sweets to get rid of chronic migraines. But today she could have done with a powerful sedative to boot. As the weeks went by, she suffered increasingly from panic attacks, living in constant fear and with the unshakeable feeling that, no matter what she did, no matter how hard she tried, she had no control over her life. Sometimes, the precariousness of her situation affected her mind and she thought she might do something crazy, like the unemployed finance executive who nine months ago had killed five members of his family before turning the gun on himself, just round the corner from here. He had left a letter for the police, putting it all down to his desperate financial situation. He'd been out of work for a number of months and had just lost the sum total of his savings in the stock market crash.

Keep going, Anna. Don't give up. Keep going!

She tried to pull herself together. She couldn't let herself give in. She knew full well that if she stopped swimming she could only sink. She had to fight with all her strength to keep her apartment. She sometimes felt like a creature hiding in its burrow, but at least she could wash and sleep safely here.

She put her iPod headphones in, walked downstairs and took a bus to the retirement home. She cleaned for three hours and spent her lunch hour browsing the internet from the staff-room computer. She had a buyer for the book she'd put up for sale who was willing to pay the asking price. Anna worked until 3 p.m. then went to the post office to send the book to its new owner: Bonnie Del Amico, Berkeley Campus, University of California.

She slid the book inside the envelope, without noticing that half its pages were blank.

*

'Hey, fellas, hurry it up a little!'

The instruction crackled from the radios of each of the eight articulated lorries crossing the industrial zone of Brooklyn. As with money transfers, the duration and route of the journey between the New Jersey depot and the recycling plant near Coney Island were strictly regulated to avoid stock being stolen on the way. Each truck was loaded with thirty pallets, carrying almost 13,000 books packed in boxes.

It was almost 10 p.m. and raining when the enormous cargo entered the pulping station inside a vast compound surrounded by high fences, reminiscent of a military training camp.

One by one, each lorry was emptied and tons of books still in their plastic wrapping were piled up on the concrete floor.

A representative of the publishing company supervised the operation, accompanied by an auditor. It wasn't every day you had to have 100,000 copies pulped because of a fault in the manufacturing process. The two men scrupulously checked the entire cargo to ensure everything was as it should be. Each time a pallet was unloaded, the auditor would take a book out of its box to check it contained the same printing error. Every one of them had the same thing missing: of the novel's 500 pages, only half had been printed. The story came to an abrupt end halfway down page 266, right in the middle of a sentence.

Three bulldozers swarmed around the sea of books, shovelling them like so much worthless rubble onto conveyor belts that sped towards the metal monster's open jaws. The pulping could now begin.

The two crushers greedily swallowed tens of thousands of books. The mechanical beast violently tore them apart and chewed them up. Ripped pages whirled around in a blizzard of paper dust.

Once they had passed through the digestive system, a pile of gutted, skinned and slashed books emerged from the beast's bowels. Then they were squashed by a press and excreted in big wire-bound bundles. Afterwards, these compressed cubes were piled up at the back of the warehouse. The next day, it would be their turn to be loaded onto more lorries. The recycled paper pulp would be reincarnated as newspapers, magazines, tissues or shoeboxes.

*

Within a few hours, it was all over. Once the entire stock had been destroyed, the factory owner, publisher

and official signed a document recording the number
of books that had been pulped in each batch.

The total came to 99,999 copies.

26

The girl who came from nowhere

*Those who fall often bring down with them those who
come to their aid*

Stefan Zweig

Hotel clinic

8 a.m.

'Well, you're doing a great job of watching over me, snoring like a pig!'

I opened my eyes with a start. I was slumped over the arm of a wooden chair and my back was killing me, my throat was tight and I had pins and needles in my legs.

Billie was sitting up in bed. Her face was beginning to get some colour back, but her hair was still white. She seemed to have a spark about her again though, which had to be a good sign.

'How are you feeling?'

'I've felt better,' she admitted, sticking out her tongue, which was back to its usual pink. 'Could you pass me a mirror?'

'I'm not sure that's such a good idea.'

But she wouldn't take no for an answer. I handed her the small mirror from the bathroom. She looked at herself in horror, lifting up clumps of hair, brushing it aside, ruffling it and inspecting the roots, appalled to see that in the course of a night her lustrous golden mane had turned into an old lady's hair.

'But... but how could this happen?' she asked, wiping away a tear.

I put my hand on her shoulder. I couldn't give her any explanations. I was trying to think of something comforting to say when the door opened and Milo and Dr Philipson walked in.

Holding a folder under his arm and looking preoccupied, the doctor muttered a swift greeting then stood for several minutes at the foot of the bed, studying the patient's charts.

'We've had most of the test results back,' he announced eventually, looking both excited and confused.

He took a felt-tip pen out of his coat and set up the little board he had brought with him.

'First of all,' he began, scribbling down a few words as he spoke, 'the thick black substance you threw up was indeed an oil-based ink. We found traces of its characteristic pigments, polymers, additives and solvents ...'

He let his sentence trail off, then came straight out and asked, 'Did you try to poison yourself, young lady?'

'No, I did not!' Billie protested.

'The reason I ask is, to be frank, I can't see how you could throw up such a substance without first having consumed it. It doesn't fit with any known pathology.'

'What else did you find?' I asked to move things along.

Mortimer Philipson handed each of us a sheet of paper filled with figures and terms I had heard on *ER* or *Grey's Anatomy*, but whose precise meaning I wasn't sure of: blood count, electrolytes, urea, creatinine, blood-sugar level, liver function, haemostasis and so on.

'As I suspected, the blood test confirmed a diagnosis of anaemia,' he explained, adding another item to the board.

'With nine grams of haemoglobin per decilitre, you're well below normal levels. This explains your paleness, extreme tiredness, headaches, palpitations and dizzy spells.'

'So what's behind the anaemia?' I asked.

'We'll need to do more tests to work that out,' explained Philipson, 'but that's not what's worrying me most.'

I was staring at the blood-test results and, despite knowing nothing on the subject, I could see straight away that one of the figures looked odd.

'It's the blood-sugar level that's out, isn't it?'

'That's right,' Mortimer agreed. 'We're looking at a severe form of hypoglycaemia, to an unheard of degree.'

'How can it be "unheard of"?' Billie asked anxiously.

'Hypoglycaemia occurs when the level of sugar in the blood is too low,' the doctor explained in simple terms. 'When the brain is unable to obtain sufficient amounts of glucose, it leads to dizzy spells and fatigue. But your glucose level is off the scale.'

'Which means what?'

'Which means that while I'm talking to you right now, you should in fact be dead, or at least in a deep coma.'

Milo and I spoke in unison. 'That can't be right!'

Philipson shook his head. 'We've repeated the tests three times. It's incomprehensible, and yet there's something even more mysterious going on here.'

He took the lid off his pen again and held it in mid-air.

'Last night, one of my interns had the idea of doing a spectrograph. It's a technique which allows you to identify molecules by mass and to characterise their chemical stru—'

I cut him off. 'Could you just get to the point?'

'It showed the presence of abnormal carbohydrates. To be clear, you have cellulose in your blood.'

He wrote the word 'cellulose' on his board.

'As you are no doubt aware,' he went on, 'cellulose is the main component of wood. Cotton and paper also contain a substantial amount of it.'

I couldn't see where he was going with all this. It became clearer when he asked us a question.

'Imagine you swallowed a bunch of cotton swabs. What do you think would happen?'

'Not much,' said Milo. 'They'd pass right through you when you did a number two.'

'That's right,' agreed Philipson. 'Cellulose is indigestible to humans. It's what marks us out from herbivores like cows and goats.'

'So if I understand this right,' said Billie, 'the human body doesn't normally contain cellulose, and so—'

'And so,' the doctor finished her sentence, 'your biological composition is not consistent with that of a human being. It's as though a part of you were becoming "vegetal".'

*

There was a long silence, as though Philipson himself were struggling to accept the conclusions of his tests.

There was still one more piece of paper in his folder: the results of the analysis of the girl's white hair.

'Your hair contains a very high concentration of sodium dithionite and hydrogen peroxide, a substance naturally secreted by the human body. When we get old, it's hydrogen peroxide that causes our hair to go white, by inhibiting the synthesis of the pigments that give it its colour. But this is usually a very gradual process; I've never seen a girl of twenty-six whose hair turned white overnight before.'

'Is it permanent?' asked Billie.

'Um,' mumbled Mortimer, 'colour can sometimes be partially regained when certain diseases are cured or aggressive treatments are stopped, but I'm afraid that's only happened in a few isolated cases.'

He gave Billie a look of genuine compassion before admitting, 'Your condition falls well outside the bounds of my expertise and those of this little clinic. We'll keep you under observation here today, but I can't recommend strongly enough that you be taken back home.'

*

An hour later

The three of us remained in the room. Having wept until she had no more tears to cry, Billie had eventually fallen asleep. Slumped on a chair, Milo was polishing off the meal tray that Billie hadn't touched, all the while keeping his eye on the board the doctor had left behind:

colour pigments
solvent additives

anaemia
cellulose

hydrogen peroxide
sodium dithionite

'I think I might have something,' he said, leaping to his feet. He took up position in front of the board, grabbed hold of the felt pen and put a curly bracket around the first two lines.

'This greasy, sticky ink stuff that your girlfriend threw up, that's what goes on printing presses, like the ones they use for your books.'

'Oh yeah?'

'And cellulose, it's the main ingredient of wood, right? And wood's used to make—'

'Er, furniture?'

'Paper pulp,' he corrected me, fleshing out Dr Philipson's notes. 'As for the hydrogen peroxide and sodium dithionite, well, both of those are used to bleach—'

'Paper, right?'
After every answer, he turned the board to me:

colour pigments > ink
solvent additives

anaemia > paper
cellulose

hydrogen peroxide > bleaching agents
sodium dithionite

'I didn't believe it at first, Tom, the whole story of the heroine falling out of the book, but the facts are staring us right in the face. Your girlfriend is turning back into a character on paper.'

He stood staring into space for a moment, then finished his scribblings:

colour pigments > ink
solvent additives

anaemia > paper book!!!
cellulose
hydrogen peroxide > bleaching agents
sodium dithionite

'The fictional world is taking back what it rightfully owns,' he concluded.

He was wandering around the room, waving his arms about wildly. I'd never seen him so worked up.

'Calm down!' I urged him. 'What exactly are you trying to say?'

'It's obvious, Tom. If Billie is a fictional character, there's just no way she can thrive in the real world!'

'Like a fish out of water…'

'Exactly! Think of the films we watched when we were kids. Why does ET get ill?'

'Because he needs to get back to his planet.'

'Why can't the mermaid in *Splash* stay on dry land, and the guy live underwater? Because every creature is different and can't just adapt to every environment.'

His argument held water, with just one exception.

'I've just spent three days with Billie and she was a total riot. Real life seemed to suit her pretty damn well. So how come she went downhill so fast?'

'It's true, that doesn't make a lot of sense,' he admitted. Milo liked things to be logical and rational. He sat back down, frowning, and crossed his legs before carrying on with his train of thought.

'We have to think of the "doorway in",' he muttered, 'the hole the fictional character came through to wind up in our reality.'

'How many times do I have to tell you? Billie "fell from a line, in the middle of an unfinished sentence",' I explained, using the very same words she had spoken when we first met.

'Ah, of course! The hundred thousand books with half the pages left blank. That's it, that's the "doorway in". Speaking of which, I'd better check that they've all been—'

He stopped halfway through the sentence, his mouth

hanging open, before pouncing on his cell phone. I saw him scroll through dozens of emails before finding the one he was looking for.

'What time did Billie's symptoms start?' he asked without lifting his eyes from the screen.

'I'd say some time around midnight, when I went back to the room.'

'So that would be 2 a.m., New York time, right?'

'That's right.'

'Then I know what set it all off,' he declared, handing me his iPhone.

I scanned over the email my publisher had sent Milo.

From: robert.brown@doubleday.com
Subject: Confirmation of destruction of defective stock
Date: September 9, 2010 02:03
To: milo.lombardo@gmail.com

Dear Mr Lombardo,

Please accept this as confirmation of the destruction by pulping of the entire defective stock of the special edition of the second volume of the *Angel Trilogy* by Tom Boyd.

Number of books destroyed: 99,999.

Operation carried out under official supervision today, between the hours of 8 p.m. and 2 a.m., at the pulping station in the Shepard factory, Brooklyn, NY.

Kindest regards,

R. Brown

'Did you see what time the email came through?'

'Yes,' I nodded, 'exactly the same time she became ill.'

'Billie is *physically linked* to the defective copies,' he hammered out.

'And by getting rid of them, we're killing her!'

We were both overexcited and terrified at the implications of what we had discovered. Above all, we felt helpless, faced with a situation that was way beyond us.

'If we do nothing, she's going to die.'

'But what can we do?' he asked. 'They've already destroyed all the stock!'

'No, if that were true, she'd already be dead. There's at least one book left that they didn't manage to pulp.'

'The copy the publishers sent me and I gave to you!' he cried. 'But what did you do with it?'

I had to rack my brains. I remembered looking at it the night Billie had turned up, soaked to the skin, in my kitchen. Then again the next morning, just before she showed me her tattoo. And then…

I couldn't concentrate. Images were flashing through my head. And then… and then… we'd argued and, in my anger, I'd thrown the book into the kitchen trash.

'We're really in the shit now!' whistled Milo when I told him where the last copy was. I rubbed my eyes. I had a fever too. It was my sprained ankle, which was becoming unbearably sore; it was the army of Mexicans who had laid into me at the bar near the motel; it was my medication-starved body; that crazy bastard's surprise right hook; and that unexpected kiss that changed everything.

My head ached so much I imagined it filled with bubbling lava. Out of the tangle of my thoughts a sudden realisation came to me.

'I need to call my cleaner and make sure she doesn't throw out the book,' I told Milo.

He held out his phone and I managed to get through to Tereza, only to learn that she had put the trash out two days earlier.

Milo read the look on my face and winced. Where was the book now? Had it wound up in landfill? Was it about to be incinerated or recycled? Might someone have picked it up in the street? We needed to get on its trail, but we knew it would be like looking for a needle in a haystack.

One thing was certain: we didn't have any time to lose.

Because Billie's life depended on finding that book.

27

Always on my mind

Loving someone means cherishing their happiness
Françoise Sagan

Billie was still asleep. Milo had gone to tell Carole what was going on. We had agreed to meet again in two hours at the hotel library to do some research and settle on a plan of action. Walking through the lobby, I came across Aurore checking out.

Her hair was artfully messy, with the obligatory celeb sunglasses. Her outfit was a lesson in boho retro chic: mini-dress, biker jacket, high-heeled ankle boots and a vintage travel bag. Most women would have had trouble carrying off the look, but on her it was faultless.

'You're leaving?'

'I've got a concert in Tokyo tomorrow night.'

'At Kioi Hall?' I asked, surprising even myself at remembering the name of the place she had played when I accompanied her on her tour of Japan.

Her face lit up. 'Do you remember that old Plymouth Fury you hired? We had such a hard time finding the concert hall I only got there three minutes before the recital was due to start. I was totally out of breath by the time I ran onstage!'

'Even so, you played really well.'

'And then after the concert we drove for hours to go

see the Hells of Beppu, those incredible hot springs!'

Talking about that night made us both nostalgic. Yes, we'd had moments of happiness together, when we had truly felt carefree – and they weren't so long ago.

Aurore broke the silence, charming, but a little embarrassed, to apologise for the way Rafael Barros had behaved. She had tried to call me that night to check I was OK, but I wasn't in my room. While a bellboy took care of her bags, I briefly explained what had happened to Billie. She listened intently. I knew that her mother had died at the age of thirty-nine from breast cancer that had been discovered too late. This sudden loss had turned her into a bit of a hypochondriac, or at least very mindful of her health and that of her loved ones.

'That sounds very serious. You should take her to see a specialist right away. I can recommend someone if you like.'

'Who?'

'Professor Jean-Baptiste Clouseau. He's the best there is, like a French version of Dr House. He's the top cardiologist in Paris and spends most of his time putting the finishing touches to a completely man-made heart. But he'll fit you in if you tell him I sent you.'

'Old flame of yours, is he?'

She rolled her eyes.

'He's a great lover... of music. He often comes to my concerts when I play in Paris. And, if you meet him, you'll see he's no Hugh Laurie to look at. But the man's a genius.'

While she was talking, she had turned on her

BlackBerry and was looking for the doctor's number in her phone book.

'I'll send you his details,' she said, getting into her car.

The car door was closed for her and I watched the sedan drive off toward the massive gate at the entrance to the complex. But after about fifty yards the taxi came to a stop in the middle of the road and Aurore came running toward me to snatch a kiss from my lips. Before she left again, she took her MP3 player out of her pocket, put the headphones in my ears and left it with me.

I had the taste of her tongue on my lips and my head was filled with the music and lyrics she had lined up for me: my favourite Elvis number, which I'd shared with her back when we loved each other enough to play each other songs.

Maybe I didn't treat you
Quite as good as I should have
Maybe I didn't love you
Quite as often as I could have …

You were always on my mind
You were always on my mind

28

Under pressure

The reader may be considered the main character in
a novel, on a par with the author, since without him,
nothing can happen
Elsa Triolet

How could a hotel have such a magnificent library?

Clearly it wasn't only the clinic that had benefited from the rich sheikh's generosity. The most striking thing about the place was its old-fashioned rarefied feel. You'd have thought you were in the reading room of a prestigious university. Thousands of beautifully bound tomes filled shelves held up by Corinthian columns. The atmosphere was hushed and intimate, the heavy carved doors, marble busts and antique panelling taking you back several centuries. The only concessions to the modern age were the latest computers built into burr walnut cases.

I would have loved to work somewhere like this when I was young. There was no study at home. If I couldn't go to Tereza's apartment, I would shut myself in the bathroom to do my homework, with a board on my lap for a desk and earplugs to block out the neighbours' shouting.

Even the librarian, with her little round glasses,

mohair jumper and tartan skirt, seemed to have been teleported in from another universe. When I handed her the list of books I wanted to look at, she confessed I was her first reader of the day.

'Most hotel guests would rather hit the beach than sit down to a bit of Hegel.'

I smiled as she handed me a pile of books, along with a mug of spiced Mexican hot chocolate.

I took them over to a seat beside a Coronelli celestial globe next to one of the large windows, so that I could read in natural light. I got straight to work.

*

The atmosphere was conducive to study. The only thing to disturb the silence was the rustling of pages being turned and the soft sound of my pen gliding over a piece of paper. Several reference books I had dissected in my student days lay open on the table in front of me, including *What is Literature?* by Jean-Paul Sartre, Umberto Eco's *Lector in fabula* and Voltaire's *Dictionnaire philosophique*. In the space of two hours, I had written ten pages of notes. I was in my element, surrounded by books, in a world of quiet reflection. I felt like an English teacher again.

'Whoa, it's like we're college boys!' Milo exclaimed, barging into the august room.

He plonked his bag down on one of the Charleston armchairs and leaned over my shoulder.

'So, have you found anything?'

'I may have a plan of attack, but I'll need your help.'

'Sure I'll help.'

'OK, we need to split up,' I said, putting the lid back on my pen. 'You go back to Los Angeles and try to track down that last faulty copy. I know it's mission impossible, but if that book's destroyed there's no question: Billie's going to die.'

'And how about you?'

'I'm going to take Billie to Paris to see the doctor Aurore recommended. Hopefully we can at least slow the illness down. But most of all…'

I gathered up my notes so I could explain myself as clearly as possible.

'Most of all?'

'It's vital that I write the third volume of the trilogy, to send Billie back to the imaginary world.'

Milo frowned.

'I don't exactly see how writing a book is going to literally send her back to her world.'

I picked up my notebook and, in the style of Dr Philipson, tried to bring together the key points I had arrived at.

'So, the real world's where you, Carole and I live. It's where we go about our real lives, surrounded by our fellow humans.'

'OK, I'm with you so far.'

'Then on the other side there's the imaginary world, the realm of fiction and dreams. It's a world that reflects the subjectivity of every reader. And it's here that Billie was developing,' I explained, making a few notes to illustrate my points as I went along.

REAL WORLD (REAL LIFE)	IMAGINARY WORLD (FICTION)
TOM - MILO - CAROLE	BILLIE

'Go on,' urged Milo.

'As you said yourself, Billie was able to cross the line between the two worlds because of a production error: the faulty printing of 100,000 copies of my book. That's what you call the "doorway in".'

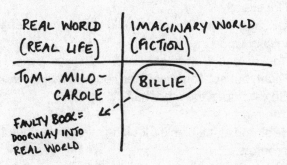

'OK,' he nodded.

'And now we wind up with Billie fading away in an environment that's foreign to her.'

'And the only way to save her is if we find the faulty book to stop her dying in real life—'

'And send her back to the fictional world by writing the third volume of the book. That's her "doorway out" of the real world.'

REAL WORLD | IMAGINARY WORLD
(REAL LIFE) | (FICTION)

TOM - MILO -
    CAROLE   WRITING OF
    BILLIE   - - -> VOLUME 3 =
              DOORWAY OUT OF
              REAL WORLD

Milo was following my diagram with interest, but I could tell something was bugging him.

'You still don't get how writing the third volume's going to let her leave, do you?'

'Not exactly.'

'OK. You'll see. So, who would you say creates this imaginary world?'

'You! I mean, the writer.'

'Right, but not only the writer. I only do half the work.'

'So who does the other half?'

'The reader.'

He stared at me blankly, looking even more confused than before.

'Look what Voltaire wrote in 1764,' I said, showing him my notes.

He leaned over and read aloud, '"The most useful books are those of which readers themselves compose half."'

I got up and confidently set out my argument.

'What's a book at its most basic? It's just letters laid out in a certain order on sheets of paper. Writing a story isn't enough to bring it to life. I've several early drafts of manuscripts in drawers, that have never been published, but they're like dead stories to me because no one else has ever set eyes on them. A book only comes to life when it's read. It's the reader who pieces together the images that create the imaginary world in which the characters develop.'

Our conversation was interrupted by the underworked librarian coming to offer Milo a mug of spiced hot chocolate. He took a sip before pointing out, 'Every time one of your books goes into stores and becomes a living thing, you tell me it doesn't really belong to you any more.'

'That's exactly it! It belongs to the reader. The reader picks up where I left off, making the characters his own and letting them come to life in his head. Sometimes he'll even put his own spin on certain passages and give them a meaning I hadn't envisaged. But that's all part of the game!'

Milo was listening intently while scrawling on my notepad.

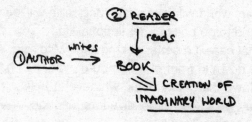

As far as I was concerned, this theory was watertight. I had always felt that a book only truly existed through its relationship with the reader. Ever since I first began to read, I had always tried to immerse myself as deeply as possible in the imaginary world of my favourite books. I'd try to guess what was going to happen, thinking of hundreds of possible outcomes, always trying to keep one step ahead of the author and even carrying on the story of the characters in my head, long after closing the book. The reader's imagination took the text way beyond the words printed on the page and allowed the story to fully exist.

'OK, so if I've got this right, you're saying the writer and the reader work together to create the imaginary world?'

'It's not me who said it, Milo. It's Umberto Eco! It's Sartre!' I replied, holding out a book open at the page where I had underlined the sentence: 'Reading is a pact of generosity between author and reader; each puts his trust in the other, each counts on the other.'

'But what does all this mean, practically speaking?'

'It means I'm going to start writing my new novel, but it'll only be once the first readers get hold of it that the imaginary world will take shape and Billie will leave the real world to go back to her fictional life.'

'In that case, I'd better get moving,' Milo said, sitting himself down in front of a computer screen. 'I have to track down that faulty book, whatever it takes. It's the only way we'll keep Billie alive long enough for you to write your new book.'

He logged on to the Mexicana Airlines website.

'There's a flight to Los Angeles in two hours. If I leave now, I can be in MacArthur Park this evening.'

'What'll you do when you get there?'

'If you're planning on taking Billie to Paris, she'll

need a fake passport pretty damn quick. I still know a few people who could help us out.'

'What about your car?'

He opened his shoulder bag and took out several wads of banknotes, which he split in two.

'One of Yochida Mitsuko's guys came for it this morning. This is all I could get for it, but it'll help us get by for a few weeks at least.'

'And then we really will be broke.'

'No denying it. Plus if you add what we owe to the IRS, we're looking at twenty years in the red.'

'Forgot to tell me that part, huh?'

'I thought you'd have realised.'

I tried to take the heat out of the situation.

'We're trying to save a life. There's no nobler cause, is there?'

'That's for sure,' he replied. 'But is this Billie girl really worth the hassle?'

'I think she's one of us,' I said, struggling to find the right words. 'I think she could be part of our "family", the family you, me and Carole made for ourselves. Because, deep down, I know she's not so different from us. Underneath that hard shell, there's a sweet, generous person inside. Behind that big mouth there's a pure heart, and life hasn't been easy on her so far.'

We hugged, and he was heading out the door when he turned back to face me.

'Are you sure you'll be able to write this new book? I thought you couldn't string two words together any more.'

I looked out the window at the sky. Thick, grey

clouds clogged the horizon, like an English landscape.

'Do I really have a choice?' I asked, closing my notebook.

29

When we're together

*I was cold in the night, so I got up to put another
blanket over her*
Romain Gary

Charles de Gaulle airport
Sunday 12 September
The taxi driver grabbed Billie's bag and stuffed it into
the trunk, crushing my laptop bag in the process. Inside
the Prius hybrid, the radio was blaring so loudly I had
to repeat myself three times to tell the driver where we
were going.

No sooner had the car left the terminal than it was
halted by the perpetual traffic jams of the Périphérique.

'Welcome to France,' I said, winking at Billie.

She shrugged her shoulders.

'Nothing you say is going to put me off this place. I've
always wanted to see Paris!'

After several miles of hold-ups, we turned off at
Porte Maillot to head down Avenue de la Grande
Armée toward the Champs-Élysées roundabout. Billie
looked out, open mouthed like a little child, as she took
in one by one the Arc de Triomphe, 'the most beautiful
avenue in the world' and the dizzy heights of Place de
la Concorde.

Though I'd been to Paris several times before with Aurore, I couldn't say I knew the city well. Always flitting between concerts, always with another plane to catch, Aurore was a nomad who had never taken the time to show me around her home town. In any case, my trips had never lasted more than a couple of days at a time, most of which were spent inside her handsome apartment on Rue Las Cases, near the Sainte-Clotilde basilica. This meant that of the entire capital I knew just a few roads in the sixth and seventh arrondissements, as well as the handful of restaurants and trendy galleries she'd taken me to.

The taxi crossed the Seine to the Left Bank, then turned down Quai d'Orsay. When the steeple and buttresses of the church of Saint-Germain-des-Prés came into view, I realised we were getting close to the furnished apartment I had found online from Mexico for us to rent. Sure enough, a few turnings later, the driver dropped us at 5 Rue de Furstemberg, opposite one of the most charming little squares I'd ever seen, with old-fashioned shops round an island in the middle.

On the island, four tall paulownias surrounded a lamppost with five lanterns. The sun bounced off the blue slate roofs. Lost amid narrow streets, far from the bustle of the boulevard, it was a timeless, romantic haven, straight out of a Peynet picture book.

*

As I write this, more than a year has gone by since that morning, but the memory of Billie getting out of the car and looking around, her eyes full of wonder, is still fresh in my mind. What I didn't know back then was that the weeks that followed would be the most painful yet precious of our lives.

*

Women's hall
Berkeley campus
University of California

'There's a package for you!' yelled Yu Chan as she walked into the room she had been sharing with Bonnie Del Amico since the start of term.

Bonnie was sitting absorbed at her computer, but raised her head and thanked her roommate before getting back to her chess game.

Bonnie was a young woman with short brown hair and a friendly face still fleshed out with a little puppy fat. But you could tell from the intense, serious look in her eyes that she had gone through more than her tender years would suggest.

The autumn sun pouring through the window illuminated the walls of the little room, which were plastered with posters of the two girls' current favourites: Robert Pattinson, Kristen Stewart, Albert Einstein, Obama and the Dalai Lama.

'Aren't you going to open it?' asked Yu Chan after a few minutes.

'Mmm,' murmured Bonnie, her mind clearly elsewhere. 'Just give me a second to outwit this machine.'

She took a gamble, moving her knight onto D4 in an attempt to take her opponent's bishop.

'It could be a present from Timothy,' guessed Yu Chan, studying the package. 'The guy's nuts about you.'

'Mmm,' repeated Bonnie. 'I really don't give a shit about Timothy.'

The computer countered her move by bringing out its queen.

'OK, I'll open it then!' Yu Chan announced.

Without waiting for the go-ahead from her roommate, she ripped open the envelope to find a large, leather-bound book bearing the words: Tom Boyd – *The Angel Trilogy* – Volume 2.

'It's the book you bought second-hand online,' she said, a note of disappointment in her voice.

'Uh-huh,' replied Bonnie.

Now she needed to protect her knight, but without making a total retreat. She clicked on the mouse to move one of her pawns forward, but in her excitement, let the piece go a bit too quickly.

Too late...

The word checkmate flashed up on screen. She'd been beaten again by that lousy heap of junk!

Not looking good for the tournament, she thought to herself, closing down the program.

The following week she was due to represent her college at the world under-18s championships in Rome. The thought of it both excited and terrified her.

She glanced at the sun-shaped clock and quickly gathered her things together. She picked up the book and stuffed it into her rucksack. She'd pack her bag for Rome later.

'*Addio, amica mia*!' she called as she walked out the door.

She took the stairs three at a time and hurried to the station to catch the BART, the commuter train that connected Berkeley to San Francisco 130 feet below the water level. She read the first three chapters of her book on the train before getting off at Embarcadero to catch a cable car on California Street. Loaded with tourists, it trundled along Nob Hill, passing Grace Cathedral.

Bonnie stepped down from the wooden carriage after a further two blocks to go to the cancer ward at Lenox Hospital, where she volunteered twice a week for a charity offering activities to help take patients' minds off their illness. She'd become all too aware of the need for this during the two years she'd watched her mother, Mallory, succumbing to the disease.

Although she was already at university, she was only sixteen, and would normally have been considered too young to take on such a task. But Elliott Cooper, the director of the hospital, was a friend of Garrett Goodrich, the doctor who had cared for her mother at the end, and he turned a blind eye to her presence.

'Hi there, Mrs Kaufman!' she sang cheerfully as she entered the third-floor room.

Ethel Kaufman's face lit up on seeing Bonnie. Until recently she had refused to take part in the art workshops or board games organised by the charity, still less the clown and puppet shows, which she found childish and silly. All she asked was to be left to die in peace. But Bonnie was different. The kid had character, and a combination of frankness and intelligence that Ethel had warmed to. The two women had taken a few weeks to suss each other out, but they had each come to treasure their twice-weekly meetings. As usual, they began with a few minutes of chit-chat, Ethel asking Bonnie about her classes at university and the approaching chess tournament. Then Bonnie took the book out of her bag.

'Surprise!' she said, holding up the attractive volume.

Ethel's eyes tired easily and Bonnie enjoyed reading to her. Over the last few weeks, both of them had become hooked on the *Angel Trilogy*.

'I couldn't resist reading the first few chapters,' confessed Bonnie. 'I'll give you a quick rundown and carry on from where I left off, OK?'

*

The Coffee Bean & Tea Leaf
A little café in Santa Monica
10 a.m.

'I think I've found something!' hollered Carole. Hunched over her laptop, the young cop had connected to the café's Wi-Fi.

Holding a mug of caramel latte, Milo peered at the screen.

After putting all kinds of keywords into search engines, Carole had eventually found the one remaining copy for sale on eBay.

'Man, that's unbelievable!' Milo exclaimed, pouring half his drink down his front.

'Do you think it's really the one we're looking for?'

'It has to be,' he said, looking at the photo. 'There was only one book left with that leather cover after the rest were pulped.'

'We're out of luck. It's already been sold,' replied Carole, frustrated.

The book had been put up for sale on eBay a few days earlier and had been snapped up straight away for the derisory sum of $14.

'We could try to get in touch with the vendor to ask who bought it.'

Putting Milo's words into action, Carole clicked on the member's profile: annaboro73, a member for six months, with positive feedback from buyers.

Carole sent a message explaining she wished to contact the person who had bought the item. They waited a good five minutes, hoping for a response they knew wouldn't come, until Milo lost patience and sent off his own straight-to-the-point message, offering a $1,000 reward.

'I have to get back to work,' said Carole, looking at her watch.

'Where's your partner?'

'Sick,' she replied, walking out of the café.

Milo went after her and got into the passenger seat of the police car.

'You can't be in here! I'm on duty and this is a patrol car.'

He pretended not to hear her and carried on the conversation.

'What was her screen name again?'

'annaboro73,' replied Carole, starting up the engine.

'OK, so her first name's Anna, agreed?'

'That would make sense.'

'And Boro's her surname. Boro… could it be a shortening of a German name?'

'More like Polish, wouldn't you say? Like Borowski or something.'

'Exactly.'

'And what about the number? Do you think that's the year she was born?'

'Could be,' replied Milo.

He had already brought up a directory website on his phone, but there were more than a dozen Anna Borowskis in the LA area alone.

'Pass me the radio,' ordered Carole as she rounded a corner. Milo picked up the microphone and couldn't resist messing around on it.

'Calling Planet Earth, this is Captain Kirk on board the *Starship Enterprise*, requesting authorisation to land at base.'

Carole looked at him in disbelief.

'What? It's funny.'

'Might have been funny when you were eight years old, Milo.' She took hold of the radio and spoke into it with authority.

'Message to base, this is Sergeant Alvarez, police number 364B1231. Can you get me the address of an Anna Borowski, born 1973?'

'OK, Sergeant, consider it done.'

*

Paris
Saint-Germain-des-Prés

Our furnished one-bed apartment was on the top floor of a little white building, with a view over the shady square. We felt at home there from the moment we arrived.

'Fancy a walk?' suggested Billie.

The Paris air already seemed to be doing her good. True, her hair was still white, her skin still pale, but she had something of her old energy back.

'May I remind you I have 500 pages to write?'

'Pah, that's nothing!' she teased, holding her face up to the sun streaming through the window.

'OK, OK. Just a quick walk round the block.'

I put on my jacket while she powdered her nose, then off we went.

We strolled along the narrow streets of Saint-Germain like the pair of tourists we were, pausing to look through the windows of every bookshop and antique dealer, reading the menus outside every café and rummaging through crates of second-hand books at the *bouquinistes* along the Seine.

In spite of the increasing number of luxury stores that were replacing the old bookshops and galleries, there was still something magical about the *quartier*. Everywhere you went in the labyrinth of back streets you breathed in a love of books, poetry and painting. Every road and every building we passed was thick with layers of rich cultural heritage. Voltaire used to write at a table in Le Procope; Verlaine would drop in for a glass of absinthe; Delacroix had his studio on Rue de Furstemberg; Racine lived on Rue Visconti; Balzac went bankrupt setting up a printer's on the same street; Oscar Wilde died alone and destitute in a seedy hotel on Rue des Beaux-Arts; Picasso painted *Guernica* on Rue des Grands-Augustins; Miles Davis played on Rue Saint-Benoît; Jim Morrison hung out on Rue de Seine... It was enough to make your head spin.

Billie was radiant, twirling about in the sunshine, guidebook in hand to make sure she didn't miss a thing.

We stopped at a café around midday. While I downed espressos, she treated herself to *fromage blanc au miel* and *pain perdu à la framboise*. I watched her tucking in, enjoying every mouthful.

Something had changed between us. Our mutual aggression had given way to a new closeness. We were in this together now, all too aware that our time together was short, the moments we shared were precious and we had to take care of one another.

'Let's take a look at that church!' she piped up, pointing to the steeple of Saint-Germain. While I got out my wallet to pay, Billie took one last gulp of hot chocolate. Then, like a child showing off, she got up and ran across the road, just as a car was coming the other way.

She landed with a horrifying thud in the middle of the road.

San Francisco
Lenox Hospital

As Bonnie closed the book she was surprised to notice that half the pages were blank.

'I'm afraid it doesn't look like we'll be able to finish the story, Mrs Kaufman.'

Ethel frowned and looked at the book more closely. It ended abruptly on page 266, right in the middle of an unfinished sentence.

'Must be some sort of printing error. You should take it back to the store.'

'I bought it over the internet!'

'Looks like you've been taken for a ride.'

Bonnie felt her face flush with annoyance. It was too bad. The book was gripping and the watercolour illustrations were really well done.

'Lunchtime!' the porter called out, pushing open the door to bring in the meal trays.

Bonnie got a meal too whenever she was here. On the menu today were vegetable soup, Brussels sprout salad and boiled cod.

Bonnie gritted her teeth and forced herself to take a few mouthfuls. Why was the cod still swimming in water? And the French bean soup such a strange brownish colour? And the unseasoned vinaigrette... ugh.

'Not great, huh?' sighed Mrs Kaufman.

'Somewhere between the frankly gross and the downright disgusting,' agreed Bonnie.

The old lady smiled to herself.

'What I wouldn't give for a good chocolate soufflé. That's my guilty pleasure.'

'I've never tried it!' said Bonnie, almost licking her lips at the thought of it.

'I'll write down the recipe for you,' offered Ethel. 'Pass me a pen and that book. It might as well be used for something.'

She opened the book. On the first of the blank pages, she wrote in her best handwriting:

Chocolate soufflé

8oz dark chocolate
2oz sugar
5 eggs
1oz flour
a quarter pint semi-skimmed milk

1) Break the chocolate into pieces and melt in a bain-marie...

*

Paris
Saint-Germain-des-Prés

'Open your eyes!'

Billie's body lay in the middle of the road. The Renault Clio had braked just in time and avoided hitting her. Traffic had stopped on Rue Bonaparte and a crowd had gathered around the girl on the ground.

I leaned over her, raising her legs to send the blood

to her brain. I turned her head to one side and loosened her clothes, following Dr Philipson's instructions to the letter. Billie eventually regained consciousness and a bit of colour came back to her cheeks. The attack had been as brief as it was dramatic, just like in Mexico.

'Hold the champagne, I'm not dead yet,' she said drily.

I squeezed her wrist. Her pulse was still weak, she had difficulty breathing and beads of sweat were forming on her brow.

We'd made an appointment to see Professor Clouseau, the doctor Aurore had recommended, the following day. I hoped against hope he would live up to his reputation.

*

Los Angeles
'Police, open up!'

Anna looked through the peephole at the police officer banging on her door.

'I know you're in there, Ms Borowski!' shouted Carole, holding up her badge.

Anna unbolted the door and peered anxiously round it.

'What is it?'

'We just need to ask you a few questions regarding the book you sold on the internet.'

'I didn't steal it!' protested Anna. 'I found it in the garbage.'

Carole looked at Milo, who took over the questioning.

'You need to give us the address of the person you sold it to.'

'I think she's a student.'

'She's a student?'

'Yeah, well, she lives on the Berkeley campus.'

*

San Francisco
Lenox Hospital
4 p.m.

Ethel Kaufman couldn't get to sleep. Since Bonnie left, she'd been tossing and turning. Something was wrong. And it wasn't just the cancer that was eating away her lungs.

It was that book, or rather what she had written on its blank pages. She sat up and took the novel from her bedside table, opening it where she had neatly written out the recipe for her favourite childhood dessert. Where had this sudden surge of nostalgia come from? Was it knowing she didn't have much time left? Yes, probably.

She couldn't bear nostalgia. Life went by so quickly she had vowed never to waste time looking back. She'd always tried to live in the moment, leaving the past behind her. She didn't hang on to memories, didn't celebrate birthdays or anniversaries, and moved house every couple of years to avoid getting too attached to people or things. That's what had kept her going all these years.

But, that afternoon, the past had come knocking.

302

She heaved herself out of bed and took a few steps over to her locker. She took out the little leather suitcase her niece, Katia, had brought with her the last time she visited. It was filled with bits and pieces Katia had found while clearing her parents' house before it was sold.

The first photo she took out was dated March 1929, a few months after Ethel was born. It showed a couple clearly in love, posing proudly with their three children. Ethel was in her mother's arms, while her brother and sister, twins four years older than her, stood either side of their father. Smiling warmly in their best clothes, they radiated happiness and togetherness. Ethel put the photo down on her bed. Several decades had passed since she'd last looked at it.

Next she lifted up a yellowed newspaper cutting of photos from the 1940s showing Nazi uniforms, barbed wire and barbarity. It brought back Ethel's own history. She was barely ten when she and her brother were sent to the US. They had managed to leave Krakow just before the Germans turned part of the city into a ghetto. Her sister was meant to join them later, but she hadn't made it – succumbing to typhus at Plaszów – and her parents had died in the Belzec extermination camp.

Ethel continued on her journey back in time. She picked up a black and white postcard of a graceful ballerina dancing on points. It was a picture of her, in New York. She'd spent her teens there with relatives of her mother, who recognised and encouraged her gift for dancing. She had soon made a name for herself and been taken on by the newly founded New York City Ballet.

The Nutcracker, *Swan Lake*, *Romeo and Juliet*: she danced the lead roles in the greatest ballets. Then at the age of twenty-eight a poorly treated fracture had left her with an awkward limp, forcing her to hang up her ballet shoes.

Her flesh tingled at the thought of what might have been. Underneath the postcard, she found the programme for a show in New York. After her accident, she had taught at the School of American Ballet and helped stage some Broadway musicals.

The next photo was still painful to look at, even after all this time. Her tall, dark, handsome lover. She had fallen for him when she was thirty-five, he ten years younger. A few moments of joyful abandon that cost her years of suffering and disillusionment.

Because then the nightmare had begun.

A nightmare that had started with the next slightly blurred photo that she had taken looking at herself in the mirror. It was a picture of her round belly. When she had given up thinking it would ever happen, Ethel had fallen pregnant at nearly forty. She had been overjoyed at the unexpected blessing and had never been so happy as during the first six months of her pregnancy. Of course, she hadn't enjoyed the morning sickness and total exhaustion, but the baby growing inside her had changed her life.

Then one morning her waters had broken, three months too early. She was taken to hospital and examined. She remembered it all so clearly. The baby was still there in her womb; she could feel it kicking and hear its heartbeat. The duty gynaecologist told her the amniotic sac had split and without amniotic fluid the child would die. The only option was to bring on labour. So then there had been the awful night when she brought her baby into the world knowing that it could not survive. After many hours of labour, she didn't give birth, but death.

She looked at him, touched him, kissed him. He was so tiny, but so beautiful. She still hadn't thought of a name for him; in her head, she had always called him 'bambino', 'my bambino'.

He lived for one minute before his heart stopped. Ethel would never forget the sixty surreal seconds when she was a mother. After that, she stopped living. She pretended to go on, but all the brightness, all the joy and faith had drained out of her in that minute. The last flame in her had died along with her son.

The tears streaming down her cheeks fell onto a small, thick envelope made from shiny paper. She was shaking as she opened it and took out a lock of her bambino's hair. She wept for a long time, but the weight she had been carrying for many years was finally lifted.

She was tired now, but before going back to bed she had a sudden urge to paste the photos, newspaper cutting, postcard and lock of hair onto the blank pages of the book. The collection of her life's key moments took up a dozen or so pages.

If she had her time again, would she do anything differently? She blocked the question from her mind. It wasn't worth thinking about. Life wasn't a video game with a choice of endings. Time passed and you went along with it, doing what you could more often than what you wanted. The rest was up to fate, and luck. And that was that.

She put the book inside a large brown envelope. Then she called the nurse and asked her to hand the package to Bonnie Del Amico the next time she came in.

*

Women's hall
Berkeley campus
7 p.m.
'Try not to eat too much tiramisu in Rome,' Yu Chan advised rather unkindly. 'There's at least a thousand calories in every portion and, you know, you have put on a few pounds lately.'

'Don't you worry about me,' Bonnie shot back, doing up her case. 'The guys don't seem to mind.'

She looked out of the window. It was dark outside, but she could see the taxi flashing its lights.

'OK, I'm outta here.'

'Good luck! Give 'em hell!'

Bonnie went out to the yellow cab and handed her bags to the driver.

'Going to the airport, miss?'

'Yes, but could we swing by Lenox Hospital first?'

Bonnie spent the journey lost in thought. Why did she feel the need to go back to see Mrs Kaufman? When she'd left her at lunchtime, she had seemed tired and a little sad. And the way Ethel had said goodbye, insisting on kissing Bonnie, was too serious; it just wasn't like her.

As though it was the last time we'll see one another.
The taxi pulled up alongside a row of parked cars.
'OK if I leave my bag here? I'll be five minutes.'
'No rush, I'll park up.'

*

Women's hall
Berkeley campus
7.30 p.m.
'Police, open up!'

Yu Chan jumped. With her roommate gone, she had leapt on the opportunity to go through her computer and try to read her emails. She sat, panicking, for a few seconds, imagining that a hidden camera somewhere in the room must have given her away.

She scrambled to turn off the monitor and went to open the door.

'I'm officer Carole Alvarez,' Carole introduced herself, knowing full well she had no authority to enter a university campus.

'We'd like to speak to Bonnie Del Amico,' said Milo.

'You've just missed her,' replied Yu Chan, relieved. 'She's gone to the airport. She's taking part in a chess tournament in Rome.'

Oh shit, Rome!

'You have her cell phone number?'

*

Lenox Hospital parking lot
7.34 p.m.

On the back seat of the taxi, Bonnie's phone was going off at the bottom of her patchwork bag. It kept on and on ringing, but the driver didn't even hear it. While he waited for his passenger, he'd turned his radio right up to listen to the Mets taking on the Braves.

Inside the building, Bonnie came out of the lift and crept down the corridor.

A nurse stopped her. 'Visiting time's over, miss!'

'I… I just wanted to say goodbye to Mrs Kaufman before I go overseas.'

'Hmm. You're the volunteer, right?'

Bonnie nodded.

'Ethel Kaufman's asleep, but she left an envelope for you.'

Feeling a little disappointed, Bonnie followed the woman to the nurses' station to pick up the package.

Opening it on the way to the airport, she was amazed to find the photos and notes Ethel had left added to the book.

Overwhelmed, it didn't cross her mind to check her phone.

*

San Francisco International Airport
Runway No.3
Flight No. 0966
9.27 p.m.

'Good evening, ladies and gentlemen. This is your chief

flight attendant speaking. It gives me great pleasure to welcome you on board this Boeing 767 flight to Rome. We have an estimated flight time of thirteen hours and fifty-five minutes this evening.

'We have now finished boarding the aircraft. In the seat pocket in front of you, you'll find a safety card setting out procedures in the unlikely event of an emergency, and we would ask that you take the time to read this carefully. The cabin crew will now carry out a short safety demonstration.'

*

San Francisco International Airport
Departures
9.28 p.m.
'The flight to Rome? Oh, I'm sorry, it's just closed,' said the girl behind the desk, looking at her computer screen.

'You're kidding me!' fumed Carole. 'We'll never get our hands on that damn book. Try that girl again.'

'I already left her two voicemails,' said Milo. 'She must have put her phone on vibrate.'

'Try one more time, please.'

*

Runway No.3
Flight No. 0966
9.29 p.m.
'We will shortly be preparing for take-off. May I ask you

now to ensure your seat belts are fastened, your seat backs are upright and all cell phones are switched off. May we also take this opportunity to remind you that this flight is strictly non-smoking, and smoking is not allowed in the restrooms.'

Bonnie fastened her seat belt and rifled through her bag to find her travel pillow, sleep mask and book. As she switched off her phone, she saw the red light was flashing, showing she had voicemail or texts. She was tempted to check, but a disapproving glare from the air hostess put her off.

*

Paris
Midnight
Our little living room was lit with the soft glow of a dozen candles. After a quiet evening, Billie had fallen asleep on the couch. As she slept, I psyched myself up to turn on my computer and open my ancient word-processing program. The awful blank page flashed up on screen, filling me with a sadly familiar feeling of queasy dread and panic.

Write something!
Write something!
I couldn't.

I went over to the couch and picked Billie up to carry her into the bedroom. She groaned and grumbled that she was too heavy, but let herself be lifted. It was a cold night and the radiator wasn't giving out much heat. I found an extra duvet in the wardrobe and tucked her in like a small child.

Pulling the door to, I heard her say, 'Thank you.'

I had closed the curtains to block out the light from the road, so I couldn't see her clearly when she whispered, 'Thank you for looking after me. No one ever looked after me before.'

*

'No one ever looked after me before.'

I was still turning Billie's words over in my head when I sat back in front of the screen. The cursor flickered, taunting me.

Where do you get your inspiration? That was the stock question I heard time and again from readers and journalists, but I'd never really come up with a decent answer. In order to write, I had to buckle down and cut myself off from the world. It took me about fifteen hours' work to fill four pages. There was no magic formula, no secret recipe for success. I just had to sit at a table, put my headphones in and listen to classical music or jazz, making sure I had a good supply of coffee to hand.

Some days, when everything was flowing right, I could run off ten pages or more in one sitting. At those times, when it seemed God was smiling on me, I could convince myself that stories were created on high and an angel was telling me what to write. But those moments were few and far between, and the idea of churning out 500 pages in the space of a few weeks seemed pretty impossible.

'Thank you for looking after me.'

I didn't feel sick any more, just a sense of nervous

anticipation, like the stage fright an actor has before the curtain goes up.

I held my fingers over the keyboard and they began to move, almost in spite of me. The first few lines appeared as if by magic.

Chapter 1

No one in Boston could remember a winter as cold as this one. The city had been groaning under a thick blanket of snow and ice for over a month. Talk in cafés turned to the topic of alleged climate change; the papers wrote of little else.

'What a crock of shit!'

In her little apartment in Southie, Billie Donelly was in a light sleep. Life hadn't exactly been kind to her up to now. She didn't know it yet, but all that was about to change.

And I was away.

I could see now that my feelings for Billie had lifted the curse. By giving me a foothold back in the real world, she'd found the key to unlock my mind. I wasn't afraid of the blank page any more.

I started typing and worked right through the night.

*

Rome
Fiumicino Airport
The next day

'Ladies and gentlemen, this is your chief flight attendant speaking. We have just touched down at Rome Fiumicino Airport, where the outside temperature is 16°C. Please accept our apologies for the slight delay. We would be grateful if you would remain seated, with your seat belt fastened, until we have come to a complete standstill. Please take care when opening the overhead lockers and ensure you take everything with you when you leave the plane. On behalf of the entire crew, we wish you a pleasant day and hope to welcome you on another United Airlines flight very soon.'

Bonnie Del Amico couldn't seem to wake up. She'd spent the whole flight in a fitful, nightmare-ridden sleep which she struggled to shake off. She was still drowsy when she walked off the plane, and didn't notice the book Ethel Kaufman had given her, left behind in the seat pocket.

30

The length of life

*There is nothing more tragic than to find an individual
bogged down in the length of life, devoid of breadth*
Martin Luther King Jr

Monday 13 September
Fifteenth *arrondissement* of Paris
9 a.m.

We got off at Balard, the last stop on line 8 of the Métro.
It was a mild, early-autumn morning and that back-to-
school feeling floated in the air.

The Hôpital Européen Marie-Curie was a huge
building on the banks of the Seine, on the edge of Parc
André-Citroën. Its glass front curved as the road bent
round and its mirrored panes reflected the surrounding
trees.

According to the brochure, the hospital had been
formed by merging the services of several departments
across the capital, and was regarded as one of the best
in Europe. The cardiovascular unit, led by Professor
Clouseau, was particularly renowned.

We eventually found the right entrance, only to get
lost in the rambling central courtyard. Finally a member
of staff pointed us in the direction of the elevators
which took us up to the penultimate floor.

Though we had an appointment, we had to wait three-quarters of an hour to see the doctor. According to his secretary, Corinne, Professor Clouseau – who lived right here in the same building as his patients – was on his way back from Boston, where he taught twice a month at the prestigious Harvard Medical School.

Under Corinne's watchful eye, we waited inside an impressive office with stylish modern furniture and a breathtaking view over the Seine and the rooftops of Paris. You could watch barges bobbing lazily down the river, Pont Mirabeau in the background and the replica of the Statue of Liberty on the Île aux Cygnes beyond.

The man who eventually burst into the room looked more like Columbo than an eminent professor of medicine. He had a crumpled trench coat flung over his shoulders like a cape, messy hair and a pasty, badly shaven face. A tartan shirt appeared from under a murky green jumper and his corduroy trousers were covered in suspicious-looking stains. If I'd passed this guy in the street, I might have thrown him a dollar. It was hard to believe that, on top of his duties at the hospital, he led a team of medics and engineers who'd spent the last fifteen years working toward the creation of an artificial heart.

He muttered a few words of apology, swapped his trench coat for an off-white doctor's coat and, no doubt suffering from jet lag, slumped into his chair.

I'd read somewhere that when we first encounter a new face, our brain takes a tenth of a second to decide whether that person is trustworthy. It's a process so quick we don't have a chance to influence this first impression with rational thoughts; it's based purely on instinct.

Despite his unkempt appearance, Professor Clouseau put me instantly at ease that morning. Billie wasn't put off by what he looked like either and launched straight into her list of symptoms: loss of consciousness, exhaustion, breathlessness, nausea, temperature, weight loss and heartburn.

While he took in all this information, murmuring, 'Hmm, hmm,' quietly, I handed him the folder of notes I had put together from the tests Mortimer Philipson had carried out. He put on a pair of bifocals straight out of the 1970s and scanned the papers. Though he pursed his lips doubtfully, his eyes behind his round spectacles betrayed a lively intelligence.

He cut Billie off. 'We're going to do all these tests again,' he announced, throwing the folder into his rubbish bin. 'These analyses carried out in some exotic hotel clinic, the whole business of being made of ink and cellulose, a "girl of paper", it just doesn't add up.'

'Why have I been blacking out then?' asked Billie angrily.

'And what about my hair—'

He interrupted brusquely.

'It seems to me that your fainting fits are linked to a sudden decrease in blood flow to the brain. A cardiac or vascular abnormality must be the cause – which is a stroke of luck, since that's my area of expertise.'

He made a list of the tests he wished her to undergo during the day and arranged to meet us again that evening.

Rome
Fiumicino Airport

The Boeing 767 from San Francisco was manoeuvring into its parking slot. The passengers had disembarked more than half an hour ago and the plane was about to be cleaned.

The pilot, Mike Portoy, finished off his post-flight report and shut his laptop.

So much damn paperwork! he thought with a yawn.

He'd rather rushed the debrief this time, but the truth was the fifteen-hour flight had wiped him out. He looked at his cell phone. His wife had left him a loving message asking how he was. To avoid having to call her back, he sent her one of the 'copy and paste' texts he kept for just such occasions. He had better things to do today than chit-chat with the wife. He was determined to take Francesca out that evening. Every time he passed through Rome, he made sure to have a shot at the hot receptionist at the lost- property office. Twenty years old, fresh-faced, sexy, with tempting curves, Francesca drove him crazy. Up to now she had always given him the brush-off, but this time would be different, he could feel it.

Mike left the cockpit, brushed his hair and did up his jacket.

Never underestimate the power of a man in uniform.

But before he got off the plane he needed to come up with a reason to approach the Italian girl.

He gave the cleaning staff their instructions. They

317

each took a section, moving quickly and efficiently through the rows of seats. On the first trolley, amid piles of discarded magazines and used tissues, he spotted a nice-looking book, bound in midnight-blue leather. He picked it up and turned it over in his hands. The cover was decorated with stars, with the name of the author and the title of the book standing out in big gold letters: Tom Boyd – *The Angel Trilogy* – Volume 2.

Never heard of it, but it'll do the trick! he said smugly to himself.

'You can't take that book, sir.'

He turned round, caught in the act. Who'd had the nerve to speak to him like that?

It was one of the cleaners, a pretty black girl named Kaela, as the regulation identity badge hanging round her neck told him. She wore a bandana over her hair depicting the Somalian flag – a white star on a blue background. Mike looked down at her with contempt.

'I'll take care of this,' he insisted, keeping hold of the book.

'I need to drop by the lost-property office anyway.'

'I'll have to speak to my supervisor, sir.'

'You can speak to the good Lord about it for all I care!' he jeered.

He turned and left the plane, book in hand.

He'd get Francesca into bed tonight, for sure.

*

Via Mario de Bernardi

As she sat in the taxi on the way to her hotel, Bonnie

suddenly remembered to turn her phone back on. It was brimming with messages. First there was a voicemail from her father checking she'd arrived safely, then a bizarre text from Yu Chan telling her the police were after her, and a whole stream of missed calls from a guy named Milo, wanting to buy the Tom Boyd novel from her.

'What the...?'

She had a feeling something wasn't right and rummaged around in her bag to find the book had gone.

'I must've left it on the plane!'

The taxi was about to get onto the motorway when Bonnie cried out, 'Stop, please! Can we turn round?'

*

Hôpital Européen Marie-Curie
Quai de Seine, Paris

'Try to relax, mademoiselle. It's a totally painless procedure.'

Billie was lying on her left side, naked from the waist up. The cardiologist stuck three electrodes onto her chest, then spread a large blob of gel over her skin.

'We're going to take a scan of your heart, which will help us to locate any potential tumours.'

He moved the probe over her from her ribs to her breastbone, taking several images. I could see her heart beating on the screen, racing with fear. And I also saw the doctor's face becoming grimmer as the examination progressed.

I came straight out and asked, 'Does it look serious?'

'Professor Clouseau will talk you through the results,' he replied rather coldly, before adding, 'I think we're going to need to do an MRI scan.'

*

Rome
Fiumicino Airport

'Francesca not here?' asked Mike Portoy, pushing open the door of the lost-property office.

The pilot struggled to hide his disappointment. Behind the counter, her replacement glanced up from her magazine to give him a glimmer of hope.

'She's on her lunch break, over at Da Vinci's.'

Mike walked out without thanking her or dropping off the book he'd picked up on the plane.

Da Vinci's was a little haven in a hidden corner of Terminal One, decorated with fake marble columns, pillars and arches covered in trailing ivy. An enormous U-shaped counter was crowded with passengers drinking strong espressos and tucking into homemade pastries.

'Hey, Francesca!' he yelled when he spotted her.

She was more beautiful every time he saw her. She was chatting to a young guy who worked there, some clown dressed in a barista's apron, paid to make pouring coffee look like an art form.

Mike walked over, smacked the book down on the counter and tried to muscle in on the conversation, changing it to his own language – American – and preferred topic – himself. But the Italian beauty only had eyes for her young companion, lapping up every word he said and fluttering her eyelashes. The kid had a winning smile, laughing eyes and angelic brown curls, like some goddamn Roman hero. Puffed up with testosterone, Mike decided to take him on, and went right ahead and asked Francesca out to dinner. He knew this little place near the Campo de Fiori that did great antipasti and—

'I'm going out with Gianluca tonight,' she replied with a shake of the head.

'Um, well, how about tomorrow then? I'm in Rome for two days.'

'It's kind of you to ask, but… no,' she turned him down, before she and her companion collapsed in helpless giggles.

Mike went pale. He didn't get it. How could the little slut choose that loser over him? He'd studied for eight years to have a prestigious career that never failed to impress people. The other guy had a shitty little part-time job. He conquered the skies, while that no-hoper took home less than 800 euros a month…

Clinging on to what was left of his dented pride, Mike forced himself to stay put and order something. The two lovebirds had long since switched back into Italian. The overwhelming aroma of coffee was going to his head. He drank his *caffè lungo* in one gulp, burning his tongue.

'Too bad, I'll just have to hire myself a hooker around San Lorenzo,' he said bitterly to himself, though he knew very well that wouldn't erase the memory of Francesca laughing at him.

He got down from his stool and skulked out of the café with his tail between his legs, leaving the leather-bound book with the fancy lettering on the counter.

*

Fiumicino Airport
Lost-property office
Five minutes later
'I'm sorry, but no one has brought in your book,' Francesca told Bonnie.

'Are you absolutely sure?' Bonnie persisted. 'It was very special to me. It had photos inside it as well—'

'OK, just fill in this form with as many details as possible about the missing item, along with your flight number. If someone brings it in, we'll call you straight away.'

'OK,' Bonnie mumbled dolefully.

She filled in the form, but a little voice inside her told her she wouldn't be seeing the book again, nor would she ever taste Mrs Kaufman's chocolate soufflé.

*

Hôpital Européen Marie-Curie
Quai de Seine, Paris
7.15 p.m.
'Corinne! Miss Donelly's results,' yelled Jean-Baptiste Clouseau as he threw open the door to his office, coming face to face with me as I stood poised to press the buzzer.

'Never understood how that thing works. Too many

buttons!' he muttered, scratching his head.

The same went for his BlackBerry, it seemed; the latest model, it flashed and vibrated every two minutes, though he paid no attention to it.

He had been operating on patients all day and appeared even less fresh than he had that morning. His face looked haggard, with dark rings under his eyes and a thick layer of stubble that seemed to have grown a quarter of an inch in the space of a few hours.

Night was falling, darkening the room, but Clouseau didn't bother to turn on the light. He pressed the middle button on a remote control to switch on a huge flat screen on the wall displaying the results of Billie's tests.

The doctor moved towards the screen to go over the first page of results.

'The blood test confirmed a lowering of your platelet count, which explains why you're so weak,' he began, peering at Billie through his odd-looking glasses.

He pressed a button to go to the next frame.

'Moving on to the scan of your heart... Well, that showed up a number of cardiac myxomas.'

'Myxomas?' asked Billie, sounding worried.

'Tumours of the heart,' Clouseau clarified abruptly.

He stood closer to the screen and pointed with the remote control toward an area of the scan showing a dark mass in the shape of a little ball.

'Your first tumour is located in the right atrium. It has the classic shape, with a short gelatinous pedicle. On first impressions, it looks fairly benign to me ...'

He let a few seconds pass before moving on to the next image.

'The second tumour is more of a cause for concern,'

he admitted. 'Its size is unusual, around four inches across, and its consistency is stringy and stiff. It's lodged close to the mitral valve, obstructing the delivery of oxygenated blood to the left side of the heart. That's what's causing your shortness of breath, your pallor and fainting fits. Your system's just not getting enough blood.'

I stepped forward to take a closer look. The tumour resembled a bunch of grapes, attached to the inside of the heart by little strings. I couldn't help but think of the roots and fibres that carry sap through wood; it was as if a tree were growing in Billie's heart.

'I... I'm going to die, aren't I?' she asked, her voice shaking.

'Given the size of this myxoma, if we don't remove it very soon, you are at great risk of cardiac embolism and sudden death,' Clouseau conceded.

He turned off the screen, switched on the lights and sat down in his armchair.

'It will require open heart surgery. There are, of course, risks involved with such a procedure, but as things stand it would be more dangerous to do nothing.'

'When can you operate?' asked Billie.

The doctor called out in his booming voice, instructing his secretary to bring him his diary. It looked pretty full already, with operations lined up months ahead. I was afraid he would pass us over to one of his colleagues, but since we were friends of Aurore he agreed to push back another appointment so that he could operate on Billie a fortnight later.

I was really getting to like this guy.

From: bonnie.delamico@berkeley.edu
Subject: The *Angel Trilogy* – Volume 2
Date: September 13, 2009 22:57
To: milo.lombardo@gmail.com
Dear Sir,

I received the many messages you left on my phone letting me know you wish to buy my copy of the book by Tom Boyd, who you say is your friend and client.

Aside from the fact the book is not for sale, I should add that I sadly mislaid it on a flight from San Francisco to Rome and it has still not been handed in to the lost property office at Fiumicino Airport.

I hope this email reaches you.

Kind regards,

Bonnie Del Amico

*

Rome
Fiumicino Airport
Da Vinci's Café

The first few passengers were beginning to come off the FlyItalia flight from Berlin. Among them was the famous painter and designer, Luca Bartoletti, returning from a short trip to the German capital. He had spent the past three days giving interviews to mark a retrospective of his work being put on by the Hamburger Bahnhof, the city's modern-art museum. Seeing his canvases hanging alongside the likes of Andy Warhol and Richard Long, he felt he had finally arrived, gaining recognition for a lifetime's work.

Luca didn't waste time waiting for a suitcase to turn up on the conveyor belt. He hated having to lug things around, so he only ever travelled with a carry-on bag.

He had hardly touched the in-flight meal of rubbery salad leaves, a revolting shrink-wrapped pasta omelette and a rock-hard pear tart. Before going to pick up his car, he stopped to grab something to eat at Da Vinci's. The café was about to close, but the owner agreed to take one last order. Luca went for a cappuccino and a toasted mozzarella, tomato and prosciutto sandwich. He sat at the counter to finish reading an article in *La Repubblica* that he had started on the plane.

When he put down his paper to take a sip of coffee, he caught sight of the blue leather book that the pilot had left on the counter earlier. Luca was a big fan of the bookcrossing scheme. He bought a huge number of books but held on to none, leaving them instead in public places for others to find.

To begin with he thought the novel had been left there on purpose as part of the scheme, but there was no sticker on the cover to indicate that this was the case. Luca flicked through the book as he bit into his sandwich. He wasn't into mass-market fiction and had never heard of Tom Boyd, but was taken aback to find that the novel was incomplete, with one of its readers having used the missing pages as a photo album.

He finished his sandwich and left the café with his find under his arm. In the underground garage, he found the old maroon Citroën DS cabriolet he'd bought at auction not long ago. He put the book down on the passenger seat and headed towards the south-west of the city.

Luca lived behind Piazza Santa Maria, on the top floor of an ochre-coloured building in the vibrant, photogenic Trastevere area. He'd turned it into a loft-style apartment and set up his studio there. When he entered his den and turned on the light, the room was flooded with the harsh brightness needed for his painting. Luca fiddled with the dimmer switch.

The place was so sparsely furnished it didn't look lived in. It was arranged around a huge central fireplace, with round windows on either side. The room was filled with trestle tables, paint rollers and brushes of all shapes and sizes, scrapers, spatulas and dozens of tins of paint. But there was no bookcase, no sofa, no TV.

Luca looked over his most recent canvases. They were all monochrome, variations on the colour white, with slashes, grooves, raised areas and brush strokes to catch the light in different ways and create unique effects. These works were very popular, with collectors paying significant sums for them. But Luca was under no illusions. He knew that commercial success and critical recognition didn't necessarily go hand in hand with talent. In this age of consumerism, tainted by noise, speed and superfluous possessions, people felt somehow purified by buying one of his canvases.

The painter took off his jacket and slowly turned the pages of Ethel Kaufman's photo album.

It had been a long time since Luca had acted on any kind of impulse. But tonight he had a real craving for chocolate soufflé…

31

Roman roads

The day you can show your weakness without the other using it to assert his strength is the day you will be loved

Cesare Pavese

Paris
14–24 September

In spite of the shadow cast by Billie's illness, the two weeks leading up to her operation were some of the best days of our relationship.

My book was coming along well. I was enjoying writing again and worked through the night, carried along on a wave of enthusiasm and creativity. My aim was to lay the foundations of Billie's future happiness. With every page I wrote, I carefully constructed the existence she had always dreamed of: a calmer way of life, free of demons and disappointments, healed of the traumas of her past.

I usually worked until dawn, heading out in the early morning when the sidewalks of Saint-Germain were being cleaned. I had my first coffee of the day at the bar of a bistro on Rue de Buci, before nipping into the bakery in Passage Dauphine to pick up some melt-in-the-mouth glazed *chaussons aux pommes*. I'd return to our little nest on Place Furstemberg, turn the radio on and make two *cafés au lait*. Billie would stroll in, yawning, and we'd eat breakfast together, sitting at the counter of our open-plan kitchen overlooking the little square. She'd hum along to the radio, trying to understand the words of the French songs. I'd brush away flakes of pastry from the corners of her mouth, while she closed her eyes against the sun shining on her face.

While I got back to work, Billie spent the morning reading. She'd found an English-language bookshop near Notre Dame and asked me to make her a list of essential reading. From Steinbeck to Salinger by way of Dickens, over the course of two weeks she devoured the novels that had shaped me growing up, making notes in the margins, asking questions about the lives of the authors and copying her favourite quotations into a notebook.

After a few hours' sleep, I'd go with her in the afternoon to a little cinema on Rue Christine that showed classic films she'd never heard of, but which were a revelation to her: *Heaven Can Wait*, *The Seven Year Itch*, *The Shop around the Corner*…

Afterwards we'd discuss the movie over hot chocolate, and every time I referred to something she wasn't familiar with she'd make a note of it in her book. We were happy.

Back home in the evening, we set ourselves the challenge of cooking some of the recipes from an old cookbook we'd dug out of the little bookcase in our apartment. With mixed results, we tried out dishes like *blanquette de veau*, duckling with pears, lemon polenta and – our biggest triumph – slow-cooked lamb shanks with honey and thyme.

And so, during those two weeks, another side of her personality came to light. She was revealed as an intelligent, complex person, determined to improve herself. I found myself unsettled by the feelings I had for her now that we'd called a truce.

After dinner, I got her to read over what I'd written that day, which sparked off long discussions. We'd found a half-drunk bottle of pear brandy in the living-room cupboard. The label had been partly rubbed off, but what we could read assured us the spirit had been 'distilled according to age-old methods' by a small producer in the northern Ardèche. On the first night, we found it undrinkable: it scorched our throats like paint-stripper. Not that that put us off having another swig the next day. By the third day we'd decided it was 'actually not that bad', and by the fourth 'pretty damn fantastic'.

After that, the liquor became part of our routine and, as the alcohol made us less inhibited, we talked more openly. Billie told me how her childhood, her miserable teens and her fear of being alone drove her toward the wrong kind of men. She told me how hard it was never to have met anyone who loved and respected her, and confided her hopes for the future and for starting a family some day. Usually she would end up falling asleep on the couch, listening to old records the owner had left behind, trying to translate the lyrics of the white-haired poet on the sleeve, who sang, cigarette in hand, that 'As time goes by, everything comes to an end... You forget the old passions and the voices that once whispered those simple words: don't be back late, be sure you don't catch cold.'

*

After taking her up to bed, I'd come back to the living room and sit in front of my screen. A night of lonely work lay ahead, sometimes fulfilling but often painful, since I knew the good years Billie had in store would be spent far away from me. She'd go back to a world I had created, but in which I didn't even exist, and be with a man who made my skin crawl.

Long before Billie burst into my life, I had dreamed up the character of Jack as a pretty repellent figure. He embodied everything I hated or that made me uncomfortable about men. Jack was my exact opposite, the kind of guy I couldn't stand and hoped never to become.In his early forties, good-looking, with two kids, he worked in Boston as vice-chairman of a large insurance company. He'd married very young and cheerfully cheated on his long-suffering wife without a second thought. He was sure of himself, smooth-talking and knew a thing or two about female psychology. When he first met a girl, he could instantly put her at ease. He went around acting just macho enough to seem like a real man, but he'd make sure he was sweet and affectionate to the girl he had his eye on. It was this contradiction they fell for, the thrill of the idea that he was showing them a side of himself he kept hidden from others.

But once he had them where he wanted them they'd soon see his true colours. Self-obsessed and manipulative, he'd take on the role of the victim to turn situations to his advantage. Every time he felt insecure, he'd put his lover down, sussing out her weak points so he could play on them.

It was into the destructive clutches of this smarmy, self-centred slime ball that I had gone and thrown my Billie. He was the one she'd fallen in love with, and the one she'd asked me to build her life with.

So now I found myself in a mess of my own making. You can't suddenly give a character in a book a completely different personality; I may have been the author, but that didn't make me God. Fiction goes by its own rules and that rotten bastard couldn't just turn into perfect son-in-law material from one volume to the next.

Each night I'd try to subtly backtrack, slowly making Jack a little more human, a little more likeable as the book went on. But even once this rather false transformation was complete, to me Jack was still Jack: the guy I hated most in the world and into whose hands, by a strange twist of fate, I had to deliver the woman I loved.

*

Pacific Palisades, California
15 September
9.01 a.m.
'Police! Open up, Mr Lombardo!'

Milo struggled to rouse himself. He rubbed his eyes and got out of bed, swaying unsteadily on his feet.

He and Carole had stayed up long into the night in front of their computers, scouring message boards and shopping sites to try to track down the missing book, without success. They left messages and set up email alerts wherever they could, extending the tedious search to every Italian site they could find with any kind of link to bookselling or literature.

'Police! Open up or—'

Milo half opened the door to come face to face with a woman from the sheriff's office. A petite brunette with green eyes, she had an Irish-American look about her and liked to imagine herself as a glamorous TV cop.

'Good morning, sir. Karen Kallen from the California State Sheriff's Department. We have an order to evict you.'

Milo came out onto the porch and saw a removal van pulling up in front of the house.

'What the fuck is this?'

'Don't make this difficult, sir,' warned the officer. 'You've been sent several formal notices from your bank over the past few weeks.'

Two removal men were now standing either side of the door, waiting for their instructions to clear the property.

'Oh and this,' continued the cop, handing him an envelope, 'is your summons to appear before court for removal of goods threatened with seizure.'

'Are you talking about—'

'The Bugatti you pawned, that's right.'

She nodded to the two heavies to get to work. In less than half an hour they had stripped the house of all its furniture.

'And this is nothing compared to what the IRS has in store for you!' Karen shouted cruelly as she got back into her car.

Milo was left alone on the pavement, with nothing but the suitcase in his hand. It suddenly struck him that he had nowhere to spend the night. He staggered one way and then the other, like a boxer who's been stunned, with no idea where to go. Three months ago he'd had to let his two employees go, along with his downtown offices. So there he was, no job, no roof over his head, no car, no nothing. He'd refused to face facts for too long, always sure that things would work out all right in the end, but this time his luck had run out.

The morning sun gleamed on the tattoos on his upper arms. Scars from his past, they took him back to life on the streets, the fights, the days when he didn't have a penny to his name … everything he thought he'd left behind.

The wailing of a siren recalled him to the present. He turned, ready to run, but it wasn't someone coming after him. It was Carole.

She could see right away what had happened and launched straight in, grabbing hold of Milo's suitcase and throwing it on the back seat of her patrol car.

'I've got a very comfortable sofa bed, but don't go thinking for one moment that you're going to squat at my place without lifting a finger. There's some wallpaper I've been wanting to take down in the living room since for ever, plus the kitchen could use a lick of paint and the seal on the shower needs fixing. I also have a tap that drips in the bathroom and some mould on the ceiling that needs seeing to. In fact, it looks like you getting chucked out is going to suit me pretty well.'

With a little nod of the head, Milo thanked her.

OK, so he didn't have a job, a house or a car, but he still had Carole.

He had lost everything. Except the thing that mattered most of all.

*

Trastevere, Rome
23 September

Luca Bartoletti walked into the small family-run restaurant down a quiet back street. You came here to sit at scruffy tables and tuck into typical no-fuss Roman cuisine. You ate your pasta on a checked tablecloth and poured your wine from a jug.

'Giovanni!' he called out.

The dining room was empty. It was only 10 a.m., but the smell of warm bread already wafted in the air. The restaurant had belonged to his parents for over forty years, though it was his brother who ran it these days.

'Giovanni!'

A figure appeared in the doorway, but it wasn't his brother.

'What you shouting for?'

'*Buongiorno*, Mamma.'

'*Buongiorno*.'

No kiss. No hug. No warmth at all.

'I'm looking for Giovanni.'

'Your brother isn't here. He's out buying *piscialandrea* at Marcello's.'

'OK, I'll wait for him.'

A heavy silence fell, as it did every time they found themselves alone together. The atmosphere was thick with blame and bitterness. They didn't speak often and saw each other more rarely still. Luca had spent many years in New York. When he returned to Italy after his divorce, he'd lived in Milan for a while before buying an apartment in Rome.

To break the tension, Luca went behind the bar and made himself an espresso. He wasn't much of a family guy. His work often gave him an excuse to skip christenings and weddings, and avoid going to Mass and those never-ending Sunday lunches. But, in his own way, he loved his family, and it upset him that he didn't know how to get through to them. His mother had never really understood his painting, or why he had been so successful. She couldn't see why people would want to spend tens of thousands of euros on plain white canvases. Luca felt she thought of him as a kind of crook, a clever rip-off merchant who managed to be comfortably off without ever doing a proper day's work. It was this lack of understanding that undermined their relationship.

'Heard from your daughter lately?' she asked.

'Sandra's just gone back to school, in New York.'

'Don't you ever see her?'

'I don't see her very often,' he admitted. 'You know her mother has custody.'

'And when you do see her it doesn't go very well, does it?'

'Look, I didn't come here to listen to this,' he said, raising his voice and getting up to leave.

'Wait a minute!' she said.

He stopped in front of the door.

'You look worried about something.'

'That's my business.'

'What did you want to talk to your brother about?'

'Some photos. Whether he'd kept them or not.'

'Photos? But you never take photos! You're always saying you don't like getting bogged down in memories.'

'Thanks, Mamma, that's a real help.'

'Who do you want pictures of?'

Luca dodged the question. 'I'll come back and see Giovanni later,' he said, opening the door.

She held him back by his sleeve.

'Your life has ended up like your paintings, Luca. Cold, empty and colourless.'

'Well, that's your opinion.'

'You know it's the truth though, don't you?' she said ruefully.

'Goodbye, Mamma,' he said, closing the door behind him.

*

The old lady shrugged her shoulders and went back to the kitchen. On the worn wooden worktop a copy of *La Repubblica* lay open at a glowing article about Luca's work. She finished reading it, then cut it out and added it to the file where for years she had collected everything that was written about her son.

*

Luca got back to his apartment. He used his paintbrushes as kindling to light a fire in the large hearth in the middle of his studio. While the flames took hold, he went around the room picking up all his canvases, his latest finished pieces as well as works in progress, spraying them one by one with white spirit before throwing them into the fire.

Your life has ended up like your paintings, Luca. Cold, empty and colourless. Luca stood entranced by the blaze, feeling a sense of release as his work went up in smoke.

The doorbell rang. Luca leant out of the window and saw the hunched figure of his mother. He went down to talk to her, but when he opened the door, she had gone, leaving a large envelope in his letterbox. He frowned and tore it open. Inside were the very photos and letters he had wanted to ask his brother for.

How had she known?

He went back up to his studio and spread the mementos from the past over his work bench.

Summer 1980: the year he'd turned eighteen and met Stella, his first love, the daughter of a fisherman from Porto Venere. Walks along the port beside the narrow, multicoloured houses looking out over the sea. Afternoons swimming in the tiny bay.

Christmas that year: him and Stella walking through the streets of Rome. A holiday romance that went on long after the sun had gone in.

Spring 1981: the bill from a hotel in Siena, the first time they'd made love.

1982: all the letters they'd written each other that year. Promises, plans, a whirl of excitement.

1983: a birthday present from Stella: a compass from Sardinia, engraved with the message, 'May life always guide you back to me'.

1984: first trip to the USA. Stella on a bicycle on the Golden Gate Bridge. Mist over the ferry to Alcatraz. Hamburgers and milkshakes at Lori's Diner.

1985…Laughter, holding hands, the untouchable couple…1986…The year he sold his first painting…1987…Should they have a baby or wait?… The first signs of doubt…1988 … The compass losing its bearings…

A tear slipped silently down Luca's cheek.

C'mon, don't start crying like a baby.

He had left Stella when he was twenty-eight. It was a dark time in his life, when frankly he was a mess. He didn't know what his paintings were about any more, and his relationship suffered for it. One morning, he'd got up and set fire to all his canvases, just as he had done today. Then he'd slipped away like a thief in the night, without a word of explanation for the pain he was causing; he could think only of himself and his painting. He'd fled to Manhattan where he changed his style, purging his pictures of the figurative until all he painted were variations on the colour white. He'd married a smart woman who ran a gallery over there and helped open doors for him in the art world. They'd had a daughter together but divorced a few years later, though they continued to do business with one another.

He had never seen Stella again. He'd heard from his brother that she had gone back to Porto Venere. He had erased her from his life, denied her existence.

So why was he dredging up ancient history now?

Maybe because it still wasn't over.

*

Rome
Babington's Tea Room
Two hours later

The tea room was right at the foot of the Spanish Steps.

Luca was sitting at a small table at the back of the room, the same one he used to sit at when he came here with Stella. The tea room was the oldest of its kind in Rome, founded 120 years ago by two English ladies in the days when you could only buy tea from chemists.

The decor, left almost unchanged since the nineteenth century, made the place feel like an enclave of Englishness right in the heart of Rome, playing on the contrast between the Mediterranean city outside and the British charm within. The panelled walls were lined with dark wooden shelves holding dozens of books and a collection of antique teapots.

Luca had opened the Tom Boyd book at a blank page, right after Mrs Kaufman's montage. He was moved by the way the various items had been put together, a succession of snippets of a life. As if it were a magic book that could make your every wish come true and bring the past back to life, Luca stuck in his own photos, with drawings and notes around them. In the last snap, he was sitting on a scooter with Stella. Roman holiday, 1981. They were nineteen. She had written to him saying, 'Don't ever stop loving me.'

He stared at the picture for several minutes. He was almost fifty now and had led a relatively full life, with its fair share of high points: he'd travelled, made a living from his art and been successful. But, when he really thought about it, nothing compared to the powerful emotions of the early years, when the future lay before you and you hadn't a care in the world. Luca closed the book and stuck a red sticker on the cover. He wrote a few words on the sticker then used his phone to connect to the bookcrossing website and left a short message on it. Then, while no one was looking, he slipped the book onto one of the shelves, between Keats and Shelley.

*

Luca went out into the piazza to find his Ducati motorbike, which he'd parked by the taxi rank. He strapped his overnight bag on the back and got on. He drove past the Villa Borghese gardens, around the Piazza del Popolo and along the river into Trastevere.

Leaving the engine running, he pulled up outside the family restaurant and lifted his visor. His mother had come out onto the pavement, as though she knew he was coming. She looked at her son, hoping that sometimes a look was enough to show that you loved someone.

Then Luca sped towards the road out of the city. He headed for Porto Venere, telling himself maybe it wasn't too late after all.

*

Los Angeles
Friday 24 September
7 a.m.

Milo was at the top of a stepladder, wearing a T-shirt and overalls and holding a roller in his hand. He was redoing the paint effects on the kitchen walls.

Carole came out of her bedroom to join him.

'Hard at work already?' she asked with a yawn.

'Yep, couldn't get back to sleep.'

She looked over his paintwork.

'You take your time, don't you?'

'What? I've been busting my gut for the past three days!'

'You're not doing too badly,' she conceded. 'Would you fix me a cappuccino please?'

Milo did as he was asked, while Carole sat down at the small round table in the living room. She got herself a bowl of cereal then opened up her laptop to check her emails.

Her inbox was full. Milo had sent her all the messages from Tom's community of readers which had built up on his website over the past three years. Pinging off group emails to all four corners of the world, she had managed to spread the word to thousands of readers. She'd been straight with them, telling them about her search for the incomplete copy of the second volume of the *Angel Trilogy*. Every morning since, she'd been inundated with words of encouragement. But the email in front of her now was more intriguing.

'Hey, come and have a look at this!' she called out.

Milo handed her a steaming cup of coffee and looked over her shoulder. Someone was claiming to have come across the famous copy on a bookcrossing site. Carole clicked on the link to the website of an Italian association which promoted reading by encouraging its members to leave books in public places for others to pick up. The rules of the 'travelling book' were simple: if you wanted to 'release' a book, you gave it a code which you recorded on the website before setting it on its course.

Carole typed 'Tom Boyd' into the search box and came up with a list of all her friend's books that could be on the loose.

'That's the one!' cried Milo, pointing to one of the photos. He pressed his nose right up to the screen, but Carole pushed him away.

'Let me have a look!'

There was no doubt about it: it had the midnight-blue leather cover, the gold stars and the title in Gothic lettering.

With another click, Carole read that the book had been left at Babington's Tea Room at 23 Piazza di Spagna, Rome, the previous day. Opening up another page, she found all the details left about the book by luca66, the screen name of the man who had released it. It said exactly where it had been put – a shelf at the back of the café – and at what time it had been released: 1.56 p.m. local time.

'We've got to go to Rome!' she announced.

'Let's not rush into anything!' said Milo, trying to calm her down.

'*What?*' she cried, outraged. 'Tom's relying on us. You spoke to him last night. Sure, he's writing again, but Billie's life is still in danger.'

Milo scowled. 'We'll get there too late. The book's already been there for hours.'

'Yes, but it's not like the guy's left it on a chair or a park bench! He's hidden it on a shelf in between loads of other books. It could be weeks before anyone notices it!'

She looked at Milo and saw that his run of disappointments had sapped his confidence.

'You do what you want, but I'm going.'

She logged on to an airline website. There was a flight to Rome at 11.40 a.m. As she filled out the online form, she came to the box asking for the number of passengers.

'Two,' said Milo, dropping his head.

*

Rome
Piazza di Spagna
The next day

In the middle of the square, next to the famous Fontana della Barcaccia, the Korean tour group hung on their guide's every word.

'For many years, Piazza di Spagna was considered to be Spanish territory. The international headquarters of the Order of Malta are also to be found here. The order enjoys a special blah blah blah…'

Seventeen-year-old Iseul Park stood staring into the fountain, mesmerised by the coins lying at the bottom of the crystal-clear water, thrown in by tourists. Iseul hated being associated with the cliché of Far Eastern tour groups and the jibes that went along with it. She felt out of place taking part in this outdated holiday formula, which consisted of seeing the sights of one European capital per day and hanging around for hours while everyone took exactly the same photo. Her ears were buzzing, she felt dazed and shaky, and she was suffocating in the middle of the crush of bodies. Feeling like a twig about to snap, she sneaked out and retreated to the first café she came across. It was Babington's Tea Room, number 23 Piazza di Spagna.

*

Rome
Fiumicino Airport

'So are they gonna open this damn door or not?' Milo exploded.

Standing in the aisle of the aeroplane, he was champing at the bit.

The journey hadn't been much fun. After leaving Los Angeles they had made stop-offs in San Francisco and Frankfurt before finally touching down on Italian soil. He looked at his watch: 12.30 p.m.

'There's no way we'll ever find this book!' he moaned. 'We'll have come all this way for nothing. I'm starving as well. Can you believe what they gave us to eat? Seriously, for the price we paid for those tickets…'

'Would you quit whining?' pleaded Carole. 'I'm so sick of hearing you complain about every little thing. You're giving me a headache!'

There was a murmur of agreement down the queue. Finally the door opened and the passengers could get off. With Milo following her, Carole raced down the escalator towards the taxi rank. But the queue was massive and the cars came and went at a snail's pace.

'What did I tell you?'

She didn't bother to respond. Instead, she took out her police badge, walked to the front of the queue and thrust the magic key that opens all doors at the guy allocating taxis.

'United States police! We need a car, right now. It's a matter of life or death!' she shouted in the manner of Dirty Harry.

Oh please, this is never going to work, thought Milo, shaking his head.

But Milo was wrong. The guy shrugged his shoulders, let them through without a second thought, and within a matter of seconds they were sitting in a taxi.

'Piazza di Spagna,' Carole told the driver. 'Babington's Tea Room.'

'And put your foot down!' added Milo.

*

Rome
Babington's Tea Room

Iseul Park was sitting at a small table at the back of the tea room. She'd drunk a large cup of tea and nibbled a scone topped with whipped cream. She liked the city, but would have preferred to take her time strolling through the streets, immersing herself in the culture, talking to people and sitting at sunny pavement cafés without having to keep a constant eye on the time and feeling pressured into taking a picture every ten seconds.

While she waited, she kept a constant eye not on the time, but on her phone. Still nothing from Jimbo. It was 1 p.m. in Italy so it must be 7 a.m. in New York. Maybe he wasn't up yet.

Maybe, but in the five days since they'd last seen each other, he hadn't rung once, or replied to any of the emails and texts she'd sent. What was going on? They'd spent a perfect month together at NYU, where Jimbo studied film. Iseul had spent the end of the summer on a study trip to the renowned university. She'd had the time of her life, finding love in the arms of her American boyfriend. He'd taken her to the airport to rejoin her group last Tuesday and they'd promised to call every day, assured each other their love would carry on growing in spite of the distance, and maybe they'd see each other again at Christmas. But after making all these promises, Jimbo had fallen off the face of the earth, leaving her torn up inside.

She put ten euros on the table to pay the bill. It really was a charming little place, with its wood-panelled walls and rows of books. It was like being in a library. She stood up and had a peek at what was on the shelves. She was studying English literature at college and some of her favourite writers were up there: Jane Austen, Shelley, John Keats and—

She frowned as she came across a book that looked out of place. Tom Boyd? Not exactly a nineteenth-century poet! She took the book off the shelf and found a red sticker on the cover. Curious, she returned discreetly to her table to look at it more closely. The sticky label carried a strange message: *Hello! I'm not lost! I'm free! I'm not just any old book – I'm destined to travel the world. Take me with you, read me and drop me off again in any public place.*

Hmm. Iseul wasn't convinced. She peeled off the label and flicked through the book to discover its bizarre contents, its blank pages filled with people's own stories. Something tugged at her. The book had a kind of magnetism. The sticker said it was free, but she still wasn't sure about putting it into her bag.

*

Rome
Babington's Tea Room
Five minutes later

'Over there!' called Milo, pointing to the shelf at the back of the tea room.

The customers and waitresses jumped at the sight of this bull in a china shop. He rushed towards the row of books and ran his hand along them so hurriedly that he sent a hundred-year-old teapot flying, which Carole managed to catch just in time.

'Between Keats and Shelley,' she told him.

This was it, they were almost there! Jane Austen, Keats, Shelley... but no sign of Tom's book.

'Damn it!' he shouted, slamming his fist angrily into the panelled wall.

While Carole carried on looking for the book on another shelf, the manager threatened to call the police. Milo calmed down and apologised. As he spoke, he looked down at an empty table where a half-eaten scone sat on a plate alongside a pot of cream. Something made him look closer, to find the red label discarded on the varnished wood of the banquette. He read what was written on it and let out a long sigh.

'We missed it by five minutes,' he told Carole, waving the little sticker at her.

32

Fight evil with evil

*I wanted you to see what real courage is, instead of
getting the idea that courage is a man with a gun in
his hand. It's when you know you're licked before you
begin, but you begin anyway and you see it through no
matter what*

Harper Lee

Brittany
Southern Finistère
Saturday 25 September

The sunny restaurant terrace looked out over the bay of
Audierne. The coast of Brittany was just as beautiful as
the coast of Mexico – even if it wasn't quite as warm.

'Brr, I'm freezing my ass off!' Billie shivered, zipping
up her anorak.

With her operation scheduled for the following
Monday, we'd decided to take our minds off things with
a restful weekend far from Paris. I'd thrown caution to
the wind and rented a car, and a cottage near Plogoff
that looked out toward the Île de Sein.

The waiter ceremoniously placed our seafood platter
in the middle of the table.

'Aren't you going to eat anything?' asked Billie,
astonished.

I eyed the assortment of oysters, sea urchins,

langoustines and clams with suspicion, wishing a hamburger with extra bacon would appear in their place.

Still, I had a go at shelling a langoustine.

'What a baby!' she teased.

She held out an oyster she'd just squeezed a lemon over.

'Try it. There's nothing better.'

I looked at it warily, put off by its slimy appearance.

'Think about that mango we had in Mexico!' she urged.

Describing the flavours of the real world...

I gulped down the mollusc's firm flesh, closing my eyes. It had a strong, salty, iodine taste, with a whiff of seaweed and a nuttiness that lingered in the mouth. Billie winked at me, laughing.

Her white hair was blowing in the wind.

Behind us, the langoustine trawlers were coming and going, along with the brightly coloured boats casting their pots into the water to catch shellfish.

Don't think about tomorrow. Don't think about what will happen when she's not here any more.

Live for the moment.

A stroll through the little winding streets of the harbour and along Trescadec beach. A drive from the Baie des Trépassés to the Pointe du Raz, with Billie eager to get behind the wheel. Falling about laughing remembering the sheriff who'd pulled us over for speeding in California. Realising we already shared a lot of memories. Suddenly wanting to talk about the future, but holding back. And then, of course, the rain came down in the middle of our walk over the rocks.

'It's like Scotland here. The rain's just part of the landscape,' she said when I started to grumble. 'Can you imagine the Highlands or Loch Lomond in the sunshine?'

*

Rome
Piazza Navona
7 p.m.

'Try a bit of this – it's to die for!' said Carole, offering Milo a spoonful of her dessert, a homemade tartufo with whipped cream on the side.

With a mischievous look in his eye, Milo took a mouthful of the chocolate ice cream. It had a dense texture and a truffly taste, offset beautifully by the cherry centre.

They were sitting outside a restaurant on Piazza Navona, an essential stop-off for any visitor to the Eternal City. With its array of pavement cafés and ice-cream parlours, the famous square was a gift to portrait painters, mime artists and street vendors.

As the sun went down, a waitress came and lit the candle in the middle of their table. It was still warm. Milo looked across at his friend and smiled. Though they were disappointed to have lost track of Tom's book, they'd felt close to one another that afternoon, exploring the city together. Several times he'd nearly told her how he really felt about her, but the fear of losing her friendship stopped him. He felt vulnerable, afraid of having his heart broken. If only she could see him in a different light. He so wished he could show her another side of himself, show her the man he could become if only he felt loved.

At the next table, an Australian couple were having dinner with their little girl, who must have been about five years old. She and Carole were making faces at each other and giggling.

'Isn't she adorable?'

'Yeah, she's good fun.'

'And very well brought up.'

'Do you want kids?' he asked rather abruptly.

She was immediately on the defensive.

'Why are you asking me that?'

'Um, because you'd make a great mom.'

'What would you know?' she barked.

'You can just tell.'

'Whatever!'

He was taken aback, stung by her angry reaction.

'Why are you being like that?'

'Look, I know you, and I'm pretty sure that's the kind of thing you say to chicks all the time to get them into bed. You think it's what they want to hear.'

'No, that's bullshit. You're being totally unfair. What is it I'm supposed to have done to make you so hard on me?' he asked, knocking over a glass as he got worked up.

'You don't really know me, Milo! You don't know anything about my life.'

'Well, for God's sake tell me then! What's this "dark secret" that's eating you?'

She stopped and studied him, wanting to believe he honestly cared. Maybe she'd flown off the handle too quickly.

Milo picked up the glass and dabbed the tablecloth with his napkin. He felt bad for having raised his voice, but he'd had enough of Carole's violent mood swings.

'Why did you get so touchy when I started talking about kids?' he asked more calmly.

'Because I've been pregnant before,' she told him, turning away as she said it. The truth had come out, like a bee escaping from a jar after years of being kept prisoner.

Milo sat totally still, stunned. All he could see was Carole's eyes glistening in the darkness.

She got out her plane ticket and put it down on the table.

'You really want to know about it? Fine. I'll tell you. But afterwards I don't want to hear a word from you. I'll trust you with a secret and then I'm going to get up and take a cab to the airport. The last flight to London leaves at 9.30 p.m., then there's a 6 a.m. flight to LA from there.'

'Are you sure you—'

'Yes, I am. I'll tell you and then I'm going. And, after that, don't call me or ask to sleep on my couch for at least a week. It's that or nothing.'

'OK,' he agreed. 'Whatever you want.'

Carole looked around her. Surrounding the obelisk in the middle of the piazza, the huge statues of the Fontana dei Quattro Fiumi stared down at her forbiddingly.

'The first time he did it,' she began, 'was the night of my birthday. I was eleven.'

*

Brittany
Plogoff – Pointe du Raz

'So, think you know how to light a fire, do you?' Billie chuckled.

'Um, yeah, I think I can manage it, thanks!' I replied edgily.

'Fantastic, well go right ahead, big man. I'll just sit back and watch adoringly.'

'If you think you're going to put me off...'

To Billie's delight, a storm had been unleashed on Finistère, rattling the shutters and sending torrential rain to lash against the windows of the house. Inside, conditions were arctic. It seemed the French expression '*charme rustique*', used in the ad for the house, could be translated as 'lack of radiators' and 'poor insulation'.

I struck a match and tried to light the pile of dead leaves I'd positioned under the logs. The little heap burst quickly into flames... then died out almost immediately.

Billie watched, trying not to smile. 'Hmm, very convincing.'

Wrapped in her dressing gown with a towel around her head, she bounded over to the hearth.

'Could you grab me some newspaper, please?'

Rummaging through the drawers of a Bigouden sideboard, I came across an old copy of *L'Equipe* dated

July 13, 1998, the day after France won the World Cup. The front page was headed 'pour l'éternité', above a picture of Zinedine Zidane throwing himself into the arms of Youri Djorkaeff.

Billie unfolded the sheets one by one before crumpling them up into a loose ball.

'You have to give the paper room to breathe,' she explained. 'My father taught me that.'

Then she sorted through the kindling, selecting only the driest bits and placing them on top of her pile of scrunched- up paper. The larger logs were then laid over the heap to make a sort of tepee.

'OK, now you can light it,' she said proudly.

Two minutes later, a good fire was crackling away.

The howling wind shook the windows so violently I thought they were going to shatter. Then a shutter slammed, just as a power cut plunged the room into darkness.

I tinkered about with the fuse box, hoping the lights would come back on.

'It'll be fine,' I said, trying to sound like I knew what I was doing. 'Must be the circuit breaker or a fuse—'

'Might well be,' she said, sniggering, 'but that's the water meter you're fiddling with. The fuse box is in the hall.'

I smiled, taking her amusement at my expense in good part. As I started to cross the room, she grabbed hold of my hand.

'Wait!'

She unwrapped the towel from around her head and

undid the belt of her dressing gown, letting it fall to the floor.

Then I took her in my arms and our distorted shadows embraced on the wall.

*

Rome
Piazza Navona
7.20 p.m.

Speaking in a low voice, Carole confided in Milo the ordeal of her traumatic childhood. She told him about the nightmarish years when her stepfather came to her bed. Years which had taken everything from her: her smile, her dreams, her innocence and her lust for life. She told him about the nights when, as the voracious animal crept from her room, his appetite satisfied, he'd repeat, 'Now you won't say a word to Mommy, will you? Don't tell Mommy.'

As if Mommy didn't already know!

She spoke about her feelings of guilt, how she'd had to keep it all in, while wanting to throw herself under a bus every day as she walked home from school. And then she told him about the abortion she'd had in secret at the age of fourteen, leaving her torn apart, drained of life, with a pain inside that would never heal.

She talked for a long time about Tom, who'd helped her keep her sanity by conjuring up the magical world of the *Angel Trilogy* for her, bit by bit.

Then she explained why she found it hard to trust men, how she'd lost faith in life and never quite regained it, and was still sometimes overcome by dark feelings when she least expected it.

Carole stopped talking, but made no move to get up.

Milo had kept his word and hadn't opened his mouth. But a question slipped out of its own accord.

'But when did it all end?'

Carole paused. She turned round and saw that the little Australian girl had left with her parents. She took a sip of water and pulled on the sweater that was draped over her shoulders.

'That's the other part of the story, Milo, but I'm not sure it's mine to tell.'

'So whose is it then?'

'It's Tom's.'

*

Brittany
Plogoff – Pointe du Raz

The fire was starting to die down, casting a flickering light around the room. Our bodies were wrapped around each other under the same tangled blanket and we kissed like teenagers.

An hour later, I got up to stoke the embers and put another log onto the grate.

We were starving, but the cupboards and fridge were bare. In the sideboard, I found a bottle of cider, 'Made in Quebec' strangely enough. It was *cidre de glace*, made from apples picked frozen off the trees in the depths of winter. I opened the bottle and looked out of the window. The rain showed no sign of letting up and you could see barely a few feet ahead.

With the blanket wrapped around her, Billie came and stood next to me at the window, holding two cider bowls.

'Would you tell me something?' she began, kissing my neck.

She lifted my jacket off the back of the chair and took out my wallet.

'Do you mind?'

I shook my head. She pulled the half-unpicked lining apart and turned the wallet upside down until a metal cartridge case fell out.

'Who did you kill?' she asked, holding up the spent case.

*

Los Angeles
MacArthur Park neighbourhood
29 April 1992

I'm seventeen years old. I'm studying in the library at high school, when a kid comes in shouting, 'They've been cleared!' Everyone in the room knows he's talking about the verdict in the Rodney King case.

A year earlier, this twenty-six-year-old black guy was pulled over for speeding by the LAPD. He was drunk and wouldn't cooperate with the police officers, so they tried to restrain him using a taser. When he resisted, they began beating him violently, unaware the whole incident was being filmed from a nearby balcony by an onlooker, who sent the tape to Channel 5 the following day. The images were quickly picked up and shown in a continuous loop by TV stations the world over. Anger, shame and indignation followed.

'They've been cleared!'

Every conversation comes to an abrupt end, to be replaced by insults flying in every direction. I can sense the disbelief and hatred growing. Black people are in the majority in this neighbourhood. I can see right away that things are going to turn nasty and I'm better off going home.

Out on the streets, news of the verdict is spreading like a virus. There's a buzz in the air and a sense it can't go on like this. Of course, this isn't the first police screw-up or the first time justice has fallen down, but this time it's been caught on camera, and that changes everything. The whole planet has seen four out-of-control cops laying into this poor guy: striking him more than fifty times with a baton and also kicking him. This incomprehensible acquittal is the last straw. The worst-off have suffered terribly during the Bush and Reagan years. People have had enough. Enough of unemployment and poverty. Enough of the scourge of drugs and an education system that entrenches inequalities.

When I get home, I switch on the TV and grab a bowl of cereal. Riots have broken out all over the place and I'm looking at the first of three days of images showing looting, arson and clashes with the police. The blocks around the intersection of Florence and Normandie are in total chaos. Guys are running off with crates of food stolen from shops. Others are pushing trolleys or rolling pallets to carry off furniture, sofas or electrical appliances. The authorities are calling for calm, but I can tell this isn't going to stop. Which actually suits me pretty well...

I gather up all the savings I've stashed inside my radio, pick up my skateboard and skate over to Marcus Blink's.

Marcus is a local thug, a 'good guy' who doesn't belong to any gangs and just flogs the odd prescription, deals a bit of weed and sells on a few firearms. We were at elementary school together and I was on the right side of him, because I'd helped his mom fill in her welfare papers a couple of times.

The whole neighbourhood's on edge. Everyone knows the gangs are going to make the most of the disorder to settle a few scores.

In return for my $200, Marcus fetches me a Glock 22; they're all over the place these days, with heaps of crooked cops selling on their weapons after reporting them lost. For another $20, he throws in a round of fifteen cartridges. I go back home, feeling the cold metal heavy in my pocket.

*

I don't get much sleep that night. I'm thinking about Carole. There's only one thing I care about, and that's making sure the abuse stops for good. Fiction is a powerful thing, but it has its limits. My stories allow her to escape to an imaginary place for a few hours, far from the physical and mental torture her tormentor is putting her through. But it's not enough. Living in a made-up world isn't a long-term solution, any more than getting high or getting drunk to forget your problems.

There's no getting around it: sooner or later, real life always catches up with you.

*

The next day, the violence returns with a vengeance, and the area's in a state of complete lawlessness. Helicopters chartered by TV stations hover over the city, broadcasting live footage of LA under siege: more looting, beatings, buildings on fire and gun battles between law-enforcement officers and rioters. Numerous reports reveal the disorganisation and inaction of the police, standing by while the stealing goes on.

With the death toll rising, the mayor goes in front of the cameras to declare a state of emergency and announce he intends to call on the National Guard to enforce a curfew from dusk to dawn. But it backfires: knowing the party's nearly over, the looting only cranks up a gear.

In our neighbourhood, it's mostly the Asian-run shops that are ransacked. Tensions between blacks and Koreans are running high, and on this second day of rioting most of the small businesses, mini-markets and liquor stores run by Koreans are pulled apart and looted, with the police nowhere to be seen.

It's almost midday. For the last hour I've been balancing on my skateboard, staking out Carole's stepfather's grocery store. He's opened up this morning in spite of the risks, hoping he'll manage to avoid the looters. But now he's feeling under threat too and I sense he's about to bring down the shutters.

That's when I choose to come out from my hiding place.

'Need a hand, Mr Alvarez?'

He doesn't bat an eyelid. He knows me and I seem like a reliable kind of kid.

'OK, Tom! Help me bring these boards in.'

I take one under each arm and follow him inside. It's a pretty lousy grocery store, of which there are dozens in the area. The kind of place that really only stocks the bare essentials, and which will soon be driven out of business by the arrival of a local Walmart.

Cruz Alvarez is medium height, quite stocky, with a big, square face; the right kind of build to play a bit-part as the pimp or night-club owner in a movie.

'You know, I always said one day those fucking—' he starts, before turning round to see the Glock 22 aimed at him.

The store's empty and there's no CCTV. All I have to do is pull the trigger. I don't want to say anything, not even, 'Drop dead, you piece of shit.' I'm not here to dish out justice or apply the law, or to hear his excuses either. There's no glory, no heroism, no courage in what I'm about to do. I just want Carole's suffering to end and this is the only way I can find to do it.

A few months ago, without telling her, I gave an anonymous tip-off at a family planning centre, but nothing came of it. I sent a letter to the police which was never followed up. I don't know what's right and what's wrong. I don't believe in God and I don't believe in fate. All I believe is that this is where I should be, standing behind this pistol with my finger on the trigger.

'Tom! What the hell's got into—'

I move closer so I can fire from point-blank range. I don't want to miss and I don't want to use more than one bullet.

I shoot.

His head explodes spattering blood all over my clothes.

I'm alone in the store, alone in the world. I can hardly stay upright. My arms are shaking.

Get out of here!

I pick up the cartridge case and put it in my pocket with the gun. Then I run home. I take a shower, burn my clothes, carefully clean the pistol and throw it into a trash can. I hold on to the cartridge so I can turn myself in one day, if an innocent man is accused of the crime. But would I really be brave enough to do it?

I'll probably never know.

*

Brittany
Plogoff – Pointe du Raz

'I've never told anybody what I did that morning. I've just had to live with it.'

'So what happened afterwards?' asked Billie.

We were lying on the couch. Billie lay behind me with

her hand on my chest, while I held on to her hip as though clinging to a raft.

Talking about it had lifted a weight off me. I knew she understood without judging me, which was all I hoped for.

'That evening, Bush senior made a speech to the nation, saying anarchy wouldn't be tolerated. The next day, 4,000 members of the National Guard were patrolling the city, with the Marines close behind. After that, things began to calm down and the mayor eventually lifted the curfew.'

'And did they investigate?'

'Around fifty people were killed and several thousand injured. There were thousands of arrests in the weeks that followed, some of them fair, some of them pretty random, but no one was ever formally accused of Cruz Alvarez's murder.'

Billie put her hand over my eyes and kissed my neck.

'We should get some sleep now.'

*

Rome
Piazza Navona

'Goodbye, Milo. Thanks for listening,' said Carole, rising to her feet.

Still in shock, he stood up too, gently holding her back.

'Wait. How do you know it was Tom if he never told you?'

'Because I'm a cop, Milo. Two years ago, I was given

access to some LAPD archives and I asked to see the file on my stepfather's death. There wasn't much in there: a couple of statements, a few photos from the crime scene and some botched fingerprints. No one really gave a damn who'd shot a small storekeeper in MacArthur Park. But in one of the pictures, you could make out pretty clearly a skateboard propped against the wall, with a stylised shooting star painted on it.'

'And this skateboard…'

'… was a present from me to Tom,' she said, turning away.

33

Sticking together

There are many things we can give to those we love:
words, peace, pleasure. You gave me the most precious
gift of all: missing you. I couldn't be without you, and
when I saw you I missed you even more
Christian Bobin

Monday 27 September
Paris
Hôpital Européen Marie-Curie
The entire surgical team surrounded Professor Jean-Baptiste Clouseau.

The professor sawed through Billie's breastbone, from the bottom right up to just below her chin.

Then he looked inside the pericardium, to examine the coronary arteries and begin the process of putting Billie on bypass. He injected a strong potassium solution to stop the heart from beating, before attaching a pump in place of the heart, along with artificial lungs.

Every time he carried out open-heart surgery, Jean-Baptiste Clouseau felt the same fascination with this magical organ that keeps us alive with 100,000 beats every day, 36 million a year and more than 3 billion in a lifetime. And all from a little blood-filled pump that appeared to be so delicate.

He opened the right auricle then the left and set

about removing the two tumours, each time cutting out the base of the growth to prevent them coming back. The fibrous tumour really was an unusual shape.

Thank God we caught it in time!

As a precaution, he explored the heart cavities and ventricles, looking for more myxomas, but there were none.

When he had finished, he reconnected the heart to the aorta, filled the lungs with air, attached drains to remove the blood and closed up the breastbone with steel wire.

Job done! he thought to himself, pulling off his gloves and leaving the theatre.

*

South Korea
Ewha Womans University

The sun was setting over Seoul. The Korean capital's roads were gridlocked, as they were every evening at rush hour.

Iseul Park exited the subway and crossed over to the campus. Nestling right in the heart of the student quarter, Ewha had more than 20,000 students and was one of the most prestigious universities in the country.

Iseul walked down the long gently sloping stairway to what everyone called 'the valley': a space surrounded by glass, with two buildings facing one another across a concrete walkway. She went into the main entrance of the translucent ocean liner of a building, whose ground floor, filled with shops and cafés, felt like a state-of-the-art shopping mall. She took the lift up to the higher levels, which housed the lecture halls, a theatre, cinema, sports hall and a huge twenty-four-hour library. She stopped to buy a green tea from the vending machine, before finding a space at the back of the room. You knew you were in the twenty-first century here: every workspace had a computer with instant access to all the books in the library in digital form.

Iseul rubbed her eyes. She could barely stay awake. She'd only got back from her study tour two days ago and was already swamped with work. She spent a good chunk of the evening writing out revision cards and going over her notes, constantly glancing at her phone, quivering every time it buzzed to signal the arrival of an email or text, but it was never the one she was hoping for.

She was cold, shivering, going crazy. Why had Jimbo suddenly gone AWOL? Had he taken her for a ride, the one time she'd really opened up to somebody?

It was almost midnight. People were gradually leaving the library, but a few students would be there until 3 or 4 a.m. It was that sort of place.

Iseul took the Tom Boyd book she'd found in the tea room in Italy out of her bag. She flicked through it until she reached the photo of Luca Bartoletti and his girlfriend, Stella, on a scooter in Rome, aged nineteen.

'Don't ever stop loving me,' the young Italian woman had written, which was exactly what she wanted to say to Jimbo.

She took a pair of scissors and a tube of glue out of her pencil case. Now it was her turn to fill up more of the blank pages, sticking in the best photos from the four happy weeks she'd spent with Jimbo. Her contribution to the selection of mementos consisted of tickets from the shows and exhibitions they'd enjoyed together, like the Tim Burton retrospective at MoMA and Chicago at the Ambassador Theater, as well as the films he'd introduced her to at the cinematheque at NYU, including *Donnie Darko*, *Requiem for a Dream* and *Brazil*.

She carried on all night, putting her heart and soul into it. Early in the morning, red-eyed and muddle-headed, she dropped by the post office in the administrative building to buy a padded envelope before slipping the midnight-blue leather book inside and sending it to the United States.

*

Paris
Hôpital Européen Marie-Curie
Cardiac intensive care unit
Billie was slowly coming around. She was still on a ventilator and couldn't speak because of the tube in her throat.

'We'll take that out in a few hours,' Clouseau promised.

He checked the little electrodes he'd placed on her chest to stimulate the heart in case it slowed down.

'No problems there,' he said.

I smiled at Billie and she winked back at me. Everything was going to be fine.

*

Wednesday 29 September
New York
Greenwich Village

'Oh God, I'm late!' the girl complained as she put her clothes back on. 'You said you'd set your alarm!'

She smoothed her skirt, slipped on her pumps and buttoned up her shirt.

The young man lay watching her from the bed, smiling in amusement.

'If you want to call me, you've got my number,' she said, opening the bedroom door.

'OK then, Christy.'

'It's Carry, jackass.'

James Limbo – who went by the name of Jimbo – grinned.

He stood up and stretched, without bothering to apologise or trying to get his one-night stand to stay. He went to make himself some breakfast.

'Shit, we're out of coffee,' he moaned, opening the kitchen cupboard.

He looked out of the window of the brownstone apartment to see Carry whoever she was heading up the road towards Houston Street.

Pretty good lay. Well, not bad. Six out of ten. He

frowned. Not good enough to give it another shot, anyway.

The door to the apartment opened and Jonathan, his flatmate, came in holding two cups of coffee from the coffee shop on the corner.

'I ran into the UPS delivery guy downstairs,' he said, pointing with his chin to the package under his arm.

'Thanks,' said Jimbo, grabbing the envelope and his double-shot caramel latte.

'You owe me $3.75,' announced Jonathan. 'Plus the 650 I lent you for the rent two weeks ago.'

'Yeah, yeah,' replied Jimbo evasively, studying the address on the back of the envelope.

'It's from Iseul Park, isn't it?'

'What's it to you?' he shot back, opening the package containing the Tom Boyd book.

Weird, he thought to himself, leafing through the book to find the photos stuck in by its various owners.

'I know you don't give a shit what I think,' Jonathan continued, 'but I have to tell you, you're really screwing Iseul around.'

'You're right, I don't give a shit what you think,' agreed Jimbo, taking a sip of coffee.

'She keeps on leaving voicemails. She's worried about you. If you want to break it off with her, you could at least have the decency to tell her. Why do you have to act this way with women? What exactly is your problem?'

'My problem is that life is short and we're all gonna die. That a good enough explanation for you?'

'No, I don't see what that has to do with anything.'

'Look, I want to be a director some day. Movies are my life, period. You know what Truffaut said? He said cinema is more important than life. Well, it's the same for me. I don't want to be tied down, married with kids. Anyone can be a good husband or father, but there's only one Quentin Tarantino or Martin Scorsese.'

'Dude, I don't think you're that good!'

'Well, if you don't get it, that's your problem. Just drop it,' replied Jimbo, retreating to the bathroom.

He took a shower and threw some clothes on.

'Right, I'm off,' he called, throwing his bag over his shoulder. 'I've a class at noon.'

'OK, cool, don't forget the re—'

Too late, he'd already slammed the door behind him.

Jimbo was hungry. He bought a falafel wrap from Mamoun's, which he wolfed down on his way to the film school. He was still a bit early, so he stopped at the café next to the school building to grab a Coke. While he was standing at the counter, he had another look at the book Iseul had sent him. There was no denying the girl was sexy and smart, and they'd had fun together, but now she was getting clingy, sending these soppy photographs.

The book itself was more interesting though. The *Angel Trilogy*? He was sure he'd heard of it somewhere. He thought about it and remembered reading in *Variety* that the rights had been sold to make it into a Hollywood movie. But how had this copy wound up full of photos? He got off his stool and sat down at one of the computers provided for customers. He typed in a few keywords about Tom Boyd and came up with thousands of results. But when he restricted his search to the last seven days, he found that someone had been flooding message boards trying to get their hands on a particular copy, half of whose pages were blank. Exactly the one he had in his bag!

He went out onto the sidewalk, mulling over what he'd just read. An idea was forming.

*

Greenwich Village
The same day
Late afternoon

Kerouac & Co. was a small bookstore on Greene Street, specialising in buying and selling second-hand and antiquarian books.

Kenneth Andrews, dressed as always in suit and tie, went over to the window display to add a signed copy of William Faulkner's *Go Down, Moses*, newly acquired from the feuding heirs of an aged collector. He placed it with an F. Scott Fitzgerald first edition, Sir Arthur Conan Doyle's framed autograph, an exhibition poster signed by Andy Warhol, and a Bob Dylan song scribbled on the back of a restaurant bill.

Kenneth Andrews had run the store for nearly fifty years. He'd been around in the bohemian glory days of the 1950s, when the Village was home to the Beat Generation, poets and folk singers. But rising rents had long ago driven the avant-garde artists out to other areas, and the inhabitants of Greenwich were now a well-to-do bunch, paying top dollar for his relics in order to get a flavour of an era they hadn't lived through.

The bell tinkled and a young man appeared in the doorway.

'Hi,' said Jimbo as he walked in.

He'd been in a few times before and found the place quaint. With its soft lighting, musty smell and antique prints, it reminded him of old movie sets and made him feel as though he were entering a parallel universe, far from the hustle and bustle of the city.

'Hi there,' replied Andrews. 'What can I do for you?'

Jimbo set the Tom Boyd book down on the counter.

'What do you think of this?'

The old man put on his glasses and inspected the book with disdain: imitation leather, mass-market fiction, faulty printing, not to mention all the photos making it even more of a mess. As far as he was concerned, this book was trash.

He was just about to say as much when he remembered reading a short item in *American Bookseller*, saying every copy of the special edition of this bestseller had had to be pulped because of a printing error. Could it be...

'I'll give you $90 for it,' he offered, following his hunch.

'You must be kidding,' Jimbo said huffily. 'This is a very special copy. I could get three times that on the internet.'

'Go ahead then. I can go up to $150, tops. Take it or leave it.'

Jimbo thought about it for a minute. 'It's a deal.'

Kenneth Andrews waited until the young man had left the store before digging out the magazine article.

Bad news for Doubleday: following a fault in the printing process, all 100,000 copies of the special edition of the second volume of the Angel Trilogy, by bestselling author Tom Boyd, have had to be pulped.

Hmm, interesting, pondered the bookseller. With a bit of luck, he might just have got hold of the one surviving copy…

*

Rome
Prati quarter
30 September
Wearing a white apron, Milo was serving arancini and pizza slices at a Sicilian restaurant in Via degli Scipioni. After Carole left, he'd decided to stay on in Rome for a few days, and this job earned him enough to pay for his tiny hotel room, plus free meals.

Milo exchanged emails with Tom every day. Over the moon to hear he'd started writing again, he'd got back in touch with Doubleday and various overseas publishers to let them know they'd been too quick to write his friend off. A new Tom Boyd book would be in the stores in no time.

'It's my birthday today,' said one of the regulars, an attractive brunette who worked in a luxury shoe store in Via Condotti.

'That's great.'

She bit into the ball of rice, leaving a lipstick mark on the outside.

'I'm having a party with some friends at my apartment. If you wanted to drop by...'

'Thanks, but I don't think so.'

A week ago, he wouldn't have needed asking twice. But after hearing what Carole had told him, things had changed.

His friend's story had knocked him for six, revealing a hidden side to the two people he was closest to. He was plunged into a whirl of contradictory emotions: enormous sympathy for Carole, feeling more strongly about her than ever; respect and pride for what Tom had done. But he was also annoyed at being left out of their circle of trust for so long, and sorry it hadn't been him who'd done the dirty work.

'I just can't say no to a slice of *cassata*,' drawled the curvaceous Italian, pointing to the cake covered in candied peel.

Milo was about to cut her a piece when his phone buzzed in his jeans pocket.

'Excuse me.'

It was a three-word email from Carole saying, 'Look at this!' followed by a link.

He clicked on the touch screen with his sticky fingers and was taken to a site where you could search the catalogues of booksellers specialising in rare or second-hand books. If the information on here was correct, a bookstore in Greenwich Village had just put the book he was looking for up for sale!

Just as he finished reading, he got a text from Carole.

```
Meet in Manhattan?
```

He wrote straight back.

```
On my way.
```

He undid his apron, put it down on the counter and bolted out of the restaurant.

'Hey! What about my dessert?'

34

The book of life

We always read in stolen moments, which probably explains why the Métro has become the biggest library in the world
Françoise Sagan

Paris
Hôpital Européen Marie-Curie
Billie was making a remarkable recovery. She was off the ventilator; the drains and various electrodes had been removed, and she was back on the ward. Clouseau came to see her every day, looking out for any signs of infection or internal bleeding, but everything seemed to be under control.

As for me, the hospital had become a kind of annexe to my office. From 7.30 a.m. to 7 p.m., I put my headphones in and worked on my laptop in the ground-floor cafeteria. At lunchtime, I got my meals from the staff self-service canteen, using Clouseau's smart card – did the guy ever sleep? Or eat? It was a mystery – and I'd been given a bed in Billie's room, which meant we could carry on spending the evenings together.

I'd never been so in love.

I'd never found it so easy to write.

Greenwich Village
1 October
Late afternoon
Carole was the first to arrive outside the little bookshop on Greene Street.

Kerouac & Co. Bookseller

She looked in the window and couldn't believe her eyes. The book was right there!

It lay open on a stand, with a label saying 'only copy', and shared the window with a collection of Emily Dickinson poems and a poster for *The Misfits*, signed by Marilyn Monroe.

She sensed Milo coming up behind her.

'I have to give you credit for keeping going,' he said as he approached the window. 'I never thought we'd find it again.'

'Do you think that's definitely it?'

'Let's find out,' he said, walking into the store.

The shop was about to close. Kenneth Andrews was putting the books he had just dusted back on the shelves. He paused to welcome his customers.

'What can I do for you?'

'We'd like to take a look at one of your books,' said Carole, pointing out Tom's novel.

'Oh yes, it's unique!' exclaimed the bookseller, taking the book out of the window and handling it as carefully as if it were written on papyrus.

Milo examined it from every angle, surprised to see how its different readers had made it their own.

'So?' said Carole nervously.

'This is the one, all right.'

'We'll take it!' she said firmly.

She felt filled with emotion and proud of herself. Thanks to her, Billie was out of danger!

'Excellent choice. I'll wrap it up for you. How would you like to pay?'

'Um, how much is it?'

Ever the pro, Kenneth Andrews had sensed how keen these customers were, and quoted an outrageous price.

'It's $6,000, ma'am.'

'*What?* Are you serious?' choked Milo.

'It's one of a kind,' the bookseller said by way of justification.

'It's daylight robbery, that's what it is!'

The old man showed them the door. 'Well, I won't hold you back.'

'Fine! You can stick your book—' fumed Milo.

'Very well, sir, and have a wonderful evening yourself,' retorted Andrews, returning the book to its stand.

'Wait a second!' pleaded Carole, trying to calm things down. 'I'll pay it.'

She took out her wallet and held out her credit card.

'That's very kind, ma'am,' he said, taking hold of the little piece of plastic.

*

Paris
Hôpital Européen Marie-Curie
The same day
'Can I go home now? I'm so bored of just lying here!' moaned Billie.

Professor Clouseau shot her a stern look.

'Does it hurt when I press here?' he asked, palpating her breastbone.

'A little bit.'

The doctor was concerned. Billie had a fever. Her scar was inflamed and hadn't knitted together properly. It might just be a superficial infection, but he ordered some tests just in case.

*

New York
'What do you mean, "declined"?' thundered Milo.

'I'm sorry,' said Kenneth Andrews, flustered, 'but there seems to be a slight problem with your wife's card.'

'I'm not his wife,' Carole corrected him.

She turned towards Milo. 'I must have maxed out my credit card buying those flights, but there's still money in my savings account.'

'This is crazy,' said Milo, urging her to see sense, 'you can't just bankrupt yourself.'

But Carole wouldn't be swayed.

'I just have to call my bank and get them to do a transfer, but it's Friday and it might take some time,' she explained.

'No problem, call in whenever you can.'

'This book is very important to us,' she stressed.

'I'll keep it aside until the end of Monday,' promised Andrews, taking it out of the window and placing it on the counter.

'Can I rely on you?'

'You have my word, ma'am.'

*

Paris
Hôpital Européen Marie-Curie
Monday 4 October

'Ow!' Billie cried out when the nurse placed a heat pad over her breastbone.

This time, the pain was more acute. She'd had a temperature all weekend and Professor Clouseau had moved her back from the ward to the cardiology unit.

The doctor stood at her bedside and examined the scar; it was all puffed up and the wound was seeping. Clouseau feared an inflammation of the bone and bone marrow: mediastinitis, a rare but serious bacterial infection that could be a complication of cardiac surgery.

None of the tests he had ordered had come back with conclusive results. The chest X-ray showed that two steel threads had snapped, but this was hard to interpret because of the bruising caused by the operation itself. Maybe it was nothing to worry about.

He thought about it, before deciding to carry out one last examination himself. He inserted a fine needle into the cavity between Billie's lungs to draw off some of the mediastinal fluid. To the naked eye, the sample looked like pus. He prescribed a course of intravenous antibiotics and sent the sample to the lab for urgent analysis.

*

Greenwich Village
Monday 4 October
9.30 a.m.

The multimillionaire Oleg Mordhorov stopped at a little café on Broome Street to order a cappuccino, just as he did every morning when he was in New York. He stepped back onto the pavement holding his paper cup and turned down Greene Street.

The autumn sun cast a gentle light on the buildings of Manhattan. Oleg liked strolling through the streets – but he wasn't just killing time. On the contrary, these were moments when he could reflect and when he sometimes took life-changing decisions.

He had a meeting at 11 a.m. to finalise a real-estate transaction. The group he headed was about to buy up office buildings and warehouses in Williamsburg, Greenpoint and Coney Island to turn them into luxury homes. The locals weren't all that keen on the idea, but that really wasn't his problem.

Oleg was forty-four, but his slightly chubby face made him appear younger. Wearing jeans, a cord jacket and a hoodie, he didn't look like one of the richest men in Russia. He didn't go in for displays of wealth, he didn't drive around in the limousine of an oligarch, and his bodyguard knew how to keep his distance and stay out of sight.

At the age of twenty-six, while teaching philosophy in Avacha Bay, Oleg had been approached to join the council of Petropavlovsk-Kamchatsky, a port city in eastern Russia. He'd become very involved in local life, until perestroika and Yeltsin's reforms led him into business. He'd become involved with some rather shady businessmen who had helped him profit from the policy of privatising state-owned assets.

At the beginning, he didn't have much in the way of business credentials, and his rivals had been taken in by the fact that he appeared to be a harmless dreamer, but this impression belied his cold, hard determination. He'd come a long way since then, cutting loose a few bothersome acquaintances in the process. He had property in London, New York and Dubai, a yacht, a private jet, a professional basketball team and a Formula 1 team.

Oleg stopped outside the window of the little bookshop Kerouac & Co. The autographed *Misfits* poster had caught his eye.

A gift for Marieke maybe. Why not?

He was dating Marieke Van Eden, a twenty-four-year-old Dutch supermodel who for the last two years had been on the cover of every fashion magazine.

'Hi,' he said, walking into the shop.

'May I help you, sir?' Kenneth Andrews greeted him.

'That Marilyn autograph. Is it genuine?'

'But of course, sir. It comes with a certificate of authenticity. It's a fantastic piece—'

'What's it worth?'

'Three thousand five hundred dollars, sir.'

'OK,' said Oleg, without trying to haggle. 'It's a present – could you wrap it for me?'

'Right away.'

While the bookseller carefully rolled up the poster, Oleg took out his Platinum card and put it down on the counter, just next to a book with a blue leather cover.

Tom Boyd – The Angel Trilogy.

That's Marieke's favourite writer.

He opened the book and flicked through it.

'How much for this?'

'Oh, I'm sorry, that's one's not for sale.'

Oleg smiled. In business, the only things he was interested in buying were those which were supposedly not for sale.

'How much?' he asked again.

His round face no longer looked so good natured. There was a worrying intensity in his eyes.

'It's already sold, sir,' Andrews explained calmly.

'If it's already sold, what's it still doing here?'

'The customer's coming back to collect it.'

'So it hasn't been paid for yet.'

'No, but I gave the customer my word.'

'And how much is your word worth?'

'My word, sir, is not for sale,' the bookseller replied firmly.

Andrews suddenly felt uncomfortable. There was

something threatening, something violent about this guy's manner. He put through the credit card and handed the Russian his package and receipt, relieved to be concluding the exchange.

Only Oleg didn't see it that way. He didn't leave, settling instead in a tawny leather armchair facing the counter.

'Everything has a price, doesn't it?'

'I don't think so, sir.'

'What was it Shakespeare said?' Oleg asked, trying to remember the quotation. '"Money makes foul fair, old young, wrong right, base noble ..."'

'You must admit that's a very cynical view of mankind.'

'Name something money can't buy,' Oleg challenged him.

'Well, it's obvious: friendship, love, dignity—'

Oleg swept his argument aside.

'Humans are weak and corruptible.'

'Surely you'd allow that there are some moral and spiritual values that escape self-interest.'

'Every man has his price.'

This time, Andrews showed him the door.

'Have a good day, won't you.'

But Oleg didn't move an inch.

'Every man has his price,' he said again. 'What's yours?'

*

Greenwich Village
Two hours later

'What the hell is this?' railed Milo, arriving outside the shop.

Carole couldn't believe her eyes. Not only had the shutters been pulled down, but a hastily scrawled sign informed potential customers:

ANNUAL CLOSURE
BEFORE CHANGE OF MANAGEMENT

She felt tears welling up. She sat on the kerb, despondent, letting her head drop into her hands. She'd just cashed the $6,000. A quarter of an hour earlier she'd been on the phone to Tom telling him the good news. And now the book had slipped through her fingers once again.

Milo shook the shutters, enraged, but Carole stood up to try to reason with him.

'You can break whatever you want – it won't change anything.'

She took out the $6,000 in bills and handed most of them to him

'Listen, I need to get back to work, but you should go and help Tom in Paris. That's the most useful thing we can do now.'

And that was that. Downbeat, they shared a taxi to JFK airport and went their separate ways: Carole to Los Angeles and Milo to Paris.

*

Newark
Late afternoon

A few miles away at another New York airport, multimillionaire Oleg Mordhorov's private jet was taking off for Europe. He'd decided to make a flying visit to surprise Marieke in Paris.

It was the first week of October and the young model was strutting her stuff in the French capital for Fashion Week. All the fashion houses fought to dress her in their new collections. A classically beautiful and sophisticated woman, she had a special spark, as if the gods of Mount Olympus had allowed a flicker of the eternal flame to pass down to Earth.

Comfortably settled in his seat, Oleg flicked through the Tom Boyd book absent-mindedly, before slipping it inside a padded envelope with a ribbon around it.

It's an original gift, he thought to himself. *I hope she'll like it*.

He spent the rest of the journey sorting out some paperwork before allowing himself a couple of hours' sleep.

*

Paris
Hôpital Européen Marie-Curie
5 October
5.30 a.m.

'Damned hospital bugs!' Clouseau cursed as he came into the room.

Knocked out by fever and fatigue, Billie hadn't woken up since the previous day.

'Bad news?' I guessed.

'Very bad indeed. We've found bacteria in the fluid we took from Billie. She's developing mediastinitis, a very serious infection which needs to be treated immediately.'

'Will you have to operate again?'

'Yes, we're taking her up to theatre straight away.'

*

Oleg Mordhorov's jet landed at Orly Sud at 6 a.m. An ordinary- looking car was waiting to take him to Île Saint-Louis, right in the heart of Paris.

The vehicle stopped on Quai de Bourbon outside a handsome seventeenth-century mansion. Holding his overnight bag, with the envelope containg the book under his arm, Oleg took the lift to the fifth floor. The duplex occupied the top two floors and had a stunning view over the Seine and Pont Marie. He'd splashed out on the place as a romantic gift for Marieke when they'd first got together.

Oleg had his own set of keys. He let himself into the apartment. It was quiet, bathed in the pale light of dawn. He recognised Marieke's fitted pearl-grey coat thrown over the white leather couch, but beside it lay a man's leather jacket which didn't belong to him...

The penny dropped immediately and he didn't bother going up to the bedroom.

Outside on the street, he tried to hide his shame in front of his driver. But in his anger he hurled the book into the river with all his might.

Hôpital Européen Marie-Curie
7.30 a.m.

Under Clouseau's supervision, the intern placed the defibrillator patches on Billie's body, which was anaesthetised. Then the surgeon took over, carefully removing all the stitches in her chest before debriding the wound, cutting out the dead and infected tissue.

The wound was oozing. Clouseau decided on closed-heart surgery. In order to drain the fluid, he put in six small drainage tubes attached to suction devices. Then he finished the procedure by stabilising the breastbone, and sewing the wound with fresh steel wire so that the movements of her breathing wouldn't interfere the healing process.

At last, the operation seems to have—

'Doctor! She's haemorrhaging!' called the intern.

*

Protected only by the padded envelope, the book with the midnight-blue cover floated down the Seine, water seeping inside as it went.

The book had covered some serious ground over the past few weeks, travelling from Malibu to San Francisco, crossing the Atlantic to Rome, continuing its journey as far as Asia before heading back to Manhattan, and eventually landing in France.

In its own way, the book had changed the lives of all the people who had held it. This wasn't just any novel.

The story it told had been dreamed up in the mind of a teenager traumatised by what his childhood friend was going through.

Years later, when the author was battling his own demons, the book had flung one of its characters into the real world to come to his aid.

But that morning, as the river water soaked through its pages, it seemed the real world had decided to fight back, determined to wipe Billie off the face of the earth.

35

The heart test

After looking for something and finding nothing,
sometimes you find it without looking for it
Jerome K. Jerome

Hôpital Européen Marie-Curie
8.10 a.m.

'Let's open her up again,' ordered Clouseau.

It was as he feared: the right ventricle had torn, causing a massive loss of blood. It was spurting out from all sides and flooding the area they were working on. The intern and nurse were struggling to contain it, forcing Clouseau to compress the heart with his hands to try to stop the flow.

This time, Billie's life was hanging by a thread.

*

Quai Saint-Bernard
8.45 a.m.

'Hey, boys, it's time for work, not time for breakfast!' spat Captain Karine Agneli, walking into the staff room at the headquarters of the river police.

Lieutenants Diaz and Capella were enjoying coffee and croissants, reading the headlines of *Le Parisien* and listening to comedy on the radio.

With her short tousled hair and charming freckles, Karine was as feminine as she was no-nonsense. She was having none of this slacking; she switched off the radio and roused her men to action.

'We've just had a call come in; there's an emergency. Some drunk's thrown himself off Pont Marie. So you'd better pull your fingers out of—'

'OK, we're going, boss!' Diaz cut her off. 'No need to lower the tone.'

Seconds later all three of them had taken their places aboard the *Cormorant*, one of the patrol boats used to police the Seine. It sliced through the waves, travelling along Quai Henri-IV and passing under Pont de Sully.

'You'd have to be totally wasted to think it was a good idea to jump in when it's this cold,' remarked Diaz.

'Uh-huh... Not looking so perky yourselves this morning,' commented Karine.

'The baby was up all night' was Capella's excuse.

'And what about you, Diaz?'

'It's my mother.'

'How do you mean?'

'It's complicated,' he said, trying to put an end to the conversation.

She left it at that. The boat carried on along Voie Georges- Pompidou, until...

'I can see him!' shouted Capella, peering through his binoculars.

They slowed down as they went under Pont Marie. A man was flailing around in the water, tangled in his raincoat, gasping as he struggled to reach the riverbank.

Karine zipped up her wet suit and dived into the water while her two lieutenants looked on sheepishly.

She swam over to the man, calmed him down and brought him back to the *Cormorant*, where Diaz pulled him on board and wrapped him in a blanket before performing first aid.

Still in the water, Karine spotted something bobbing on the surface. She reached for it. It was a large padded envelope lined with bubble wrap – not exactly biodegradable. Since tackling pollution was also within the remit of the river police, she took it with her as Capella hauled her up on deck.

*

Hôpital Européen Marie-Curie

The surgical team spent the whole morning trying to save Billie.

Clouseau used a piece of the lining of the peritoneum to patch up the tear in the ventricle.

It was a last-ditch attempt to keep her alive.

Her chances were looking slim.

*

Quai Saint-Bernard
9.15 a.m.

Back at HQ, Lieutenant Capella was emptying the boat before hosing it down.

He picked up the padded envelope, which was sodden as a sponge. Inside was a book in English in pretty shoddy condition. He was just about to throw it into the skip when he changed his mind and placed it on the quayside.

*

A few days went by...
Milo had come to meet me in Paris, helping me through a difficult period.

Teetering between life and death, Billie had been in intensive care for over a week under the watchful eye of Clouseau, who came by to monitor his patient every three hours.

He was incredibly understanding, allowing me to come and go whenever I wanted. And so I spent a good part of each day sitting on a chair, my laptop on my knees, feverishly tapping away on the keyboard to the beat of the heart monitor and whirr of the ventilator.

Drugged up on painkillers, Billie was intubated and had drains and drips coming out of her arms and chest. She hardly opened her eyes, and when she did I could see the suffering and anguish in them. I wanted to be able to comfort her and dry her tears, but all I could do was carry on writing.

*

In the middle of October, Milo sat outside a café and finished a long letter to Carole. He folded the sheets and put them in an envelope, paid for his Perrier-menthe and crossed the road to Quai Malaquais, on the banks of the Seine. As he walked in the direction of the Institut de France, where he'd spotted a letter box, he slowed down to glance over the racks of the *bouquinistes*.

Old books were displayed with black and white Doisneau postcards, vintage Chat Noir posters, 1960s vinyl, and hideous Eiffel Tower key-rings. Milo stopped at a stall specialising in comic books. From *The Incredible Hulk* to *Spiderman*, his imagination had been filled with the heroes of Marvel comics as a child, and that afternoon he took pleasure in looking through the Astérix and Lucky Luke books. The last rack was 'Everything for 1 euro'. Milo had a rummage: dog-eared paperbacks, torn magazines and, in amongst all this junk, a tattered midnight-blue leather hardback …

No way!

He studied the book: the binding had buckled and the pages were stuck together and bone dry.

'Where … where did you get this book?' he asked.

The bookseller, who spoke just a little English, explained that he had found it on the quayside. Still, Milo couldn't understand by what miracle the book he'd lost track of in New York had ended up in Paris ten days later.

Still flummoxed, he kept turning the book over in his hands.

Yes, he'd found the book, but what a state it was in.

The *bouquiniste* could see he was puzzling over it.

'If you want to get it mended, I can recommend someone,' he suggested, handing him a business card.

*

Annexe of Saint-Benoît Priory
Somewhere in Paris

In the craft bookbinding workshop of the priory, Sister Marie-Claude was examined the book she had been charged with mending. The body of the book was battered and bruised, its imitation leather cover badly damaged. It was going to be difficult to restore, but the nun prepared to do her best.

She began by carefully undoing the binding. Then, using a humidifier barely bigger than a pen, she sprayed a very fine mist over the book, at an exact temperature displayed on a digital screen. The cloud of humidity sank into the paper and the pages came unstuck. Because they had got wet, they were very delicate and faded in places. Sister Marie-Claude carefully inserted sheets of blotting paper between each of them before standing the book upright and drying it very gently with a hairdryer. A few hours later, you could turn the pages more or less smoothly. The nun carefully checked each of them in turn, making sure she'd done a good job. She stuck in the photos that had fallen out, along with the little lock of hair that looked as if it had come from the head of an angel. Then, to get the book back to its original shape, she placed it inside a press for the night.

The next day, Sister Marie-Claude set about making

a new skin for the book. In the peace and quiet of the workshop, she worked through the day with surgical precision, creating a cover from dyed calfskin with a lambskin label, on which she inscribed the title in gold leaf.

At 7 p.m., the young American with the strange name knocked at the door of the priory. Sister Marie-Claude returned the book to Milo, who complimented her so wholeheartedly on her work that she couldn't help but blush.

*

'Wake up!' ordered Milo, shaking me.

What the—

I had fallen asleep in front of my computer again, in the hospital room Billie had occupied before her operation. I spent every night there, with the unspoken agreement of the staff.

The blinds were down and the room was lit by a dim nightlight.

'What time is it?' I asked, rubbing my eyes.

'Eleven o'clock.'

'And what day is it?'

'Wednesday.'

He couldn't help adding in a sarcastic tone, 'And before you ask, yes, it's 2010 and Obama's still the president.'

'Hmm.'

I had a tendency to lose track of time while concentrating on my writing.

'How many pages have you written?' he asked, reading over my shoulder.

'Two hundred fifty,' I replied, folding down the screen. 'Halfway there.'

'And how's Billie?'

'Still in intensive care. They're watching her closely.'

With great solemnity, he took a sumptuously bound book out of a bag.

'I've a present for you,' he said mysteriously.

It took me a little while to register that this was none other than my book, which he and Carole had chased across the four corners of the earth.

It had been expertly restored and its leather cover was warm and smooth to the touch.

'Billie's out of danger now,' Milo reassured me. 'Now all you have to do is finish your story to send her back to her own world.'

*

Weeks and months went by.
October, November, December...
The wind carried away the yellow leaves that had fallen on the sidewalks, and the mellow autumn sun gave way to the harsh chill of winter.

Cafés brought their chairs indoors or turned on their heaters. Stalls selling roasted chestnuts sprang up around Métro exits, enticing commuters as they put on hats and tightened scarves against the cold.

I was on a roll, writing faster and faster, pressing the keys almost without pausing for breath, carried along by a story of which I was now the plaything as much as the creator, hypnotised by the page numbers at the bottom of my screen: 350, 400, 450...

Billie had pulled through and passed the 'heart test'.

First, they had replaced the tube down her throat with an oxygen mask. Then Clouseau gradually reduced the dose of painkillers and took out the drains and drips, breathing a sigh of relief when her samples came back clear of any new infections.

After that, her bandages were taken off and her wounds covered with transparent film. As the weeks passed, her scar faded.

Billie began eating and drinking by herself again. I watched her take her first steps, then climb a flight of stairs, supervised by a physio.

Her hair had returned to its normal colour, and she had gone back to her usual smiling, vibrant self.

On 17 December, Paris woke up to its first flakes of snow, which carried on falling all morning.

And on 23 December I finished my novel.

36

The last time I saw Billie

True love is when two dreams meet and escape, hand in hand, from the real world
Romain Gary

Paris
23 December
8 p.m.

With one shopping day left, the Christmas market was in full swing. As Billie and I walked arm in arm, I guided her through the little white stalls that had been set up between Place de la Concorde and the Champs-Élysées roundabout. The big wheel, the lights, ice sculptures and wafts of mulled wine and gingerbread gave the avenue a magical fairytale feel.

'You're buying me a pair of shoes?' squealed Billie as we passed the luxury boutiques on Avenue Montaigne.

'No, I'm taking you to the theatre.'

'To see a play?'

'No, to eat!'

We arrived outside the white marble facade of the Théâtre des Champs-Élysées, taking the lift up to the top-floor restaurant.

Sparsely furnished with wood, glass and granite surfaces, the room was painted in pastel shades, offset by plum-coloured columns.

'Would you care for something to drink?' asked the maître d', after showing us to a cosy silk-draped booth.

I ordered two glasses of champagne and took a tiny silver case out of my pocket.

'I kept my promise,' I said, handing it to my dinner companion.

'It's not a ring, is it?'

'No, don't get carried away.'

'Aha, it's a USB stick!' she discovered, pulling the cap off.

'You've finished your book!'

I nodded. The waiter set our drinks down.

'I've got something for you too,' she said mysteriously, taking a cell phone out of her bag. 'I wanted to give this back before we say cheers.'

'But that's my phone!'

'Yeah, I know, I pinched it this morning,' she confessed openly. 'You know how nosy I am ...'

I took it back, grumbling, while she sat looking pleased with herself.

'I hope you don't mind but I read a few of your texts. I see things are back on track with Aurore!'

Though she wasn't entirely mistaken, I shook my head.

Over the last few weeks, Aurore's messages had become more frequent and affectionate. She told me she missed me, said she was sorry for some of the things she'd done and hinted at giving our relationship 'a second chance'.

'She's fallen for you again! Didn't I tell you I'd stick to my side of the bargain?' Billie declared, taking the crumpled piece of tablecloth from her pocket.

'Those were the days,' I said, thinking back nostalgically to when we'd made our pact.

'Yes, I seem to remember giving you a good slap!'

'So…' I paused. 'This is it then, the adventure stops here.'

She looked at me, trying to keep things light-hearted.

'That's right, mission accomplished times two! You've written your book and I got you back the woman you love.'

'You're the woman I love.'

'Please, don't make this complicated,' she begged as the waiter came over to take our order.

I turned away so she wouldn't see I was upset. I looked out through the dizzying glass wall, taking in the incredible view over the rooftops of the city.

I waited until the waiter had gone before asking, 'So what exactly's going to happen now?'

'We've been over this a million times, Tom. You're going to send your manuscript to your editor and, when he reads it, the imaginary world you describe in your story will form in his head. And that imaginary world is where I belong.'

'You belong here, with me!'

'No, there's no way that can happen. I can't be in two places at once, the real world and the fictional one. I can't live here; I almost died – it's a miracle I'm still here at all.'

'But you're better now.'

'I'm living on borrowed time and you know it. If I stay, I'll get ill again, and I won't be so lucky next time.'

I couldn't believe she was giving up so easily.

'It's like… you're happy to be leaving me!'

'I'm not happy at all, but we've known from the beginning this couldn't last. We always knew we couldn't have a future together, that our relationship couldn't go anywhere.'

'But things have happened between us!'

'I know they have. The last few weeks have been like a dream, but the fact is we're worlds apart. You're living a real life; I'm just a "figment of the imagination".'

'Fine,' I said, standing up from the table, 'but you could at least act like you care.'

I threw my napkin down on my chair and slammed the last of my money on the table before walking out of the restaurant.

*

The biting cold that had set in over the city chilled me to the bone. I turned up the collar of my coat and hurried up the avenue to the Plaza, where three taxis were waiting.

Billie ran after me, grabbing hold of my arm.

'How dare you walk off like that? How can you spoil everything we've been through together?'

She was shivering violently. Tears were running down her cheeks and you could see her breath in the icy air.

'What do you you think?' she shouted. 'That I'm not devastated at the thought of losing you? You poor fool, you have no idea how much I love you!'

She was really wound up, outraged at my accusations.

'What do you want me to say? That I've never been so happy with a man in my entire life? I didn't even know it was possible to feel this way about someone! I didn't know you could feel passion at the same time as respect, and laughter, and tenderness! You're the only one who ever got me to read. The only one who really listens to me and doesn't make me feel like too much of an idiot. The only one who's as interested in what I have to say as in my legs. The only one to see me as something more than an easy lay... But you're too stupid to realise.'

I took her in my arms. I was angry too. Angry at the way I'd behaved, and at the barrier between fiction and reality that stood firmly in the way of the happiness we deserved.

*

For the last time, we went back to 'our place', the little apartment on Place de Furstenberg which had been the setting for our burgeoning love.

For the last time, I lit a fire in the fireplace, showing her I remembered what she'd taught me: scrunched-up paper first, then kindling and finally the logs, piled up like a tepee.

For the last time, we drank a mouthful of the infamous – and delicious – pear liqueur.

For the last time, Léo Ferré sang to us, '*avec le temps va, tout s'en va*'.

*

The fire began to take hold, throwing flickering reflections onto the walls. We were lying on the sofa; Billie's head was resting on my stomach and I was playing with her hair.

'I want you to promise me something,' she said, turning toward me.

'Whatever you want.'

'Promise me you're not going to fall back down that black hole. And tell me you won't go back to popping pills.'

I was moved by her pleas, but not convinced I'd actually be able to comply once I was back on my own again.

'You've got your life back on track, Tom. You've started writing again, and you've learned to love again. You have friends. Be happy with Aurore, have lots of babies. Don't be—'

'I couldn't care less about Aurore!' I cut in.

She stood up and continued, 'Even if I lived ten lifetimes, I'd never be able to thank you enough for what you've done for me. I have no idea what's going to happen to me or where I'm going to end up. All I know is, wherever I am, I'll always love you.'

She walked over to the desk and opened the drawer. She was holding the restored book that Milo had brought me.

'What are you doing?'

407

As I tried to go over to her, I was overcome with dizziness. My head felt heavy and I was suddenly overwhelmingly sleepy.

What's happening to me?

I took a few shaky steps. Billie had opened the book and I guessed she had turned to the notorious page 266, which came to an abrupt end with 'she cried, falling'.

I couldn't keep my eyes open, I had no strength left, and suddenly I understood.

The liqueur! Billie only touched her lips to it, but I…

'Did you… did you put something in the bottle?'

She didn't try to deny it, taking from her pocket a bottle of sleeping pills she must have stolen from the hospital.

'But … why?'

'So you'd let me leave.'

The muscles in my neck were frozen and I felt a strong urge to be sick. I tried to fight it, struggling to stay upright, but everything was falling to pieces around me.

The last clear image I have is of Billie stoking the embers before throwing the book into the flames. She'd arrived through the book, and it was through the book that she would leave again.

Helpless to stop her, I fell to my knees, my vision becoming more and more blurred. Billie had opened my laptop and I sensed rather than saw that she was going to connect the silver USB stick to …

Though everything was swimming around me, I

408

heard an email being sent from my computer. Then, as I passed out on the floor, a little voice whispered, 'I love you,' the words melting away as I drifted into a deep sleep.

*

Manhattan
Madison Avenue

Meanwhile, in New York, it was just gone 4 p.m. when Rebecca Tyler, editorial director at Doubleday, picked up her phone to take a call from her assistant.

'The new Tom Boyd manuscript has just come in!' Janice told her.

'About time!' exclaimed Rebecca. 'We've been waiting for it for months.'

'Shall I print it off for you?'

'Yes, quick as you can.'

Rebecca asked for her next two meetings to be cancelled. The third volume of the *Angel Trilogy* was a big priority for the publishing house, and she was anxious to see what the text was like.

She started reading just before five and carried on late into the evening.

Without a word to her boss, Janice had printed off her own copy of the novel. She left the office at six to get the subway back to her little apartment in Williamsburg, telling herself she must be crazy to have taken such a risk. It was the kind of professional misconduct that could get her fired. But she simply couldn't wait to read the last part of the trilogy.

And so it was in these first two readers' heads that the imaginary world described by Tom began to take shape.

The world in which Billie's life would now be played out.

*

Paris
24 December
9 a.m.
I woke up the next morning feeling sick and with a horrible taste in my mouth. The apartment was cold and empty. There was nothing but ashes in the fireplace.

Outside, the sky was dark and rain was beating against the windows.

Billie had left my life as suddenly as she had come into it, like a bullet ripping through my heart, and once again I was left broken and alone.

37

My best friends' wedding

It's the friends you can call up at 4 a.m. that matter
Marlene Dietrich

Eight months later
First week of September
Malibu, California

The estate, a replica French château built by an eccentric multimillionaire in the sixties, sprawled over the cliff tops above Zuma beach. With fifteen acres of field, garden and vineyard, it felt more like deepest Burgundy than a city of surfers and white beaches beside the ocean.

These were the exclusive surroundings in which Milo and Carole had chosen to celebrate their marriage. Since our adventure had come to an end, my two friends had been blissfully in love, and I couldn't have been more delighted to see them so happy at last.

Life was getting back to normal. I'd paid off my debts and sorted out my legal problems. The third volume of my trilogy had come out six months earlier and been well received by readers. The first film adapted from my novels topped the box office for three weeks in the summer. The wheel of fortune turned quickly in Hollywood: I'd gone from zero back to hero, once again the bestselling author who could do no wrong. *Sic transit gloria mundi*.

Milo had opened up our offices again, and this time he was playing it safe with my affairs. He'd got back the Bugatti, but when he found out his wife-to-be was expecting, he'd traded it in for a Volvo.

In short, Milo was not the old Milo any more.

Although it seemed as if life was smiling on me again, I was in a kind of mourning for Billie. I was still in love with her. I had stayed true to my promise, keeping off the cocktail of antidepressants, tranquillisers and crystal meth, and trying to live as clean a life as possible. To keep busy, I'd embarked on a massive book-signing tour, which took me all over the world in the space of a few months. Just meeting people did me good, but whenever I found myself alone I thought of Billie and remembered our extraordinary meeting, the way we sparred and sparked off each other, and the warmth when we touched.

After Billie, I'd drawn a line under my love life and broken off all contact with Aurore. There was no point giving it another go. I'd stopped thinking about the future, taking each day as it came.

But I knew I couldn't afford to buy another one-way ticket to nowheresville. If I broke down now I'd never get up again. I couldn't let Carole and Milo down when they were doing all they could to help me. So as not to put a damper on their happiness, I did my best to hide my feelings, turning up to their matchmaking dinners on Friday nights when they hoped to find me a soul mate. They were determined to track down 'that special someone' and got everyone they knew on the case. Thanks to their efforts, I met a hand-picked assortment of single Californian girls over the next few months, including a college professor, a scriptwriter, a teacher and a psychologist – but the game soon wore thin and our conversations never carried on beyond dinner.

*

'A speech from the best man!' shouted one of the guests inside the reception marquee.

The tent was filled almost entirely with cops, firemen and ambulance drivers, people Carole knew through work who had come along with their families. On Milo's side, it was pretty much just me and his mom. The mood was relaxed and laid-back. The canvas curtains flapped in the breeze, bringing in wafts of cut grass and sea air.

'Speech!' they all clamoured, clinking their glasses and forcing me to my feet. I could have done without this. The feelings I had for my friends were not easily expressed in front of a crowd of forty people.

Still, I played the game, and everyone went quiet as I began. I turned to face Carole. She looked incredible in her corseted dress threaded with tiny crystals.

'Carole, we've known each other since we were kids – pretty much all our lives. Our paths are inextricably linked and I could never be happy knowing you weren't happy too.'

I smiled at her and she winked back at me. Then I turned to Milo.

'Milo, we've been through everything together, from the tough times growing up, right up until we 'made it to the top' and all that jazz. Together, we've made mistakes, and fixed them. Together, we've lost everything, and won it all back. And I hope that's how we'll carry on our journey through life – together'

Milo gave me a little nod. I could see his eyes were shining.

'Over the last year, the two of you have shown me that I can always count on you, no matter what. You've shown me that the old saying about friendship doubling joy and halving grief is more than just a neat phrase.

'From the bottom of my heart, I want to thank you, and to promise you that I'll always be there for you too.'

Then I lifted my glass. 'To the bride and groom!'

I saw Carole wiping away a tear, as Milo walked over to hug me.

'We need to talk,' he said into my ear.

*

We snuck off to a quiet spot, a boathouse on the edge of a lake patrolled by an army of swans. The little building, topped with a pediment, was home to a collection of varnished wooden boats, and had a cool, timeless feel that was very New England.

'So, what did you want to talk about?'

Milo loosened his tie. He was trying hard to look

calm, but it was clear from his face he was feeling uncomfortable.

'I can't keep on living a lie, Tom. I know I should have said something sooner but—'

He stopped and rubbed his eyes.

'What is it?' I asked, anxious to know what was going on.

'Don't tell me you've lost on the markets again?'

'No. It's Billie.'

'What about Billie?'

'She… she's real. Well, kind of…'

I had no idea what he was trying to say.

'Man, are you wasted?'

He breathed deeply to try to regain his composure, sitting down at a workbench.

'You have to look at the whole picture. Remember what a state you were in a year ago. You were all over the place. It was one thing after another: speeding fines, drugs, trouble with the law. You'd stopped writing and you were sinking into a deep depression that nothing could drag you out of; not therapy, not medication, not our support.'

I sat down next to him, feeling suddenly uneasy.

'One morning,' he went on, 'I got a call from the publisher about an error in the latest print run of the second book. He sent a copy over by courier and I saw that the book stopped right in the middle, on the words, "she cried, falling". The sentence went round and round in my head the whole day, and I was still thinking about it at my meeting with Columbia that afternoon. The producers were wrapping up the casting

415

for your film adaptation, and they were auditioning for the supporting roles that day. I hung around for a while on the set where they were trying out actresses for the part of Billie. And that's where I met this girl—'

'What girl?'

'Her name was Lilly. A messed-up-looking girl whose script was shaking while she read her lines. She was pale, her eyes were plastered with mascara and she mooched about looking flaky, like a Cassavetes heroine. From what I saw, I thought her audition was out of this world, but the assistant director made it clear she didn't stand much chance. The guy must have been blind; it was so fricking obvious the girl was your Billie. So I asked her for a drink and she told me about her life.'

Milo went quiet for an unbearable length of time, waiting to see my reaction, measuring his words – but I'd had enough of him beating around the bush.

'Go on, for God's sake!'

'In between waitressing jobs, Lilly was doing some modelling while trying to get into acting. She'd done a few photo shoots for magazines, appeared in some tacky commercials and played bit-parts in short films, but she was no Kate Moss.

'Even though she was still young, she gave the impression she was already coming to the end of her career. She seemed out of place in the cut-throat world of fashion, where new girls were always arriving on the scene and if you hadn't made it big by twenty-five, forget it...'

I felt a shiver go down my spine and the blood

pounding in my temples. I didn't want to hear what he was about to say.

'What is it you're trying to tell me, Milo? What did you offer that girl?'

'I offered her $15,000,' he finally admitted. 'Fifteen thousand dollars to play the part of Billie, but not in a movie. In your life.'

38

Lilly

We cannot change the cards we are dealt, just how we play the hand
Randy Pausch

'I offered her $15,000 to play the part of Billie, but not in a movie. In your life.'

Milo's revelation was like an uppercut landing on my chin.

My head was spinning and I felt like a boxer collapsing in the middle of the ring.

While I sat in stunned silence, Milo tried to explain himself.

'I know it's crazy, but it worked, Tom! I couldn't sit back and watch you fall to pieces. I had to grab hold of you and shake you into action. It was the only card I had left to play to get you out of your depression.'

I couldn't take it in.

So Billie was just an actress? And the whole thing had been a lie? Then how the hell had I fallen for it?

'I don't believe you,' I said. 'It doesn't add up. It's not just that she looks exactly like her, but there are so many other things that prove she must be Billie!'

'Like what?'

'Her tattoo, for one.'

'It was a fake. A transfer we got from the on-set make-up artist.'

'She knew absolutely everything about Billie's life.'

'I got her to read all your books and she pulled them apart. I didn't give her the password to your computer, but she had access to your character biographies.'

'And how exactly did you get hold of those?'

'I hired someone to hack into your machine.'

'You're one heck of a bastard.'

'No. I'm your friend.'

No matter what he said, there was no way I could believe it.

'But you tried to have me committed! You drove me to the psychiatrist yourself!'

'Because I knew that, if my plan worked, you'd refuse to go along with it and you'd try to escape.'

Pictures ran through my head of everything I'd been through with 'Billie'. I sifted through them, trying to find something to catch Milo out.

'Hang on a minute! She knew how to fix the car when it broke down! Where did she learn to do that if her brothers aren't mechanics?'

He batted it back.

'That was just a wire I'd disconnected. We rehearsed it; it was a way of clearing up any doubts you might still have had. Don't waste your time trying to question it; there's only one thing that could have given her away, but luckily it passed you by.'

'What?'

'Billie's left-handed, but Lilly's right-handed. Obvious when you think about it.'

I was racking my brains, but I just couldn't remember if he was right about that or not.

'OK, that's all very well, but you've missed the most important part: Billie's illness.'

'Well, when you arrived in Mexico, things did begin to move faster,' Milo admitted. 'Though you still weren't ready to write again, it was obvious you were feeling better – and, more to the point, that something was going on between you and her. Though neither of you would admit it, you were falling for each other. I thought about telling you everything then, but Lilly was determined to carry on. The whole business with the illness was her idea.'

Now I really was confused.

'But... why?'

'Because she loved you, you idiot! She wanted you to be happy; to start writing again and win Aurore back. And she did it!'

'So, the white hair was—'

'Hair dye.'

'The ink in her mouth?'

'Just the contents of an ink cartridge emptied under her tongue.'

'And what about the test results in Mexico? The cellulose they found in her body?'

'The whole thing was a wind-up, Tom. Dr Philipson was three months from retirement. I told him you were my friend and I wanted to play a trick on you. He was bored stiff sitting around in his clinic; getting in on the joke kept him entertained. But you know how it is – the best-laid plans and all... The whole thing could have fallen apart when Aurore suggested taking Billie to see Professor Clouseau.'

'But he would never have got mixed up in some game of smoke and mirrors. Billie wasn't putting it on in Paris. She almost died, I know it.'

'You're right, but that's when something unbelievable happened. She didn't know it, but Billie really was sick. Thanks to Clouseau, her heart tumours were discovered. So, in a way, you could say I saved both of your lives.'

'OK, so how about the book you spent weeks chasing all over the world?'

'Well, I had to go along with that one,' he admitted. 'Carole was still in the dark about the whole thing and believed in the story 100 per cent. It was her in the driving seat. I just went along with it, playing the g—'

Before Milo could finish his sentence, I'd floored him with a punch.

'You had no right!'

'No right to save you?' he asked, getting back on his feet.

'It's not a question of rights. It was what I had to do.'

'At what cost?'

'Whatever it took.'

He wiped away the blood trickling from his mouth, before rapping out how he saw it.

'You'd have done the same for me. You were ready to kill to protect Carole, so don't try to lecture me! It's the story of our lives, Tom: when one of us cracks, the others come running. That's the one thing that's saw us through.

'You got me off the streets. I'd still be locked up if it wasn't for you, not marrying the woman I love. If it wasn't for you, Carole might have wound up hanging from the end of a rope, not about to give birth. And what about you?' he asked. 'Where would you be now if we'd let you tear your life apart? In rehab? Or dead?'

A white light shone in through the frosted-glass windows. I left his question hanging. My mind was on something else.

'Where is she now?'

'Who, Lilly? No idea. I gave her the dough and she took off.

I think she left LA. She used to work weekends at a nightclub on the Sunset Strip. I went back to look for her, but no one had seen her.'

'What's her surname?'

'No idea. I'm not even sure Lilly's her real name.'

'You've got nothing else to go on?'

'Hey, listen, I can understand you wanting to find her, but you have to realise that the woman you're looking for is a second-rate actress, a waitress in a strip joint – not the Billie you fell in love with.'

'You can keep your advice to yourself. So that's all you have on her?'

'Sorry, that's it. But I want you to know that I'd do it all again if I had to.'

I walked out of the boathouse, trying to make sense of what Milo had just told me, and took a few steps onto the wooden landing stage jutting out over the lake. White swans swam among wild irises, indifferent to human suffering.

*

I picked up my car from the parking lot and drove along the coast to Santa Monica. My head was all over the place as I made my way into the city. I felt I was cruising aimlessly through Inglewood, onto Van Ness and down Vermont Avenue, before realising that some invisible force had guided me back to where I grew up.

I parked the convertible near the plant tubs, which, for as long as I could remember, had never contained anything other than cigarette butts and empty bottles.

In the shadow of the high rises, everything and nothing had changed. There were still the same guys shooting hoops on the basketball court and others leaning against the walls, waiting for something to happen. For a second, I was sure one of them was going to shout out, 'Hey, freak!' But I was a stranger here now and no one bothered me.

I walked past the wire-fenced court to the parking lot. 'My' tree was still there. It looked even scrawnier now, with even fewer leaves, but it was still standing. I sat down on the dry grass and leaned back against the trunk, just like I always used to.

Just then, a Mini Cooper screeched to a halt, right across two parking spaces. Carole got out of the car, still in her wedding dress. She walked toward me, a large sports bag in her right hand, the beautiful white train of her dress in her left to keep it from getting dirty.

'Check this out, there's a wedding in the parking lot!' hollered one of the players from the court.

They all stopped to take a look, before getting back to business.

Carole joined me under the tree.

'Hey, Tom.'

'Hey. I think you've got your dates mixed up though; today's not my birthday.'

She smiled, a tear running silently down her face.

'Milo told me everything a week ago. I swear that's the first I heard of it,' she told me, sitting down on the low wall.

'Sorry I ruined your wedding.'

'It's OK. How are you feeling?'

'Like someone who's been taken for a ride.'

She took out a pack of cigarettes, but I held her back.

'Are you crazy or something? You're pregnant, remember.'

'Well, don't talk like that then! That's not the way you should look at it.'

'How else do you expect me to look at it? I've been treated like a fool, by my best friend of all people.'

'Look, I saw the way she was with you, Tom. I saw the way she looked at you and I'm telling you she wasn't faking it.'

'No, just raking it in to the tune of $15,000!'

'Now hold on. Milo never asked her to sleep with you!'

'Well, she couldn't wait to get out of here as soon as her contract was finished, could she!'

'Just put yourself in her shoes for a second. You think it was easy for her to untangle it all? As far as she knew, you'd fallen in love with a character – a character that wasn't really her.'

There was something in what Carole was saying.

Who had I really fallen for? A character I'd created, which Milo manipulated like a puppet on a string? Or a failed actress playing the biggest role of her life?

Neither. I'd fallen in love with a girl in the middle of the Mexican desert, when she made me see that everything was richer, more flavoursome, more colourful when she was with me.

'You've got to find her, Tom, or you'll regret it for the rest of your life.'

I shook my head. 'It's impossible. We've got nothing to go on, not even a name.'

'You'll have to do better than that.'

'What do you mean?'

'You see, I could never be happy knowing you weren't happy too.'

I could hear in her voice that she really meant it.

'So I brought you this.'

She reached over to her bag and handed me a bloodstained shirt.

'It's a lovely gift, but I think I preferred the computer,' I joked, to ease the tension.

She couldn't help smiling, before explaining the reason behind it.

'You remember the morning I turned up at your place with Milo and you first told us about Billie? Your apartment was a mess and the terrace had been turned upside down. There was blood on the window and all over your clothes.'

'Yes, that's when "Billie" gashed open her hand.'

'Seeing the blood really worried me. All kinds of

425

thoughts were going through my mind, like maybe you'd killed or hurt someone. So, the next day I came back to clean up all the traces of blood. I found this shirt in the bathroom and took it away to remove the evidence. I held on to it, and when Milo told me the truth, I took it to the lab for a DNA test. I checked it against the database and...'

She produced a folder from her bag.

'... and I found out your lady friend has form.'

I opened the wallet to find a photocopy of the FBI file, which Carole summarised for me.

'Her name's Lilly Austin, born 1984 in Oakland. Arrested twice in the last five years. Nothing too serious: once for failure to comply at a pro-choice march in 2006, and again in 2009 for smoking pot in a park.'

'Is that all you need to do to get a record?'

'I'm guessing you don't watch *CSI* then? California state police routinely take DNA from people who've been arrested for or suspected of committing certain offences. If it makes you feel better, you're part of the club too.'

'Do you have her new address?'

'No, but I put her name into our database and came up with this.'

She handed me a sheet of paper. It was an enrolment form for Brown University, for the current academic year.

'Lilly's studying literature and dramatic arts,' explained Carole.

'How did she get into Brown? That's one of the best schools in the country.'

'I called them. She won a place on the basis of her written application, skipping the usual process. I guess she must have spent the last few months studying.'

I looked at the two documents, fascinated by Lilly Austin, the stranger whose picture was slowly forming before my eyes.

'I'd better get back to my guests,' said Carole, looking at her watch. 'And you've got someone to see too.'

*

I took the first flight to Boston the following Monday. I arrived in the capital of Massachusetts at 4 p.m., hired a car at the airport and headed toward Providence.

The Brown University campus was made up of impressive redbrick buildings surrounded by lush green lawns. It was the end of the day for many of the students. Before setting off, I'd looked up the timetable for Lilly's courses online, and I was waiting outside the doors of the hall where her lecture was about to finish, my heart thumping.

I was standing far enough back so that she didn't see me when she came out with a crowd of other students. I didn't quite recognise her at first; she'd cut her hair and dyed it darker. She was wearing a tweed cap and an outfit – short grey skirt over black tights, fitted jacket over turtleneck sweater – that gave her the look of a London girl.

I'd made up my mind to go over, but I wanted to wait until she was on her own. I followed the group of two guys and another girl until they got to a café not far off campus. Drinking her tea, Lilly launched into a passionate debate with one of the male students – an intellectual type with Latin good looks. The more I watched her, the happier and calmer she seemed to me. Moving far away from LA to continue her studies seemed to have restored her sense of balance. Some people were good at that, starting over; all I could ever do was carry on.

I left the café without approaching her and got back in the car. Dipping back into college life had left me feeling low. Sure, I was glad to see her looking happy, but the girl I'd seen today wasn't 'my' Billie any more. She'd clearly turned a page, and eeing her chatting to that twenty-year-old made me feel old. Maybe the ten-year age gap wasn't so easily bridged after all.

As I drove back to the airport, I kicked myself for a wasted journey. And, worse, I felt like a photographer failing to capture that once-in-a-lifetime image; I had let the crucial moment pass, when my life could have swung from darkness into laughter and light.

*

On the plane back to LA, I switched on my laptop. Though I was maybe only halfway through my life, I knew I'd never meet a girl like Billie again. A girl who, in the space of a few weeks, had got me to believe in the impossible, and had led me away from that dangerous

428

place where I had been on the edge of despair.

My adventure with Billie was over, but I didn't want to forget a single moment of it. I needed to tell our story. It would be a story for everyone who has been in love, is still in love, or looking out for love. So I opened a new document and gave it the title of my next novel: *The Girl on Paper*.

During the five-hour flight, I wrote the whole first chapter in one go. It began:

Chapter 1

The house by the ocean

'Tom, open the door!'

The shout was drowned out by the wind and there was no reply.

'Tom! It's me, Milo. I know you're in there. Come out of your hole for crying out loud!'

Malibu
Los Angeles County
A beach house

For the last five minutes, Milo Lombardo had been hammering incessantly on the wooden shutters overlooking the terrace of his best friend's house.

'Tom! Open up or I'll kick the door down. You know I'm strong enough!'

39

Nine months later ...

The novelist destroys the house of his life and uses its stones to build the house of his novel
Milan Kundera

A light spring breeze was blowing over Boston Old Town. Lilly Austin was wandering through the steep narrow streets of Beacon Hill. With its blossom-covered trees, gas lamps and brick houses with heavy wooden doors, the area oozed charm.

She stopped outside the window of an antique dealer on the corner of River Street and Byron Street, before heading into a bookstore. Inside, space was tight, with novels snugly lined up alongside essays. A pile of books caught her eye: Tom had written a new novel.

For a year and a half, she had made a conscious effort to avoid the fiction shelf, so she wouldn't come across him. Because every time she did come across him on the subway, on buses, on billboards or outside a café, she was overwhelmed with sadness and felt like crying.

Whenever any of her college friends talked about him (or, rather, his books), she had to bite her lip to stop herself saying, 'I drove a Bugatti with him; I crossed the

Mexican desert with him; I lived in Paris with him; I've slept with him.'

Sometimes, when she saw readers immersed in the third volume of the trilogy, she couldn't help feeling a bit smug and wanted to call out, 'It's because of me that you're reading that book! He wrote it for me!'

She read the title of the new book: *The Girl on Paper.* She scanned the first few pages, eager to know more. It was her story! It was their story! Her heart thumping, she rushed to the till, paid for the book then carried on reading on a bench in the Public Garden, a large park in the centre of the city.

*

Lilly nervously turned the pages, not knowing how the tale would end. She was reliving the whole adventure through Tom's eyes, amazed to discover how his feelings had developed. The story as she had lived it ended with chapter 36, and she approached the final two chapters with trepidation.

The novel was Tom's way of recognising she had saved his life, but, more than that, it was a sign that he'd forgiven her for lying to him and had carried on loving her after she'd left.

She was almost in tears when she read that he had come to Brown University the previous autumn, leaving without speaking to her. The same thing had happened to her, the year before!

One morning, she had decided enough was enough

and got on a flight to Los Angeles, determined to tell him the truth, secretly hoping things weren't over between them.

She'd arrived in Malibu in the early evening, but the beach house was empty, so she took a cab to try Milo's house at Pacific Palisades. As the lights were on, she'd walked up to the house and seen through the window two couples having dinner: Milo and Carole, looking very much in love, and Tom, with a young woman she didn't recognise.

At the time, she'd felt incredibly sad and almost ashamed at having allowed herself to imagine that Tom wouldn't have found somebody else. Now she understood it must have been one of those Friday night 'matchmaking dinners' that his friends organised in the hope of finding him a soul mate.

By the time she closed the book, her heart was pounding. This time it was more than just a hope; she knew for certain their love story was far from over. What they had been through was only the first chapter and she was determined they would write the next one together!

It was getting dark on Beacon Hill. Crossing the road to the subway station, Billie passed a rather prim-looking Bostonian with a Yorkshire terrier under her arm.

She was so happy she couldn't help declaring it to the world.

'I'm *The Girl on Paper*!' she shouted, holding up the cover for the woman to see.

The Ghosts and Angels Bookstore is pleased to invite you to meet the author Tom Boyd on Tuesday 12 June, 3 – 6 p.m., when he will be signing copies of his latest novel, The Girl on Paper.

*

Los Angeles

It was almost 7 p.m. The queue of readers was shrinking and the signing session nearly over. Milo had stayed the whole afternoon, chatting with customers and cracking jokes. His good humour and light-heartedness helped make their wait less tedious.

'Jeez, is that the time?' he exclaimed, looking at his watch. 'I'd better leave you to finish up on your own. It's feeding time!'

Milo's daughter had been born three months earlier and, predictably he was smitten.

'I've been telling you to go for over an hour!' I pointed out.

He flung on his jacket, said goodbye to the store staff and hurried back to his family.

'Ooh, I booked you a cab,' he shouted to me from the door. 'It'll be waiting the other side of the junction.'

'OK. Send Carole my love.'

I stayed another ten minutes to sign the last few books and have a quick chat to the store manager. With its warm, soft lighting, creaking floorboards and wax-polished shelves, you didn't come across bookstores like Ghosts and Angels very often these days. It was somewhere between *The Shop around the Corner* and *84 Charing Cross Road*. The store manager had supported my first novel long before the press picked it up, and I'd stayed faithful to the place ever since, kicking off every book signing tour there.

'You can go out the back,' she told me.

She'd started bringing down the metal shutter when there was a knock at the window. A tardy reader was waving around her copy of the book and clasping her hands together, praying to be let in. The manager waited for my nod before opening the door. I took the lid off my pen and sat back down at the table.

'It's Sarah!' the reader said, holding out her book.

While I was writing the dedication, another customer slipped in through the open door. I handed back Sarah's copy and took the next one, without looking up.

'Who's it for?' I asked.

'Lilly,' a calm, gentle voice replied.

I was hurrying along, on the verge of writing her name on the title page when she added, 'Or Billie, if you like.'

I lifted my head to find life had just handed me a second chance.

*

A quarter of an hour later, the two of us were standing outside on the pavement, and this time there was no way I was letting her go.

'D'you want a ride?' I asked. 'There's a taxi waiting for me.'

'No, it's OK, my car's just here,' she said, pointing behind me.

I turned round and, to my amazement, saw the clapped-out bubblegum-pink Fiat 500 that had carried us across the Mexican desert.

'I got quite attached to the old thing, would you believe?' she explained.

'How did you get it?'

'If you only knew! There's a story in that…'

'Go on then.'

'A long story.'

'I've got all the time in the world.'

'OK, maybe we could have dinner somewhere.'

'Sounds good to me.'

'But I'll do the driving,' she said, getting behind the wheel of her old banger.

I paid the cab driver for his time before getting into the car beside Lilly.

'So, where are we headed?' she asked, turning on the ignition.

'Wherever you want.'

She put her foot down and the old crate rattled into action, as shaky and uncomfortable as ever. I hardly noticed; I felt as if I was walking on air, as if we'd never been apart.

'How about I take you for some lobster and seafood?' she suggested. 'I know this great place on Melrose Avenue.

But only if you're paying … I'm not exactly rolling in it at the moment. And no pulling faces this time, none of your "I don't eat this, or that, and, urgh, oysters are all slimy." Surely you like lobster? Oh my God, I absolutely love it – the best is when it's grilled and flambéed with brandy – yum! And what about crab? A few years ago, when I was working at this restaurant in Long Beach, they served these things called robber crabs. They can weigh more than thirty pounds, can you imagine? They climb trees, knock off the coconuts and then crack them open with their pincers to eat the flesh! Isn't that *insane*? You get them in the Maldives and also the Seychelles. Have you been to the Seychelles? It'd be such a dream to go there, all those lagoons, the crystal-clear water, the white sand… And those giant turtles on Silhouette Island, they're just incredible. Did you know they can weigh as much as 400 pounds and live for over 120 years? Pretty cool, huh? How about India? Have you been? One of my girlfriends told me about this amazing guesthouse in Pondicherry that…'

Where Would I Be Without You?
Guillaume Musso

Over 1 million copies sold worldwide

Sometimes, a second chance can come out of
nowhere…

Parisian cop Martin Beaumont has never really got
over his first love, Gabrielle. Their brief, intense affair
in San Francisco and the pain of her rejection still haunt
him years later.

Now, however, he's a successful detective – and
tonight he's going to arrest the legendary art thief,
Archibald Maclean, when he raids the Musée d'Orsay
for a priceless Van Gogh. But the enigmatic Archibald
has other plans.

Martin's pursuit of the master criminal across Paris
is the first step in an adventure that will take him back
to San Francisco, and to the edge of love and life itself.

ISBN: 9781906040345
Price: £7.99

PRAISE FOR
WHERE WOULD I BE WITHOUT YOU?

'A pulsating read which features romance, thriller and fantasy.' *Metro*

'The French have brought us berets, baguettes and Beaujolais, and now we can thank them for bestseller Guillaume Musso.' *The Sun*

'Musso shows he is a master at creating mystery' *Paris Match*

'His stories blend emotion, suspense and the supernatural' *L'Express*

'A non-stop thriller, a romance, a hair-raising fantasy but one which is also very readable.' *Le Figaro Littéraire*

Guillaume Musso on
Where Would I Be Without You?

I had two ambitions when starting to write *Where Would I Be Without You?* Firstly, I wanted to tell a story that would inspire readers, with characters who looked to the future and who tried hard to make something of themselves instead of giving up to destiny or fate. Secondly, I wanted to include something about my passion for paintings and sculptures as there are some works of art which mean as much to me as books.

These were my two points of reference for the moment when Archibald, the art thief, and Martin, the flic, come face-to-face.

I also have a soft spot for Gabrielle, the main character in the book; a young woman torn apart by her abandonment by these two men who meant so much to her and who reappear at the moment where she has nearly given up. I wanted *Where Would I Be Without You?* to be an optimistic book.

Coming in Summer 2013

The Angel's Call
Guillaume Musso

When they accidentally swap smartphones at an airport, Madeline Green and Jonathan Lempereur are total strangers. By the time they realize what's happened, they're on opposite sides of the Atlantic, and have begun to learn rather more about each other.

Mild curiosity turns to obsession as their mobiles reveal secrets from their past lives: Jonathan was once a world-famous chef whose glittering career collapsed overnight; Madeline abandoned her police career in the wake of a harrowing case, to become a Parisian florist.

Having never met properly, they begin to feel intimately acquainted and, as their lives draw closer, events and feelings begin to race out of control…

ISBN: 9781908313041
£7.99

GALLIC